# MADELINE BAKER

**Winner of the *Romantic Times* Reviewers' Choice Award for Best Indian Series!**

**"Madeline Baker is synonymous with tender Western romances!"**
**—*Romantic Times***

## Critical acclaim for Madeline Baker's previous bestsellers:

### *WARRIOR'S LADY*

"Readers will be enchanted with *Warrior's Lady,* a magical fairy tale that is to be devoured again and again."

—*Romantic Times*

### *THE SPIRIT PATH*

"Poignant, sensual and wonderful....Madeline Baker fans will be enchanted!"

—*Romantic Times*

### *MIDNIGHT FIRE*

"Once again, Madeline Baker proves that she has the Midas touch....A definite treasure!"

—*Romantic Times*

### *COMANCHE FLAME*

"Another Baker triumph! Powerful, passionate, and action-packed, it will keep readers on the edge of their seats!"

—*Romantic Times*

### *PRAIRIE HEAT*

"A smoldering tale of revenge and passion as only Madeline Baker can write...without a doubt one of her best!"

—*Romantic Times*

### *A WHISPER IN THE WIND*

"Fresh, powerful and exciting, a time-travel novel taut with raw primal tension and rich in Indian history and tradition!"

—*Romantic Times*

# STORMY SURRENDER

"I can give you all the experience you need," Caleb muttered.

Callie smiled at him uncertainly. "What do you mean?" she asked and felt the warm afterglow of the whiskey turn suddenly cold and sour.

"You can start at the saloon tomorrow," he said, his voice taut. "You can stay here tonight."

The words seemed to echo in the stillness of the room. Callie stared at him, her heart pounding in her ears. "What...what do you mean?"

"I mean I intend to give you some experience."

Without warning, he grabbed her and kissed her, his lips warm against hers, his arms holding her body to his chest. He smelled of smoke and leather, of whiskey and wanting. She tried to push him away, but it was like trying to move a mountain.

Other *Leisure Books* by Madeline Baker:
**WARRIOR'S LADY**
**THE SPIRIT PATH**
**MIDNIGHT FIRE**
**COMANCHE FLAME**
**PRAIRIE HEAT**
**A WHISPER IN THE WIND**
**FORBIDDEN FIRES**
**LACEY'S WAY**
**FIRST LOVE, WILD LOVE**
**RENEGADE HEART**
**RECKLESS DESIRE**
**LOVE FOREVERMORE**
**RECKLESS LOVE**
**LOVE IN THE WIND**
**RECKLESS HEART**

# MADELINE BAKER

LEISURE BOOKS  NEW YORK CITY

*For my cousin, "Sweet" Susie Spiceland,*
*I love you cuz.*
*You're the best!*
*(See, all you had to do was ask!)*

A LEISURE BOOK®

March 1994

Published by

Dorchester Publishing Co., Inc.
276 Fifth Avenue
New York, NY 10001



Printed in the United States of America.

# RED FEATHER

"Red Feather."
She hears it spoken from afar.
It has been a long time since she heard her name.
Her hair, once black as a raven's wing,
Is touched with silver; the stars have left her eyes.

Her deerskin dress has been replaced by gingham;
Strange shoes adorn her feet.
No longer, she tarries from first light across the
horizon, until last golden ray merges with campfire;
Gone, also, is the laughter of children at play,
Babbling voices of friends,
Men preparing for the hunt.

Gone, the love she has known.
If she closes her eyes, maybe she can escape
The bonds of time, and not be here
In this contraption
Called a rocking chair.

"Red Feather."
If she did not know better, it could be his voice,
Soft upon the wind.
She closes her eyes; tired and weary,
She wants to rest as the chair gently rocks
To and fro.

"Come, Red Feather, it is time."
She is once more where she belongs—
in another time with all she loves.

"At last, Red Feather, you are home."

—Mary Lou VonMeter

CHEYENNE
SURRENDER

# Chapter One

*Wyoming Territory*
*1883*

He was going home—back to the Land of the Spotted Eagle. Back to the tall grass and the slow-talking streams. Back to the land where he'd been born.

Home.

Caleb took a deep breath, filling his lungs with draughts of the cool, clear air. He caught the warm rich scent of Mother Earth, of sun-kissed pine trees and prairie grass. He could have taken the train to Cheyenne. It would have been faster, but he felt the need to be alone with his thoughts, to listen to the ancient voices in the wind as he rode across the vast prairie, to remember who he was.

He was going home.

Had it really been twelve years since he'd left Wyoming? Twelve years since he'd turned his back on his father and broken his mother's heart?

Twelve years. Where had the time gone?

The cry of a hunting hawk cut across the stillness of the open prairie, sending a shiver of exhilaration and excitement down his spine. Gazing upward, he watched the bird soar in ever-decreasing circles until it plummeted to earth, only to take to the skies a moment later with a luckless rabbit clutched in its talons.

Life and death.

The hunter and the hunted. He'd been both in his time. But that was all behind him now.

Reining the buckskin to a halt, he withdrew a sheet of paper from his coat pocket. The writing was small and neat, the message was short.

> Dear Mr. Stryker:
>
> Your father passed away in June, your mother followed three months later. According to the terms of your mother's will, the house on East 17th Street and the Rocking S Ranch now belong to you.
>
> Please advise me as to your wishes regarding the disposal of these properties as soon as possible.

It was dated the thirtieth of September and signed by Orville Hoag, Attorney at Law, Cheyenne, Wyoming.

With a sigh, Caleb jammed the wrinkled sheet of paper into his pocket. It had taken five months for the letter to find him.

He stared out across the prairie for a long moment, his eyes narrowed against the bright noonday sun. His mother was dead. The thought tugged at his heart, bringing to mind feelings he hadn't acknowledged in years, resurrecting memories he'd thought buried and forgotten long ago.

Red Feather, daughter of He Dog and Shell Woman, was dead. The knowledge of her passing left him feeling empty and alone. How many times had she written, begging him to come home? How many times had he promised to visit, knowing in his heart that he'd never go back as long as the old man lived? And now they were both gone.

He felt no grief at Duncan Stryker's passing, only relief that he would never again have to face the man who had fathered him.

Muttering an oath, he urged the buckskin into a mile-eating lope, wondering what the devil a half-breed bounty hunter who'd spent the last eight years chasing outlaws on both sides of the Mexican border was going to do with a twenty-room mansion on 17th Street.

# *Chapter Two*

*Spring, 1883*

Caleb rode down 16th Street to Hill, past the Inter-Ocean Hotel and the Cheyenne Opera House, marveling at the changes that had occurred in his absence.

Cheyenne was a booming town, growing rich on grass and cattle. Situated roughly a hundred miles north of Denver, the city had first been settled in the summer of 1867 by the Union Pacific Railroad. It had been the end of the line then. "Hell on Wheels", they had called it, and deservedly so. But it had been a city destined to flourish—lots that the Union Pacific originally sold for a hundred and fifty dollars were resold for over two thousand dollars each a few months later.

In 1869, Cheyenne had been selected as the

capital of Wyoming Territory; in the same year it had been almost completely destroyed by fire. But you'd never know that now.

Caleb shook his head as he turned down 18th Street.

There were electric lights in the heart of the city now, the first in any town west of the Mississippi, and he'd heard that the Inter-Ocean had recently installed some new-fangled invention called a water closet. There were two on each floor of the hotel, and it was said people came from miles around just to have a look at what many considered to be just a passing craze. Caleb shook his head. Indoor plumbing. What would they think of next?

He found the law office of Hoag and Linderman on 18th Street, sandwiched between Buckley's Mercantile and Holman's Gun Shop.

Dismounting, Caleb brushed the trail dust from his clothes as best he could, squared his hat on his head, and opened the glass-paneled door.

The office was small and square. Most of the floor space was taken up by an oversized desk that dwarfed the man sitting behind it. There was a four-drawer oak file cabinet to the right of the desk. A bookshelf crammed with law books lined the wall on Caleb's left.

Orville Hoag looked up from the pages of his law book as a tall, broad-shouldered man filled the doorway. He felt a twinge of unease as he took in the man's appearance—the dusty black hat with its beaded headband, the faded black shirt, buckskin pants, and knee-high moccasins. He sat up a little taller, squaring his shoulders as he did so. "May I help you?"

"I'm looking for Orville Hoag."

Hoag swallowed hard, hoping the half-breed wasn't looking for trouble because he looked like he knew how to dish it out sure as death and hell.

"You've found him," Orville admitted. He returned the big man's stare, hoping he hadn't just made the biggest mistake of his life.

Caleb grunted softly as his gaze bored into Hoag. The lawyer was a middle-aged man with wavy brown hair, guileless blue eyes, and soft hands. He wore a dark blue suit, a striped vest, and a silk cravat.

Orville Hoag cleared his throat. "How can I help you, Mr. . . ."

"Stryker."

"Ah, Mr. Stryker." Relief washed through Hoag as he stood up to shake the man's hand. The man was here on business, but not *that* kind of business.

Orville Hoag gestured at the padded leather chair situated on the other side of the desk as he resumed his own seat. "Won't you sit down? I trust you had a pleasant journey."

"Pleasant enough."

"Yes, well, your mother left quite an estate. There are some papers for you to sign. I . . . uh . . . that is, are you planning to stay in Cheyenne?"

"I haven't decided. Does it make a difference?"

"Of course not. It's just that . . . well, there are several parties interested in buying the Rocking S."

Caleb nodded impatiently. He was in no mood to make decisions at the moment.

"And I'm sure you wouldn't have any trouble

finding a buyer for the mansion, either," Hoag went on. "They're both situated on prime parcels of land."

"You in the real estate business, too, Mr. Hoag?"

"Why, no, sir."

"Just eager to have me out of town?" Caleb asked the question without malice. There were a lot of people who didn't cotton to half-breeds and he couldn't fight them all.

Orville Hoag flushed under the half-breed's penetrating stare. "Of course not, I . . . it's just that . . ."

"Can I have a look at those papers now?"

"Yes, of course." Hoag rummaged through the files stacked on his desk for several moments, acutely conscious of the half-breed's cold gray eyes following his every move.

It took several moments before the lawyer found what he was looking for, and by then his hands were trembling. Sliding the file across the desk top, he waited patiently while Caleb Stryker perused his mother's will.

"I can assure you everything is in order," Hoag remarked. "Your father's will, dated the tenth of April, 1871, left everything to your mother."

A muscle twitched in Caleb's jaw. So the old man had written Caleb out of his will the very day Caleb left Cheyenne.

Hoag licked his lips, then tugged at his collar. "Originally, your mother's will stated that your father was to be the sole beneficiary, and that if she outlived him, the estate was to be sold and the proceeds sent to your father's sister in England. Your father's will read the same."

Hoag paused, wondering what had caused the rift

between the gunman and Duncan Stryker. "Your father began ailing back in the spring of eighty-one. Shortly after that, your mother changed her will so that you would be the sole beneficiary should anything happen to your father."

"Did the old man know that?"

"No, I don't believe he did." Hoag dipped his pen in the inkwell on the corner of the desk and handed it to Stryker. "If you'll just sign here. And here."

Hoag cleared his throat again, eager to finish his business with Stryker's son and be done with it. "Yes, that should take care of it."

The lawyer blotted Caleb's signatures, folded one of the documents in half, and slipped it into a large brown envelope. "I believe that takes care of everything. You'll find the deeds to the ranch and the house in the envelope, as well as the key to the mansion and a copy of your mother's will. Joe Brigman is still the foreman of the Rocking S. He's been looking after things since your mother passed away."

"Thanks."

"You'll need to stop at the bank. I believe the note on the Rocking S is due sometime this year. You'll want to take care of that."

"Note?"

"Yes, your mother borrowed against the ranch and sent the money to Washington." Hoag shook his head in obvious disapproval of women meddling in men's affairs. "She also drove over a hundred head of cattle to the reservation last year. Several people tried to talk her out of it, but she said the Indians needed the meat."

With a curt nod, Caleb scooped up the envelope

and left the office. *Good for you, Ma,* he mused. *Good for you.*

Orville Hoag stared after Stryker for several minutes. *So,* he thought, *that's the heir.* He'd heard of Caleb Stryker, but then, who hadn't? The man had earned himself quite a reputation as a bounty hunter in the course of the last eight years. It was rumored he had a draw like greased lightning and that he didn't care much if he brought his quarry in sitting up or face down across a saddle.

Hoag shook his head. The man looked more Indian than white with his swarthy skin and long black hair. And those eyes, as cold and gray as gun metal. Hoag shook his head again. After looking into Stryker's eyes, he believed everything he'd ever heard about the man.

Caleb stood on the boardwalk outside the law office, debating what to do first. The promise of a drink decided him and he took up the buckskin's reins and walked across the street to the Three Queens Saloon. There was plenty of time to go home and visit old ghosts.

Tying the mare to the hitch rack outside the saloon, he took a deep breath, then stepped through the swinging doors.

The Three Queens was located in a large rectangular building. He paused inside, surprised to find everything as he remembered it.

A gleaming mahogany bar spanned the wall opposite the swinging doors. A painting of a red-headed woman wrapped in a gossamer blue dressing gown hung behind the bar; a three-tiered glass shelf held an assortment of bottles and fancy glasses. There was a small stage and a piano to the left, a faro layout to the right, and a dozen or so poker tables in between.

With a faint nod of approval, he walked up to the bar and ordered a shot of whiskey, downing it in a single swallow. It was good whiskey, the best he'd had in months.

Taking the bottle, Caleb made his way to a table located in the back of the room. Sitting with his back to the wall, he poured himself another drink and sipped it slowly, letting the whiskey's warmth flow into him while he looked around.

He saw Erasmus Nagle, I.C. Whipple, and W.A. Robbins sitting with their heads together at a table across the room and wondered what big deals were in the making. Nagle had come to Cheyenne in 1868 and was known as "The Merchant King of Wyoming". In 1875, he'd founded the Cheyenne and Black Hills Telegraph Company, along with W.H. Hibbard. They were all rich men.

Caleb grinned wryly. He'd made a lot of money himself in the last eight years. Blood money, his mother had called it, but he'd never owned more than a fast horse and a good rifle—until now. He'd spent his money almost as fast as he made it, on good whiskey and bad women, on the turn of a card, a roll of the dice.

He chuckled softly as he refilled his glass. And now he owned the mansion and the ranch, all because his mother had outlived his father.

His old man must be rolling in his grave, shouting at the devil to let him out of hell so he could burn the ranch and salt the land before his son took over.

"But it's too late, you old reprobate," Caleb murmured. "Too late."

He closed his eyes and for a moment he was fifteen years old again, flinching under the whip, refusing to cry because he knew just how much his tears would please the old man.

*Never speak that heathen language again!* He heard the old man's voice echo inside his head. *You're not a bloody savage. You're my son!* And then he heard his mother's voice, soft and pleading, *Duncan, stop, please stop. You'll kill him.*

But he hadn't died at the old man's hand. Not that day or in the ones that followed. Foolish as it was, he had openly defied Duncan at every turn, speaking Lakota instead of English whenever the old man was around, refusing to wear a shirt and pants in favor of buckskin leggings and moccasins. The old man got his revenge though. He always did.

Caleb would never forget the day out at the ranch when the old man had hacked off his hair. It had taken four cowhands to hold Caleb down and when the old man laid the scissors aside, Caleb had little more than a quarter inch of stubble. It was the worst humiliation of his life. Two years later, when he turned seventeen, he ran away. His mother had begged him to stay, promising things would get better, but he knew he had to go, had to get away before he killed the old man with his bare hands. When he'd first left Cheyenne, he'd had every intention of going back to his mother's people, but he'd gotten sidetracked along the way, and then it was too late. He'd been away too long. . . .

Opening his eyes, Caleb removed his hat and raked his fingers through his hair, hair that was as thick and long and black as his mother's had been. His hair. It had become a symbol of his independence.

With a sigh, he poured himself another drink. For a moment, he gazed at the dark amber liquid, and then a faint smile tugged at the corners of his mouth.

"Here's to you, Duncan Bradley Stryker," he muttered as he lifted the glass in a mock salute. "May you rot in hell for all eternity."

# Chapter Three

Callie McGuire watched the tall half-breed exit through the batwing doors of the Three Queens Saloon. He paused a moment and then walked toward the hitchrack. Yes, she thought, he was Duncan Stryker's son, no doubt of that. The resemblance was there in the hooded gray eyes that gave nothing away, in the way he walked, as if he owned the very air he breathed and the earth beneath his feet.

He was an exceptionally tall man, with the broadest shoulders she'd ever seen and long, long legs. His profile was sharp and clean, the nose a trifle large, the cheekbones high and prominent, as if to boast of his Indian blood. His mouth was wide and well-shaped, his brows straight.

The fact that he was quite the handsomest man

she had ever seen barely registered. She wasn't interested in him as a man, only as a means to an end—an end to working as a chambermaid in Mrs. Colton's boardinghouse and as a serving girl in the adjoining restaurant.

She experienced a moment of anxiety when he swung aboard a big buckskin mare and headed out of town. He couldn't be leaving, not so soon! But then she saw him turn down Oak Street, and she breathed a sigh of relief. No doubt he was going to the mansion. It was just as well, she thought. She couldn't very well discuss her business in the middle of 18th Street.

Picking up her skirts, Callie made her way back to the boardinghouse. As soon as she finished serving the evening meal, she'd go see Duncan's son, say her piece, and be done with it.

Caleb stared at the house his father had built for his mother. Located in the 200 block of East 17th Street, it was constructed of red brick, three stories high. A big bay window faced the street. There was a wide front porch, a large round tower on the north front corner, and an upstairs balcony off the bedroom that had belonged to his mother.

Dismounting, he ran his hand along the wrought-iron fence that surrounded the house, remembering the first day they'd moved in. His mother had adjusted to living the white man's way by then and she'd been proud of the house, which had been the biggest and finest on the block.

She'd been proud of the house, Caleb remembered bleakly, but she'd never truly been happy here. Duncan had dressed her up in silks and satin. He had hired someone to tutor her in the English language so she would speak correctly; he'd made sure she learned how to read and write and that she knew how to behave in polite society. She had learned to be a gracious hostess because it pleased her husband. She had lived in his house, entertained his friends, attended his church, accompanied him to parties. But none of it had made her happy. There had been an abiding sadness in the depths of her eyes, a yearning for the old days, the old ways.

Caleb swore softly. It hadn't made him happy, either, learning how to talk and dress and act like a white man. But he'd done it for her.

Tossing the buckskin's reins over the hitching post inside the front gate, he walked up the four steps that led to the veranda, slipped the key into the lock, and opened the massive front door.

For a moment, he stood in the entry hall, listening to the ghosts of the past; then he took a deep breath and walked toward the parlor, his footsteps echoing on the parquet floor.

The parlor was decorated with dark wood furniture and dark colors. A large gilt-edged mirror hung over the fireplace; a sepia-toned photograph of his mother and father hung on the opposite wall. He stood for a moment, taking in the thick layer of dust that covered the furniture, listening to the hollow silence.

He went to the dining room next. It was papered in blue and gold. A long rectangular table ringed by eight chairs stood in the middle of the room. The chairs were covered in the same pattern as the wallpaper. A chandelier hung from the ceiling, its prisms dull, a lacy spider web stretching from the top to the bottom.

The kitchen had been his favorite room because his father never went there. Caleb paused inside the door and rolled a cigarette, remembering the hours he'd spent sitting at the table, teasing Fanny, the cook. She'd been a good old soul, the only one in the house who hadn't been afraid of Duncan's temper.

Extinguishing his cigarette, he left the kitchen and went into the music room. A wry grin tugged at his lips. No one in the Stryker family had a bit of musical talent, yet the room contained a piano, a harp, a violin, and a cello. And in one corner, gathering dust, a Lakota war drum and the flute Duncan had used to court his bride.

He spent a few moments in his mother's sewing room and smoked another cigarette in the library, wondering if anyone had ever read the books that filled the shelves. He walked the length and breadth of his father's den and took a quick look at the billiard room, which still reeked of Duncan Stryker's brand of tobacco, before he walked up the carpeted stairway to the second floor.

And the voices of the ghosts grew louder.

He opened the door to his old room and stepped inside. Nothing had changed since he left that night twelve years ago. A table and chair of dark walnut stood in one corner; a matching four-drawer chest still held his clothes. A fine layer of dust covered everything. The same dark blue drapes hung at the window, and the same brown-and-blue print counterpane covered the bed.

How many nights had he lain in that bed and wished they were back with the Lakota? Life had been so much simpler there. His parents had been happy. He'd been happy. He'd never understood why his father had decided to leave the Indians. Duncan had always seemed content to live the Lakota way.

Admittedly, Caleb knew very little about his father's past, only that Duncan had wandered into the Lakota camp in the midst of a raging blizzard, spent the rest of the winter with the Indians, and married Red Feather the following autumn.

Then, in the summer of sixty-six, Duncan had changed. He'd become irritable, restless. Perhaps he'd felt life was passing him by. Perhaps he'd just grown bored with the Lakota's way of living. Whatever the reason, he had made the decision to go back to his own people.

Life for a man with an Indian wife and a half-breed boy would have been unbearable in any town west of the Mississippi if Duncan Stryker had been some dirt-poor farmer. But by the time they settled in Cheyenne, Duncan was a rich man. Caleb had to admire the old man's grit. He had parlayed the small stake he'd earned selling beaver skins into a tidy little fortune at an all-night poker game, and then he'd taken his winnings and bought a small herd of cattle. He sold them at a good price, bought another bigger, better herd, and sold it for enough cash to buy the ranch on Crow Creek.

In just over a year, Duncan had doubled his investment. Six months later, he built the mansion in town so he'd have a place to spend the cold Wyoming winters. As soon as they moved into the mansion, Duncan's attitude toward his wife and child underwent a drastic change. It was then he insisted that Red Feather change her name to Faith and learn to behave like a proper white woman. He had insisted Caleb forget everything he'd learned from the Indians. A rich man and a proud one, Duncan never expressed a moment's shame or embarrassment because his wife and child were Indian. Instead, he made sure everyone knew it and accepted it. And people were polite to his Indian wife because Duncan Stryker was one of the richest men in town.

Caleb knew there had been men who cursed Duncan behind his back, calling him any number of nasty names. They had made jokes about his Injun wife and breed kid, but nobody had the guts to say a derogatory word to the old man's face. Caleb had heard them, though. He'd heard the snickers, the taunts, the jibes, and he had hated the white men who made fun of his Indian blood, and he had hated his father for taking them away from the Lakota.

If Duncan knew what men said behind his back, he didn't let it show. But Caleb knew that, where his father had once been proud of him, he was now ashamed. Ashamed to have a son who was a half-breed, ashamed to have an Indian woman for a wife even if she was one of the most beautiful women in town. And that knowledge had festered inside Caleb like a wound that wouldn't heal.

Pushing his hat back on his head, Caleb walked out of his room and crossed the hall to his mother's room. Taking a deep breath, he opened the door and stepped inside. She'd been dead for months; he hadn't seen her for nearly twelve years, yet he fancied that he could smell her perfume, that faint scent of wildflowers that had always clung to her hair and clothes.

Caleb moved slowly about the room, his hand reaching out to smooth the cover of his mother's bed, to caress the back of her favorite rocking chair, to touch the silver-backed brush he'd given her for Christmas the year before he ran away. He closed his eyes, remembering how pleased she'd been with his gift, remembering the nights when Duncan had been away from home and the two of them spent the evening together in her room. He'd sit in her rocking chair in front of the fireplace, watching while she brushed her hair, listening as she told him stories from her childhood, ancient tales about Coyote, the trickster, about the ghost with two faces, and Arrow Boy. She spoke to him in Lakota, and the soft guttural sounds made him homesick for the People, for the life they had left behind. He had often begged her to leave Duncan, to go back to her people, but she would not go. Duncan was her husband, and she loved him.

Muttering an oath, Caleb stalked out of the room. He paused on the landing, tracing random patterns in the dust that covered the hand-carved oak banister. Might as well see it all, he mused, and climbed the stairs to the huge ballroom that took up the entire third floor. Lustrous oak benches lined two of the walls, and there was an alcove for the orchestra. An enormous chandelier hung from a solid gold chain.

How many times had he stood in this room, clad in a dark suit, stiff white linen shirt, and string tie and watched Cheyenne's most influential citizens waltz around the floor? Men like E. W. Whitcomb, who had also married an Indian woman. Men like Joseph Maul Carey, who had been appointed Assistant Supreme Court Justice in 1871. Men like M.E. Post, who'd come to Cheyenne in 1867 and become so successful in banking and ranching that he'd been known as the "Sheep King of the Territory". His wife, who had come West in a covered wagon, could often be seen riding around Cheyenne in a fancy carriage driven by a liveried coachman. So many rich and influential men, Caleb mused, like Nathan Baker, publisher of the *Cheyenne Leader,* and Alexander Swan, who was known from coast to coast as "The Cattle King of the West."

With a thoughtful frown, Caleb returned to the first floor, wondering how many of those men still lived in Cheyenne. He took off his hat and tossed it on a table, then dropped down on one of the sofas and ran his hands through his hair. What was he doing here, resurrecting old ghosts, old memories? He felt a fresh wave of guilt as he thought of his mother. She had died here, in that bed upstairs. Alone.

He frowned as he heard a knock at the front door. Who the devil would be coming to see him?

He decided he didn't care and settled back on the sofa, but the knock came again, louder, more insistent.

Scowling, he went to the front door and opened it, his eyes narrowing as he stared at the girl standing on the porch.

"What do you want?"

Callie blinked at him. Up close, Caleb Stryker was even taller, broader, and more fierce-looking than he'd appeared from a distance. The gray wool shirt was stretched taut over shoulders as wide as a barn door, and his legs were encased in buckskin pants that fit like a second skin.

"Well?" he asked, his tone cold and impatient.

"I'm Callie McGuire."

Caleb's gaze ran over her in a quick, appraising glance. She was young and slender. A riot of red-gold curls framed an oval face.

Hooking his thumbs in his gunbelt, he raised his gaze to her face again. "You say that like it should mean something."

She stared at him through eyes as blue and clear as a high mountain stream. "Doesn't it?"

"Not to me."

"My mother was Leila McGuire."

"So?"

Suddenly out of steam, Callie stared up at him, intimidated by his size, by the apparent dislike in his eyes, by the gun that looked so at home on his right hip.

"I . . . that is, my mother . . . I thought . . ."

"Spit it out, girl. What do you want from me?"

"Money." She blurted the word, too desperate to be tactful.

"Money?" A hint of a smile played over his mouth. "I didn't know Cheyenne's tarts made house calls."

Callie's face went white, then red. He was calling her a whore! Without thinking, she stood on tiptoe and slapped him as hard as she could. The sound of her hand striking his flesh seemed to echo in the ensuing silence.

Caleb swore in surprise as her small palm cracked against his cheek. It didn't really hurt, of course—she was too diminutive to inflict any real damage—but he had to admit it did sting a little.

Callie stared at him, her eyes growing wide with fear as the print of her hand blossomed on his cheek. Appalled by what she'd done, she turned on her heel and ran for home, certain she'd rather meet the devil himself than face the anger she'd glimpsed in the half-breed's cold gray eyes.

Caleb stared after the girl, his hand still pressed to his cheek. Shaking his head, he walked down the stairs, took up the buckskin's reins, and led the horse to the barn located behind the house.

Duncan had set a store by his horses and didn't hold with leaving them in the livery barn in town. Caleb shook his head as he put the buckskin in a box stall and closed the door. He'd seen houses in the panhandle that weren't as big or as comfortable as the old man's barn.

After seeing to the buckskin's needs, he returned to the house. In the parlor, he sat on the high-backed sofa and removed his moccasins, then rolled another cigarette and sat staring into the fireplace, wondering who the devil Leila McGuire was and why her daughter had come to him for money.

One corner of his mouth lifted in a wry grin as he thought of the girl with the red-gold hair. Cheeky little thing, drumming up business outside the saloon. She didn't look to be more than fifteen, sixteen at the most. Pretty eyes, though, he mused, contemplating the glowing end of his cigarette. Deep and blue, like a summer sky. Pretty skin, too, kind of soft and creamy-looking.

With a shake of his head, he flicked the cigarette butt into the fireplace, then rummaged through his saddlebags. Tonight he'd eat jerky and hard biscuits, but tomorrow he'd order in plenty of supplies to stock the pantry.

Tomorrow. In the morning he'd go find out how things stood at the bank, and in a day or two, or a week or two, he'd ride out to the ranch and have a look around. There was no hurry, not if

Joe Brigman was in charge. The man loved the Rocking S as if it were his own.

Dragging his hand over his jaw, Caleb admitted to a vague reluctance to go out to the ranch. Once it had been the only place in the white man's world that seemed like home. Would he still feel the same, or had growing up changed all that?

With a sigh, he wondered if he'd ever really feel at home anywhere again.

Digging the makings from his shirt pocket, he rolled another cigarette and took a deep drag, bemused by all the decisions that had come with his inheritance.

Sooner or later he'd have to decide what to do with the ranch and the mansion. He'd have to decide if he was ready to settle down here in Cheyenne, or anywhere else, for that matter. He'd been on the move for the last twelve years, never staying long in any one place, never feeling the need to put down roots. Never having a place to call his own, until now. . . .

It hit him then, really hit him for the first time. Duncan Stryker was dead, and the Rocking S belonged to him, lock, stock and barrel.

"It's mine," he mused aloud, and a thrill of exhilaration rushed through him, potent as hundred-proof whiskey. "All mine!"

He knew then what he was going to do. He was going to keep the ranch, and every year he'd take cattle to the Indians, just like his mother had. It would be his final revenge against the old man, his way of honoring his mother's memory.

Caleb glanced around the room, thinking how peaceful it was to be home again now that the old man was gone. He could feel his mother's spirit hovering over him, promising him that things would get better.

And this time he believed her.

# *Chapter Four*

Callie brushed a stray wisp of hair from her forehead, then, with a sigh, carried a tray of dirty dishes into the kitchen. Grabbing a damp rag, she returned to the dining room to wipe off the oilcloth that covered the table before setting it with clean silverware.

It was just after noon, the busiest time of the day. Most of the tables were occupied, filled with single men who stopped at Maude Colton's Family Restaurant twice a day for a taste of home cooking and some of Fanny Monroe's sassy talk. Fanny was the cook, and though she wasn't pretty and she weighed almost two hundred pounds, the men loved her, gray hair, wrinkles, and all. She came out of the kitchen several times a day to say hello to her favorite customers. Mrs. Colton didn't like the way Fanny carried on with the customers, but she knew better than to make an issue of it because Fanny Monroe was the best cook in the territory.

Callie was clearing one of the tables when a hush fell over the restaurant. Glancing over her shoulder, she saw the reason for the sudden silence. Caleb Stryker was coming through the door.

Callie shook her head in despair. What a day! First Richard Ashton had come into the restaurant—smiling his smug smile, flirting outrageously, making unseemly suggestions—and now Caleb Stryker was here.

She felt her cheeks flush as she recalled how she had slapped him the night before. Merciful heavens, had he come here to get even?

Her mouth went dry as she watched him cross the floor to an empty table. He moved with all the sinewy grace of a wolf on the prowl. He was dressed as he had been last night, in a gray shirt, buckskin pants, and moccasins.

Apparently unaware of his impact on the room, he tossed his hat onto the chair beside him and reached for the menu. He seemed to be unaware of her presence as well, and yet she had the feeling that he knew exactly how many people were in the restaurant and why they had all stopped talking the minute he walked in. It was his eyes, she thought, those cold gray eyes. They didn't miss a thing.

She wished futilely that there was another serving girl to take his order so that she wouldn't have to go near him. She'd hoped never to see that odious man again. All her hopes and dreams had been shattered when he refused to give her the money that Duncan Stryker had promised her mother. She'd been counting on that money to get her out of Cheyenne, to give her a start at a new life in a town where no one had ever heard of Leila McGuire.

She took her time setting the table she'd just cleared, stalling for time, hoping that maybe Fanny would come out of the kitchen and decide to wait on the half-breed.

Gradually, the conversation in the restaurant picked up again, but she noticed that the men's voices remained hushed, as if they were afraid to call attention to themselves. They all sent furtive glances in Stryker's direction, though, their gazes coolly assessing, wondering if he was as dangerous as he was purported to be, wondering if it was true that he'd killed near a dozen men in the last eight years.

Gathering her courage, Callie walked up to the gunman's table. "Can I help you?" she asked curtly.

Caleb looked up, his brows drawing together in a frown as he recognized the girl who had slapped him the night before.

"Got a day job too, I see," he drawled.

Callie curled her hands into fists as she felt the hot color climb up her neck and wash into her cheeks.

"I am not a street girl," she hissed, keeping her voice low so no one else could hear.

One black brow arched upward in silent skepticism. "You could have fooled me."

"Listen, mister, do you want something to eat or not?"

"A steak. Rare."

She glared at him. What a brute he was. She was

surprised he didn't want his steak raw. Pivoting on her heel, she stormed into the kitchen, her fingers itching to scratch his eyes out. Darn him! Why did he have the power to irritate her so?

Caleb sat back in his chair, watching the waitress swish around the room, taking orders, clearing tables, avoiding an occasional hand that slid in her direction. A number of the men flirted with her, but she didn't respond except to blush now and then. She was a funny kind of street girl, he mused, or maybe she just liked to play hard to get.

She refused to meet his eyes when she served his meal, staying at his table only long enough to pour him a cup of coffee and ask if he needed anything else.

He shook his head, amused at her anger. Hell, he was the one who should be angry. She'd slapped him for no good reason, then run down the steps as though the hounds of hell were snapping at her heels.

The steak was just the way he liked it, thick and rare; the fried potatoes were plentiful and well-seasoned, the biscuits hot and fluffy. It was, in fact, the best meal he'd had in months, and he sat back in his chair, happy to have nothing to do and no place to go. The coffee was strong and black, and he asked for a second cup just to annoy the girl. What was her name? Callie something.

Gradually, the restaurant emptied as the customers went back to work, until only Caleb remained, sipping at a third cup of coffee. The girl looked different than he remembered. Her hair was coiled in a knot at the nape of her neck. The blue of her dress deepened the blue of her eyes. She wore a white apron over her skirt, tied in back in a big bow. It made her look like a little girl playing dress-up.

Callie cleared the other tables, acutely conscious of the half-breed's gaze on her back as she moved around the room, replacing the oilcloths with red checked gingham for the dinner crowd. Why didn't he leave? He couldn't possibly want more coffee. He'd had three cups already!

"What've you got for dessert?"

His voice was deep and dark and rich, reaching out to her from across the room, making all her senses come alive.

"Apple pie."

"My favorite. Think you could bring me a slice?"

Muttering under her breath, Callie cut a wedge of pie and carried it to his table.

"I need a fork."

She grabbed one from the next table and slammed it down in front of him. "Anything else? A clean napkin? Another cup of coffee? A glass of water?"

"Another cup of coffee would be nice," he allowed, his lips twitching in what looked suspiciously like a grin.

In a huff, she poured him another cup of coffee, then went into the kitchen to escape his mocking grin.

"Lunch crowd all gone?" Fanny asked, tucking a wisp of hair behind her ear.

"Not quite. That gunman is still out there." Callie washed her hands and dried them on her apron. "I think he's planning to spend the day."

"Gunman?" Fanny asked, frowning. "What gunman?"

"The one at table two."

"Is he bothering you?"

"Not in the way you think."

Fanny planted her hands on her ample hips and eyed Callie intently. "What's that mean, sugar?"

"He . . . nothing."

Fanny nodded. "He's a fine lookin' man," she mused. "Tall as a tree. Broad shoulders and slim hips. I always liked a man with broad shoulders and slim hips."

Callie stared at her, aghast. "What are you talking about?"

"Caleb Stryker, of course. I saw him through the door. I ain't seen him in, oh, must be twelve years by now. I used to cook for the Strykers, you know, but when Missus Stryker passed on, I quit. But that boy, well, he's not the kind a woman would forget."

"Well, I'd like to forget him," Callie retorted emphatically. "I'm going to my room. I'll be back in time for the dinner crowd."

"Okay, sugar. Don't be late."

Caleb took a last bite of pie and drained his cup, wondering what was keeping the girl. She hadn't given him his bill yet.

But it wasn't Callie who came through the kitchen doorway.

"How ya doin', Caleb?"

"Fanny!"

Rising, Caleb reached for her hand, but she caught him in a hug and gave him a squeeze.

"Welcome home, Caleb."

"Thanks." He grinned at her. "You haven't changed a bit. How've you been?"

She patted her ample girth. "Fine, as always. I'm surprised to see you here."

"Yeah, well, I'm surprised to be here."

"I'm sorry about your ma. I know how you loved her."

Caleb nodded.

"You been giving my girl a bad time out here?"

"Not me. I just stopped by for lunch."

"Well, you've got her spooked. You be nice to her, hear? She's had some rough times."

"Who hasn't?" he muttered under his breath. "You still taking chicks under your wing, Fanny?"

"Now and then. You mind what I said now."

"Okay, Fanny, I hear you. How much do I owe you for lunch?"

"This one's on the house."

"Thanks, Fanny. See you at dinner."

Callie shook her head. He was there again, sitting at the same table. She knew it didn't mean a thing. Lots of men took their meals at the restaurant, but it annoyed her just the same. She couldn't help but feel he'd come back just to irritate her.

She tried to pretend he wasn't there, but she could feel his eyes watching her. Distracted, she spilled a glass of water in Milt Dugan's lap, dropped a plate on the floor, and upended Mr. Paul's soup bowl.

She'd never been this clumsy, not even her first day. Her face was red with embarrassment when she served Caleb Stryker his dinner. She didn't miss the amusement in his eyes, or the way he held on to his water glass when she set his plate on the table.

"Anything wrong?" she snapped.

"No, ma'am. You just seem a mite fidgety, and I already had one bath today."

A clear image of that long lean body reclining in

a tub popped into Callie's mind, causing an odd fluttering in her stomach.

"Do you need anything else?" she asked, her voice emerging in a high squeak.

"No, ma'am."

Relieved, she turned away from the table, only to trip over his outstretched leg. Arms flailing, she tried to regain her balance, only to reel backward and land in his lap.

She wanted to die. Laughter erupted all around her as she flailed her arms, trying to get up. And then she felt his hands on her waist, effortlessly lifting her, placing her on her feet. He was laughing, too. The sound flowed over her like warm honey, making her want to scream because she liked the sound of his laughter, and she didn't want to like anything about him.

She whirled around to face him, her hand lifting of its own accord.

"I wouldn't," he warned, and his voice was as cold as the look in his eyes.

Chastened, Callie slowly lowered her arm and then, with as much dignity as she could muster, she swept out of the room, hoping she'd never lay eyes on Caleb Stryker again as long as she lived.

# Chapter Five

Callie stared at Mrs. Colton. "You can't mean it!"

"I do mean it, miss. I heard about the spectacle you made of yourself today. Spilling water in Mr. Dugan's lap, breaking dishes, knocking over Mr. Paul's soup. Why, he might have been badly burned. And then falling into a customer's lap! I run a respectable restaurant, and I won't have anyone who works for me behaving in such an unseemly fashion."

"It won't happen again."

"That's right." Maude Colton swept Callie's room with a long assessing glance. "You're paid up until tomorrow night. I'll expect you to find other accommodations by then."

"But . . ." Callie bit down on her lower lip, refusing to beg. "Yes, ma'am."

With a curt nod, Maude Colton turned on her

heel and left the room, closing the door firmly behind her.

Callie stared at the door. What was she going to do now? Where would she go? She had worked in the restaurant in exchange for room and board and two dollars a week. What little money she'd saved, she'd spent on clothes, which she'd needed badly after the fire.

"Oh, Mama," she murmured. "What am I gonna do now?"

Sitting on the edge of the bed, Callie gazed at the rag rug at her feet as she contemplated her future. There were very few businessmen in Cheyenne who employed outside help; most of the shops were owned and run by a man and his family. Except for the saloons. She shuddered at the idea of working in one of the gambling halls that lined the main street, serving drinks, letting drunken cowhands paw her, taking them upstairs. . . .

She shook her head. She couldn't do that. She'd starve first, she thought adamantly, and then sighed. Maybe she was tainted somehow. Maybe that kind of life was in her blood. Maybe there was no point in fighting it any longer. Her mother had worked in the Miner's Rest. It was where Leila had met Duncan Stryker. He'd become her favorite customer. And then her only customer.

Callie felt the sudden sting of tears. Everyone in Cheyenne knew her mother had been Duncan Stryker's mistress. For the last four years, everywhere Callie went, she'd seen the knowledge in the eyes of the women, the speculation in the eyes of the men as they wondered if she'd follow in her mother's footsteps when she was old enough.

Callie wiped the tears from her eyes with the

backs of her hands. Well, she was old enough, she thought bleakly, though she sometimes felt far older than her seventeen years. Old enough and needy enough, but she'd never do it. Never!

She sat up straight, rubbing the ache in her back as she gazed at her mother's photograph. Leila had been a beautiful woman. Why had she held herself so cheaply? Why had she dragged her daughter from town to town, selling her favors in mining camps and cheap saloons? There had been many men who wanted to care for her, a few who had even offered to marry her. But it had been Duncan Stryker who captured her heart. He had been handsome, rich, powerful. He could have set Leila up in a fine house and showered her with wealth, yet he'd kept her in a suite of rooms above the Miner's Rest, and Leila had put up with it for almost five years because she loved him, refusing to believe his promises were lies.

And now her mother was dead, and Duncan was dead, and she was alone.

*He'll look after you, baby. He promised me he would.*

Those had been her mother's dying words. But three days after the fire that had killed her mother, Duncan Stryker had died of a heart attack. Callie had gone to the funeral, intending to ask Mrs. Stryker if Duncan had left her anything, but she had taken one look at the widow's grief-stricken face and changed her mind. She'd known, somehow she'd known, that Duncan Stryker's wife didn't know anything about Leila or the promises Duncan had made, and Callie didn't have the heart to tell her.

Even now she could remember how beautiful

Mrs. Stryker had been, with her tawny skin, almond-shaped eyes, and coal-black hair. The widow had carried herself regally, looking elegant in her long black dress and veil. She had stood at the graveside, her gloved hands folded, her head bowed, as the priest said the last rites over her husband. She had accepted the condolences of the mourners and thanked Father Cardella for coming. She had remained at the grave long after everyone else had left, silent tears streaming down her face. Looking at her had made Callie hate Duncan Stryker even more. Why had he been unfaithful to such a beautiful woman, a woman who had obviously cared for him deeply?

Callie let out a long sigh. Her mother had said that no man, be he gentle or mean, handsome or homely, rich or poor, could be trusted to remain faithful to one woman. It was in a man's nature to stray, Leila had said, her voice filled with sadness, and there was nothing a woman could do about it.

Well, there was something she could do about it, Callie thought. She'd never love a man the way her mother had loved Duncan Stryker, never trust a man with her heart.

"You owe me, Duncan Stryker," Callie muttered. "Darn it, you owe me, and I mean to collect!"

Rising, she smoothed her dress, brushed her hair, and left the boardinghouse, walking resolutely toward Orville Hoag's law office.

Ten minutes later, her determination had turned to defeat.

"I'm sorry," Mr. Hoag said again. "I'm afraid any promises Duncan Stryker made to your mother died with him. If you had something in writing, if he'd mentioned you or your mother in his will . . ." The lawyer shook his head. "Even then, I'm afraid you'd have a hard time collecting, since Mrs. Stryker's will superseded his. I'm sorry."

"But it's not fair. Everything my mother owned burned in the fire at the Miner's Rest. All her things, the money she'd saved, my clothes . . . isn't there anything I can do?"

"I'm afraid not."

Discouraged, Callie thanked the lawyer for his time and left his office. She kept her gaze lowered as she passed the saloons, hating the tinny music that blared from within, hating the smell of smoke and whiskey that drifted through the open doors. It was all so familiar. Maybe she was foolish to fight it. Maybe it would be easier just to walk into the Three Queens and ask for a job. The pay was good, she could set her own hours, pick her own customers. . . .

Callie swallowed the bile that rose in her throat and hurried down the boardwalk. Slipping her hand into her pocket, she clutched the letter she'd received earlier that day. It was from Molly Faye, an old friend of her mother's. Molly Faye had saved enough money to leave the Miner's Rest and now she had a chance to buy a millinery shop in Denver, but she needed another thousand dollars. She'd written to Callie, offering her a partnership in the business if she could come up with enough money.

Callie let out a sigh. If Duncan Stryker had kept his promise to look after her, she wouldn't be in this mess now. She'd have the money she needed to leave Cheyenne and start a new life where no one knew who her mother had been.

She was so preoccupied with her thoughts she didn't see the man emerge from the bank, wasn't even aware of his presence until she slammed into his back.

"Oh! Excuse me," Callie said, her face flushing with embarrassment. "I didn't see you. I'm sor— you!"

Caleb shook his head as he gazed into Callie McGuire's flushed face.

"I might have known it would be you," he drawled.

Callie glared at him. He looked prosperous in a pair of black trousers and a dark gray shirt, both of which were obviously new. He seemed to like gray, she noted absently.

"You gonna stand there staring daggers at me all day?" Caleb asked dryly.

Impotent fury pulsed through Callie's veins. She wished she could scream at him, slap him, shoot him with the big ugly pistol he wore tied low on his right hip.

Instead, she gathered her composure and said, with as much dignity as she could muster, "Indeed, no. If you'll kindly step aside and let me pass, I'll be on my way."

"Late for work at the restaurant, I guess," Caleb remarked, amused by the anger in her eye and her rigid stance.

"No," she retorted. "Thanks to you, I was fired."

"Me? What did I do?"

Callie shook her head. How could she tell him that it had been his presence in the restaurant that made her so clumsy?

He shrugged, as if the fact that she had lost her job was of no importance. "Now you can devote more time to your other job."

"I don't have another job," Callie said, biting off each word. "Thanks to you, I probably won't be able to find other employment once people learn that Mrs. Colton fired me for being incompetent. And I've lost my room at the boardinghouse. And I don't have any money. . . ."

To her horror, she started to cry. Tears cascaded down her cheeks, and she was helpless to stop them. She saw several women pause to stare at her, saw them putting their heads together, whispering about her, as they moved on. Soon the whole town would know she'd been crying in the middle of 16th Street.

"Here." Caleb thrust a kerchief into her hand. "Dry your tears."

She pressed the cloth to her eyes, but the tears kept coming, harder and faster. She'd held them back for so long, and now it was like trying to turn the tide.

With an oath, Caleb grabbed her by the arm and propelled her down the boardwalk. Lifting her onto the back of his horse, he swung up behind her and headed for the mansion.

Callie started to struggle, but the grip of his arm around her waist was sure and solid, comforting somehow. With a strangled sob, she collapsed against the hard wall of his chest and let the tears flow unchecked.

Caleb had called himself every kind of fool there was by the time they reached the mansion. Swinging down from the saddle, he took the girl in his arms and carried her inside, depositing her none too gently on the damask-covered sofa in the parlor. Tossing his hat on a chair, he poured two hits of scotch and placed one into the girl's hand.

"Drink it," he ordered curtly.

Obediently, she put the glass to her mouth and took a big swallow, then dissolved into a fit of coughing.

"That's not water, you know," Caleb muttered. "It's twelve-year-old Scotch. You're supposed to sip it slowly."

Callie gasped as the liquor hit her stomach like a hot rock, suffusing her with heat from head to foot. She'd never so much as tasted alcohol, and she decided then and there that she would never drink it again, if she lived.

With a shake of his head, Caleb took the glass from her hand and set it on the table beside the sofa. "You through crying now?"

Callie nodded, certain she'd never speak again. Her eyes burned, her throat burned, but somehow things didn't seem as bad as they had earlier.

"You want to tell me what this is all about?"

She nodded and as coherently as she could, she told him about her mother and Duncan Stryker's promise to look after them.

Caleb listened intently, swearing under his breath as the girl's tale unfolded. So, he thought bitterly, it wasn't enough that Duncan had taken Red Feather away from her own people, he had humiliated her by keeping a mistress. No doubt everybody in the whole town knew he'd been unfaithful. If the man wasn't already dead, Caleb would have killed him with his bare hands.

"And so," Callie finished, "I need some money so I can get out of town. A friend of my mother's has a chance to buy a millinery shop in Denver. She said if I had a thousand dollars, I could go into business with her, as her partner. I have to have the money by next week, or she's going to find someone else."

Caleb whistled softly. She didn't want much, just a thousand dollars in a week's time.

Callie sniffed, his silence spurring her hope. At least he hadn't said no. "I want to go someplace where no one knows who I am or what my mother did for a living."

Caleb nodded. He could understand her shame. He'd been ashamed of having Duncan Stryker for a father ever since he was old enough to know what kind of man his father really was.

He glanced up to find the girl staring at him, her tear-stained eyes wide and filled with hope.

"Don't you have any other family? Brothers or sisters?"

"No." She smiled wistfully. "I was a mistake, you know. Children weren't welcome in my mother's line of work."

Caleb grunted softly, a twinge of pity stirring within him. She looked like a little girl, lost and alone. But looking after little lost girls wasn't his stock in trade.

"I'd like to help you, Miss McGuire," he said, not meeting her gaze. "But I'm a little short of cash right now."

"That's impossible. Your father had more money than anyone in town."

"He did, but I'm afraid my mother made some rather bad investments after he died. What little actual cash he had left was used to buy blankets and medical supplies."

Callie frowned. "Medical supplies? For what?"

"It seems she sent a wagon train of supplies

and several hundred head of cattle to the Lakota reservation to help see the Indians through the winter."

Caleb smiled, pleased by what his mother had done.

"You're broke?"

Caleb hesitated. He wasn't really broke. He had a few hundred dollars cash, and he could easily borrow a thousand or so from the bank, but he was suddenly, unaccountably, reluctant to provide a way for Callie McGuire to leave Cheyenne.

"I'm not exactly broke, I just don't have much ready cash to speak of. It seems my mother mortgaged the Rocking S to raise money to lobby for Indian rights in Congress."

Caleb rubbed a hand across his jaw. The banker, George Webster, had advised him that the note would be due the end of the year.

Caleb laughed softly, thinking how outraged Duncan would be if he knew what Faith Stryker had done.

Callie's shoulders slumped in defeat. She'd humbled herself, humiliated herself, and for what? Caleb Stryker didn't have any more money than she did despite the fact that he owned a ranch and a mansion.

Too bad he didn't own a saloon. He might have given her a job!

"Well, thanks for nothing," she muttered.

"What are you gonna do now?" he asked.

Callie shrugged. Defeat weighed heavily on her shoulders. Maybe she should just quit fighting it and take over where her mother had left off.

"I guess I'll go see if the Three Queens has room for another girl."

Her words, softly spoken, seemed to hover in the air, like smoke.

Caleb frowned. "You ever done anything like that before?"

"No." She shrugged again. "Does it make a difference?" She was caught between a rock and a hard place, she thought bleakly. It was either go to work at one of the saloons, or give in to Richard. Neither thought was particularly appealing, but it was better to belong to no one than to belong to someone she didn't love.

The thought of Richard made her frown. He'd been after her ever since her mother died, trying to get her alone, telling her that he'd take good care of her if she'd just say the word. No matter how many times Callie told him no, he always came back, offering her more money each time, predicting that sooner or later she'd give in because she was no better than her mother.

But she didn't intend to be *that* kind of girl. She'd serve drinks in the Three Queens, that was all. It might take longer to save enough money to get out of Cheyenne, but she'd leave with her virtue and her integrity intact.

Caleb experienced a sudden sinking sensation in the pit of his stomach when he thought of Callie working at the Three Queens. The saloon girls were hired to wait on the customers, nothing more, but sooner or later they all made their way into one of the cribs upstairs, tempted by the promise of more money, lured by the false hope that they'd meet the man who would give them a better life.

He thought of giving Callie the money she wanted and letting her go, but for some inexplicable reason he couldn't bear the thought of never seeing her again.

"You haven't answered my question," Callie said. "Do you think my lack of experience will matter?"

Caleb swore under his breath. She was young and pretty. Her skin was like smooth cream; her red-gold hair glowed as though it had an inner fire. And her eyes—they were as wide and blue as a midsummer sky. She wouldn't have any trouble earning a living.

"I can give you all the experience you need," he muttered.

Callie smiled at him uncertainly. "What do you mean?" she asked, and felt the warm afterglow of the whiskey turn suddenly cold and sour.

"You can start at the saloon tomorrow," Caleb said, his voice taut. "You can start here tonight."

The words seemed to echo in the stillness of the room. Callie stared at him, her heart pounding in her ears. "What . . . what do you mean?"

"I mean I intend to give you some experience."

Without warning, he grabbed her and kissed her, his lips warm against hers, his arms holding her body to his chest. He smelled of smoke and leather, of whiskey and wanting. She tried to push him away, but it was like trying to move a mountain.

She moaned softly as his tongue slid across her lower lip, felt a fevered stirring in the pit of her stomach as his tongue gained entrance to her mouth. She was dying, drowning in the taste of him.

Hardly aware of what she was doing, she pressed her breasts against his chest, wanting to be closer. Her tongue met his, and she felt the wonder of it clear to her toes. Heat stirred in her belly and exploded outward, hotter than any flame, more potent than the whiskey she'd consumed earlier, and she was helpless to fight him.

Caleb drew a ragged breath and then kissed her again, more gently this time, drinking from her lips as though he were a man who had long been deprived of nourishment. She tasted of Scotch, yet her kisses were more intoxicating than any whiskey known to man. Her skin was like satin in his hands, her lips as soft as the velvet of a butterfly's wings.

Spellbound by his touch, Callie let him hold her and kiss her. Time and place ceased to exist. There was no right or wrong, there was only this moment, this man, and the wonder of his touch. And then his hand caressed her breast, and reality came crashing down. She opened her eyes and stared at him, seeing a man who was a stranger, a man who didn't care who she was.

With a sob, she tried to push him away.

Caleb's heart was pounding like a runaway train; his blood was on fire, molten with need. He drew back to take a breath and it was then that he saw the fear in her eyes, heard the whimpers of terror that had fallen on deaf ears.

With an oath, he let her go and she sank down on the sofa. He stood there, staring down at her, his chest heaving, his hands clenched at his sides.

"I think you'd better go before you get into real trouble."

He never should have touched her, he thought. She was trouble looking for a place to happen, a brushfire waiting for a spark.

"I don't have anyplace to go."

"Go home," Caleb said, his voice brittle with longing and self-disgust.

"I have no home. Mrs. Colton turned me out."

He was lost and he knew it. Whether her story about Duncan having promised to look after her was true or not no longer mattered. He couldn't turn her out into the street with nowhere to go.

Gazing into her shimmering blue eyes, he knew, deep in his soul, that Callie McGuire was about to turn his life upside down.

# Chapter Six

"You can stay here tonight," Caleb said curtly. "Tomorrow we'll get your things from the boardinghouse."

She stared at him, her heart pounding with trepidation. Oh, Lord, what if he meant to seduce her? What if he meant to keep her, the way Duncan Stryker had kept her mother? She knew then that she couldn't do it. She'd rather starve than become what her mother had been.

She gathered her tattered dignity around her. "I can't."

"Can't what?"

She felt the heat creep into her cheeks again. "I can't be your . . . your . . . you know."

"I'm not looking for a live-in whore, Miss McGuire. I'm looking for a housekeeper, someone to do the cooking, someone to keep an eye on things when I'm out at the ranch."

Callie stared up at him, unable to believe her good fortune. She wouldn't have to work at the saloon. She could work here, in this beautiful house, and as soon as she had saved enough money, she'd leave Cheyenne and never look back. She'd make a fresh start in a town where no one would know who she was or what her mother had done for a living. And she'd never have to see Richard Ashton—or Caleb Stryker—again.

"Are you sure?" she asked breathlessly.

"Quite sure. The bedrooms are upstairs. Take any one you want except the one at the end of the hall. That's mine."

"Thank you, Mr. Stryker. You've been very kind."

Caleb snorted. He'd been called a lot of things in his day, but kind wasn't one of them. He stood in the doorway, watching as she walked up the carpeted stairway. He heard the sound of her muffled footsteps as she went from door to door, pausing to peer into each room. He could almost see her frown when she tried the door to his mother's room and found it locked.

He swore softly when he heard her enter the next to the last room at the end of the hall and close the door. She'd made a good choice, he mused as he listened to her footsteps overhead, then felt his stomach knot with tension as he realized she'd chosen the room next to his.

Callie paused beside the big brass bed, her hand dropping to stroke the blue velvet counterpane. She'd never seen such a beautiful bedroom in her life. There were white lace curtains at the windows, a flowered carpet on the floor, blue-and-white striped paper on the walls. There was even a fireplace with a mantel of cherry wood. She found a white enamel bathtub behind a folding screen, and there was a mirror over a dainty oak dressing table. It was more luxury than she'd dreamed existed.

With a soft sigh of pleasure, she fell back on the bed, running her hands over the soft velvet. She was going to live here, in Duncan Stryker's mansion. With Duncan Stryker's son . . .

She felt the heat climb into her cheeks as she remembered the incredible strength of his arms around her, the taste of his mouth, the scent of his heated flesh. No one had ever kissed her like that, as if he wanted to devour her, to draw out her very soul until she stood naked and vulnerable before him. She had gone up in flames, like a tree in the midst of a forest fire, unmindful of right or wrong.

It couldn't happen again. It *wouldn't* happen again. She was going to be his housekeeper and cook, nothing more.

Turning on her side, she closed her eyes and fell asleep dreaming of seven-course meals and bathtubs filled with hot water and fragrant bubbles.

Sunlight warmed her face and she sighed as she turned over, reluctant to awake from the beautiful dream she'd been having.

For a moment, she snuggled deeper into the covers, reliving the fantasy. She'd been a princess, living in an enormous castle. She'd had servants to do her bidding, more money than she could ever spend, closets filled with expensive clothes and shoes and hats and gloves. And she'd been loved by a tall, dark, handsome prince, loved and cherished in a way few women ever knew. . . .

A sharp rap on the door scattered the last images and she sat up. For a moment, she wondered where she was, and then it all came back to her. She was in Caleb Stryker's mansion.

"Are you in there, Miss McGuire?"

The harsh sound of his voice made her jump.

"Yes. What is it?"

"It's way past time for breakfast, that's what it is," Caleb muttered irritably. "Do you always sleep this late?"

"No, I'm sorry. I'll be right down."

She scrambled out of bed only to stare at her reflection in the mirror. She looked awful. Her hair was a tangled mass. Her dress was badly wrinkled from sleeping in it all night. How could she possibly go downstairs and face him looking as she did?

Well, there was no help for it. Squaring her shoulders, she opened the bedroom door and marched resolutely down the stairs and into the kitchen.

For a moment, she could only stand there, staring. It was a spacious room, awash with light from the morning sun. A big square table ringed by four chairs stood in one corner. There was a large cast-iron stove and a sink with an indoor pump. She found a large pantry beside the back door, the shelves stocked with a wide variety of tinned fruits and vegetables and meat, sacks of sugar and flour and corn meal, jars of preserves and honey. One cupboard was filled with translucent china and crystal glassware, another held the dishes she assumed were for everyday use.

"Oh, Fanny," she murmured, "I'll bet you miss this kitchen!"

Thirty minutes later, she called Caleb Stryker to breakfast. He took his place at the dining room table, one black brow arched in curious amusement as he waited for her to serve him.

Callie refused to meet his gaze as she set his plate on the table. She poured him a cup of coffee, then stood back, watching him anxiously. She had never done much cooking.

Caleb eyed his plate as if he expected the food to attack him; then, with a sigh, he took a bite. The scrambled eggs were hard, the bacon burned, and the baking powder biscuits looked like little rocks.

Worry spread through Callie as she watched his expression.

"It's not bad," Caleb said charitably. "Aren't you going to eat?"

"In here?" Callie's gaze swept around the room, taking in the blue-and-gold wallpaper, the carved oak table, the crystal chandelier. "With you?"

Caleb shrugged. "Why not?"

"What would people think if they knew you ate breakfast with the hired help?"

He looked up, his deep gray eyes suddenly hard and cold. "I don't much care what people think," he retorted. "But you can eat in the kitchen if that's what you want."

It *was* what she wanted, Callie thought, but she didn't want him to think she was afraid of him, so she fixed a plate for herself and sat down across from him.

They ate in silence.

Though he didn't look at her, Caleb was acutely aware of Callie's presence at the table. He knew each time she slid a glance in his direction, just as he knew she was uncomfortable sitting there with him. She didn't think it was fitting, the hired help eating with the lord of the manor. It made him uncomfortable, too, but not for the same reasons. He felt fidgety because she was close, so close he could smell the scent of her hair, hear the whisper of her skirts when she moved.

He'd hardly slept at all the night before. Every time he closed his eyes, he'd seen her face, her eyes wide and scared, her lips full and pink, like a rose in full bloom. He remembered all too well how she'd felt in his arms, how tiny her waist, how soft her skin.

He'd tossed and turned all night long, thinking of her, imagining her in his bed. It had been a mistake to let her stay, and a bigger mistake to give her a job, but he didn't have the heart to tell her he'd changed his mind. It was obvious she needed someone to look out for her. It surprised the devil out of him to realize that he wanted to be the one to do it.

Abruptly, he pushed his plate aside and stood up. "We're leaving in ten minutes."

"Leaving?"

"To get your things from old lady Colton."

"Oh."

"Be ready," he muttered, and left the room.

Outside, he saddled the buckskin, then walked up and down the yard, waiting for the time to pass, waiting for his blood to cool. He'd done a lot of stupid things in his time, he thought bleakly, but inviting a temptation like Callie McGuire to live under his roof had to be the dumbest move of all.

She was young.

She was innocent.

She was trouble.

She stepped outside five minutes later. He could see she'd tried to smooth the wrinkles from her skirt and do something with her hair, but to no avail. She looked as if she needed to be ironed from head to foot, and yet he thought she looked mighty appealing in her wrinkled dress and fly-away hair.

"Ready?"

At her nod, he boosted her into the saddle, then swung up behind her. He wrapped one arm around her waist, his nostrils immediately filling with her scent as her hair swept his cheek.

A muscle twitched in his jaw as he touched his heels to the buckskin's flanks. Neither of them spoke as they rode down 17th Street and turned left on Ransom.

When they reached the boardinghouse, Caleb dismounted and tossed the buckskin's reins over the fence, then lifted Callie from the saddle, his hands lingering at her waist far longer than was necessary. For a timeless moment, his eyes met hers.

Callie swallowed hard, the heat of his gaze searing her soul even as the touch of his hands seemed to burn through the material of her dress.

He muttered something unintelligible under his breath as he turned away, and after a moment Callie followed him up the walkway toward the front door.

Maude Colton answered their knock, her pale

brown eyes showing her disdain as she admitted Callie to the parlor. She looked like a prune, Caleb thought, with her mouth twisted into a sneer and her face all pinched-looking and suspicious as Caleb followed Callie up the stairs to her room.

Callie opened the bedroom door and stepped inside. "It isn't proper for you to be up here with me, you know."

"Why?" he muttered, sending a withering glance in Maude Colton's direction. "We've got the best chaperon in town."

"And the one with the biggest mouth, too," Callie whispered, and then shrugged, knowing it was useless to argue with him. He'd do what he pleased whether she liked it or not.

Caleb stood in the doorway, watching while Callie placed her meager belongings in a battered carpetbag.

"Is that it?" he asked. "That's everything?"

Callie nodded, embarrassed to confess that she owned so little.

"We'll stop at Brewster's and you can buy whatever you need."

"I . . . but it isn't . . ."

"I suppose it isn't proper for me to buy you clothes, either," he remarked. "Well, consider it part of your wages, which, by the way, we never discussed."

"I'm sure you'll be fair."

One black eyebrow rose in a questioning arch. "Are you?"

Callie nodded. Fastening the carpetbag, she took a last look around the room, then walked out the door. She could feel Mrs. Colton's narrow-eyed gaze on her back as she left the house, and she knew it would be all over town by nightfall how Callie McGuire had let a man into her bedroom in the middle of the day.

At Brewster's, Caleb bought her three new dresses, two pairs of shoes, stockings, a bonnet, a blue velvet jacket, a lacy pink parasol, a pair of gloves, a fan made of feathers, and a white lawn nightgown. He also bought her a new hairbrush, combs, and pins and ribbons for her hair. He insisted that she buy undergarments as well, and then tossed a bottle of rose water onto the pile because he liked the way it smelled.

Callie's cheeks flushed a deep crimson as Caleb told Ed Brewster to charge her purchases to his account. She didn't miss the speculative look in Mr. Brewster's eye as he wrote the amount in his account book, nor did she miss the disapproving frown on Martha Brewster's face as she wrapped Callie's merchandise in brown paper and placed it in a string bag.

"I feel like a kept woman," Callie muttered as they left the store, then wished she'd kept her mouth shut because a kept woman was exactly what her mother had been.

But Caleb only shrugged as he followed her out of Brewster's.

"Wait here," he said. "I forgot to buy cigars."

Callie nodded. She was watching two boys play jack straws when she heard a familiar voice. Turning, she saw Richard Ashton walking toward her. He looked prosperous as always, decked out in a dark brown suit, a brown-and-white striped shirt, and a black bowler hat. He was a handsome young man, with wavy blond hair, dark brown eyes, and an engaging smile, and she might have liked him if he'd treated her with respect instead of scorn.

"Well, looks like this is my lucky day," Richard drawled as he came to stand beside her. "I've been looking all over town for you. Where've you been hiding?"

"Nowhere."

Richard's hand slid up her arm. "My folks left town yesterday," he said, giving her shoulder a squeeze. "We could have ourselves a little party tonight, if you know what I mean."

Callie shook her head, hoping that no one could overhear Richard's odious proposition.

"I'll pick you up about eight. What do you say?"

"She's busy."

Relief washed through Callie at the sound of Caleb's voice.

"This man bothering you, Miss McGuire?"

"Yes . . . no." Callie looked up at Caleb, not knowing what to say. Richard Ashton's father was not only rich, he was a judge, as well.

"He's bothering me," Caleb remarked.

He thrust the box of cigars into Callie's hands, then grabbed Richard by the shirtfront and lifted him off his feet.

"Miss McGuire is my housekeeper," Caleb said, biting off each word. "I don't want you accosting her on the street again. Is that clear?"

Richard glared at Caleb, his eyes glinting with defiance. "And just who are you?"

"I'm the man that's gonna whip you to within an inch of your life if you ever lay a hand on Miss McGuire again."

The color drained from Richard's face, but he couldn't back down. There were too many people watching now. Callie saw the Brewsters standing on the porch, along with several townspeople.

"I'm not afraid of you, you dirty half-breed," Richard said, sneering. "Let me go."

Caleb's punch came hard and fast. Richard grunted, then groaned as blood spurted from his nose.

"Caleb, his father is Judge Charles Ashton!"

"I don't care if his father's the president of the United States," Caleb retorted as he released Richard. "He'd better keep that mouth of his shut until he learns some manners." Caleb glared at Richard. "And keep your hands to yourself."

With a last warning glance in Ashton's direction, Caleb lifted Callie onto the back of the buckskin, slung the string bag over the pommel of the saddle, then swung effortlessly up behind Callie and turned the horse toward home.

Callie kept her head down, not wanting to see the inquisitive looks on the faces of the townspeople. What reputation she had left was going to be in shreds before the day was out. As soon as Mrs. Brewster got together with Mrs. Colton, the story would grow and spread, and by sundown everyone would know that Caleb and Richard had been fighting over her in the street and everyone would think she was following in her mother's footsteps. For a moment, she considered telling Stryker that she'd changed her mind, that she didn't want to work for him, that she was leaving town, money or no money.

But then the cool hand of caution took over. She didn't have enough money to buy a horse or a train ticket out of town. She didn't have any family to turn to, and she had nowhere else to go. And, if the truth be told, she didn't want to leave Caleb Stryker's house, or Caleb Stryker. She felt safe with him, which was positively foolish. Putting herself in his care was like trusting a lion to protect a lamb, and yet he had put Richard Ashton in his place. True, she was afraid of the dark secrets that hid behind Caleb's deep gray eyes, afraid of the violence that she'd witnessed only moments ago, afraid the stories she'd heard about him were all true. But she wasn't afraid of him.

At home, Caleb helped her from the saddle, handed her the string bag and box of cigars, then led the horse toward the barn.

Callie watched him go, then hurried into the house. In her room, she spread her new clothes on the bed, marveling at the rich bounty. Three new dresses! She'd never had three new dresses all at once. And two pairs of shoes—a plain brown pair for everyday and a pair of kidskin for dress-up, though when she'd be dressed up she didn't know.

Her fingers caressed the velvet jacket, then moved to stroke one of the plumes on the hat. Impulsively, she put on the bonnet and tied the bow under her chin, then posed in front of the mirror.

It was a becoming bonnet. The roses were pink, the plumes white, the ribbon that tied under her chin was a deep blue that made her eyes seem brighter, deeper.

She reached for the fan and held it in front of her face, pouting at her reflection in the mirror.

Standing at the door, unnoticed, Caleb felt a sudden clenching in his gut as he watched Callie preen in front of the looking glass. Her eyes were a smoky blue, filled with the promise of fire; her lips, slightly parted, issued an invitation to an unseen admirer. He felt a tightening in his groin as she began to sway back and forth, her hips moving in time to music only she could hear.

"May I have this dance?"

Callie whirled around, startled to see Caleb watching her, an amused expression lurking in his eyes. He was dressed all in black; it was the perfect foil for his swarthy skin and slate-gray eyes. She noticed that he was still wearing his gunbelt. It was of black leather, unadorned, showing signs of wear. The Colt rode easily on his hip, as if it were a part of him, reminding her that he was a dangerous man, one who was constantly prepared for trouble, even in his own house.

"How long have you been standing there?" she asked, conscious of the tremor in her voice. He seemed to fill the doorway, and as he stepped into the room, she felt dwarfed by his presence.

"Not long." He crossed the floor toward her, his hand reaching for hers.

Wordlessly, he took the fan from her hand and tossed it onto the bed, then drew her into his arms and waltzed her around the room. He held her as propriety demanded, leaving a discreet distance between them, yet her whole body burned at his nearness.

She risked a glance at his face, felt her breath catch in her throat as she read the thinly veiled hunger in the depths of his turbulent gray eyes.

"We shouldn't . . ." She swallowed past the rising lump in her throat. "It isn't . . ."

His right eyebrow arched upward in a gesture that was becoming familiar. "Proper?"

Callie nodded. He was a wonderful dancer, but it was hard for her to follow his lead when all she could think about was that they were alone in the house and he was in her bedroom.

He twirled her around and she caught a glimpse of the bed out of the corner of her eye. It seemed to fill the whole room. Cheeks flushing, she glanced up at him, her mouth as dry as day-old toast.

"You're safe," he said, his voice quietly reassuring. "We're just dancing."

"You're very good."

"My mother insisted I learn the white man's dances."

"She was Indian, wasn't she?"

"Lakota."

"Fanny said you lived with the Indians until you were twelve."

Caleb nodded, all expression gone from his eyes.

"Did you like living with them?"

"Yeah, I did."

"Did you ever go back?"

"No."

"Why not?"

"I don't know. I guess I was having too good a time drinking and gambling and whor—"

He cut the word in half, remembering her mother's chosen occupation. "When I wanted to go back, it was too late. There was a lot of fighting going on, and I didn't want to be involved because I was sympathetic to both sides."

Caleb stopped twirling her around, though he didn't let her go. Callie felt his gaze move over her face, soft as a caress.

"A lot of half-breeds are never happy in either world," he remarked, his expression pensive. "They never seem to know who they are, or where they belong, but I've never felt that way. I have a deep respect for my mother's people, but there's also a lot of things I admire about the whites."

"Fanny said you left town because of your father."

Caleb nodded.

"Did the two of you have a fight?"

"Every day for five years."

"Five years! What were you fighting about?"

"Everything. He wanted me to forget that I was half Indian. He wanted me to think like him, believe what he believed." Caleb shook his head. "I couldn't do it. I was young and proud and just as stubborn as he was, and the harder he tried to mold me into his image, the harder I resisted. I knew he was ashamed of my mother because she was an Indian, ashamed of me because I was a half-breed, and I hated him for it."

Callie looked up at him, wishing she could think of something to say, some words of comfort, of consolation.

Caleb gazed into her eyes, reading her thoughts as easily as print on a page. She was feeling sorry for him, and he wondered whatever had possessed him to tell her so much of his past. It wasn't something he usually shared. He didn't want her pity or her sympathy.

A soft sigh whispered past her lips. Her breath was warm and sweet, her lips a temptation he was hard pressed to resist. He wanted her. Then and there. Wanted her for reasons that made no sense. Or perhaps they did. She was lonely and he was lonely, and maybe that was reason enough.

And maybe it wasn't.

Abruptly, he released her and headed for the door.

"I won't be home for dinner," he muttered, and left her standing there in the middle of the room.

## Chapter Seven

Caleb sat at a back table in the Three Queens Saloon, his hand fisted around a glass of bourbon, trying to imagine himself as a member of the Stock Growers Association, attending church, contributing to the school building fund.

The citizens of Cheyenne had accepted Duncan Stryker because he was a rich man when being rich wasn't commonplace. Caleb sensed they would not welcome the half-breed son who'd made his living as a bounty hunter.

A few days ago, he'd been certain he wanted to move out to the ranch and raise cattle, but now he found himself having second thoughts.

Caleb finished his drink in a single swallow, then stared into the empty glass. Was that what he wanted, to try to fit in, to deny his heritage and his past?

He poured himself another drink and rolled the glass back and forth between his palms, watching the amber liquid slosh against the sides of the glass. Why hadn't he given Callie the money to leave town? Why did he want her to stay? She was too young for him. Too innocent. Too trusting. He'd had no business asking her to work for him, none at all. But he didn't want her to go, didn't want to think of her in another town. With another man.

Didn't want to sit here alone any longer.

Outside, Caleb took a deep breath. For a moment, he considered going back inside and playing a few hands of poker, but the idea didn't appeal to him near as much as going home.

He rode by the Cheyenne Club, which was located on East 17th Street, on the way to the mansion, wondering if it was as sumptuously furnished as he'd heard. He'd been told there was a large dining room, card rooms, a reading room, a billiard room and a lounge on the first floor. The chef had been imported from Canada. There were apartments for members on the second floor.

Caleb counted nineteen hitching posts as he rode by. He'd heard the rules of the club were strict—no profanity, no drunkenness, no fighting, no cheating at cards, no games on Sunday. And no ladies allowed.

He'd expected Callie to be in bed when he got home, but she was in the parlor, a train schedule on her lap.

"Kind of late for you to be up, isn't it?" Caleb remarked.

"No later than it is for you."

Caleb grunted. Dropping into one of the wing-back chairs across from the sofa, he gestured at the timetable. "You goin' somewhere?"

"Just as soon as I can."

"Where do you want to go?"

"I'm not sure. Durango, maybe. Or California. I'd like to see San Francisco."

"I've been to Durango. And Frisco. One place is pretty much like another."

"Maybe."

"And people are the same all over."

She didn't miss the note of bitterness in his voice, or the sudden hard look in his eyes. "What do you mean?"

"Nothing. Forget it." He frowned when she didn't say anything more, just sat there staring at him, her eyes looking as deep and blue as the ocean. "You'll like Frisco."

"Did you?"

"I wasn't there to have a good time. I was looking for somebody. I found him and we left."

Callie bit down on her lip, wondering if Caleb had brought the wanted man in alive. There were so many rumors about Stryker, the ruthless bounty hunter, the man without a heart, the man who didn't care if he brought his prisoners in dead or alive.

She wanted to ask him who he'd been after, how many men he'd killed, but California seemed like a safer subject. "Did you see the Pacific Ocean?"

"Yeah."

"Was it beautiful?"

"It was big." He saw the disappointment in her eyes. "And beautiful."

He knew she was seeing it in her mind from the way her eyes sparkled, and he thought again how lovely she was with her smooth, creamy skin and sky-blue eyes.

"It's late," he said. And rising to his feet, he headed for the stairs.

"Mr. Stryker."

He paused, glancing at her over his shoulder.

"Tomorrow's Sunday. Will you be going to church?"

A wry grin tugged at the corners of Caleb's mouth. "I think I'll pass."

Callie felt that every eye in the chapel was on her as she walked down the aisle and took a seat. Smoothing her skirt, she folded her hands in her lap and stared at the stained-glass window behind the pulpit. It depicted the Savior as the Good Shepherd, with a staff in his left hand and a small white lamb gently enfolded in the crook of his right arm.

A few minutes later, Father Cardella arrived and the service began. Callie sang softly but clearly, loving the words of the hymns, the feeling of peace that filled her soul as she listened to Father Cardella's promise of forgiveness in this life and joy in the life to come.

She left the church as soon as the service was over, but not before she overhead bits and pieces of the conversation between Mrs. Brewster, Mrs. Colton, and Mrs. Avery.

". . . her mother's footsteps."

"He's just as bad, taking up with the daughter of his father's mistress. . . ."

". . . living in that house alone . . ."

"The apple doesn't fall far from the tree . . ."

". . . her mother's footsteps . . ."

". . . she'd be ashamed to show her face in church."

Callie blinked rapidly, fighting the tears that burned her eyes. She shook Father Cardella's hand, then hurried down the street. Money or no money, she was leaving Cheyenne tomorrow if she had to walk!

Caleb looked up from his newspaper as he heard the front door slam. Moments later, he heard Callie banging the pots and pans in the kitchen.

Curious, he set the paper aside and went into the kitchen. Pulling a chair from the table, he straddled it, then folded his arms across the back and watched as Callie cracked eggs into a bowl, then proceeded to stir them furiously.

"Hey," he called softly. "Who do you have in there?"

"Martha Brewster," she replied through clenched teeth.

Caleb stared pointedly at the bowl, one brow arched in amusement. "I think she's dead now."

"Well, she ought to be!"

"Callie, what's wrong?"

"Nothing. I'm leaving in the morning."

"Oh?"

"Yes."

"How much do you figure I owe you for two days' work?"

"I don't know. We never talked about my wages." She looked up at him, blinking rapidly. "You said you'd be fair."

"So I did."

He stood up in a fluid movement and walked toward her. Taking the bowl from her hands, he placed it on the table, then put his hands on her shoulders. "What is it? What's bothering you?"

"Martha Brewster. She said I was just like my mother, that I didn't have any business being in a church."

A muscle worked in Caleb's jaw. "She said that to you?"

"Not to my face. But I heard her just the same."

"And that's why you want to leave town?"

"Yes."

"Running away won't solve anything."

"You're a fine one to talk. *You* ran away."

"Yeah, and it didn't solve anything. I've lived a hard life, Callie, and I've learned a lot of hard lessons. And one thing I know for sure is that you've got to stand up for yourself because no one else will."

"That might be easy for you. You're a man. But I'll never be able to hold my head up in this town again. Everyone will believe the worst because they believed it about my mother, and it was true."

Caleb took a deep breath. "I lied to you before, Callie. If you really want to leave town, I can give you the money."

Her blue eyes sparkled with excitement. "Really?"

He nodded. "But I wish you'd stay."

"Why?"

His hands slid from her shoulders to lightly grasp her arms. "I think you know why."

His words, the rough edge in his voice, sent a shiver down her spine. But it was the smoldering heat in his hooded gaze that drained the strength from her limbs.

"I can't . . ."

She felt his hands tighten on her arms, saw the heat turn to flame. He wanted her, she thought. Wanted her in the same way Duncan Stryker had wanted her mother. The knowledge filled her with anger, and a perverse sense of pleasure.

"I've never begged anyone for anything," he said, his voice gruff. "But I'm begging you to stay. And not just for the reason you think, although that's part of it."

"I can't . . . please don't ask me."

"Do I have to get down on my knees?"

Her eyes grew wide with wonder and doubt. "Would you?"

"I'd rather not," he said dryly. "At least think about it overnight."

"No." She shook her head, refusing to let the sound of his voice weaken her determination. "I'm leaving in the morning."

It was for the best, she thought bleakly. She didn't want to stay in Cheyenne where everyone knew what her mother had been. She didn't want to face Mrs. Brewster's scorn, or Mrs. Colton's self-righteous indignation. She didn't want to have to dodge Richard Ashton's company any longer.

Caleb let out a sigh. He hadn't really expected her to stay. And perhaps her leaving was for the best, after all. "Call me when breakfast is ready."

In spite of her decision to leave the next morning, Callie thought about what Caleb had said. All that day and all that night, she thought about why she wanted to leave Cheyenne, about starting over in a new town, seeing faces that wouldn't be filled with derision or accusation. If she had money, she could go to California, see the ocean, find a job . . . Some of her enthusiasm waned. She wasn't qualified to do anything. She had no references. She could probably get a job in a restaurant, or maybe as a housekeeper.

*You're a housekeeper now,* she reminded herself. *So why leave?*

She stared out the window. In the yard below, she could see Caleb pacing back and forth, his face illuminated in the faint red glow of a cigar.

She didn't want to leave Caleb Stryker. Why was she letting an old biddy like Mrs. Brewster chase her out of town? Whose business was it what she did or who she worked for, anyway? She wasn't hurting anyone. She wasn't doing anything wrong. If people wanted to think the worst about her, that was their problem, not hers. Caleb had hired her to be his housekeeper, nothing more. Her conscience was clear.

With a smile, she slid into bed and closed her eyes, asleep almost before her head hit the pillow.

# *Chapter Eight*

"Good morning." Callie bestowed her brightest smile on Caleb as she hurried into the kitchen.

"Good morning." He looked at Callie speculatively as she donned a crisp white apron. "I thought you'd be packing."

"I've decided to stay."

"Oh? Why?"

"Because I . . . I decided you were right. Running away won't solve anything."

Callie felt her cheeks grow warm under his intense scrutiny.

"Is that the only reason?" he asked.

The color in her cheeks deepened under his probing gaze. "It's the main one."

"Is it?"

Callie grinned impudently. "If I leave town, Mrs. Brewster won't have anyone to gossip about."

"So you're doing her a favor by staying?"

"Exactly. What would you like for breakfast?" she asked before he could think of any more questions.

"Bacon and eggs."

"And fried potatoes?"

"Sounds good."

To Callie's discomfort, he sat there watching while she fixed breakfast. She could feel his gaze on her back, and as it had once before, it made her clumsy. She dropped a knife on the floor, knocked over the salt shaker, let the coffee boil over.

She refused to look at him until she heard the sound of his laughter, then she whirled around, her hands on her hips. "What's so funny?" she demanded.

"Are you always this clumsy in the kitchen?"

"No."

"Just when I'm around?"

The sudden color in her cheeks told him he had guessed right.

"What is it about me that bothers you?"

"I don't know. That gun, maybe. Or the way you look at me."

"How do I look at you?" he asked, his voice suddenly soft and hypnotic.

"Like you want to devour me," Callie blurted, then clapped her hand over her mouth, horrified that she'd said such a thing to his face.

"Well, you've got that right," he admitted, keeping his voice light. "I might just have to serve you up for breakfast if you don't take those eggs off the fire."

"Oh!" Callie whirled around, grabbing the handle of the frying pan, shrieking as the hot metal seared the palm of her right hand.

Caleb was beside her in an instant. Removing the pan from the fire, he took her hand in his and examined the burn. "Where do you keep the lard?"

"Under the cupboard," Callie replied through clenched teeth. "Oh, it hurts!"

She bit down on her lower lip as he smeared a thin coat of lard across her reddened palm, then wrapped her hand in a clean cloth pulled from one of the drawers.

"Sit down," he said. "I'll fix breakfast."

Feeling like a child, Callie sat down, her hand cradled in her lap, while Caleb threw out the burned eggs and washed the frying pan.

"How do you like your eggs?" he asked.

"Scrambled, please."

"How many?"

"Just two."

He was a good cook. The bacon was cooked just right, the eggs were light and fluffy, the potatoes lightly browned. Even his coffee was better than hers.

"Where'd you learn to cook?" she asked, disgruntled because he seemed to do everything so well.

"Taught myself. I spent a lot of time on the trail in the last eight years, you know. It was learn to cook or starve."

"It's good," she admitted grudgingly.

"I know. Here, have some more eggs. You're too thin."

"I am not!"

"Have some anyway."

When breakfast was over, he washed the dishes and left them on the counter to dry. "You can put them away later," he said. "Come on, let's go into town. We need to stock up on a few things, and I'm out of cigars."

"You just bought cigars," Callie reminded him.

Caleb nodded, readily understanding her reluctance to go into town. It was never any fun, being the subject of gossip and speculation. He knew all about it. Rumor and small talk had followed him everywhere he went. "You've got to face them sometime."

"I faced them yesterday."

"Then it's time to do it again. Come on."

Before they left the house, Caleb removed the cloth from Callie's injured hand and examined her palm. It was still red, but it hadn't blistered. Likely it would be sore for a day or two, he thought as he bandaged her hand, but no real damage had been done.

It was all Callie could do to make herself enter Brewster's Mercantile. She felt Martha Brewster's accusing gaze the minute she stepped into the building, felt the woman's eyes follow her every move as she walked up one aisle and down the other.

Brewster's was a large, square building, filled with everything anyone could possibly need: coal oil and candy, wedding clothes and McGuffey's Readers, castor oil and camphor, opium and snake root. The air was fragrant with a myriad of smells: the aroma of plug tobacco, the leather smell of boots and saddles, the odor of freshly ground coffee. There were cracker barrels and pickle barrels, open and inviting. Fifty-gallon barrels of vinegar and kerosene rested on their sides so customers could fill their jugs. Slabs of sidemeat, cooking pots and pans, bridles and bits hung from the rafters. There were bins of sugar and flour, beans and coffee.

Callie passed the drug counter, reading the labels on some of the bottles: John Bull's Worm Destroyer, Dr. Sherman's Prickly Ash Bitters, Dr. Kilmer's Female Remedy and Blood Purifer.

She saw enamel wash basins, brass cuspidors, copper tea kettles, frying pans, milk pails, flour sifters, foot warmers, and washboards, all piled together in a heap.

By the time she'd finished shopping, she had a sizable order. Waiting her turn at the counter, Callie read the signs tacked to the back wall: Peaberry Coffee, 13 cents a pound; lemons, 12 cents a dozen; P&G White Naptha Soap, 5 cents per bar; fresh country butter, 23 cents a pound; fresh country eggs, 5 cents a dozen; 50-pound sack of flour, 89 cents; Silver Leaf Pure Hog Lard, 8-pound bucket, 49 cents.

"Will that be all?" Ed Brewster's voice was stiff and polite and Callie knew that Martha had been talking to him, spreading her lies.

"I'd like a box of your best cigars," Caleb said.

"Yessir."

"This is a nice store," Caleb remarked as Mr. Brewster added up their purchases. "I'd hate to have to take my business elsewhere—say, over to Killian's."

"I don't understand," Brewster remarked with a frown. "Why would you want to patronize another store?"

"My housekeeper overheard your wife and Mrs. Colton saying some rather unkind things about her at church yesterday," Caleb said, his voice hard. "I suggest you tell Mrs. Brewster and her friends to mind their own business."

"I understand, sir. You can be sure it won't happen again."

"Obliged." Caleb paid for their supplies, gave Ed Brewster a last warning glance, and walked out of the store, his arms laden with packages.

Callie heard Mr. Brewster hollering at Martha before they reached the street. She knew then that they hadn't come into town for supplies *or* cigars. "Thank you, Mr. Stryker," she said quietly, grateful that he would defend her reputation.

"Call me Caleb."

"It wouldn't be—"

"Proper," he interjected.

"That's right."

He was scowling when he dumped the parcels into the back of the buggy, then lifted her onto the black leather seat. The buggy, shiny and black, was brand-new. Their first stop that morning had been the livery barn, where Caleb had bought the buggy and a pair of dappled gray geldings to pull it. His buckskin, tied to the back, followed along behind.

When they reached home, Caleb carried the groceries into the kitchen, then went outside to unharness the horses.

Callie hummed softly as she put things away. Using only one hand made the task last longer, but she didn't mind. It had been so nice, wandering through Brewster's, buying whatever she wanted.

After she put the groceries and the breakfast dishes away, she went into the parlor and began dusting the furniture, loving the feel of the smooth wood beneath her cloth. She let her fingers caress the soft velvet of the draperies, the lush fabric that covered the sofa and chairs. She studied the paintings and admired the delicate Chinese vase that stood in one corner. Such luxury, such riches. And it was hers to enjoy for as long as she worked here.

Callie paused before the sepia-toned photograph of Caleb's parents. His mother was seated in an elaborately carved chair, her hands folded in her lap. She was wearing an evening gown, the bodice fitted, the neckline square and edged with lace, the sleeves long, the cuffs also trimmed with lace. A faint smile touched her lips.

But it was Caleb's father who held Callie's attention. He stood behind his wife, one hand resting on her shoulder. He'd been a tall man, with light hair and a sweeping moustache that made him look a little like a pirate. His expression was stern. They were both handsome people, Callie mused. It was obvious that Caleb had inherited his coloring from his mother and his build from his father.

Going into the hallway, she polished the banister, then went into her room and made the bed and dusted the highboy and bedside table. Then, feeling as if she were prying, she went into Caleb's room.

It was large, as were all the rooms in the mansion. There was a fireplace on one wall, a massive walnut chest of drawers, a matching table and chair, a big bed covered with a brown and blue quilt. A painting of a buffalo stampede hung over the bed.

Callie studied the artwork carefully, noting the dark gray clouds that were gathering in the vast blue sky, the buffalo running flat out across the prairie, their eyes wide, their nostrils flared to drink the wind. She could almost feel the earth shake, smell the rain promised by the clouds, taste the dust churning beneath hundreds of cloven hooves.

It was obviously the painting of an amateur, lacking the vivid detail and perfection of a professional, yet it captured the mood of the scene perfectly.

It was a painting that suited a man like Caleb Stryker, she mused, a painting filled with passion and tumult, with the harsh beauty and reality of life.

She whirled around at the sound of his footsteps, feeling as if she had been caught prying into something that was none of her business.

"I . . . I just came in to clean. I . . . is it all right?"

"That's what I'm paying you for," he said, glancing around. "Doesn't look like you've done much, though. Is your hand bothering you?"

"No. I haven't really started in here yet. I was admiring the painting over your bed. It's wonderful."

"Thanks."

She stared at him, her head tilted to one side. "You painted it?"

"Yeah. Surprised?"

"A little. Do you have any others?"

"No. That's the only one I kept."

"That's too bad. It's quite good."

"I was happy with it at the time."

"And you're not now?"

"Let's just say I've been around enough to know I made a lot of mistakes."

Callie stared at him, knowing intuitively that he wasn't referring to the painting alone.

For a taut moment, her gaze met his and the tension in the room grew until it was almost painful. Callie clutched the dust rag in her hand tighter, aware of the bed behind her, of the man standing in front of her, close enough to touch. Her hand tingled with the need to reach out to him, to erase the lines of trouble and heartache from his brow, to wipe the pain of the past from his eyes.

For a moment, she thought he would reach for her, but then the heat left his gaze. "I'll let you get to work," he said, his voice thick, and she felt the tension drain out of the room.

Callie watched him walk out the door, admiring the way he moved, the width of his shoulders and back, the length of his stride. He was a fine figure of a man, she thought, tall and strong and straight.

With a sigh, she began to dust the top of the highboy, her imagination filling with thoughts of Caleb Stryker's mouth on her own.

Their days fell into a routine of sorts, and as the days slipped by, Callie discovered, to her surprise, that Caleb was a rather easy-going man to live with. He made few demands on her time, and when she'd done her work for the day, she was free to do whatever she wished. She rarely left the house except to go shopping with Caleb on Friday and to church, alone, on Sunday.

She read the books in the library, fascinated by stories of far-off lands, enchanted by tales of sorcery and witchcraft. She spent long hours in the kitchen, learning to cook a decent meal, to bake cookies and pies. Fanny was a big help, stopping by now and then to show her how to make a flaky pie crust, how to bake a loaf of bread that was lightly brown on the outside and soft, but not doughy, on the inside.

Fanny had nothing but good things to say about Caleb Stryker, although she admitted she'd only known him for a few years before he ran away from home. He'd been a quiet lad, Fanny had remarked one morning, with a smile to melt hearts and a deep sadness always lurking in the back of his eyes.

It was a sadness that was still there, Callie thought as she waited for the cake she'd baked to cool. She'd seen it lurking behind Caleb's eyes on occasion, though he tried to hide it.

She couldn't help wondering what Caleb's life as a bounty hunter had been like, and how he got started in a way of life that seemed to work on both sides of the law. Mostly, she wondered if he'd put that way of life behind him for good, or if he intended to dispose of his property in Cheyenne and go back to being a bounty hunter. It didn't seem like a particularly enjoyable way to earn a living, but he must have liked it, to have done it for so long. And she supposed the fact that he was still alive proved that he'd been good at it.

It was all too easy to picture Caleb with a gun in his hand, so easy to imagine him hunting wanted men, shooting them. So easy it made her a little afraid, not of Caleb himself, but of the violence he was obviously capable of, the savagery she sensed lurking just beneath the surface of his civilized facade. But he would never hurt her. She knew that as surely as she knew the sun would rise in the morning, that the flowers would bloom in the spring.

She looked up from the cake she was frosting as he entered the kitchen. He'd left the house shortly after noon and she hadn't seen him since. Of course, it was none of her business where he spent his time, but she couldn't help wondering where he'd been and what he'd been doing.

She wrinkled her nose with distaste as he passed by her. He'd been at the saloon. The smell of stale cigar smoke clung to his clothes; she could smell the faint odor of whiskey on his breath.

"You missed dinner," she said.

"Yeah." Removing his hat, he sat down in one of the chairs and grinned up at her. She was wearing a blue dress with a white lace collar. Her hair was drawn back, tied with a strip of wide white ribbon. "Any coffee in the pot?"

Callie nodded. "Just what's left from breakfast. I'll make you a fresh pot."

"What's there will be fine."

Callie lifted the lid to the coffeepot and peered inside. "It looks like mud."

"The stronger the better."

She finished frosting the cake while she waited for the coffee to heat, conscious of Caleb's gaze on her back.

"What'd you do all day?" he asked after a while.

"The usual. What did you do?" She hadn't meant to ask. It was none of her business how he spent his days. Or nights.

Caleb snorted softly. "What did I do? Well, missy, I'll tell you what I did. I won better than a thousand dollars from Erasmus Nagle and his cronies."

"A thousand dollars." Callie turned to stare at him. "You won a thousand dollars playing cards?" A thousand dollars. You could buy a world full of dreams—or a partnership in a millinery shop—with a thousand dollars.

"Yep. And then I lost it."

Callie stared at him. "You lost it! How?"

"Playing billiards at Dillman's Saloon."

Callie stared at him, aghast. "You lost it. Just like that?"

"Just like that." He propped his elbows on the table and pressed his hands against his temples. "That coffee ready? I've got a devil of a headache."

"Serves you right, drinking and gambling. A thousand dollars! How could you?"

"You act like it was your money I lost," he retorted. And suddenly a bell went off in his head and he knew why she was so upset. A thousand dollars would have taken her to Denver to start a new life.

Callie turned away, busying herself with washing the bowls and pans she'd used in making the cake. What was she doing, reprimanding him? He was her employer. She had no right to castigate him for his actions. What if he got mad and told her to leave? But a thousand dollars! It was more money than she'd ever seen, the exact amount she had needed to start a new life, and he'd lost it in one afternoon.

Biting down on her lower lip, she poured him a cup of coffee

His fingers brushed hers as she handed him the cup. "Thanks."

The coffee was hot and bitter, but he drank it without complaint, wondering why he'd spent the better part of the day wandering from saloon to saloon when he could have been here, with Callie. And yet it was Callie's presence that drove him out of the house. She was too young. Too sweet. Too naive.

And he wanted her too much.

Caleb shook his head. How had she managed to retain her virginity, her innocence, growing up as she had? Despite her youth, her upbringing should have left her hard and worldly-wise, yet she possessed an air of vulnerability that made him ache inside. He'd never been that young, that innocent.

He stood up, his legs unsteady as he walked toward her. She'd been a girl long enough. It was time she learned what it meant to be a woman.

Callie whirled around as Caleb pulled the ribbon from her hair, felt her heart skip a beat as she gazed up into his eyes, dark gray eyes that were filled with heat.

She'd seen that look before, in Duncan Stryker's eyes when he looked at her mother, in Richard Ashton's eyes the last time he'd caught her alone.

Before she could think or speak, he was kissing her, his mouth hard against hers. He tasted of whiskey and coffee. And desire. She could taste it, feel it where his body pressed against hers.

"No." She pushed away from him, only to come up short against the counter. "Don't."

Caleb took a deep breath and let it out in a long sigh, the fear in Callie's eyes smothering his desire as effectively as dirt thrown over a campfire.

Unable to help himself, he lifted a lock of her hair and rubbed it between his thumb and forefinger. It was soft and silky, and he swore under his breath. He hadn't had a woman in a long time, he mused, too long. He'd have to do something about that soon, he thought grimly, for Callie's sake, and his own.

Abruptly, he turned on his heel and left the kitchen, knowing he had to get away from her before he did something they'd both regret.

# *Chapter Nine*

Callie stared after Caleb, her heart racing, her whole body trembling from the force of the desire that had blazed in his smoky gray eyes. He wanted her, as Richard Ashton wanted her, as Duncan Stryker had wanted Leila.

She left the kitchen and wandered through the downstairs, her hands skimming the tops of tables, the arm of the high-backed settee, a tassel that hung from a heavy velvet drapery. As much as she loved this house and the privacy and security it represented, she would have to leave. She'd seen that look in Caleb's eyes too many times not to know what it meant.

Callie shuddered. She hated that look, hated it because she feared it.

Going to the window, Callie gazed out into the darkness. How many times had men pawed at her, made promises, brought Leila presents, in the hope of taking her to bed? There had been times, before Duncan, when Callie feared her mother might not be able to stop them. And then Duncan Stryker came along and everyone knew better than to touch Leila or her daughter. But the men hadn't stopped looking.

They still looked, but no one dared approach her because she lived in Caleb's house. Callie clenched her fists. She knew what the men thought, what everyone thought, but it wasn't true and never would be. She'd seen enough of that kind of life and no man alive would ever sweet-talk her out of her virginity. It was a promise she'd made to herself the first time she realized what it was that her mother did for a living, a promise she had vowed to keep no matter what the cost.

She drew back from the window as Caleb came into view. He paused at the foot of the steps to roll and smoke a cigarette, his profile sharp and clear in the moonlight. She lifted her skirts, intending to turn away, but the sight of him held her there.

A tiny flame fluttered deep within her as she looked at him, at the spread of his shoulders, the way the light of the moon shone on his hair. He began to pace back and forth in front of the steps and the tiny flame within her grew stronger, brighter, as she watched the play of muscles in his arms and legs.

Too vividly, she recalled the strength in those arms, the touch of his mouth on hers, the way her whole body had come alive at his nearness. Had Duncan made her mother feel like that?

The memory of her mother, of what she had been, cooled the heat in Callie's cheeks.

"Never," she murmured, tearing her gaze away from Caleb's profile. "Never." And turning on her heel, she ran up the stairs to her room and closed the door.

Caleb prowled the front yard, driven by a restlessness that wouldn't let him alone. He needed a woman, needed to feel the comfort of soft arms, the taste of sweet lips, to revel in the total surrender of a woman and hear her tell him he was the most wonderful man in the world, even if it was a lie.

He thought of going to the saloon, of losing himself in the warm oblivion of a bottle and the heat of a woman. Once, the idea would have appealed to him, but not now, not when he knew Callie was asleep upstairs.

Callie, with her misty blue eyes and her warm pink lips. Callie, who'd come alive in his arms, surprising him with the depth of her response, eager yet shy, willing yet afraid.

He felt his blood heat as he thought of her and he cursed under his breath. Why was he standing here daydreaming about a girl when he could be at the saloon, wrapped in the arms of a woman!

He stared at the buckskin. The horse was saddled and ready to go. For a moment Caleb stood there, uncertain; then he crushed his cigarette beneath his boot heel and swung into the saddle, heading for the Three Queens Saloon.

Callie slid out of bed at the sound of hoofbeats. Going to her window, she saw Caleb riding down the street. She knew intuitively where he was going, and why, but she hadn't expected it to hurt so much.

She chided herself for being foolish. Caleb Stryker was a bounty hunter, a drifter, and she hardly knew the man. Yet she couldn't smother the feeling of betrayal when she thought of him in another woman's arms.

With an effort, she turned away from the window and went back to bed, only to lie awake in the darkness, listening to the downstairs clock chime the passing of each hour.

She felt awful in the morning. There were dark shadows under her eyes from lack of sleep; she was cranky and out of sorts as she filled the coffeepot with water.

Her stomach muscles clenched when she heard Caleb's footsteps coming down the stairs.

His voice was low when he bade her a good morning.

"Morning," she replied.

"Breakfast about ready?"

"No. I was just making coffee."

He looked at her quizzically, noticing the dark shadows under her eyes for the first time.

"Looks like we're both off to a late start."

"Yes."

"Didn't you sleep well?"

"I slept fine," she retorted.

"Lucky you," Caleb muttered under his breath.

He hadn't slept at all. Going to the saloon hadn't solved a thing. The girls all looked overblown and coarse when compared to Callie's youthful exuberance; the whiskey had tasted flat, and playing cards had been a waste of time and money.

Callie frowned at him. "Did you say something?"

"Forget it. I'm sorry about last night, Callie. I'd had too much to drink and . . ." He shrugged. "It won't happen again."

She nodded, wordlessly accepting his apology. When breakfast was ready, she sat down across from him. She ate in silence, tasting nothing. He looked awful, she thought. Dark bristles shadowed his jaw, and his eyes were bloodshot. She knew it had been after midnight when he came home because she'd still been awake.

Caleb pushed his plate away. "I'm going out to the ranch," he remarked. "I'm leaving this afternoon."

"Leaving?"

"Yeah." He should have gone out to check on things days ago, but Callie's presence had kept him in Cheyenne.

"Why?"

Caleb dragged a hand across his jaw, wishing she wouldn't look at him like that.

"I need to see how things are going out there," he replied, but that wasn't the reason at all and they both knew it.

"How long will you be gone?"

She sounded like a little girl being left home alone for the first time. It tore at his heart, making him feel lower than a snake because he was afraid he wasn't strong enough to keep his hands off her.

"I don't know. A few days, a week maybe."

"Oh." She glanced around the kitchen. What would she do in this big house all alone?

"You can come with me if you like." The words were out before he realized he'd spoken, and then it was too late to take them back.

"Really? Do you mean it? Oh, I'd like that!"

Caleb forced a smile, wondering what on earth had prompted him to invite her along. Hell, one of the reasons he was going out to the Rocking S was to get away from her, but he felt a sudden pleasure at the thought of showing her the ranch.

"We'll leave first thing in the morning," he said, rising from the table. "Be ready."

Callie's smile lit the room. "I'll be ready," she promised.

She twirled around the floor when she was alone. The ranch! She was finally going to see the ranch that Duncan Stryker had bragged about. He'd always promised to take her there, but of course he never had. All her life, she'd wanted to live on a ranch, to be surrounded by horses and cattle and pigs and chickens, to see things grow, to be a part of the land. Maybe Caleb would teach her how to ride a horse and milk a cow. Maybe she'd be able to see chicks hatching, pick vegetables fresh off the vine, plant flowers. . . .

Abruptly, she stopped twirling. It was just for a visit. He was going out to check on things, not to make her dreams come true.

But she couldn't stay her excitement as she went up to her room and began to pack her few belongings. She was getting away from Cheyenne, away from Richard Ashton and gossip, if only for a few days. She felt lighthearted and free for the first time in months.

They left shortly after dawn. Callie sat beside Caleb, admiring the beauty of the day, as he drove out of town. His big buckskin was tied to the back of the carriage.

They rode in silence for a while. Callie couldn't keep from stealing glances in Caleb's direction. He was dressed all in black again, and while the color seemed to suit him, it made him seem forbidding, somehow, dangerous and out of reach. Her gaze was drawn toward his gun, and she wondered how many men he had killed and if his conscience ever bothered him and if he had trouble sleeping at night.

After a time, Callie drew her gaze and thoughts away from the man sitting beside her and admired the scenery. The country was beautiful, green and lush as they neared the river. The sky seemed wider and more blue away from town. She had always loved the sense of wonder that rose within her whenever she saw the vastness of the land unbroken by fences or houses.

It was spring, and the earth was new and alive. Closing her eyes, she drew in a deep breath, inhaling the sweet scent of new grass and earth. And with those scents came the scent of tobacco and leather and man.

She felt Caleb's gaze upon her face, as tangible as a touch.

A blush warmed her cheeks as she opened her eyes and looked up at him.

"Were you sleeping?" he asked.

"No." Callie shrugged self-consciously. "I was just . . . you know, enjoying the countryside."

Caleb grunted softly. Few women he'd ever known had taken the time to appreciate the beauty of the land. Most of them had been more interested in the latest fashions, or how much money a man had to spend on them.

"It is pretty," he agreed.

As pretty as red-gold hair and summer-sky eyes.

"What's your favorite time of the year?" Callie asked, and then felt foolish for asking a grown man such a silly question.

"Winter."

"Really? Why?"

"I like the silence."

Callie shook her head. "I like spring, when the world is new and you feel like anything is possible."

"You're so young," Caleb muttered.

"What?"

"I said you're young. At your age, anything *is* possible."

Callie smiled. Away from town, away from Richard Ashton's innuendos and Martha Brewster's wagging tongue, she did feel as if anything was possible.

"What are you thinking now, Miss McGuire? No, don't tell me, let me guess. You're dreaming of a prince and happy-ever-after."

"What's wrong with that?" Callie asked defensively.

"Nothing, honey. Hang on to your dreams as long as you can."

"Why are you so cynical, Mr. Stryker? You've got everything anyone could want. Surely all your dreams have come true."

"Yeah. Ever since I was a little boy, I dreamed about becoming a bounty hunter."

"Why did you? Become a bounty hunter, I mean?"

"I don't know. I guess I just sort of fell into it."

"You aren't going to do it any more, are you?"

Caleb shrugged. "I don't know. I kind of enjoyed it."

"Enjoyed it! You're not serious!"

"It beat shoveling manure, or swamping saloons." He grinned at her. "The first man I captured was an accident. I was working for a freight company in some little hick town in New Mexico at the time. I was driving a wagon across town when something spooked the horses. The wagon turned over and one of the horses knocked some guy down. Turned out he was wanted for robbing a bank in El Paso. The reward wasn't big, but it seemed like a better way to earn a living than hauling freight. I was pretty good at tracking, thanks to my Indian grandfather, and I learned how to handle a gun without much trouble. Fortunately, most of the men I went after weren't of a mind to shoot it out."

"You could have been killed."

"I could have been killed driving that wagon when it overturned."

"But your father was a rich man."

Caleb turned to face her, his expression dark. "So what?"

"So, you could have lived in that beautiful house."

"No. I'd have had to be someone else to do that."

"I don't understand."

A shadow flicked in the depths of his eyes and was gone. "I don't, either. I just know I had to get out. I couldn't be what my father wanted me to be. He refused to let me stay with the Lakota when he decided to return to his own people, and after I'd been in Cheyenne a few months, I knew I couldn't be the kind of son he wanted. If I'd stayed, we would have wound up killing each other." He shrugged, as if it didn't matter. "So, I left."

"My mother loved him."

Anger sat like a stone in his belly. "Did she?"

Callie nodded.

"And did he love her?"

"She said he did."

Caleb drew the team to a halt in the shade of a cottonwood tree. "Did he visit her often?"

"Whenever he came to town. Usually once a week or so. I always wondered why my mother was content to live above a saloon, why she didn't want a house of her own, but she said it didn't matter. All that mattered was that Duncan came to see her whenever he could."

"And my mother never knew?"

"I don't think so. I saw her at your father's funeral. She was a beautiful woman, the most beautiful woman I've ever seen."

"Yeah." She'd been beautiful, generous, caring. And Duncan had betrayed her.

"I'd like to have known your mother," Callie said, toying with a fold of her skirt, "but of course that was impossible."

"I reckon." He wrapped the reins around the whip and vaulted to the ground. "Do you want to stretch your legs a bit?"

Callie nodded, placing her hands on his shoulders as he reached up for her. He lifted her easily from the seat, his hands strong and sure around her waist, his touch making her tingle from head to foot. Their faces were only a breath apart as he swung her to the ground.

He held her for several seconds longer than necessary, and Callie felt her breath catch in her throat. His eyes were gray and stormy, and try as she might, she couldn't take her gaze from his. She was keenly aware of his hands circling her waist, could feel the strength in his fingers, the warmth in his touch. She knew she should pull away, but she seemed rooted to the spot, held by the fierce gleam in his deep gray eyes, unwilling, somehow, to let him go.

A dozen thoughts and emotions exploded through Caleb as he gazed down at Callie. She stood on tiptoe, her hands still resting on his shoulders. He watched the pulse beating rapidly in her throat, felt a sudden rush of heat as the tip of her tongue dampened her lips. He had a sudden urge to press his mouth to hers, to taste the sweet promise of those rosy lips, to watch her eyes grow dark with passion and desire. It would be so easy, so easy to draw her down onto the grass and pleasure himself in her sweetness.

He groaned softly as she licked her lips again. Lordy, did she know what she was doing to him? Maybe she wasn't as innocent as she professed to be. Maybe it was all an act. It would be no trouble to find out, no trouble at all.

Callie's heart began to race as Caleb bent toward her, his face and the heat in his eyes blocking everything else from view. He was going to kiss her. She knew it with every fiber of her being. Fear and excitement mingled with dread and anticipation. She started to protest, but her words were swallowed in his kiss. For a moment, she was too stunned to think. His lips were warm and firm, filled with knowledge and promise, and she surrendered to his touch, surprised at how pleasant his kiss was. Richard Ashton's kisses, taken by force in an alley behind the feed store, had filled her with revulsion, but Caleb's kiss made her feel warm and weak all over.

She gasped as his tongue slid over her lower lip, shocked that he would take such a liberty, shocked that she liked it. Only when she felt his hands sliding over her breast did sanity return.

She acted instinctively, driving her knee into his groin with all the force at her command. It had the desired effect.

Caleb released her immediately, a low groan rumbling deep in his throat as he doubled over. She heard him swear, heard the harsh rasp of his breathing as he fought the pain.

Callie stared at him, silently blessing her mother for showing her how to defend herself against a man's unwanted advances, and perversely wondering why she felt so awful.

"Mr. Stryker, are you all right?"

He didn't look at her, only muttered a ferocious curse that made her ears burn.

Remorse filled Callie's heart. She hadn't really meant to hurt him, only to make him stop caressing her because she liked it far too much. Her mother had warned her that men could not be trusted, that many a girl lost her innocence because, in the heat of the moment, all her good intentions could be swept away by the touch of a man's hand. And Callie had sworn to hang on to her virginity no matter what. She wasn't going to make the same mistake her mother had. She wasn't going to trade her innocence for a few brief moments of pleasure.

"I . . . I'm sorry."

Still doubled over, he only grunted softly.

"Is there anything I can do?"

"Just leave me the devil alone."

With a nod, Callie turned away. She hadn't meant to hurt him, but it was his own fault, after all. He should have kept his hands to himself.

*And you should have said no.*

Walking to the narrow creek, Callie sank down to her knees and rinsed her hands and face in the cool water. He probably hated her now. He might even send her away. And then what would she do? He hadn't paid her wages yet. What if he refused to pay her? She'd have to go back to Cheyenne and beg, borrow, or steal enough money to get out of town.

"Miss McGuire?"

She glanced over her shoulder to see Caleb walking slowly toward her. "I really am sorry," she told him.

"Your mother teach you how to do that?"

A faint hint of color rose in her cheeks. "Yes, among other things." Callie lifted her chin a little higher, her voice filled with accusation. "Some men won't take no for an answer."

"I don't remember asking a question," Caleb muttered, and then a wry grin cut across his features. "Do you want to draw your wages?"

"What? No, I mean . . . not unless you want me to go."

Letting her go would be the best thing all around. He knew it. He knew he should never have hired her in the first place. But he had, and now he couldn't let her go.

"No." He took a deep breath. Damn, but she had the sharpest, pointiest little knee he'd ever encountered. "Come on," he said, reaching for her hand. "Let's have lunch. If we hurry, we can make the ranch before dark."

# *Chapter Ten*

The ranch was everything Callie had ever dreamed of and more. The main house was rectangular in shape, with a pitched roof to shed water and snow and a wide front porch.

There was a big red barn, several corrals, a bunkhouse, a cookhouse, a tool shed, and a smokehouse. She saw a couple of hay wagons, an old buckboard, and a new plow. But it was the animals that caught her eye—horses and cattle, sheep and goats, chickens and dogs, even a couple of pigs.

Caleb drew the buggy to a halt near the front steps. He alighted with a great deal of care, then helped Callie down.

"Well, here we are," he said. "Let's go see if anybody's home."

The front door was unlocked, and Callie followed Caleb inside, her eyes widening at what she saw.

Mrs. Colton's restaurant would have fit into the parlor. The furniture was of solid walnut, the upholstery a rich dark red. There were several colorful Indian rugs on the floor and another on one wall. A huge fireplace filled one corner. A rack of antlers hung over the hearth, and an oak cabinet held a half-dozen rifles.

She followed Caleb from room to room. The kitchen was large and square, with a window that faced east to take advantage of the morning sun. There was a large pantry, several shelves over the kitchen sink, and a spacious cupboard. A dining room adjoined the kitchen. Down the hall, there were four medium-sized bedrooms, all decorated in different colors and types of wood, and one very large one that had blue-flowered paper on the walls, blue curtains at the windows, and a matching spread on the bed. She caught a glimpse of a small den paneled in dark wood that held a roll-top desk, several chairs, and a small table. The last room contained a bathtub.

Returning to the parlor, Caleb tossed his hat on the rack beside the front door, then ran his hands through his hair. "Might as well make yourself at home."

"Where is everybody?"

"Likely in the bunkhouse. I don't think anybody's been living here, though I imagine Emily's been keeping an eye on things."

Callie glanced around the room, noting the thin layer of dust on the furniture and the small, lacy cobweb that hung in a corner of the ceiling. It was obvious, at least to her, that the place needed a good cleaning from top to bottom. Someone might have been taking care of the house, but they hadn't been doing a very thorough job.

"Why don't you look in the kitchen and see if there's anything to eat?" Caleb suggested.

With a nod, Callie headed for the kitchen, mentally making a list of things to do as she went. Dusting would be her first priority; then she'd sweep the floors, shake out the rugs, and clean the lamps.

Caleb walked from one end of the room to the other, then stood beside the fireplace, his shoulder against the rough stone. The ranch house was pretty much as he remembered it. His mother had always preferred the mansion to the ranch, but Caleb had always loved the Rocking S. If they'd been allowed to live at the ranch year-round, he might never have left home, but Duncan Stryker had loved Cheyenne. He'd liked rubbing elbows with the big shots; he'd liked talking to the other cattlemen about the ranch and about grazing rights and beef prices. He'd liked being seen with other wealthy men. And he'd liked showing off his wife, who'd been the prettiest woman in town, Indian or not.

Caleb rolled and lit a cigarette. Taking a deep drag, he gazed around the room. He'd come home, he thought, and wondered why he'd put it off for so long. The mansion had never been home, would never be home. But the ranch . . . he had roots here whether he liked it or not.

His gaze settled on the blanket he'd brought with him when they left his mother's people, surprised to see that it still hung on the wall. Surprised his father hadn't burned it long since.

"Why couldn't we have just stayed here?" he mused aloud.

He'd been happy, those summers they spent on

the ranch. He'd worked the cattle, liking the big, tough-talking cowhands he rode with, liking the long hours in the saddle, the thrill of chasing down a bunch-quitter, the quiet nights around a campfire listening to the old timers tell about chasing longhorns in the Texas *brasada*. Brush-popping, they called it. He'd picked up a lot of their lingo. *Kak* was cowboy talk for saddle, *chinks* were chaps. He'd ridden night-hawk, drunk coffee so thick you could float a horseshoe in it, eaten sonofabitch stew and learned to like it.

He took a last drag on the cigarette before flicking it into the fireplace. It was a hard life, being a cowboy, but it had been a good life, full of action and adventure, and men to ride the river with. But it hadn't lasted. He'd been the boss's son and after a while, that made a difference.

He looked up as Callie entered the room. "Supper's ready. I thought we'd eat in the kitchen, if that's okay."

"Fine."

She'd gone to a lot of trouble. There was a yellow cloth on the table. The soft glow of candlelight. There was cold ham, green beans, and tinned peaches for dinner. He caught the rich aroma of coffee brewing.

"Looks good," he remarked, taking a seat at the table.

Callie sat down opposite him. For a moment, they ate in silence.

"Where'd you get the ham?" Caleb asked after a while.

"Joe Brigman brought it. He saw us ride up. He said he'd stop by to see you later."

Caleb grunted. Joe Brigman was the ranch foreman. Duncan had hired him soon after they arrived in Cheyenne. Joe had a wife and six kids. The kids would be grown by now, Caleb mused, and wondered how Joe's youngest had turned out. Angela Brigman had been a pretty girl, with braids the color of honey, light green eyes, and a sprinkling of freckles across her cheeks. His mother had always teased him about Angela, saying she thought Angela would make him a fine wife someday, but he'd left home while Angela was still just a kid.

She wouldn't be a kid any more, he thought soberly. He'd been away for twelve years. Twelve years. It still didn't seem possible that he'd been gone that long, that his parents were dead, that he'd killed more men than he cared to remember.

Callie watched Caleb surreptitiously, wondering what was bothering him. He wasn't usually so quiet, and she wondered if he was still mad at her for what had happened that afternoon. He wasn't walking funny any more, so she assumed he was feeling better.

She poured him a cup of coffee, then cleared the table, a little miffed because he didn't even seem to notice that she was there.

"What?" Caleb looked up, aware that Callie was speaking to him.

"I'm tired," she repeated. "Where should I sleep?"

He ignored the answer that immediately came to mind. "Wherever you want."

"Good night, then. I'll see you in the morning?"

"Yeah."

He noticed the coffee for the first time. It was cold, but he drank it anyway, his expression thoughtful as he watched Callie leave the room.

What was he going to do about her? She was young and innocent and just looking at her aroused him in ways he wasn't sure he liked. He should have given her a thousand dollars and sent her on her way. She was trouble looking for a place to happen, a snare he'd best avoid. But just being near her made him feel good all over.

Grimacing, he shoved away from the table and went out the back door.

A full moon illuminated the yard. Caleb walked away from the house to stare out at the land. He heard a calf bawling, the lowing of a cow in reply, the sharp bark of a coyote. He'd walked about a half mile when he heard the muffled sound of footsteps coming up behind him. Instinctively, he melted into the shadows, drawing his gun as he did so.

"Caleb, that you?"

He slid his gun into the holster as he stepped into a pool of moonlight. "Hi, Joe."

The foreman of the Rocking S held out his hand, and Caleb took it. Joe Brigman had been around a long time, and it was beginning to show. His hair, once black as coal, was now gray. His skin was the color of old saddle leather, lined by years in the sun and the wind. But his green eyes were still sharp, and his grip was still strong as he shook Caleb's hand.

"I was just coming up to the house to see you," Brigman remarked. He looked Caleb over from head to toe. "It's been a long time."

"Yeah. How've you been, Joe?"

"Fine, just fine."

"How's Emily?"

"She's well. She gets a touch of the misery in her back now and then, but she don't complain."

"Kids doing all right?"

"Yeah. Joe Junior's got his own spread down in Texas, Kyle's working for a law firm in Denver, and the girls are all grown and gone, except for Angela. Her husband, Ira Bristol, passed on two years ago and she came back home. She's engaged to a fine young man now. Thomas Watts. He works at the Stock Growers' National Bank over on Carey."

Caleb nodded. Joe Brigman and his family lived in what everyone referred to as the "old house." It was the house that had been on the property when Duncan took over the Rocking S, but it hadn't been big enough, or grand enough, for a man like Duncan Stryker. A year after they bought the ranch, Duncan built a new house about a mile and a half from the old one. The old house didn't belong to Joe, but it was his for as long as he worked for the Rocking S.

"How's the ranch doin'?" Caleb asked.

"We're getting by. Got a good calf crop this year, and we should do as well next year. I guess you heard your mother sent several hundred head of cattle over to the reservation last year?"

"I heard. I plan to do it again this year."

Brigman grunted noncommittally. "She mortgaged the ranch, but I guess Orville Hoag told you about that."

Caleb nodded, ignoring the faint note of disapproval he detected in the foreman's voice. He couldn't blame Joe for feeling the way he did. The man had been a part of the Rocking S for a good many years. It wasn't just a place to work any more, it was home.

"Angela's been looking after things up at the main house," Joe remarked after a while. "She's been goin' up once a week or so to dust and make sure everything's all right."

"Thank her for me, will you? And tell her it won't be necessary for a while."

Brigman nodded. "That pretty little gal gonna keep house for you?"

"Yeah."

Caleb saw the flicker of curiosity in Brigman's eyes as the foreman wondered what his relationship with "that pretty little gal" might be, but Joe knew better than to question the boss about his personal life.

"I'll tell Angela. I know she'll be glad to see you."

"Thanks, Joe. I'll see you in the morning. I want to ride out and look the place over."

"I'll have your horse ready."

Caleb swore softly. "The horses . . ."

"It's been taken care of, boss. The animals have been fed, and the buggy's behind the barn."

"Thanks."

Joe Brigman touched his hat brim with his fingertips. "'Night, boss. See ya in the morning."

Caleb let out a long sigh. *Must be getting old,* he thought, *forgetting to look after the stock.* But then, he'd had other things on his mind, like summer-sky eyes and lightning-quick knees that were as sharp as an axe.

He returned to the house to find it dark save for a lamp Callie had left burning for him on the kitchen table.

Caleb picked up the lamp with his left hand, keeping his gun hand free, then grinned wryly. Old habits died hard, he thought, remembering how he'd automatically moved into the shadows earlier that night. During the last eight years, he'd made it a habit to sit with his back to a wall, to look over the crowd in a saloon before he stepped inside, to sleep with his gun close at hand.

They were habits he'd cultivated in order to survive as a bounty hunter, habits that were now ingrained deep within him.

As he walked down the hall, he wondered which bedroom Callie had chosen. The pink one, maybe, or the yellow one. He didn't think she'd care much for the brown one that had been his.

Or maybe she'd taken the big bedroom at the end of the hall, the one that had belonged to his parents.

Heat uncurled in his loins as he pictured Callie reclining in the middle of the big bed, her red-gold hair spread out on one of the satin-covered pillows, her eyes as blue as the counterpane.

He was holding his breath when he turned the knob and opened the door. He refused to admit disappointment when he saw that the bed was empty. And then he laughed. A woman who'd kicked him square in the groin in the afternoon wasn't likely to be waiting to seduce him tonight.

Undressing, he drew back the covers and slid between the sheets, his back propped against the big carved headboard. It seemed odd to be in his parents' room, to be sitting on their bed. It hit him again, harder this time. They were gone, both of them. Duncan wouldn't come storming into the house, cussing a blue streak while he upbraided him for something he'd done wrong. His mother wouldn't be there at breakfast, her face calm and serene as she listened to Duncan outline the day's activities.

With a sigh, Caleb doused the lamp and stared into the darkness. He was a grown man, far past the age when he needed mothering, but he wished suddenly that he could go to Callie's bed and crawl in beside her, that he could rest his head on her breast and fall asleep in her arms.

He woke to the sound of singing. For a moment, he lay there, his eyes closed, just listening, letting Callie's voice wash over him. She was singing a tune he'd heard in a dozen cribs and cantinas from Colorado to Texas, and he smiled faintly. Most girls learned hymns and lullabys at their mother's knee, but not Callie.

She had a nice voice, kind of low and husky, and for a moment he visualized her in a skimpy little black lace costume with paint on her cheeks and feathers in her hair. He could imagine her strutting across the stage, a pout on her lips as she flirted with the crowd. He could almost hear the catcalls, see the lust in the eyes of the spectators.

Opening his eyes, he wiped the image from his mind. He'd kill any man who looked at her too long, beat her within an inch of her life if she even thought about prancing around on a stage.

Caleb grimaced as he threw back the covers and swung his legs over the side of the bed. Callie had never mentioned wanting to sing in a saloon. It was only his imagination running wild.

He dressed quickly, lured into the kitchen by the aroma of frying bacon.

Callie was standing at the stove, scrambling eggs in a cast-iron skillet. Her hair was pulled back and tied at the nape of her neck, and he had a sudden urge to take her in his arms and kiss her good morning.

He swore softly as he pulled a chair from the table and sat down.

Callie looked over her shoulder and smiled at him. "Good morning."

"Morning."

"Breakfast is almost ready."

He grunted, wondering how she could always be so cheerful in the morning. Personally, he didn't care much for company or conversation until he'd had about a dozen cups of black coffee, but Callie always had a smile and a cheerful greeting.

"I made biscuits," she remarked.

Caleb grunted again, forcing a smile as she placed a plate in front of him. The bacon was crisp, the eggs light and fluffy, and the biscuits almost melted in his mouth.

He looked up to find her watching him from across the table, an eager expression in her eyes.

"It's good," he said in surprise.

Callie smiled. "Fanny's teaching me to cook." She ate in silence for a moment. "She likes you."

"Fanny? Yeah, we got along all right. She was one of the few women in town who didn't look at me like I was a cross between Satan and Blackbeard."

"Was it really as bad as all that?"

"In the beginning. Tensions were high between the Indians and the whites back in those days. Soldiers massacred a village in a place called Cedar Creek, and then Chivington attacked a peaceful village at Sand Creek. Naturally, the Indians retaliated. Eventually, the townspeople decided I wasn't going to murder them in their beds or scalp them on the street, but they always looked at me a little suspiciously."

"That must have been hard for you."

"I got used to it. And things got easier when I left home. Nobody really knew who I was, and the men I was hunting didn't care."

"Did you . . . have you killed very many men?"

"Enough."

The tone of his voice and the look in his eye warned her not to pursue the matter, and they finished the meal in silence.

"Thanks," Caleb said, rising.

"You're welcome."

He looked at her for a moment, wishing she were older, wiser, or that he was younger and less hardened. *She's just your cook and housekeeper,* he reminded himself. *Don't get involved.*

"Can you ride?"

"Yes," she said quickly. It was lie, but he wouldn't know that.

"I'm goin' out and have a look around. Do you wanna come along?"

Callie nodded eagerly. "I'd like that."

"Meet me down in the barn in twenty minutes."

"All right."

She was grinning from ear to ear as she hurried down the hall to her room to change her clothes. She was going riding! On a horse! The idea filled her with excitement and trepidation. She'd always loved horses. They were so beautiful. And so big.

He was waiting for her outside the barn. A docile-looking bay gelding stood beside Caleb's big buckskin mare.

"I'm ready," she said brightly.

Caleb nodded. She was wearing a calico skirt and a long-sleeved white blouse buttoned up to her throat. There were gloves on her hands, and a straw hat shaded her face.

"Let's go," he said gruffly. "Come on, I'll give you a leg up."

She looked at Caleb askance for a moment, then moved cautiously toward the horse. The gelding looked much bigger when she was standing beside it.

Caleb laced his fingers together. "Put your foot here and I'll give you a boost."

Callie looked at his hands and then looked up at the saddle, which seemed to be about a mile above the ground. Resolutely, she placed her left hand on Caleb's shoulder and her right foot in his hands.

Caleb grimaced. "Are you sure you've ridden before?"

"Of course."

"Do you always ride backwards?"

"What?"

"Put your *left* foot here and swing your right leg over the saddle when I boost you up."

"Oh. Of course. How silly of me."

She did as she was told, and a moment later she was sitting on the back of the horse. Caleb glanced at her speculatively as he adjusted the stirrups, then handed her the reins.

Callie took them gingerly, hoping the horse knew what to do.

"That bay's got a soft mouth," Caleb remarked, patting the horse's neck, "so don't go yanking on the reins."

"Okay," Callie replied, wondering what he meant. Did the horse have some kind of infirmity?

Caleb swung aboard the buckskin and led the way out of the barnyard. Callie breathed a sigh of relief when the bay followed.

It was a beautiful day, but Callie was so busy trying to maintain her balance that she hardly noticed. She felt as though she was sitting on a mountain.

After the first rush of excitement passed, Callie found that horseback riding was even more wonderful than she'd imagined. There was something peaceful about riding across the grassland. Sitting so high gave her a wonderful view, and the rocking motion of the gelding was pleasant.

But most pleasant of all was watching Caleb. He rode easy in the saddle, moving in perfect rhythm with the buckskin. Of course, he *was* part Indian, and everyone knew Indians were practically born knowing how to ride. She envied him that easy grace and vowed that someday she'd be able to ride every bit as well as he did. Maybe better!

She realized just how much she had to learn a few minutes later when Caleb put the buckskin into a lope. The bay lined out in a run, and the unexpected forward momentum threw Callie off balance so that she tumbled over the gelding's rump and landed on her backside in the grass. The gelding came to a halt a few yards away, turning to look at her as if to say "what happened to you?"

Callie stood up with a groan, one hand massaging her bruised posterior. She had no recollection of falling off the horse, or of hitting the ground, but she'd obviously landed hard. No doubt she'd be black and blue tomorrow.

She looked up, red-faced, as Caleb trotted toward her.

"What happened?" he asked.

Callie glared at him. What kind of stupid question was that?

"Have you ever been on a horse before?"

She shook her head, her expression sullen.

"Why didn't you tell me?"

"I was afraid you'd leave me home."

"Callie, you could have been hurt."

"I am hurt."

"I mean seriously hurt. You could have broken an arm or a leg or something."

Dismounting, he walked toward her. "Are you all right?"

"Yes."

He looked at her a moment, his gaze running over her from head to toe. Except for the faint blush in her cheeks, she seemed unhurt.

Taking up the bay's reins, he lifted Callie into the saddle again.

"Okay, lesson one. Never run before you can walk."

"Very funny."

For the next half-hour, she listened attentively as he explained to her that a soft mouth meant the horse was responsive to the bit. He taught her how to neck rein and how to pull back on the reins to bring the bay to a stop, and how to squeeze the horse's sides to make it go forward. He told her to lean forward when going uphill to ease the weight on the bay's hindquarters, and to lean back when going downhill to help the horse keep its balance. He advised against riding downhill at an angle, saying that going straight was better so that if the horse lost its footing, it would sit down on its hocks. He showed her how to sit, straight but not stiff.

By the end of an hour and a half, Callie no longer felt like she was going to fall off every time the horse changed direction, but she was smart enough to know that she still had a lot to learn.

She protested when Caleb said it was time to head for home, but as soon as she stepped out of the saddle, she was glad he hadn't agreed to stay out any longer. Her rump was numb, and the insides of her thighs didn't even bear thinking about.

"You'll feel better after a long hot bath," Caleb promised.

"I doubt it," Callie said with a groan.

"Trust me. We'll ride again tomorrow morning."

"Tomorrow?"

"Gotta toughen up those muscles."

"Tomorrow?" Callie repeated, wondering if she'd ever be able to walk normally again.

"After breakfast."

With a nod, she hobbled down the hallway to her room, one hand pressed to her aching back. Somehow, she doubted Caleb knew how she was feeling. He'd probably never had a sore muscle in his life.

Minutes later, Callie sank down in the bathtub. The hot water did make her feel better, but she was still stiff and sore when she climbed out of the tub a half-hour later. Slipping into a loose-fitting robe, she went into the kitchen to prepare the midday meal, only to find Caleb sitting at the table, a platter of cold meat, cheese, and fruit spread before him. There was also a loaf of fresh-baked bread and a pitcher of lemonade.

"Cookie brought it up," Caleb replied in answer to her unspoken question. "Seems someone told him you didn't look too spry after our ride."

"Someone named Caleb Stryker?" Callie guessed.

"No, someone named Joe Brigman."

"I guess everyone knows I fell off my horse," Callie muttered. "The cowboys are probably all laughing about it."

"Probably," Caleb acknowledged with a grin. "Are you gonna sit down?"

Callie looked at the chair with trepidation, biting back a groan as her bruised tailbone made contact with the hard wood. "I'm not sure I ever want to sit on a horse again."

"You're not giving up already?"

"I'm not?"

"It's up to you."

"I'm not," she agreed. "I really did like the ride, but I don't care much for the aftereffects. Is your—are you sore all over, too?"

"No. And riding won't make you sore, either, once the newness wears off."

They ate in companionable silence. Callie was ever aware of the tall, dark man sitting across from her. There was something about Caleb Stryker, she mused, wishing she could put her finger on just what it was that fascinated her so. It was more than his rugged good looks, though she never tired of looking at him. He seemed so self-assured, in complete charge of his emotions at all times. He knew who he was and what he wanted, and yet she couldn't help feeling that he was hurting deep inside.

He looked up from his plate to find her staring at him. Callie tried to draw her gaze away from his face, but she couldn't break the hold of his eyes on hers.

She felt the heat climb in her cheeks and still she couldn't look away. His eyes were a deep, cool gray, mesmerizing in their intensity. She had the feeling that he knew what she'd been thinking, that he could see into her heart and soul.

Caleb watched the color blossom in Callie's cheeks. She looked at him through eyes as wide and innocent as those of an angel, completely unaware of the effect she had on him. He wasn't ignorant of the fact that she found him attractive. Many women had looked at him like that, their eyes filled with curiosity as they wondered if he was like other men, or if his being a half-breed made him different somehow, if he'd be more savage, more demanding. In the beginning, he'd been offended by such glances, and then, as he grew older, his anger had turned to amusement.

And yet, when Callie looked at him like that, he wasn't insulted or amused. He wanted only to take her in his arms and show her that he was no different from any other man.

The silence between them grew taut. Callie's mouth went dry, her palms were damp, her pulse was racing. Her gaze drifted to Caleb's lips—firm warm lips that had touched her own—and then she quickly glanced away. But not quickly enough.

"Callie." He murmured her name as he stood up. Leaning across the table, he cupped her face in the palms of his hands and kissed her lightly.

Her eyelids fluttered down as his mouth covered hers. A storm of emotions raged within her as his kiss deepened. She was helpless to withstand the sweet probing of his tongue. He tasted of butter and cheese and tangy lemonade. His calloused hands were warm against her cheeks. She was drowning in sunlight, suffocating in pleasure. She inhaled, a deep, shuddering breath, and her nostrils filled with the scent of tobacco and leather and the musky scent of man. The taste of him, the scent of him, the touch of his hands, intoxicated her.

A soft moan filled her ears and she couldn't tell if it came from her own throat or his. His hands were moving, his fingers caressing her neck, kneading her shoulders. Gasping for air, she opened her eyes to find him staring down at her, their mouths only a breath apart.

His face filled her vision. His nose was hawk-like and straight, his lips were slightly parted, and he was breathing hard, as if he'd just run a great distance. There was a tiny cleft in his chin that she hadn't noticed before, a faint white scar near his hairline. But it was the look in his storm-gray eyes that held her, that made her stomach tremble and her heart pound.

"Mr. Stryker . . ."

He smiled down at her, his expression slightly bemused. "Don't you think you should call me Caleb?"

"Caleb, I . . ."

"What?" His voice was soft and rough, like velvet rubbed the wrong way.

"I . . ."

He lifted one hand to stroke the curve of her cheek, and the touch of his hand and the look in his eyes made her toes curl with pleasure.

"What is it, Callie?"

"I don't know. I . . . I've never . . ."

She heard him mutter something that sounded suspiciously like a curse as he straightened up and turned away, but not before she saw the visible evidence of his desire.

She stared at his broad back, not knowing what to say. She knew what went on between a man and a woman. But until that moment, she'd never really known what desire was, or how strong it could be.

She was wondering what she could possibly say to break the tension between them when Caleb grabbed his hat and left the room.

# *Chapter Eleven*

Caleb stood in the yard, taking deep breaths of cool air while he waited for his heart to stop hammering.

He shook his head, wondering what it was about her that made him feel like a young stud with his first mare. For all her youth and innocence, Callie McGuire heated his blood faster than hundred-year-old brandy on a cold day.

Caleb swore softly. He'd made love to a lot of women, young and not so young, pretty and not so pretty, but none of them had ever affected him like this inexperienced girl with her red-gold hair and cornflower-blue eyes. He supposed it was her inexperience that captivated him. Every time he looked at her, he wondered what it would be like to be the man who showed her how good it could be between a man and a woman. Only she wasn't a woman. She was just a kid with a smile that could melt ice and a laugh that could charm the birds out of the trees.

He walked across the south meadow, cursing himself for being so weak, telling himself that it wasn't really Callie he wanted, it was just that he hadn't had a woman in a long time.

"Hi, Caleb. I heard you were back."

He looked up, surprised to find that he'd walked all the way to the Brigman place, and even more surprised to find himself face to face with Joe's daughter.

"How are you, Angie?"

"Fine. And you?"

"Fine." He removed his hat and ran a hand through his hair, wondering why it was suddenly so hard to talk to Angela. Years ago, she'd tagged at his heels. Once he'd even stolen a kiss out behind the barn. Now he couldn't think of a thing to say to her.

"I'm sorry about your mother. She always treated me like family."

Caleb nodded. Angie had grown into a pretty young woman. Her hair was a darker shade of blond, long dark lashes fringed light green eyes, and there was still a dusting of freckles across her cheeks and nose.

"Are you here to stay?" she asked.

"I don't know. I've got a few things to work out. I hear you're getting married soon."

"Yes." She smiled at him. "When I was a little girl, I always thought I'd marry you."

Caleb shifted uncomfortably, remembering that his mother had always expected him to marry Angela. "I guess life never turns out the way you think it will."

"I guess not. You're quite famous in these parts, you know. We've kept up with you through the newspapers."

"Pretty boring reading, I should think."

"Not to me. Have you put that kind of life behind you, Cal?"

Cal. No one had ever called him that except Angie. It brought to mind warm summer nights and moonlit swims. And a beating he'd gotten from his father for swimming in the nude with Angie late one night.

"Have you?" She took a step toward him, lifting a hand as if she meant to touch him, then changed her mind.

"I don't know."

"You never forgave your father, did you?"

"No."

"He only wanted the best for you."

"Did he?"

"You know he did. He loved you. They both loved you."

"Sure. That's why the old man cut me out of his will the day I left home. Because he loved me."

"He was hurt. We all were."

Caleb drew a deep sigh and let it out in a long shuddering breath. Raking over the past had never solved anything.

"I still love you, Cal."

"Angie . . ."

"It's true. I always hoped you'd come back for me."

"There's been no place in my life for a woman. Not then. Not now."

"Oh? That's not what I hear. Dad says there's a woman at the ranch."

"She's just a housekeeper, someone I hired in town."

Disdain flickered in the depths of Angela's eyes. "She's Leila's daughter, isn't she?"

"How do you know about Leila McGuire?"

"Everyone in town knows who she was. What she was."

He saw the question lurking in Angie's eyes, and he shook his head. "Her daughter's not like that. She's a nice girl who needed a job, that's all."

"Would you like to come to dinner tomorrow night?"

"I don't think that's a good idea."

"Why not?"

"You're engaged to another man."

"Tom won't mind." And she wouldn't care if he did. Tom was a wonderful man, kind, attentive, and thoughtful. But he was also boring and predictable, not like Caleb. With Tom, she'd have a settled life and a modest home; with Cal she'd have excitement, the ranch, the mansion in town.

Angela closed the distance between them and this time she did touch him, her hand reaching up to stroke Caleb's cheek, to trace the faint white scar near his hairline.

"I missed you, Cal. All these years, I never forgot about you."

She stood on her tiptoes, leaning into him until he could feel her breasts crushed against his chest. Her lips, when she kissed him, were warm and soft, and for a moment he thought of taking what she was offering. She was a woman. She was willing.

But she was the wrong woman.

Gently, he put her away from him. "It's too

late, Angie. I'm not a kid anymore, and neither are you."

"You could still come to dinner," she urged. "Mother would love to see you."

"Maybe another time."

Caleb rubbed a hand across his jaw as he watched Angela walk away, wondering what his life would have been like if he'd stayed in Cheyenne, gone to work for his father, and married Angela, like everyone expected. She was a pretty woman. No doubt she'd have made him a fine wife, just like his mother always said. But whatever affection he'd felt for her all those years ago no longer existed. She'd grown up while he was gone, been married and widowed, and now she was engaged again. He didn't know the new Angela, wasn't sure he wanted to know her. He'd aged as well, he thought ruefully, aged in ways Angela would never understand.

Shoving his hands in his pants pockets, Caleb turned around and headed back to the main house.

It was dusk when he reached the house. Lamplight glowed in the windows; a curl of fat gray smoke rose from the chimney. The front door was slightly ajar, and as he stepped up on the porch, the aroma of roasting meat tickled his nostrils.

He stood on the porch for a moment, pretending he had a wife waiting for him inside, someone who would welcome him with a hug and a kiss, someone who would ask how his day had been, someone who would smile as she sat across the table from him.

He shook the image aside as he stepped into the parlor. Removing his hat, he tossed it on a chair, then crossed the room to the kitchen.

Callie was at the stove, stirring something in a pot. She'd changed out of her robe into a green dress with short puffy sleeves. Her hair was piled on top of her head, but several tendrils had escaped to trail down her back. He watched her for several minutes, bemused that he could find such pleasure in simply watching her.

Callie moved the pot to the back of the stove to simmer. She was turning, reaching for a tea towel, when she saw Caleb standing in the doorway, an odd expression on his face.

"Is something wrong?" she asked.

"No."

"I was beginning to think you weren't coming back."

"Not likely, since this is my house."

"I know, but you were gone a long time."

"I went for a walk."

She was looking up at him, waiting for him to go on, but he didn't want to tell her about Angela, didn't want to answer the questions that were sure to be forthcoming if he mentioned another woman. Still, the two were bound to meet.

Caleb sighed. "I ran into Joe's daughter, Angela. Her husband died a while back, and she's been living with her folks. What's for dinner?"

"Roast beef, mashed potatoes, fresh-picked peas, apple pie."

"I'll go wash up."

Callie nodded, wondering what he wasn't telling her about his run-in with Angela, but before she could pry into something that was none of her business, he left the room.

He seemed preoccupied during dinner. Time and again Callie started to ask about Angela, but she couldn't quite summon the nerve. She immediately jumped to the conclusion that Angela was beautiful, a woman who knew all the right things to say to a man. The mere idea made her blood boil furiously even though she had no right to be jealous. She was just his housekeeper, after all, nothing more.

They were having coffee in the parlor when someone knocked at the door. Callie looked at Caleb, wondering if he was expecting company, but he shrugged as if he didn't have any idea who it might be.

It was his house and she let him answer the door, heard the sound of voices, then footsteps nearing the parlor.

"Angela, this is my housekeeper, Callie McGuire. Callie, this is Joe Brigman's daughter, Angela Bristol."

The two women stared at each other for a moment, then both spoke at once.

"How do you do?" Callie murmured.

"Pleased to meet you," Angela said, her voice cool.

The ensuing silence was louder than thunder.

"Come in and sit down, Angie," Caleb said, thinking he'd rather face down all three members of the Price gang than try to make polite conversation with the two women who were staring at each other like angry cats. He could almost hear them unsheathing their claws.

"Would you like some coffee, Angie?" Caleb asked.

Angela Bristol smiled at Caleb, displaying even white teeth and a dimple in her cheek. "Yes, that would be nice."

"Callie, would you mind?"

She almost blurted out that she minded very much when she remembered that she wasn't here as Caleb's guest. She was his housekeeper and cook, nothing more.

Rising stiffly to her feet, Callie made her way into the kitchen, thinking she'd rather serve Angela Bristol a cup of poison than a cup of coffee.

She shut the kitchen door with a bang. It was obvious why Mrs. Angela Bristol had come to call. She wanted Caleb Stryker. And she was pretty enough to get him, Callie thought bitterly. Angela was tall and shapely. Angela had beautiful skin and hair. Angela was his guest, his equal, not his employee.

Callie slammed the coffeepot on a tray, added cups and saucers, cream and sugar, two spoons, and carried the tray into the parlor, placing it on the table beside the sofa.

"Will that be all, Mr. Stryker?" she asked.

"Yeah. Thanks, Callie." He frowned when she turned to leave the room. "Where are you going?"

"I'm going to retire for the night if you won't be needing me for anything else."

"But . . ."

"Let her go, Caleb," Angela said, smiling sweetly. "It's obvious the poor girl's tired."

"Very well," Caleb agreed reluctantly. "Good night, Callie."

"Good night, Mr. Stryker."

He watched her leave the room, cursing the fact that he was now alone with Angela. She was smiling when he turned to face her. Smiling like a lion about to bring down a lamb.

To fill the silence, he started to pour himself a cup of coffee.

"Here, let me do that," Angela said. She took the coffeepot from his hand and filled a cup for him and one for herself. "Cream? Sugar?"

"Just black."

She handed him a cup, then added cream and sugar to her own, smiling at him all the while. "This is a lovely room," she remarked. "You'll probably think me silly, but sometimes, when I was here tidying up, I pretended that we lived here."

"Angie . . ."

"Oh, I know, it's foolish. But it's what I always wanted. What your mother wanted."

"My mother's dead."

"Cal, I'd make you a good wife."

"Angie, you're supposed to be getting married soon."

"I know, but Tom's nothing compared to you."

"You don't know anything about me. I'm not the same boy who left here twelve years ago. I've changed. You've changed."

"I like the changes I see," Angie purred. "Do you?"

"Dammit, woman, there was never anything between us!"

Tears pooled in her eyes. "Cal, how can you say that? You kissed me! Have you forgotten?"

"I was just a kid. *You* were just a kid. It didn't mean anything."

"Well, it meant something to me."

Caleb sighed heavily, defeated by her tears. "Angie, I'm sorry."

Angela sniffed loudly and then, sensing that he was weakening, she slid into his arms and kissed him.

For a moment, he was too startled to do anything but kiss her back. After all, she was warm and willing and in his arms, kissing him as if she'd never let go.

Sanity returned at the same time that Callie entered the room.

"Excuse me," Callie said, her eyes widening in surprise at finding Angela in Caleb's arms. "I . . . I . . . excuse me," she said again, and fled the room, the sight of Angela kissing Caleb branded in her mind.

Caleb swore softly as he disentangled himself from Angela's arms. "I think you'd better go home, Angie."

"But why?"

"I'm not the right man for you. You always said you wanted to be respectable, to marry a man who'd give you a house in town." He shook his head ruefully. "You know I've never been very respectable. And I don't want to live in town."

"You're respectable enough for me, Caleb Stryker. You're more of a man than any other man in shoe leather."

"It's getting late. Your father will be worried."

"No, he won't. He knows where I am."

"Angie, please." He didn't want to hurt her feelings, but he was remembering now why he'd never seriously thought about marrying Angie. And he remembered something else, too. That kiss behind the barn had been her idea, not his.

"All right, Cal, I'll go." She smiled up at him, knowing better than to push too hard. But she didn't intend to give up, not without a fight. "We can still be friends, can't we?"

"Friends," he muttered. "Sure."

"Good night, then."

"Good night."

He walked her to the door, endured her parting kiss. Returning to the parlor, he braced his hands on the mantel and stared into the fireplace, wishing it was Callie who'd thrown herself into his arms, Callie who thought he was the pick of the crop. But Callie didn't have much use for men, and he was too old and too weary to pay court to a blushing virgin.

# *Chapter Twelve*

Callie was ready for her riding lesson shortly after breakfast. She wore the same calico skirt she'd worn the day before, and a blue shirtwaist that matched her eyes.

She'd almost decided not to ride at all, certain that Caleb would rather go riding with Angela Bristol, but when she mentioned it to him, he'd just shaken his head and told her that Angela Bristol was a friend, nothing more. They hadn't been kissing like they were "just friends" the night before, Callie thought, but she hadn't said so out loud.

At the barn, the first thing Caleb taught her was how to saddle a horse. Then he stepped back and watched while she saddled the bay.

Acutely aware that he was observing her every move, Callie made sure the blanket was smooth before she lifted the heavy saddle into place. She'd expected him to saddle her horse for her. No doubt he would have saddled the widow Bristol's horse.

Caleb frowned at the grim expression on Callie's face. She looked mad enough to spit nails.

He boosted her into the saddle, mounted his own horse, and led the way out of the yard.

Finding a flat stretch of ground, he had Callie put the bay through its paces. Walk. Trot. Lope. First left, then right. He watched her carefully, thinking that she had a natural seat and light hands. A few more lessons and she'd be riding like a Lakota warrior.

"That's enough for now," Caleb called twenty minutes later. "There's a lake just east of here. Do you like to fish?"

"I don't know."

"I brought some string and a couple of hooks. Are you game to try?"

Callie nodded. She put her heels to the bay's flanks and set out after Caleb. It was a beautiful morning. The sky was blue and clear; a faint breeze stirred the tall grass.

There were cattle everywhere, tan ones, red ones, black and white ones, all with doleful brown eyes. Some had calves at their sides. They looked up only briefly as the riders passed by.

Remembering that Caleb had said that his mother had sent several hundred head to the Indians, Callie was surprised to see so many cows, and said as much.

Caleb grinned. "We'd never sell them all," he explained. "Likely Joe sent some of the older cows and young bulls to the reservation."

The lake, spawned by an underground stream, was located in a small valley, ringed by trees and low-lying shrubs. She fell in love with the place the moment she saw it. Sunlight danced on the face of the water. Birds sang in the trees. Several ducks were sunning themselves on the shore.

Callie dismounted near the water's edge. Following Caleb's lead, she tethered the bay to a nearby tree, then stood watching as he cut two long slender branches and quickly fashioned a pair of fishing poles using the string and hooks he'd brought with him. He dug up a couple of worms for bait, then handed Callie one of the poles.

For a time they stood side by side, but when nothing happened right away, Callie sat down on the grass, the fishing pole clutched in both hands. After a moment, Caleb sank down beside her.

"Have you ever caught any fish in this lake?" Callie asked, her expression dubious.

"When I was a boy."

"Maybe they've all been caught by now."

"Maybe."

"Why were you kissing Angela Bristol?"

Caleb made a sound of disgust low in his throat. "She was kissing me. Angie thinks she's in love with me."

"How do you know she isn't?"

"For one thing, I haven't seen her in twelve years. And she's supposed to be engaged."

"Really?" Callie looked at him in surprise. What kind of woman was Angela Bristol, to be engaged to one man and kissing another?

"That's what her father told me."

"She's pretty, isn't she?"

"I guess so." Caleb's gaze drifted over Callie's

face. Her cheeks were the color of ripe peaches, her eyes as blue as a robin's egg; her lips, slightly parted, were as pink as a wild rose. He'd never seen anything more lovely, or more desirable, in his life.

"Would you want to kiss her if she wasn't engaged?"

"Who?"

Callie looked at him in exasperation. "Angela, of course."

"No."

A whisper of a breeze blew over the water, stirring a lock of Callie's hair and ruffling the hem of her skirt. As always, she looked more like a little girl than a grown woman, and Caleb cursed under his breath, wishing that she was more knowledgeable about men. If she were older, wiser, he'd tell her bluntly that he wanted to make love to her; perhaps he'd even try to seduce her.

But he couldn't seduce Callie. Her very innocence was like a boundary—a barrier he refused to cross. He'd done a lot of things he wasn't proud of, but he'd never deflowered a virgin, and he didn't intend to start now.

Callie slid her tongue over her lips. It made her nervous, when Caleb looked at her like that, his dark eyes hot and hungry. She knew what it meant, and the thought that he wanted her filled her with fear and excitement.

For a moment, she held her breath, waiting, wondering if he would kiss her again, hoping he would, and yet, at the same time, afraid of his touch because she knew that most men weren't content to stop with kissing. They always wanted more, and she had no more to give.

She let her breath out in a long sigh as she recalled the night Richard Ashton had trapped her in the alley. She remembered the way his hand had squeezed her breast until it hurt, the smell of liquor on his breath as he kissed her, his mouth hot and wet and repulsive.

Caleb had been watching Callie, trying to discern what she was thinking. He frowned as her expression grew wary.

He was about to ask her what was wrong when the end of the fishing pole in Callie's hand began to vibrate.

"Hold tight," he exclaimed. "You've got a bite!"

"What should I do?"

"Just hang on."

"Here, you take it," Callie said. She thrust her fishing pole into Caleb's hands and took his in exchange, then watched as he backed away from the shore and began drawing in the line.

She squealed in delight when she saw the fish wriggling on the end of the string. "I caught one!" she crowed. "My first fish!"

"It's a beauty," Caleb said, extracting the hook from the trout's mouth.

"You've got one, too," Callie exclaimed as she felt a pull on Caleb's fishing pole. "Hurry, bring it in."

"You do it."

Face flushed with excitement, Callie took a step back and began to pull the line in, hand over hand. "Your fish isn't as big as mine," she remarked as she drew the fish out of the water.

"Beginner's luck," he retorted with a grin. "I'll bet you my next one will be bigger than yours."

"What do you want to bet?"

His gaze moved over her face to settle on her lips. "A kiss." It sounded foolish, childish, spoken aloud. He was a grown man, far too old to play kid's games. But he waited on tenterhooks for her answer.

"A kiss?" Suddenly, there was a lump in her throat and it was hard to breathe.

Caleb nodded. "If I win, I get to kiss you."

"And what do I get if I win?"

All the humor drained out of his face. "You get to kiss me."

Callie stared at him for a long moment, and then she nodded.

He put fresh bait on their hooks, threw her line in the water for her, then walked a few feet away and threw in his own line.

She stood at the water's edge, stealing furtive glances in Caleb's direction, hoping that he would catch the biggest fish because she didn't think she had the nerve to kiss him, but she very much wanted him to kiss her.

Time seemed to crawl by, but then there was a tug on the line and she was pulling in another fish, bigger than the first. Twenty minutes later, Caleb pulled in his second catch of the day. It was half the size of hers.

She looked up at him, mute, as he tossed his fish with the other three.

"Looks like you win," he said.

Callie nodded, her heart pounding like a blacksmith's hammer.

"Are you ready to collect?"

She was warm all over, as though all her blood was on fire. He was standing in front of her, his dark eyes intent upon her face, his breathing suddenly as erratic as her own.

"It's all right, Callie," he said, his voice rough, "you don't have to collect."

"I want to." She had to force the words past her lips, could hardly hear them over the fierce beating of her heart.

He took a step toward her. "Are you sure?"

She nodded, unable to speak for his nearness. It always surprised her how tall and broad he was. The top of her head barely reached his shoulder.

Swallowing hard, she placed her hands on his chest and stood on tiptoe. Obligingly, he lowered his head toward her, one arm circling her waist. His hair, as black as night, fell across his shoulders like a dark curtain.

For a moment, she stared into his eyes, felt herself melting in the heat of his gaze. And then, unable to withstand the hunger in his eyes any longer, she closed her eyes and touched her lips to his.

Lightning. It was like being touched by lightning. She felt the heat of it, the shock of it, right down to her toes.

And he felt it, too. He groaned as if he were in pain. His arm, as inflexible as iron, tightened around her waist, and then he was drawing her body against his, crushing her close, holding her so hard she thought her ribs might crack. His tongue delved into her mouth as he lifted her up, pressing her hips to his, shamelessly letting her feel the strength of his desire.

For a timeless moment, she forgot everything but the thrill of his kiss, the power of his touch. She tasted his tongue with her own, felt him shudder against her, heard him whisper something in a soft, guttural language she could not understand. But she understood the tone of his voice, the look in his eyes when he took his mouth from hers to draw in a ragged breath.

Unbidden, into her mind came the memory of her mother and Duncan Stryker sprawled across an unmade bed in the Miner's Rest, and hard upon the heels of that recollection came the memory of her mother's tear-filled voice warning her that men all wanted the same thing from a woman. Then she heard Richard Ashton shouting at her, predicting that sooner or later she'd end up just like her mother.

"Let me go!" She pounded on Caleb's chest with her fists, and it was like hitting a stone wall. "Let me go!"

"Dammit, Callie—"

"No! No! Let me go!"

"You're playing with fire, Callie," he warned, his voice husky with barely restrained desire. "Don't turn me away, not this time."

He stroked the curve of her cheek with one calloused finger. "I know you don't trust me, but I see the hunger in your eyes, I can smell it on you.

"And when I kiss you . . ."

He lowered his head and kissed her again, hard and brutal this time, and she responded with a moan that was filled with both pleasure and pain.

"Callie . . ." His voice was like dark fire, beckoning her closer, daring her to touch its heat.

"No. No, please, I can't."

Caleb drew a deep breath, thinking that letting Callie go now would be one of the hardest things he'd ever done.

But he didn't want to take her by force, and he didn't want to seduce her into something she'd regret later. He wanted her warm and eager, wanted to hear her admit that she wanted him, too. He didn't want any doubts or misgivings between them.

He swore a vile oath as he released her, cursing her for being nothing but a tease, cursing himself for wanting her so bad that it hurt.

For a moment he thought of throwing her down on the ground and taking what he wanted, what he needed. Instead, he clenched his hands at his sides and took deep, even breaths, trying to ignore the throbbing ache of unfulfilled desire.

Callie stared at him for stretched seconds, her breathing harsh and uneven.

Caleb saw her eyes widen, heard the gasp of her indrawn breath as she saw the very visible evidence of his desire.

Before he could say anything, she whirled around and ran for her horse. Scrambling into the saddle, she picked up the reins and drummed her heels into the bay's flanks, lighting out for home just as fast as she could go.

Caleb cursed softly as he threw the fish into one of his saddlebags, then vaulted into the saddle and rode after Callie.

# Chapter Thirteen

Callie reined the bay to a gravel-scattering halt near the porch steps, threw the reins over the hitch rack, and ran into the house.

In her room, she closed the door, turned the key in the lock, and hurled herself, face down, on the bed. She pounded the pillow with her fists, angry with Caleb Stryker for arousing her passion, angry with herself for liking it. She would not surrender her virtue to Caleb, or to any man, not until she had a ring on her finger and a piece of paper that said she was duly and legally wed.

She would not become what her mother had been.

She would not be a whore. Not for Caleb. Not for any man.

Oh, but it was so easy to see why her mother had given up everything for Duncan Stryker. Duncan had been tall and handsome, but his son was more so. Duncan had exuded an aura of virility and masculinity, but now his attraction seemed weak in comparison to Caleb's. Duncan had been forceful, powerful, and rich, accustomed to having whatever he wanted, and she feared Caleb was cut from the same cloth.

What was she to do?

She told herself that she would have to leave, that she couldn't stay in the house with him after what had happened today.

She would take the money she had earned working as Caleb's housekeeper and leave Cheyenne. She had enough to get her to Denver. Perhaps, if she couldn't be Molly Faye's partner in the millinery shop, she could work for her doing odd jobs, cleaning and sweeping up.

She didn't want to leave the ranch.

Tears of frustration welled in her eyes, and she pounded her fists on the pillow again, railing at fate, furious because life had become so complicated.

A harsh knock on the door sent her thoughts scattering and she sat up, her heart pounding.

It had to be Caleb.

"Callie? Open the door."

She shook her head, unable to speak past the lump in her throat.

"Callie? You'd better open this door before I kick it in!"

"Go away."

"Open the damn door."

He spoke each word slowly and distinctly, and she cringed at the anger in his voice.

"Now, Callie."

She slid out of bed and crossed the floor as if going to meet her doom. Twisting the key in the lock, she reached for the door knob, but it was already turning, the door was opening, and Caleb Stryker stood in the doorway, his face as dark as a thundercloud, his gray eyes ominous.

"Mr. Stryker . . . Caleb, I . . . I'm sorry. I didn't mean to make you . . . to let you think that I . . . please don't hurt me."

He swore under his breath, his anger evaporating in the face of her fear. "I'm not going to hurt you. Why would you think such a thing?"

"My mother . . ."

"Duncan hit your mother?"

"No, not Duncan. Other men, before him. Sometimes they hit my mother when she wouldn't let them . . . let them have their way with me."

She looked away, too embarrassed to face him. "Sometimes they hit me, too."

"Callie."

He breathed her name, his heart aching for the life she'd led, the pain she must have suffered. No wonder she was afraid of him. No wonder she wanted to get out of Cheyenne.

A single tear rolled down her cheek. "I don't want to be like my mother."

"I know."

Slowly, so as not to frighten her, he crossed the space between them and drew her into his arms. "Relax, Callie. I'm not going to hurt you." *I just want to hold you. I need to hold you, to know that you're safe.*

She stood unmoving in his arms, her body as stiff and unyielding as a statue. He could feel her trembling, and he cursed the men who had made her afraid .

"It's all right, Callie," he murmured. "No one will hurt you while I'm here. It's all right, girl. It's all right."

His voice was deep and low, soothing. Gradually, the tenseness drained out of her body and she rested her head against his chest.

He held her for a long while, rocking her gently back and forth.

"What do you want, Callie?" he asked after a while.

She blinked up at him. "I don't know."

"Do you want to leave?"

"I did, but . . ."

"But?" He held his breath as he waited for her answer.

"I like it here, on the ranch."

"Then stay. Stay as long as you like, Callie."

"Thank you, Mr. Stryker."

"Caleb."

"Caleb."

She repeated his name hesitantly, remembering the last time she had used his Christian name, the day they'd gone riding together for the first time. When he'd kissed her for the first time.

Caleb drew a sharp breath. Her nearness was starting to affect him in ways he wouldn't be able to hide for long. After giving her a slight squeeze, he let her go and took a step backward.

"If I clean those fish, do you think you could fry 'em up for dinner?"

Callie nodded, a faint smile lighting her tear-streaked face. "Just let me wash up and I'll be right there."

"Take your time," he said gruffly, and got out of her room just as fast as he could, before the urge to kiss her became overpowering, before he carried her to bed and showed her there was nothing to be afraid of.

Caleb stayed away from the ranch house as much as possible during the next two weeks, riding out with the cowhands to check the cattle and the condition of the range. He spent a day hauling debris out of the creek, and another day riding the southern boundary of the ranch because one of the hands had seen the tracks of a mountain lion.

If Callie knew why he spent so much time away from the house, she didn't remark on it. It was obvious how she spent her days, for the house had never looked better. The floors had been waxed so thoroughly that it was almost dangerous to walk on them. The windows were squeaky clean, all the bed linens had been changed, and the curtains were washed and starched. There wasn't a speck of dust to be found anywhere in the house, and heaven help the poor spider who tried to find a place to spin a web.

The only time they spent together was at supper. Callie made small talk, telling Caleb about her day, because she didn't like the silence between them.

Caleb felt guilty for not spending more time with her. He knew she was probably lonely, since she had no one else to talk to, but her nearness was a constant torment. He dreamed of her at night, dark erotic dreams that often caused him to wake in a sweat. More than once, he left the house in the middle of the night, making his way to the creek to cool his desire in the chill water.

He'd been fighting his desire for Callie for three tension-filled weeks when Angela Bristol came to call again.

Callie decided that Ira Bristol must have left his widow a wealthy woman, for Angela was dressed in a costly dark pink wool suit and matching hat. Callie glanced down at her blue gingham dress and felt every inch the servant she'd been hired to be.

Angela breezed into the house as if she had every right to be there. She nodded briefly to Callie and then ignored her completely, all her attention focused on Caleb. Callie took the hint and left the room, wishing she had the nerve to tell Angela Bristol exactly what she thought of her.

Caleb frowned irritably, wishing Callie hadn't left him alone with Angela. He'd seen that predatory look on the faces of too many women not to recognize it for what it was, and he was in no mood to play cat and mouse with Angie, not tonight.

For a time, Angela and Caleb made small talk about the ranch and about next year's calf crop. Then Angela dropped her bombshell.

"I broke my engagement to Tom." She smiled at Caleb as if expecting him to be thrilled by her news.

"Why would you do that?"

"I just can't marry him, not now that you're back."

"Angela . . ."

"I know, I know, you think you don't want to marry me, but it's meant to be, Cal, you'll see."

Caleb shook his head. "You're making a big mistake, Angie." He took a deep breath. "I haven't decided what I want to do yet. I might sell everything and go back to bounty hunting."

Angela pressed a hand to her heart. "You wouldn't!"

"I might."

Angela shook her head. "You won't. Your place is here, on the ranch, and my place is with you."

She stood up, her smile firmly in place. "Will I see you in church tomorrow?"

"No."

"I'll save you a place in case you change your mind."

"Good night, Angie."

"Good night, Cal." She brushed her lips across his, murmured a second "good night" and was gone.

Caleb stared after her, wondering what he was going to do about Angela Bristol.

"Is she gone?"

He glanced over his shoulder to see Callie standing in the doorway between the parlor and the kitchen.

"Yeah."

"You wouldn't really go back to bounty hunting, would you?"

Caleb shrugged. "I don't know. I might."

"But why?"

"I liked it." He grinned at her look of horror. "It was exciting."

After closing the front door, he crossed the room and sat down in a corner of the sofa.

"Exciting," he repeated. "Kind of like hunting big game. It's dangerous, but there's something exhilarating about pitting your strength and your wits against an adversary and knowing that one mistake could cost you your life."

Callie sat down on the other end of the sofa. "And that's why you liked it, because it was dangerous?"

"Partly."

He wondered how he could explain it to her, how he could make her understand what it had been like for a half-breed to try and make his way in the white man's world where everyone who wasn't white was viewed with suspicion.

"I tried holding down regular jobs," he went on with a shrug, "but I hated them all. I didn't like working for someone else, taking orders, living my life by a clock. Bounty hunting let me be my own man. I could work when I felt like it, keep my own hours, be my own boss."

"But you don't need to work any more. You've got the ranch and the mansion."

"I know."

It was more responsibility than he'd ever had or wanted, and he wasn't sure he liked it. That was another reason he'd liked bounty hunting. All he'd owned was a horse, his saddle, his weapons, and the clothes on his back. And it had been enough.

But then he looked around the room and knew that this was what he wanted, where he wanted to be. Where he needed to be.

Callie took a deep breath, gathering her courage to ask the question that had been haunting her all night.

"Are you going to marry Angela Bristol?"

"Marry her! Whatever gave you that idea?"

"She did. It's obvious she's just waiting for you to pop the question."

"She's got a long wait. I don't want to marry Angela. Hell, I don't want to marry anybody."

"Why not?"

It was her biggest dream, to marry a man who would love her and cherish her, a knight on a shining steed who would carry her away to his castle where they'd live happily ever after. But it was just a dream, and she knew all too well that fantasy and reality were as far apart as the shores of the Pacific and the Atlantic.

"I guess I've never seen a good marriage," Caleb replied. "Even the ones that start off right seem to turn sour somewhere along the way."

"I guess you're right," Callie admitted reluctantly.

Many of the men who had frequented the cribs in the saloon had been married men. Duncan Stryker had been a married man, married to the most beautiful woman Callie had ever seen, but it hadn't kept him home at night. Her mother had said over and over again that men wanted only one thing from a woman, but it seemed one woman wasn't enough for most men.

"There must be some happy marriages," Callie murmured. "Fanny's, for one."

Caleb grunted in soft agreement.

"I don't think Angela's going to take 'no' for an answer," Callie remarked, returning to their original topic.

Caleb scowled. Angela Bristol was about as tactful as a double-barreled shotgun, as subtle as a mare in heat, and as hard to get rid of as a bad habit.

In the course of the next two weeks, she turned up everywhere—in the barn, on the range, at the lake. Whether he was rubbing down his horse, checking the cattle, or riding the boundary of the

Rocking S, Angie was there, all smiles and sweet words, inviting him to dinner, reminiscing about old times. It got so he was afraid to step out of the house.

Callie watched it all with a faint hint of amusement. Caleb Stryker was a hard man, self-sufficient, always in control of his emotions, yet Angela Bristol's constant attention had him as flustered as a school boy.

"I told you she wasn't going to give up," Callie reminded Caleb one afternoon as he was prowling the parlor floor, cursing Angela's stubbornness. "I don't think she's used to taking 'no' for an answer."

"Well, she'd better get used to it," Caleb growled.

Callie laughed softly. "I think you'd better start thinking about what to wear to the wedding."

Caleb swore under his breath as he glared at Callie. She thought it was funny, but Angela was driving him crazy.

And so was Callie. His gaze moved over her, admiring the way the lamplight glistened in her red-gold hair, the soft innocence in her deep blue eyes, the delicate curve of her cheek, the graceful line of her neck. He took a deep breath as he let his gaze linger on her mouth, remembering all too clearly the taste of her lips.

"I have an idea," he said, thinking aloud. "You'll probably think it's crazy, but how would you like to pretend we're engaged?"

"What?"

"You heard me. If Angela thought I'd asked you to marry me, maybe she'd leave me alone."

Callie stared at him, her mind reeling. Pretend to be engaged to Caleb Stryker? She thought of the kisses they'd shared at the lake, of the hypnotic pull of his deep gray eyes, of the ever-present attraction that hummed between them even now. Pretending to be engaged might lead to other things, things she wasn't prepared to deal with.

Slowly, she shook her head. "No, I don't think so."

"Nothing would really change between us," Caleb assured her. "I just want to get Angie off my back. She's got the tenacity of a wolf on the scent of blood."

Callie gazed up at him, her heart racing. He was tall and broad and more handsome than any man had a right to be. "I don't know . . ."

"Just think of it as another facet of being my housekeeper. You know, cooking, cleaning, pretending to be my fiancé. What do you think?"

"I think it's insane."

"It'll just be for a little while, until Angie catches the scent of other game." Caleb shrugged. "I'll make it worth your while, Callie. As my fiancé, you can buy whatever you like in town and put it on my account. Clothes for yourself, do-dads for the house, whatever you want."

She was weakening; he could see it in her eyes. So he played what he thought was his ace in the hole.

"With my money behind you, you'll be able to thumb your nose at Maude Colton and Martha Brewster and everybody else who ever gave you a bad time."

It was crazy, the craziest thing she'd ever heard, but suddenly it made a bizarre kind of sense. Not only would Angie have to stop pestering Caleb, but if Richard Ashton thought she was engaged, he'd have to leave her alone as well.

Callie smiled to herself. It might be fun, to pretend she was the future Mrs. Stryker, to waltz into Brewster's Mercantile and buy whatever caught her fancy, to wear silky underthings and skirts that rustled instead of cotton and muslin.

"What happens when our little charade is over? I won't be able to stay on as your housekeeper if people think our so-called romance is finished."

"I'll look after you, Callie, I promise."

Unbidden came the memory of her mother's voice. *He'll look after you, baby. He promised me he would.*

Slowly, Callie shook her head. "No."

Caleb frowned. He'd been so certain she'd see things his way. After all, she had nothing to lose. "Why not?"

Callie lifted her chin and squared her shoulders, determined to say what was on her mind no matter what the consequences might be.

"I'll tell you why not," she said with more courage than she felt. "Your father promised to look after my mother, but he didn't. He never gave her anything but empty promises."

A muscle worked in Caleb's jaw. "I'm not like my father."

"My mother said all men were the same."

"Maybe all the men she knew were the same. But you have to consider the type of men she met in her line of work."

"I want something in writing."

"Like what?"

"I don't know. Something written in your own hand, something signed and dated that says you'll give me a thousand dollars in cash when our charade is over."

Caleb stared at her. "You're serious, aren't you?"

"Yes. I may not know much, but I don't intend to make the same mistakes my mother did."

Caleb swore under his breath, but inwardly he couldn't help admiring Callie McGuire. She had the gumption and the determination to look out for herself, and he knew that wasn't easy because he'd been doing it for most of his life.

"All right, Callie. I'll write it up tonight and you can look it over in the morning before we go into town. We can even stop by Hoag's office and have him witness it if it will make you happy."

Callie nodded. "One more thing. I want you to go to church with me next Sunday."

"Church!" Caleb swore under his breath. "All right, Callie, I'll take you to church if it will make you happy."

"Then I'll be your make-believe fiancé for as long as you think it's necessary."

She smiled up at him, her blue eyes twinkling. "As soon as you sign the paper."

# Chapter Fourteen

She looked radiant, Caleb thought as he quickly wrote out the terms of their agreement. What with her blue eyes sparkling and her luscious mouth curved in a smile, she looked like the proverbial cat that had swallowed the canary.

"Maybe we should seal our bargain with a kiss," Caleb mused, his voice sounding as rusty as an old hinge.

And before she could protest, before he could talk himself out of it, he tossed the pen on the table and wrapped his arms around her.

His kiss was as soft as dandelion down, as explosive as dynamite.

Unable to help herself, Callie leaned toward him, a soft sigh rising in her throat.

Caleb gazed into the depths of Callie's eyes,

groaned deep in his throat as he pulled her up against him and kissed her again.

She was fire and honey in his arms, an angel clothed in hair like silk and skin like satin. He had a sudden, totally irrational wish that their engagement was real, that in a month or two she would be his wife. His to hold, to touch, to grow old with.

A heavy heat settled in his loins as he imagined her in his bed. He'd make love to her from sundown to sunrise, he thought, and then start all over again.

A long shudder ran the length of Callie's body when he released her. It had been a mistake to agree to be his fiancée, she thought hazily, a mistake even to agree to work for a man like Caleb Stryker. He was much too attractive, much too persuasive, and she sorely feared that she wouldn't be able to resist him for long if he kissed her like that very many more times.

He was watching her, his dark eyes unfathomable, his hands shoved into his pants pockets. His whole body was taut, like a mountain lion getting ready to pounce. And she was the prey.

Thoroughly shaken by his kiss, she took a step backward. "I . . . uh, think I'll go fix dinner."

A deep breath hissed through Caleb's teeth, and then he nodded. "Yeah, that's a good idea."

He watched her leave the room, admiring the shapely curve, the gentle swaying, of her hips. Then he headed for the barn, where he spent the next thirty minutes currying the horses until their coats gleamed like polished brass.

Reluctant to be alone in the house with Callie, he lingered in the barn, checking the harness, wiping the dust from the buggy, examining the cinch on his saddle. Finally, when he couldn't think of anything else to do, he returned to the house.

Callie was in the kitchen, singing "Onward, Christian Soldiers" as she prepared dinner.

She whirled around at the sound of his footsteps, her smile a little rough around the edges. "Dinner will be ready in a minute."

Caleb nodded, then slid into a chair, feeling like a slack-jawed kid on his first date. He couldn't stop watching her, couldn't help remembering the taste of that kiss, or the way she'd felt in his arms.

Callie set the table, wondering at the escalating tension between them. She'd prepared numerous meals for him since she'd agreed to be his housekeeper. This afternoon was no different than a dozen other times, so why was she so nervous, so conscious of the way his gaze followed her as she moved around the kitchen?

Callie was shaking inside by the time she sat down across from him. She avoided his gaze as she filled her plate, felt her heart catch as his hand brushed hers.

Reluctantly, she looked up, and their gazes met and locked.

His eyes were stormy with desire, dark and gray as thunderclouds. The heat of his gaze was like lightning, sizzling through her veins, making all her senses spring to life.

Good Lord, she thought, if a sham engagement made the sparks fly between them like this, what would the real thing do?

"Callie . . ."

She shook her head, afraid of the longing she heard in his voice, afraid of the silent, answering cry that rose in her heart.

"No. We can't . . . I can't."

Caleb dragged a hand across his jaw. He had no right to want her, but want her he did, with every fiber of his being. But he could not, would not, force her.

"It's all right, Callie."

"I'm sorry," she stammered, though she wasn't sure why she was apologizing.

"You don't need to apologize," he said gruffly. "You haven't done anything wrong."

He fought down the urge to drag her across the table and into his arms. Instead, he gestured at the meal spread before them.

"Looks good."

Callie tried to concentrate on what she was eating, but she didn't taste a thing.

Later, while washing and drying the dishes, she couldn't remember whether she'd eaten or not. All she could remember was the look in Caleb's eyes, the husky tremor in his voice.

Callie went to her room early that night, her mind fantasizing about what it would be like if she were really engaged to Caleb. She'd have security then, all the security in the world. She'd never have to worry about being hungry, never have to worry about where her next meal was coming from. She'd have someone to take care of her, a place to live, the means to buy whatever caught her fancy.

In bed, she drew the covers up to her chin, then stared up at the white-washed ceiling, wondering if anyone would ever truly love her, if she'd ever have a home of her own, children, respectability. A husband . . .

With a sigh, she closed her eyes, her mind filling with Caleb's swarthy image. He was made of copper and ebony, she thought.

As though he had materialized out of her secret yearning, he was suddenly there beside her. His hand, big and calloused, was gentle as it stroked her cheek, moved through the hair at her temple. He whispered her name, and the sound of his voice went through her like liquid fire. With a soft whimper, she reached for him and he stretched out beside her on the bed.

For a moment, they gazed into each other's eyes, and then he was kissing her. His mouth was hot and tasted of brandy; his hands played over her flesh, touching where no one else had ever touched, causing her to burn with desire. She had never known such ecstasy, such pleasure, such torment. She held him close, closer, seeking for something she didn't quite understand.

"Show me," she begged. "Teach me."

He smiled, and his teeth were very white against the deep bronze of his skin, and then he was laughing at her and she heard a voice ringing in her head, saw Richard Ashton's finger pointing in her direction as he accused her of being no better than her mother, no better than a two-bit whore on a Saturday night. . . .

Callie woke in a cold sweat, her own cry echoing in her ears. It had all been a dream, nothing but a bad dream.

She sat up, her heart pounding in her breast as her bedroom door swung open.

"Callie? You all right?"

She breathed a sigh of relief as she recognized Caleb's voice.

"I'm fine," she said, her voice shaky. "I had a nightmare, that's all."

He crossed the room, a tall, dark figure moving through a sea of blackness. Instinctively, she drew the covers up to her chin even though she knew he couldn't see her clearly in the darkness.

"Can I get you anything?" he asked.

"No, thank you."

He paused, wanting to say more, wanting to take her in his arms and comfort her, but he made no move toward her, knowing that once he touched her, he'd never be able to let her go.

"Good night, then," he said.

"Good night."

He heard the soft rustle of the bedclothes as she slid down between the sheets.

It would be so easy, he thought, so easy to crawl into bed beside her and awaken the passion sleeping in her soul. It flared to life every time he touched her. All she needed was someone to unlock the floodgates, someone to show her how good it could be between a man and a woman. And he wanted to be that someone.

His feet were like lead as he crossed the room and stepped into the hall. Muttering an oath, he closed the door behind him.

He hoped like hell that she'd be able to sleep, because he knew he wouldn't.

# Chapter Fifteen

True to his word, Caleb took Callie to church the following Sunday. He wore dark gray pants, a light gray coat, a dazzling white shirt that emphasized his swarthy complexion, and a black silk cravat.

It would likely be his only appearance in the small, wood-framed chapel, he mused as he stood before a mirror straightening his cravat, so he might as well set a few people back on their heels. They would no doubt expect him to appear in fringed buckskins, or maybe in a fancy gambler's suit and gaudy brocade vest. It would be amusing to see their reaction when he appeared looking like any other respectable citizen.

And, indeed, people did turn to stare as he drew the shiny black carriage to a halt beside the building, though he couldn't be sure if they were staring at the carriage, at him, or at Callie, who looked like a vision in a demure dress of dark blue velvet. Black kidskin boots hugged her feet, and her red-gold hair was tucked beneath a wide-brimmed hat that sported a long white feather. A pair of dainty white gloves added the finishing touch to her attire. He thought she looked like she'd just stepped out of the pages of Godey's Lady's Book.

Vaulting to the ground, he helped Callie alight from the carriage, then took her arm and escorted her into the church and down the center aisle to a pew near the front of the church.

He could hear people whispering behind them, but he didn't care. People had always talked about him for one reason or another, lamenting his heritage, speculating on how many men he had killed, wondering if he'd ever scalped anyone or shot anyone in the back.

It had stopped bothering him long ago, but he could feel the tension in Callie; he took her hand in his and gave it a reassuring squeeze.

"They're just jealous because you're the most beautiful woman in the place," Caleb whispered.

Callie smiled, pleased by his compliment even though she didn't believe it for a minute. Still, she knew the dress was pretty, the prettiest she'd ever owned, and it gave her a small measure of confidence. The dress had materialized in her closet as if by magic, along with several others. She knew they were from Caleb, though when he'd ordered them or how he'd known what size she wore remained a mystery. She had a sneaking suspicion that Fanny had something to do with it.

Callie pasted a stiff smile on her face as Martha and Ed Brewster sat down in the opposite pew, then felt her smile fade a little as Maude Colton slid in beside them.

Maude and Martha immediately put their heads together, and Callie looked straight ahead, her cheeks burning with the knowledge that they were gossiping about her.

She hardly heard a word of the service, but in spite of her uneasiness at being surrounded by people who thought she was no better than she ought to be, she found a measure of comfort within the walls of the church. The hymns filled her with gladness, the closing prayer touched her heart, and she was feeling much better about herself and everything else by the time the meeting was over.

Outside, she had just shaken hands with the minister and was turning to speak to Caleb when she saw Angela Bristol walking toward them.

"Just smile," Caleb said, and taking her hand firmly in his, he turned to greet Angela.

"Caleb!" she gushed, totally ignoring Callie, "why didn't you tell me you were coming to church? I would have saved you a seat."

Callie took a step closer to Caleb, annoyed by the woman's rudeness.

Slipping her arm through his, she smiled up at Caleb. "Why don't you tell Angela our news, dear?"

"News?" Angela's gaze darted from Callie's smug smile to Caleb's impassive visage. "What news?"

"Caleb has asked me to marry him." Callie looked up at Caleb and batted her eyelashes.

"He has?"

Callie nodded as she gave Caleb's arm a squeeze. "Isn't it wonderful?"

"Yes, wonderful." Angela's voice held all the enthusiasm of a man just condemned to death. "When's the wedding?"

"We haven't set the date yet," Caleb said. He placed his hand over Callie's and smiled down at her.

The heat in Caleb's smile made Callie's heart go all soft and mushy. *Only make-believe,* she reminded herself. *Only make-believe.*

Angela looked briefly at Callie, then returned her attention to Caleb.

"You always were the impulsive one, Cal, but asking your housekeeper to marry you—really, what will people say?"

"Pretty much what they would have said if I'd proposed to my foreman's daughter, don't you think?"

Caleb's words left Angela speechless, and Callie fought back the urge to laugh out loud.

Caleb gave Angela a cool smile. "You'll excuse us if we're in a hurry," he said, giving Callie a quick hug, "but we've got a lot to discuss."

He didn't wait for Angela to reply, but swept Callie into his arms and carried her to the buggy, where he placed her gently on the seat, then swung up beside her.

Callie glared at him as she smoothed her skirts into place, not knowing whether to be pleased because he had put Mrs. Angela Bristol in her place, or angry because he had embarrassed her in front of the whole congregation.

Anger won.

"How could you make a scene like that, and in front of the minister, too! What will people think?"

His grin was wicked. "They'll think I can't wait to get you home."

"Oh!" Her cheeks flamed as she realized exactly what he meant, and exactly what people would think.

She could feel Angela Bristol's gaze boring into her back as Caleb clucked to the team.

At home, she took refuge in the kitchen, preparing an elaborate afternoon meal because it would keep her busy and give her an excuse to avoid Caleb.

She'd thought he'd seek her out sooner or later, and when he didn't, she peeked into the back parlor to see what he was doing. He wasn't there.

Frowning, she walked through the house, wondering where he'd gone. A noise from the den caught her attention, and she paused outside the door. It was closed and she pressed her ear to the wood, listening intently. She heard him moving about the room, heard the clink of glass against glass as he poured himself a drink.

Relieved, somehow, she went back into the kitchen and began mixing up a cake batter, hoping that Caleb liked chocolate.

Caleb glanced at the door, grinning when he heard Callie's footsteps. So, she'd come looking for him. He waited, wondering if she'd join him in the den, but after a moment he heard her footsteps moving away from the door.

It was just as well. She'd looked so pretty today it had been all he could do to keep his hands off her.

He studied the whiskey in his glass before downing it in a single swallow. Refilling the glass, he sat down at his father's desk, contemplating the papers piled in neat stacks.

He picked up the closest one and perused it quickly. It was a bill of sale for a hundred head of cattle Duncan had bought shortly before his death.

Caleb browsed through the other papers, wondering why no one had ever put them away. There were a number of letters from distant cattle buyers; receipts for goods purchased in Denver, New York, San Francisco, and Paris; and a letter from an English nobleman who was interested in buying the mansion.

Caleb sat back in his father's chair and sipped his drink. Apparently, his mother hadn't taken the time to go through his father's correspondence before she passed away, or maybe she hadn't made a trip out to the ranch after Duncan died. She'd always preferred the mansion to the ranch. He supposed Joe Brigman had taken care of any urgent business that had come up after Duncan passed on. Likely, Joe had put aside the matters that could wait, thinking that Faith would look after them when she'd finished mourning.

Setting the empty glass aside, Caleb opened the top left-hand drawer. Inside were several account books, a couple of bank books, and, of all things, a Bible.

Caleb grinned as he ran his hand over the volume of scripture. Duncan had never been a church-going man. Had he found religion in his old age?

Lifting the Bible, Caleb turned it over in his hand. The pages didn't show much wear; the cover was still new and shiny.

He was about to toss it back into the drawer when he noticed there was something sticking out between the pages.

Opening the Bible, he found two envelopes. The one addressed to Leila McGuire was sealed; the unsealed one was addressed to Orville Hoag, Attorney at Law.

Frowning, Caleb turned the sealed envelope over and over in his hands and then, very carefully, he slit open the envelope and removed a single sheet of white paper.

It was a letter, dated June 2, 1882, eight days before his father had passed away.

*Dearest Leila, I think the end is near. I had hoped to see you one last time, but I fear that will not be possible now. Be assured that I will provide for you and Callie. When I go to Cheyenne on Wednesday, I intend to stop at Hoag's office and give him a codicil to my will, stipulating that, upon my death, all interest and ownership in the Rocking S will pass to you or your heirs.*

*I know this will be a bitter blow to Faith, but she never cared for the ranch, and I know it was always Callie's dream to come here for a visit, although that was never possible. Perhaps this will help to make up for any slight she might have felt.*

*As I look back on my life, I realize that I made many mistakes. I should have taken better care of you. I should have tried to patch things up with Caleb. I should have been a better husband, but looking back solves nothing. Only now, when it's too late to make amends, do I realize how stubborn and selfish I've been. Please forgive this old man, and remember that I loved you. Duncan.*

Caleb stared at the letter, written in his father's familiar bold scrawl, and then opened the second envelope.

Inside he found a codicil to Duncan's will, written in his father's hand and dated June 1, 1882, stating in clear, crisp terms that the Rocking S ranch, its furnishings and livestock, were to be transferred to Leila McGuire or her heirs in the event of his death.

Caleb's first thought was that Callie had told the truth. Duncan had promised to provide for her and her mother, and he had done so.

Tossing the codicil on the desk, Caleb softly cursed his father. If Duncan had wanted to leave his mistress something, why hadn't he left her the mansion? What would a whore know about running a cattle ranch? Dammit, the Rocking S should have been his! Aside from a Lakota lodge deep in the heart of the Black Hills, the ranch was the only place that had ever felt like home.

Sitting forward, he propped his elbows on the desk top and rested his chin on his clasped hands.

So, the Rocking S belonged to Callie. She'd never have to worry about money again, he thought with a wry grin. She'd be able to buy and sell Maude Colton a hundred times over.

The ranch should have been his.

He stared into the fireplace, wondering if Callie would be willing to trade the ranch for the mansion. She didn't know anything about ranching, but she loved the ranch. He'd seen the look in her eyes when they arrived, the wonder, the awe. She loved the cattle, the horses, the chickens, even the pigs.

Picking up the letter and the codicil, he folded them and slid them both into one of the envelopes, then slipped the envelope back into the Bible. He put the Bible back in the desk drawer, behind the account books, and closed the drawer.

Next time he went into town, he'd stop at Hoag's office and find out if the codicil was valid.

Until then, Callie didn't need to know anything about it.

# *Chapter Sixteen*

Caleb sat across the kitchen table from Callie the following Friday afternoon, only half-listening to what she was saying.

Five days had passed since he'd found the addition to his father's will and he hadn't had a good night's sleep since. His conscience, which didn't bother him too often, had kept him awake night after night, urging him to tell Callie about the codicil to the old man's will. Whether he liked it or not, the ranch belonged to her. He could stall as long as he liked, could put off telling her about it until he went into town and checked it out with Hoag, but he knew that the codicil, written in his father's own hand, was perfectly legal. And binding.

Caleb clenched his jaw, his anger at his father increasing with every beat of his heart. Damn the old man! He'd known how much the ranch meant to Caleb, so he'd left it to Leila McGuire, knowing there was no way Caleb would be able to get his hands on it. So much for all that twaddle the old man had spouted about patching things up between them!

He glanced up as he realized that Callie had asked him a question.

"What?"

"I asked if you'd like a piece of cake?"

"Yeah, sure."

He watched her skirts sway as she crossed the kitchen floor to the counter to cut the cake. Every movement she made enticed him—the way she walked, the little habit she had of smoothing the hair at her temple with the back of her hand, the way she sometimes tilted her head to one side when she was curious about something.

The little chit had bewitched him so completely that he couldn't seem to think of anything but her. She'd captured his imagination, and now she had his ranch as well.

Caleb scowled blackly, then forced himself to smile as Callie slid a plate in front of him and poured him another cup of coffee.

"I hope you like it," Callie said as she took her seat.

She looked at Caleb askance, wondering what was bothering him. He'd been preoccupied since they got home from church last Sunday. She wondered briefly if he was angry because she'd asked him to take her to church, but that seemed ridiculous.

Still, if he was mad at her, she wanted to know why. "Is something wrong?"

"No. Why do you ask?"

"I don't know, you just seem so . . ." Callie lifted a hand and let it fall. "I don't know, angry somehow."

"I'm fine."

She looked at him for a moment, then shrugged. If he didn't want to tell her what was bothering him, then it was none of her business.

Caleb scowled into his coffee cup. So, the ranch belonged to Callie. But she didn't know that. And she didn't need to find out. All he had to do to keep control of the ranch was destroy the codicil.

Or marry Callie.

He swore softly. Marry Callie, and the ranch would be his. And Callie would be his. He'd be free to touch her, hold her, bury himself in her sweetness.

But he didn't want to get married.

Feeling Callie's gaze, he glanced up to find her watching him, her eyes narrowed, her brow furrowed.

"What?" Guilt and desire made his voice sharp.

She drew back as if she'd been slapped. "Nothing. I . . . I just wish I knew what was bothering you. Maybe it would help if you talked about it."

"It wouldn't help," he replied curtly.

"I'm sorry. You're not upset about taking me to church, are you?" she queried, and when he shook his head, she summoned her courage and asked if they could go again next Sunday.

A wry grin twitched at Caleb's lips. "Are you trying to turn me into a saint?"

Callie smiled beguilingly. "I don't know. Do you think I could?"

"I think you could turn me into anything you darn well pleased," he muttered.

Callie smiled at that.

"I think I'd like to turn you into a church-going man," she mused, and then, seeing Caleb frown, she added, "It wasn't that bad, was it?"

Caleb grunted softly. "Not if you don't mind listening to some old man who's probably never done a thing wrong in his entire life spout off about hell and damnation."

"Don't you believe in hell?"

"No. I believe most people make their own hell right here on earth."

"I guess that means you don't believe in heaven either."

"Oh, I believe in heaven, all right," Caleb drawled softly.

His gaze moved over Callie's face, lingering on her lips, then moving downward to caress her breasts. "I definitely believe in heaven."

Callie's heart seemed to stop, then start with a rush. Her face felt hot, her hands were cold, and there was a curious fluttering deep in her belly that radiated outward until she was trembling from head to foot.

"You're driving me crazy, Callie. You must know how much I want you."

She nodded slowly, unable to draw her gaze from his, unable to stop the quivering heat that pulsed through her.

"What if I asked you to marry me, for real?"

"What?"

The word emerged from her throat as a small squeak.

"You heard me. Why don't we get married? You'll have all the security you've ever wanted, and I . . ."

His voice trailed off and he left the sentence unfinished, knowing that she understood what he would get, what he wanted.

"But you don't love me."

Caleb shrugged. "You don't love me, either. What difference does it make?"

"I don't want my marriage to be a business deal. Marriage is forever. It should be meaningful. Beautiful . . ."

Caleb stood up and moved away from the table.

"Come here, Callie."

"No."

"I won't hurt you."

"Won't you?"

He shook his head, then held out his hand. "Come here."

"No."

The word slipped out of her mouth, meaningless and empty as she stood up and walked toward him.

"Please, Mr. Stryker . . . Caleb."

"Don't talk."

He took her hand and drew her to him, holding her lightly within the circle of his arms.

Callie gazed up into his eyes, those dark gray eyes that held secrets she yearned to know, promises she knew he wouldn't keep.

"Say yes, Callie."

His voice was like the wind on a dark summer night, whispering over her skin, mesmerizing her with its touch.

"I . . . I hardly know you," she stammered.

"You know me." His voice grew deeper, huskier. "You've always known me."

"I'm afraid."

"Of me?"

His hands slid over her arms, his calloused palms making her skin tingle.

She shook her head. "No. Of what you were."

"What was I?"

The backs of his knuckles grazed her cheek.

"A bounty hunter." She met his gaze boldly as her hand slid down to rest on the butt of his pistol. "You've killed men. Lots of men."

His mouth curled up at the corner. "But never a woman."

"Caleb, I want . . ."

The words died in her throat. What did she want?

"I'll be good to you, Callie. I won't beat you. I won't take a mistress. What more do you want from a husband?"

"Love! I want love. All your money can't buy me that."

"I don't know what love is," Caleb murmured, his finger tracing the outline of her lower lip. "But I know what this is."

He bent toward her, his mouth claiming hers in a long, searing kiss that drove everything else from her mind. His lips were warm and firm and demanding, stealing the breath from her body, the strength from her limbs.

She moaned softly as his tongue delved into her mouth, seeking the sweetness within, and when her tongue met his, it was like tasting fire, fire that was hot enough to burn yet cool enough to touch. Liquid fire that made her blood flow hot.

His arms tightened around her, holding her close, so close she could scarcely breathe. So close she could feel every masculine inch of his body imprinted against her own.

It was madness to let him kiss her, to let his hands caress her. His voice whispered in her ear, his words sweet, filled with passion and promise.

She couldn't think, not with his hands lingering near her breasts, not with his lips scorching hers. His tongue was like a brand, sizzling hot, marking her as his.

He drew back, but only a little, so that she could see nothing but his face. His eyes were smoky, like dark fire on a rainy night.

"Say yes, Callie."

Her mind said no. All reason, all sanity, all logic, said no. But her heart said, "Yes."

Caleb stared down at her, a bemused expression on his face. "How soon?"

She stared up at him, unable to think coherently. "Soon?"

"The wedding, Callie. How soon?"

"Couldn't we wait a while? We just told people we were engaged." A blush crept into her cheeks. "I'd hate for them to start counting on their fingers."

He grinned at her. "Sure, Callie, whatever you want."

"Could we . . . could we be married by a priest?"

"If you like."

"And a dress? Could I have a dress?"

"The best money can buy."

"Really? Could I order one from New York?"

"You can order one from Paris," Caleb said, suddenly pleased by the thought of marrying Callie, of giving her everything she had ever wanted, everything she'd never been able to have. Everything but love.

The hopeful look in Callie's expression drove

the knife a little deeper. For a moment, he was tempted to tell her he'd changed his mind. She deserved better than she was getting. She wanted moonlight and romance and happy-ever-after, and all he wanted was the right to call the ranch his own and to have Callie's luscious body in his bed.

The thought of possessing her quickly overrode his guilt.

"We need to drive the cattle to the reservation in the next week or two," Caleb said, drawing his thoughts from Callie's dangerous curves. "How about if we set the date for the first of September? That'll give you time to order a dress and give me plenty of time to get out to the reservation and back."

Callie nodded, too numb to speak.

In a few months, she'd be Mrs. Caleb Stryker, for better or for worse.

# Chapter Seventeen

Callie sat on the sofa, watching Caleb as he cleaned and oiled his Colt. In the last week, while she'd been ordering a dress for the wedding and thinking about redecorating the bedroom they would share, he'd been making preparations for the cattle drive—hiring extra hands, looking over the cattle, and checking the horses.

They spent their evenings together, talking about what they'd done that day, planning for the future, discussing whether they should keep the mansion or put it up for sale.

Now, listening to Caleb as he warned her again not to go riding off to town unless she took someone with her, she realized that she didn't want to stay at the ranch without him.

"I want to go with you."

Caleb glanced over his shoulder, not certain he had heard her right.

"What?"

"I said I want to go with you. To the reservation."

"No, Callie. This isn't a pleasure ride. We'll be spending long hours in the saddle and bedding down on the ground. Besides, a trail drive is no place for a woman."

"Please, Caleb. I want to go. I won't be any trouble."

*Stubborn woman,* he thought irritably, torn between the thought of worrying about her if he left her behind and the constant torment of having her bedroll spread near his, knowing she was sleeping within the reach of his hand when he'd be unable to touch her.

"We'll be leaving the first of the week. You got any pants?"

"Pants!" she exclaimed, as startled as if he'd asked her if she had any tobacco. "Of course not."

"I'll get you some."

"Whatever for?"

"I think you'll find it a lot easier to ride in pants than in a dress and petticoats. You'll need a good hat, too, and some gloves. I'll take care of it."

Callie watched him leave the room, then grinned at her reflection in the mirror. Pants, indeed!

She wasn't grinning a week later. Clad in a pair of men's Levi's, a plaid shirt, a wide-brimmed Stetson hat, and boots, Callie stared at her reflection. Surely Caleb didn't intend for her to go outside looking like this? The pants were a trifle snug, very clearly outlining her legs and derrière. The shirt, though loose-fitting, did little to conceal her bosom.

Callie shook her head. She simply couldn't leave the house wearing such outlandish attire.

A familiar rap on the door drew her attention from the mirror, and she turned around to find Caleb standing in the doorway. "You're late," he said curtly.

Callie let out a sigh of exasperation. "You'll have to wait while I change. I can't wear these clothes."

"Why not?"

"Why not! Just look at me."

A slow smile spread over Caleb's face. "You look fine to me."

"No decent woman would ever be caught wearing pants."

"Nobody that matters is gonna see you out on the range," he remarked, "but if you've changed your mind, that's fine with me."

"I haven't changed my mind."

Callie grabbed the sheepskin jacket draped over the back of a chair. "They make riding *skirts,* you know," she muttered as she left the room.

Caleb grinned as he followed Callie down the hall. To tell the truth, he'd never thought of a riding skirt; now, watching the sway of her hips in the tight-fitting denim, he knew he'd made the right choice.

Caleb's big buckskin mare and a blaze-faced black mare stood waiting outside the back door.

"Do you need a leg up?" Caleb asked.

"No, thank you." Callie placed her foot in the stirrup, grasped the saddle horn with both hands, and pulled herself into the saddle.

With a grunt of approval, Caleb swung onto the

back of the buckskin. *Stubborn,* he mused. But he wouldn't have her any other way.

"Where's the herd?" Callie asked.

"They left at first light. We'll catch up. George Geary will help Joe look after things at the ranch until we get back."

"How long will we be gone?"

"As long as it takes." He lifted one black brow. "It's not too late to change your mind."

Callie shook her head. She'd ordered her wedding dress, and there really wasn't much else to do. Neither she nor Caleb had many friends in town, so the ceremony would be small, probably just the two of them and Fanny.

She looked at Caleb and smiled. She was going on a trail drive! She remembered hearing Duncan talk about driving cattle to the railhead, about the long hours in the saddle, the dust, the recalcitrant cattle. He'd been complaining, but she'd always thought it sounded like great fun.

As they rode along, Caleb stopped now and then, dismounting to check on the grass or to pull a deadfall from the middle of a stream.

Callie never tired of watching him. His every move was quick and sure and somehow sensual. She was aware of his strength as he pulled the log from the stream, felt her heart skip a beat as she watched the play of muscles in his back and arms and legs.

The sun was barely in the sky when he drew rein beneath a cottonwood.

"Did you have breakfast?"

Callie shook her head, wondering if he could hear the loud rumbling in her stomach.

Dismounting, Caleb offered to help Callie from

her horse, but she declined, determined to do for herself. They ate a cold meal of beef and beans and buttermilk biscuits that Cookie had prepared, washing it down with water from their canteens.

Fifteen minutes later, they were riding again. Callie felt a little thrill of pride as they passed scattered bunches of cattle. They were Rocking S cattle. Soon they'd be hers. Many of the cows had calves at their sides. She remembered that Joe Brigman had said something about a good calf crop next year, too.

She slid a glance in Caleb's direction. He'd said he didn't love her, but surely he must care for her if he wanted to marry her. And she cared for him, more than she'd let on. People had started marriages with less. She'd make it work. And maybe, someday, he'd fall in love with her. At least, she hoped he would, because she was afraid she was falling in love with him—helplessly, hopelessly, in love.

She felt Caleb's gaze on her face, felt her pulse race when she saw his smile. Things would work out, she just knew they would.

She saw the dust and heard the cattle long before the herd was in sight.

As they drew near, Caleb tied a bandanna over his nose and mouth and urged Callie to do the same. He waved at the man riding drag, then urged his horse into a trot to get past the main body of the herd.

Callie followed close on his heels, a little frightened to be riding so near so many cattle. Close up, they were bigger than she'd thought.

By late afternoon, she began to wonder if maybe she should have stayed home after all. It was one thing to go out for a pleasure ride, quite another to spend five hours in the saddle, surrounded by cattle and dust and five tobacco-chewing cowboys she'd never seen before.

When they made camp at dusk, she was dead on her feet, and only her pride kept her from admitting she'd made a mistake. She managed to keep her eyes open long enough to eat supper, then she rolled into her blankets, not caring what anyone, including Caleb Stryker, thought. She was asleep almost before she closed her eyes.

After several days on the trail, Callie wondered why she'd been so eager to tag along. What had sounded like great fun was, in reality, just plain monotonous. Day after day it was the same. Up at dawn, eat a quick but hearty breakfast, bunch the cattle, then ride for several hours.

At midday, they took a break so the cattle could graze. The cowboys all kept a string of four or five horses, and they changed mounts every three or four hours to give their horses a rest. The quietest, most dependable animals were used to ride herd after dark. After the afternoon break, it was back in the saddle until dusk. On the best of days, they made twenty miles; on the worst, less than ten.

It seemed like a lot of work for little reward, Callie mused, since cowboys only made about twenty-five dollars a month. Most of them owned little more than their saddles and a change of clothes. And their hats. She soon learned that a cowboy took his hat off last thing at night and reached for it first thing in the morning.

A couple of the cowboys dreamed of owning their own spreads; the others seemed content to drift from ranch to ranch, riding for the brand.

She picked up some of the cowboys' quaint words along the way. A buckeroo was a cowboy who hailed from Nevada. When a cowboy talked about cutting the dust, he wanted a drink, not necessarily water. Slow elk was a term for meat from another man's cow. The biscuit line was where out-of-work cowboys could draw a free meal.

To her disbelief, one of the hands told her that the best way to collect a scattered herd was by the "bloody hide roundup." When she learned what it meant, she was sorry she asked.

"Wal, you kill yerself a steer," one of the hands told her, "then you skin it and hang the bloody hide from a tree. The smell will bring them other cattle running from miles around." He grinned at her, showing a row of tobacco-stained teeth. "Then you jest round 'em up and get on with it."

She also learned that if a cow gave birth to a dead calf on the trail, the cow had to be allowed to smell it, apparently to convince the animal the calf was dead, otherwise the cow would keep leaving the herd to go back for its offspring.

When she looked doubtful, Caleb told her both stories were true.

For the most part, the cowboys treated Callie with respect. The youngest, a sandy-haired young man named Whitley, insisted on saddling her horse each morning, while Cookie made sure she was the first to be served and that her coffee cup was always full. Callie rather liked being waited on, though she could tell by Caleb's expression that he didn't approve in the least, but he kept his thoughts to himself.

Whitley, especially, seemed to make an effort to be near her. He was a tall, thin young man, perhaps nineteen years old, with unruly straw-colored hair and the palest blue eyes Callie had ever seen. Like every other man present, he wore a gun on his hip and carried a rifle in a scabbard on his saddle.

She had seen Caleb eye Whitley speculatively on several occasions, but so far he hadn't said anything about the time Callie spent with the boy. Secretly, she hoped Caleb was jealous, though she thought that was doubtful. To be jealous, he would have had to care, and though Callie knew Caleb desired her, she didn't think his feelings for her went much deeper than that.

Personally, Callie found Whitley's attentions rather flattering. The man asked about her past, about life on the ranch, about Caleb. Friendly questions that helped pass the time.

Whitley hailed from Texas, he had remarked proudly, the oldest of seven children. His father was dead—Whitley's voice had hardened and his mild blue eyes had filled with rage when he said this—but his mother was still alive, struggling to make ends meet on a poor dirt farm outside of El Paso.

Callie removed her hat and wiped the perspiration from her brow and the back of her neck. They'd been on the trail for over two weeks and she felt every mile of it. But there were compensations. Her riding ability had improved a hundred per cent. She loved the vast prairie, the gently rolling hills, the slender cottonwoods that grew alongside the water holes and streams.

Caleb remarked that fire from a cottonwood tree was used to drive away *Anog-ite,* the Two-Faced Woman, during a young girl's coming-of-age ceremony. *Anog-ite* was the goddess of shameful things.

Out here, in the midst of the wild country, she saw things she'd never seen in the city—small herds of deer and elk; eagles soaring overhead, their wings spread as they rode the tail of the wind in search of prey. There were rabbits and skunks, squirrels and lizards.

Once, in the distance, she saw a big brown bear. Another time, she spied a wolf skulking through a stand of timber. On one occasion, she noticed tracks near a water hole, and Caleb told her they were the tracks of a mountain lion. At night, she heard the bark of a coyote.

Caleb was always near at hand, sometimes riding silently beside her, sometimes telling her how it had been years ago, before the whites flooded the land.

He was beside her now, telling her about the vast herds of buffalo that had once roamed the land, his voice melancholy as he talked of herds so big they had covered the earth like a great brown blanket. Herds that numbered in the millions. The Indians had been a proud people then, counting their wealth in ponies and buffalo robes, free as the wind that blew across the plains.

Caleb's eyes took on a faraway look when he talked of his mother's people. Once the Lakota had been the bravest, most warlike tribe on the plains. They had ruled from the Rocky Mountains to the Missouri River. Many of their women had married French traders, who had kept the warriors supplied with the best firearms and quantities of ammunition.

They had fought fiercely to hang on to their lands, but they had been no match for the ever-growing numbers of whites who had made the long trek westward, searching for land, for riches, for gold. The Army, at first pledged to protect treaty lands from invasion, soon realized that it was like trying to stop a flood with a sieve. Then the battles began: Ash Hollow, Cedar Canyon, Sand Creek, the Washita, the Rosebud, the Little Big Horn.

Listening, Callie could see it all clearly in her mind: the proud warriors riding to hunt and to fight, the vast herds of Indian ponies, the conical lodges pitched along a quiet river. She saw women at work and children at play, and then, as time went on, she saw burning lodges and mutilated bodies, the horrors and tragedy of war being played out on both sides. So much killing, so much death.

And now these once proud people were living in poverty on the reservation.

Callie slid a glance at Caleb as he fell silent. She tried to picture him clad in a buckskin breech clout, his long black hair in braids, his face streaked with war paint, but the image wouldn't come. She'd always been told that Indians were godless savages, that they weren't the same as white people, that they couldn't take care of themselves and must therefore be kept on reservations and looked after by those in authority. She'd never questioned the logic of it. It was simply the way things were.

They were only three days from the reservation when two things happened to mar what had otherwise been an uneventful journey.

The first happened on Friday morning. Caleb was riding drag when a big brindle cow with a crooked horn suddenly decided to go exploring on her own. Caleb wheeled the buckskin around, and the gelding broke into a gallop. Callie watched, grinning, as Caleb closed in on the errant cow. One minute he was turning the cow back toward the herd, and the next he was flying through the air.

Callie screamed as he hit the ground, hard, rolling over several times before coming to a halt.

She raced toward him, hollering his name, breathing a sigh of relief when he sat up, shaking his head to clear it.

"Are you all right?" she asked anxiously. Dismounting, she knelt beside him. "What happened?"

"Beats the devil out of me. Cinch must have snapped."

Whitley and a stocky cowpoke named Granger rode up just then.

Granger leaned forward, his arms crossed on the saddle horn. "You all right, boss?"

"Yeah." Caleb stood up. Feeling a little shaky, he retrieved his hat, settled it on his head, then brushed the dust from his jeans and shirt.

Callie followed him as he walked to where his saddle lay in the dirt and began to examine the cinch.

"It's been cut," Caleb said to no one in particular.

"Cut?" Callie frowned. "I don't understand."

"It was done deliberately."

"But why? Who?" Callie shook her head. "You might have been killed."

"Yeah." His gaze strayed toward Whitley and Granger, and then he stared thoughtfully at the haze that marked the cattle's whereabouts. "I reckon that was the idea."

Lifting the saddle, Caleb handed it up to Whitley. "Throw that in the back of the chuck wagon, will you? I'll have Cookie repair the cinch after supper."

Whitley nodded and reined his horse toward the trail.

Caleb stared after him for a moment, then swung aboard the buckskin's bare back.

The next night was a night Callie would never forget. She'd spread her bedroll beside Caleb's as she did every night, feeling safe with him there beside her. She was sitting on her blankets, brushing her hair, when Caleb pulled back the top cover of his bedroll.

Callie frowned as a soft hissing sound issued from the fold of the bottom blanket, then let out an ear-piercing shriek. She'd never been close to a rattlesnake before, but she knew this had to be the biggest snake ever created, and it was coiled in the middle of Caleb's blankets, poised to strike.

But it was the speed of Caleb's reflexes that would be forever etched in her mind. She'd heard the phrase "quick as lightning." Once, she'd even seen a bolt of lightning hit a tree, lancing through the dark sky to strike with a speed that seemed unreal, leaving the tree in flames.

Caleb's draw was as fast, as smooth, and as deadly as that lightning bolt. A single well-placed shot neatly sliced the rattler's head from its body.

Her scream had drawn the attention of the men, and they had all come running. They gathered around, talking excitedly about the size of the snake and Caleb's marksmanship.

"It's all right, Callie," he said. "It's not uncommon for rattlers to crawl into the first warm place they find."

He offered her a quick smile as he punched the spent cartridge from the chamber, slid another in its place, and holstered the Colt.

"That's why we check everything so carefully on the trail. Boots in the morning, for spiders." Caleb's gaze settled on Whitley's face. "Blankets at night, for snakes."

Callie nodded, her heart still pounding wildly. She checked her bedroll three times before she crawled inside.

When she'd finally relaxed enough to close her eyes, Caleb's image rose in her mind, his dark gray eyes narrowed as he drew and cocked his gun in one smooth, swift movement. She'd never seen anything like it.

Even now, it seemed incredible that a man could draw a gun, aim, and fire so quickly and so accurately. There had been no hesitation, no uncertainty. In a way, it had been a beautiful thing to watch, his hand streaking for his holster, withdrawing the Colt, cocking the hammer, squeezing the trigger. All done in the blink of an eye. No wonder he had survived eight years as a bounty hunter, she thought. She'd never seen anything so fast—or so deadly.

Callie didn't know what she had expected to find when they reached the reservation, but she was appalled at what she saw. Lodges were pitched randomly, some made of old buffalo hides, the newer ones made of canvas. The men looked at her through eyes empty of life, of hope; the women stared at her suspiciously; the children looked at her with something akin to fear.

Caleb rode to one of the lodges and dismounted, telling Callie to stay on her horse. A moment later, a tall man with a hawklike nose and deep-set black eyes emerged from the lodge.

The two men clasped forearms, there was a quick exchange in a tongue Callie assumed was Lakota, and then the Indian nodded, a slight smile playing over his face.

Turning, Caleb lifted Callie from the saddle. "This is Iron Calf. We grew up together."

Callie nodded at the Indian. He was wearing a faded blue cotton shirt, a breechclout that hung to his knees, and moccasins.

Iron Calf nodded in Callie's direction. "*Owanyeke wasse.*"

Caleb grinned, then nodded.

"What did he say?" Callie asked.

"He said I have good taste in women."

A faint blush tinged Callie's cheeks as Caleb took her hand and followed Iron Calf into the lodge.

Callie had never felt so out of place in her life. The interior of the lodge was dim and cool. A woman with long black braids sat in the rear of the tipi, a child at her breast. Caleb told Callie to sit down and be quiet. It was in her mind to argue, but she couldn't quite summon the nerve.

For the next half hour, Caleb and Iron Calf talked back and forth. Caleb told Iron Calf where he had left the cattle and learned that things on the reservation weren't as bad as he had believed. McGillicuddy, the Indian Agent, seemed a fair man.

Iron Calf remarked that many of the Indians on the other side of the reservation were trying to adapt to the white man's ways. Over six hundred houses had been built, there were a hundred and thirty-five miles of telegraph line, and six day schools, where the children went to learn the white man's tongue, had been opened. Some of the Indians had turned their hands to farming. However, there were about four hundred Cheyenne on the reservation who stubbornly refused to try the white man's way. And Iron Calf sympathized with them. He and his people had no desire to turn from their old life, the old ways.

"I thank you for the beef," Iron Calf remarked. "It is easier to accept charity from a brother than an enemy."

"Do not think of it as charity," Caleb replied. "It is the Lakota way to share one's wealth. *Wakan Tanka* has been good to me. I would be ungrateful if I turned my back on my people."

Iron Calf nodded. "We will talk again, my brother."

The two men exchanged farewells, then Caleb helped Callie to her feet and they left the lodge.

"What was that all about?" Callie asked.

"He was telling me a little about conditions on the reservation, and I told him where we'd left the cattle and warned him not to tell the Indian Agent they were there."

"Why?"

"Most of the agents are dishonest, though this one, McGillicudy, seems fair enough. Still, a lot of them take goods meant for the Indians and sell them and pocket the money. Sometimes they lie about the allotment they need and sell the difference."

"That's awful!"

"Yeah."

"Why doesn't someone do something?"

"Because nobody cares. The Army'd be happy if the Indians just disappeared. As for the agent, he doesn't have to answer to anybody but the government, and they're too busy lining their pockets to care what's going on here."

Callie shook her head in dismay. "Can't *you* do something?"

"I brought them enough cattle to see them through the winter."

"I meant . . ."

"I know what you meant." How could he explain to her about all the graft and corruption on the reservation? There were trading posts on the reservation, given permission to be there by the government. Most of the traders were in cahoots with the Indian Agents. They raised the prices of the goods they sold to the Lakota, but the Lakota had no concept of money, no inkling of what a pound of sugar or coffee should cost. He put the dismal thought from his mind.

"We've been invited to spend the night."

Callie glanced around uneasily. "Here?"

"Yeah."

"Is it . . . safe?"

"You'll be fine. Here's our lodge."

Callie looked at the hide lodge, then blinked at Caleb.

"*Our* lodge? Are you going to stay here, too?"

Caleb grinned wryly. "Do you want to be by yourself?"

She quickly shook her head.

"That's what I thought. We're to be Iron Calf's guests for dinner tonight. And tomorrow we're going on a hunt."

"A hunt? What are we going to hunt?"

"The white man's buffalo."

"White man's buffalo," Callie repeated. "What kind of buffalo is that?"

"You'll see," Caleb answered with a mysterious grin, and refused to say more.

# Chapter Eighteen

When Callie stepped out of the lodge the following morning, she was certain every Indian this side of the Missouri had somehow made his way to the reservation during the night. Dozens of Indian men, most clad in little more than breechclouts and moccasins, their faces painted in bizarre designs, were gathered in the center of the village.

Callie couldn't stifle the tremor of fear that sped along her spine as she stared at them. This was the same tribe, no doubt some of the same Indians, who had taken part in the Custer massacre only a few years ago. Yesterday, they had looked pathetic, beaten, and defeated. Today they looked like the ferocious warriors the Eastern newspapers had declared them to be.

She wished Caleb would come back from wherever he'd gone earlier that morning. She'd never been more aware of being white, of being a woman, than she was at the moment.

She felt her heart begin to pound as a tall Indian walked toward her. She was about to turn and duck inside the lodge when the man spoke her name.

It was Caleb, dressed in a skimpy clout and moccasins. Several slashes of black paint adorned his cheeks. There was a beaded choker at his throat, a slash of paint across his naked chest, and a formidable-looking knife sheathed in his belt.

"What . . . why are you dressed like that?"

"I'm going on the hunt. I don't know a lot of these men, and I don't want them to think of me as an outsider. It's part of who I am, Callie," he said, seeing her look of dismay, "part of what I am. Maybe the best part."

She didn't understand, not really, but she wanted to. She moved closer to Caleb, her heart pounding with trepidation, as more men joined the group. It almost seemed like a holiday, Callie thought. The women were wearing what she assumed were their best dresses, and the children ran through the camp, shouting and chasing each other, obviously in high spirits.

An aged Indian wearing a buffalo-horn headdress walked among the men, chanting slowly as he sprinkled some sort of powder in the air.

"What's he doing?" Callie asked, her voice hushed.

"He's blessing the hunt, offering sacred pollen to the earth and the sky and the four directions."

"Praying, you mean?"

"I guess you could call it that."

"I thought the Indians were heathens."

"No. Their god is *Wakan Tanka.*"

"There's only one God."

"Not to the Lakota. They believe in many gods. They believe that everything has a spirit of its own. The rocks. The trees. The water. They believe the animals are their brothers, and that all are related through the great circle of life."

Callie was about to say such a thing was ridiculous, but something in Caleb's eyes stilled her tongue. He believed it, she thought, every word.

In moments, the Indians were mounted. Caleb boosted Callie into the saddle, then swung aboard his own mount, and they followed the warriors out of the village.

A short time later, they reached the place where the cattle were grazing peacefully.

"Where are the buffalo?" Callie asked, frowning.

"There," Caleb said, pointing to the herd.

"Those aren't buffalo."

"That's right," Caleb said, his voice tinged with anger and bitterness.

Callie shook her head. "I don't understand."

"You will. The white man killed off most of the buffalo for their tongues and hides, and so the Lakota are making do with what they've got. And what they've got are cattle."

"The white man's buffalo," Callie said, understanding at last.

What followed was a sight Callie knew she'd never forget. Several Indians fired their rifles into the air to stampede the herd, and then the Indians lit out after the cattle, yelling and brandishing lances and a few ancient rifles.

Callie followed behind with the women, who were mounted and leading pack horses, her gaze riveted on Caleb. He rode a bare-backed paint pony, his long hair flying behind him, his body glistening in the sun.

Sometimes she lost sight of him in the billowing clouds of dust, but unerringly she picked him out again and again. She marveled anew at his horsemanship. He gripped the single horsehair rein in his teeth, guiding the sure-footed paint with the pressure of his knees. She wondered that he didn't fall off as the paint rode in and out of the cattle. Caleb was armed with a rifle, and he brought down two cows in quick succession.

As quickly as it had begun, the stampede was over. A half-dozen warriors rounded up the remaining cattle and herded them toward the village, while the other men rode back to their kills to wait for the women to come up and begin the butchering.

Callie watched Caleb ride toward her, his face exultant, his body sheened with sweat. She felt a peculiar fluttering in her stomach as she watched him approach. There was something about the sight of all that sweating male flesh that appealed to something earthy deep within her. She'd have had to be blind or dead not to notice the spread of his shoulders, the inherent power in his muscular arms and legs, the proud set of his head, the blue-black sheen of his hair. This was a Caleb she had never seen before—wild, untamed, with the thrill of the hunt still shining in the depths of his dark gray eyes.

She stared at him as he slid from his horse to stand beside her. Her stomach muscles quivered at his nearness; her nostrils filled with the pungent scent of sweat. Here was a man, a warrior, primal and uncivilized. She wanted to run away from him, and at the same time she wanted to throw her arms around him and let him carry her away to a hide lodge. She swallowed hard, reminding herself that Caleb was not a wild savage. Just a bounty hunter.

"Why?" she asked when she found her voice. "Why stampede the herd away from the village? Why chase the cattle and kill them here, then haul the meat all the way back home?"

Caleb grinned. "Partly for the thrill of the hunt. For hundreds of years, the Lakota chased the buffalo. But that's not the only reason. The Lakota believe the meat isn't any good unless the animal runs for several miles before it's killed."

"Oh."

She looked past him to where the women had begun butchering, then turned away, sickened by the sight of their knives slicing into still-warm flesh.

"Who's going to . . ." She waved her hand in the direction of cattle he had killed. "You know."

"I gave my kills to Iron Calf. His woman will take care of it and share the meat with her sister, whose husband was killed at the Little Big Horn."

Callie nodded. She had never thought of the Indians as having sisters, of sharing, or caring. Perhaps they weren't the godless, soulless savages everyone said they were.

That night, there was a huge celebration. The aroma of roasting beef filled the air. Dogs fought over the bones. Women laughed as they tended the meat, their faces alight with anticipation. The men built a bonfire in the middle of the camp. Callie sat beside Caleb, watching as some of the warriors danced.

At first, she was shocked by their wild gestures, by their scant attire, by the paint on their faces. But then, gradually, she saw the dance for what it was, a celebration of life.

She was even more shocked when Caleb joined in. For some reason she couldn't explain, she had expected, had hoped, that he would look out of place among the wildly gyrating men, but he was one of them, in heart and soul and blood. His steps were as intricate and finely executed as theirs, his skin as dark, his voice as loud and exultant.

A warm glow spread through Callie as she watched him, a heat that had nothing to do with the warm summer night, or the campfire, or the crowd of people pressing around her.

Abruptly, she rose to her feet and made her way to the lodge. She had to get away from Caleb, away from the beat of the drums that so nearly matched the beat of her heart. She'd held on to her virginity this long. She didn't intend to lose it now. Not until she had a ring on her finger and that all-important piece of paper in her hand.

Fully clothed, she stretched out on the robes in the rear of the lodge, reminding herself that he was just a man like any other man, a man who wasn't to be trusted no matter how attractive he might be.

"Just a man, not to be trusted." *Did any other man look so desirable?*

"Just a man, not to be trusted," she repeated, more firmly this time. *Did any other man have muscles like his, muscles that rippled like liquid steel sheathed in satin?*

"Just a man! Not to be trusted!"

But they were going to be married soon. Surely that changed everything. Surely she'd be able to trust him then.

She had to believe that, or it was never going to work.

Her eyelids grew heavy, heavier, and in spite of the beat of the drums and the doubts that wouldn't let her go, she drifted off to sleep.

When she woke, it was daylight and she was alone in the lodge. On the floor beside her sleeping pallet, in a neatly folded pile, she found a cream-colored doeskin dress and a pair of hard-soled moccasins.

She also found a note, written with charcoal on a piece of buckskin. It read:

> *Good morning, sleepy head. The dress and moccasins are a gift from Iron Calf's woman. She'll be insulted if you don't wear them.*

It was signed with the initial C.

Rising, Callie removed her shirt, camisole, and pants and slipped on the dress. It was as soft as velvet against her bare skin. She pulled on the moccasins, smiling as she wished for a mirror so she could see how she looked.

Pulling her hairbrush from her saddlebag, she brushed the tangles from her hair and then, feeling more than a little self-conscious, she lifted the door flap and peered outside.

The sun was already high in the sky. Smoke from a few cookfires made lazy spirals as they floated upward. A short distance away, she could see several women bent over cowhides pegged to the ground. A handful of men were gathered in front of the lodge across the way, deeply engrossed in a gambling game played with sticks and two colored stones. A trio of little girls were playing with dolls made of corn husks and buckskin.

There was no sign of Caleb.

She was wondering what to do when she saw him walking toward her. He was wearing the same skimpy clout he'd worn at the dance, and a pair of moccasins. His hair, held away from his face by a narrow strip of red cloth, fell past his shoulders. It irritated her, the way her heart turned over at the mere sight of him. She didn't want to care. Caring meant vulnerability. Caring meant pain.

But she couldn't help but admire the bare expanse of his chest, the width of his shoulders, or the masculine beauty of his finely chiseled features.

"Morning," he said, handing her a bowl. "I thought you might be hungry."

"Thank you." Callie gazed at the bowl, a frown on her face.

"They were all out of biscuits and gravy," Caleb remarked, grinning at her.

"I've never had beef stew for breakfast." Callie looked at him suspiciously. "It *is* beef, isn't it? I've heard the Indians eat their dogs."

"It's beef, Callie," he replied, a hard edge to his voice. "They only eat their dogs when there's nothing else."

Callie had never really believed the Indians ate their dogs, and now she looked at him in horror.

"If you're hungry enough, you'll eat just about anything," Caleb said, his voice harsh.

He'd been that hungry, she thought, and wished she'd never said anything.

"Sorry," he muttered, remembering winters when food had been scarce, when the cries of hungry children had sounded throughout the village day and night. He recalled watching his own grandfather refuse to eat so that his daughter's family wouldn't starve.

With an effort, he pushed the grim memories from his mind.

"You look pretty in buckskins," he murmured.

"Do I?"

"Yeah."

The dress fit a little snugly on top, outlining her breasts and defining her waist, then flaring over her hips. The seams of the sleeves and the hem of the skirt were adorned with fringe that swayed with every move she made.

Callie flushed under Caleb's admiring gaze, pleased that he found her attractive.

"You look pretty, too," she said, and blushed to the roots of her hair.

"Pretty, huh?" He laughed softly. "I've been called a lot of things in my time, but pretty wasn't one of them."

"Where are the men who came with us?"

"I paid them off and sent them home. They weren't too eager to hang around, and the Indians didn't want them here."

Callie nodded. Sitting down, she began to eat. The meat was tender, the broth seasoned with sage and wild onions. She wished she had some bread and milk to go with it, then felt ashamed for being ungrateful. These people had so little, she almost felt guilty for taking one bowl of soup, even if Caleb had provided the beef.

She gestured at the women with her spoon. "They work so hard. I don't understand why they cling to their old habits, why they refuse to embrace our ways."

"Life was good in the old days, Callie. We didn't have to beg the white man for food then. The men spent the summer hunting and raiding, while the women gathered vegetables and repaired their tipis. In the fall, there was a last big hunt, and the women dried a lot of the meat for winter.

"I liked the winters. We camped in the shelter of the Black Hills, close to wood and water. On long winter nights, the old men would tell the ancient tales of the People, stories about *Unktehi,* the Water Monster, and *Iktome,* the Spider Man. My favorite stories were about *Wakinyan Tanka,* the Thunderbirds, and the creatures who guard their sacred mountain."

"What kind of creatures?" Callie asked, curious even though she didn't believe in sorcery and magical birds.

"A bear, a deer, a beaver, and a butterfly."

"A butterfly?"

"It was no ordinary butterfly."

Callie looked skeptical, though she couldn't help but be charmed by such fanciful notions as Thunderbirds and supernatural butterflies.

"Are you going to do this every year?" Callie asked.

Caleb nodded. "Yeah. Why?"

"I thought maybe next year we'd bring some blankets," Callie remarked as she watched two nearly naked little boys wrestling in the dirt. "And maybe some other things, like sugar and flour, calico, things like that. It wouldn't cost much, and we'd be sure they got it instead of some unscrupulous agent."

She glanced at Caleb to find him looking at her intently.

"What's the matter?" she asked. "Don't you think it's a good idea?"

"I think it's a wonderful idea, Callie," he replied softly,

The admiration in his eyes, the appreciation in his voice, sent little shivers down her spine.

The next two-and-a-half weeks were like a long holiday. The men shook off their lethargy, the women put their endless tasks aside, and the days were filled with foot races for men, women, and children alike. There were contests where the men showed off their skill with bow and lance.

Early one morning, there was a horse race, the longest, most grueling race Callie had ever seen. The course, almost two miles long, went up a steep hill, through a shallow river, winding through a grove of trees. There were fallen logs to jump, boulders to navigate.

Callie cheered for Caleb, yelling as loudly as any of the Lakota women. Caleb rode as if he were a part of the horse, leaning low over the buckskin's neck, urging the big horse on.

Watching the animal as it galloped toward the finish line, Callie could see how Caleb had managed to catch all those wanted men he'd pursued, for the big buckskin ran like the wind, easily outdistancing the other horses.

She was jumping up and down when Caleb crossed the finish line first, her heart pounding with excitement. Man and beast were dripping water from crossing the river. The horse's neck was lathered with sweat. She thought they looked magnificent.

Caleb was grinning exultantly when he drew rein beside her and swept her up into the saddle. Caught up in the exhilaration of the moment, Callie threw her arms around Caleb and kissed him, blushing furiously when the other warriors whooped in approval.

Embarrassed, Callie tried to slide back to the ground. She had never seen the Indians express any affection in public, though she had seen Iron Calf hug his wife in the privacy of their lodge.

Caleb grinned at her and then, to the delight of the other men, he grabbed Callie in his arms and kissed her long and hard.

"To the victor belong the spoils," he murmured in her ear.

"You haven't won a battle," Callie said, disengaging herself from his embrace and slipping off the buckskin's back. "Only a horse race."

"Then I guess I'll have to win a battle," Caleb remarked, and the look in his eyes sent a little frisson of anticipation skating down her spine.

During those long, carefree days, Callie saw Caleb in a whole new light. He stripped off the layers of civilization as easily as he stripped off the clothes of the white man, and she watched, fascinated, as he blended in with the other warriors.

Eventually, Callie realized the Indians were celebrating more than the arrival of the cattle, they were celebrating Caleb's return to his mother's people.

Each night, there was a feast with great quantities of food, followed by dancing into the wee hours of the morning. The men wore clouts and moccasins and finely beaded shirts or vests; the women wore doeskin dresses adorned with elks' teeth and fringe and brightly colored beads.

Callie loved the dancing. She loved the hypnotic beat of the drums, the singing. But mostly she loved watching Caleb. He looked dark and mysterious in the light of the flickering fire. His skin glowed like smooth copper, his hair swirled around his shoulders, as dark as the sky at midnight.

One evening Caleb took her by the hand and urged her to join him in the dance circle. Callie felt tremendously self-conscious as she tried to follow the steps, but gradually she relaxed. The steps were simple, no one seemed to be making fun of her, and after looking into Caleb's eyes, she forgot everyone else.

They danced facing each other, back and forth and side to side, the drum beat like the echo of Callie's heart. She was sorry when the dance was over, but then Caleb took her by the hand and led her away from the crowd.

For a time, they walked in silence, occasionally passing other couples who had also sought refuge in the dark quiet away from the campfire.

"I can see why you liked living with the Indians," Callie remarked after a while. "They're such friendly people, not at all what I expected."

"What did you expect?"

Callie shrugged. "I'm not really sure."

"Savages in war paint? Barbarians who spoke in grunts and ate raw meat off the ground?"

"Nothing like that exactly," Callie protested. "Although I had been told that Indians weren't like other people, that they weren't capable of loving or caring. But I can see now that's not true. Iron Calf loves his wife and children. Anyone can see that. I wish we could do more for them."

"You've got a heart bigger than Texas," Caleb murmured, touched by her feeling for his people.

Callie glanced up to see Caleb gazing down at her as if she was the most wonderful person in the world. She swallowed hard, then took a deep breath. He was going to kiss her. She knew it. and even then he was bending toward her, one long arm circling her waist.

"*Pilamaya,* Callie," he whispered.

"*Pilamaya?*" she repeated.

"It's Lakota for thank-you."

"For what?" She licked her lips as his head bent closer to hers.

"For liking my people. For wanting to help me make life easier for them. For being beautiful . . ." he murmured, and kissed her, his lips warm and gentle, filled with gratitude.

Callie wondered what would have happened next if a half-dozen young boys hadn't come running toward their hiding place, whooping and yelling in a wild game of tag.

Caleb let out a long sigh of disappointment as he took Callie's hand in his. It was probably just as well that they'd been interrupted, he mused, for Callie was sorely tempting in the moonlight. Her eyes sparkled like sapphires, and her lips, slightly parted, begged to be kissed again. And again. But this wasn't the time or the place.

He chuckled as the boys began to circle them, shooting at them with guns made out of sticks and child-sized bows and arrows.

"It's late," Caleb said, grinning as the would-be warriors broke into a mock war dance. "Come on, I'll walk you home before we get scalped."

# Chapter Nineteen

The following morning after breakfast, they went to tell Iron Calf and his family good-bye.

They spent the next hour in Iron Calf's lodge. Callie smiled a little when Caleb told Iron Calf that they would be back with more cattle next year, unaccountably pleased to have been included in his plans.

Callie held Iron Calf's baby while the men talked. She'd had little opportunity to be around children when she was growing up and couldn't remember ever holding a baby. The infant looked up at her through deep black eyes, its tiny arms waving.

Tentatively, Callie reached out to touch the baby's cheek, marveling at its softness. She smiled when the boy's tiny hand curled around her finger.

Her arms felt strangely empty when Iron Calf's

wife took the child. A short time later, she followed Caleb out of the lodge.

*"Toksha ake wacin yanktin ktelo,"* Iron Calf said, grasping Caleb's forearm.

Caleb nodded. "And I shall see you again. Walk in peace, my brother."

By midafternoon, they were on their way home. For the first few miles, Callie thought about the people she had met, about the supplies they would bring next year: warm blankets, cooking pots, corn meal, sugar, salt, candy for the children, calico and flannel. It gave her a sense of satisfaction, of purpose, to know that they had made life a little easier for Caleb's people. She'd never really done anything for anyone else before; now that she was about to marry a wealthy man, she intended to share her good fortune with others.

It was almost dark when Caleb made camp. Callie offered to help, but he said it wasn't necessary. He had everything under control, and in a very short time, he had a small fire going and two large steaks frying in a pan.

It wasn't until dinner was over that Callie realized just how alone they were. The night wrapped around them, enfolding them in darkness. In the distance, she heard the howl of a wolf, and a few moments later, the answering call of its mate. Other night sounds reached her ears—the croak of a frog, the song of a cricket, the quiet swish of an owl's wings as it searched for prey.

Callie sat beside the fire, her hands folded in her lap as she gazed into the flames. It hadn't occurred to her that Caleb would send the other men away when they reached the reservation. Had she known she'd be alone with Caleb on on the ride back, she would have stayed home. His mere presence was enough to play havoc with her nerves. His scent reached out to her, strong and uniquely masculine, tickling her senses, making her think of the kisses they had shared, reminding her that his arms had held her close, that her heart had beat in time with his.

She should have stayed home.

She felt the force of his gaze, compelling her to look at him. Slowly, hardly daring to breathe, she met his hooded stare. His eyes were dark, clouded with desire. She looked at him as if she'd never seen him before, her gaze lingering a moment on his strong, square jaw, the cleft in his chin, the faint scar near his hairline. His nose was as straight as a blade, his cheekbones high and pronounced, his lips full and finely sculpted. His brows were straight, his lashes short and thick. He looked ruggedly handsome in the orange glow of the flames, reminding her of some ancient mystic warrior whose glance had the power to mesmerize.

Caleb sucked in a deep breath as Callie's gaze met his. She looked beautiful in the firelight. Her hair, freed of its braids, fell over her shoulders in soft waves that took on the color of the flames, tempting his touch. Her lips, slightly parted, promised the nectar of the gods. The firelight bathed her skin in a warm golden glow, making her look other-worldly, like a goddess taking a vacation from heaven. Her eyes were as blue as the sky at midday, as wary as those of a doe poised for flight. Was she afraid of him? Or was it her own feelings that made her uneasy?

"Callie?"

"What?"

"It's time to turn in. I want to get an early start in the morning."

She blinked at him as if she didn't understand.

Caleb resisted the impulse to draw her into his arms. "Is something wrong?"

"No." She shook her head, refusing to admit that she wanted him to hold her, to kiss her. He was a man, not to be trusted. If she wasn't careful, Caleb Stryker would steal her heart and her innocence, and she'd be left with nothing.

She stood up, wrapping her arms around herself. "Good night."

"Good night, Callie."

His voice, low and resonant, enveloped her like dark silk, drawing her slowly toward him.

Without quite knowing how it happened, she was in his arms, her head tilted back so she could see his face. His eyes were glowing, like the coals of a fire, transmitting their heat to her.

She swallowed hard as his grip tightened. The silence between them was heavy and she wished he would say something, anything, but he only looked at her, his expression naked with desire, his hands light as they stroked her back. She shivered as one hand slid up under her hair and caressed the sensitive skin of her nape.

Callie opened her mouth, intending to tell him it was a mistake, that she hadn't meant to entice him in any way, that she'd changed her mind, but the words died on her lips as his head bent toward hers. And then he was kissing her, the touch of his mouth suffusing her with heat, heat that spread through her like warm honey, thick and sweet.

She looked up at him blankly when he took his mouth from hers. Bereft of his lips, she felt suddenly cold, abandoned, and she slipped her arms around his waist, unconsciously drawing him closer, gasping when she felt the evidence of his desire.

"Sweet dreams, Callie," he murmured sardonically, and left her standing there in the darkness.

Callie stared after him as he disappeared into the shadows, his footsteps as soft as a cat's.

She was trembling when she crawled into her bedroll. Her last conscious thought was that she should have stayed home.

Callie groaned softly as someone shook her shoulder. "Go away," she mumbled.

"Time to get up."

"No."

She pulled the covers over her head, willing him to leave her alone. It had been hours before she fell asleep last night. Every time she closed her eyes, she saw Caleb's image, saw the desire that lurked in his eyes, heard the longing in his voice. And when she did get to sleep, it was to dream of him as he'd looked dancing around the campfire, his long, lean body clad in nothing but a bit of buckskin, his swarthy skin glistening in the light of the flames.

"Come on, Callie," he coaxed, shaking her shoulder again. "Breakfast is ready."

"I'm not hungry."

"You will be in an hour or two. Might as well eat it while it's hot."

With a low groan, she tossed the covers aside and sat up. Sullen-faced, she accepted the plate and cup Caleb handed her. It wasn't much of a breakfast, just beans, bacon, and coffee. But the beans were hot, and the bacon was crisp. As for the coffee, it was strong and hot and black, just the way *he* liked it.

Caleb watched Callie frown as she sipped the bitter brew. They'd be married soon. The thought warmed him more quickly than the coffee. She'd be his, and the ranch would be his. He'd pay off the mortgage, maybe sell the mansion, unless Callie wanted to keep it. Personally, he had no interest in living in Cheyenne, but some women didn't like spending the long cold winters on the range. They liked to winter in town.

When breakfast was over, Callie washed the dishes while he saddled the horses, combed her hair while he doused the fire.

She shook her head when he offered to help her mount. "I can do it."

She was proud of her ability to mount by herself. Stepping into the stirrup, she pulled herself into the saddle and then smiled with pleasure. If nothing else, the trip had toughened her muscles, and while she knew she'd never ride as effortlessly as Caleb, long hours in the saddle no longer left her stiff and sore.

They traveled much faster without the cattle. Callie enjoyed the bright summer days. There was always something to see: a skunk leading her young ones to water, an eagle soaring in the sky, birds dusting their feathers. Caleb told her about living with the Indians when he was a boy, about learning to hunt and use a bow and arrow.

Though the days were wonderful, Callie dreaded the nights. There was something vastly intimate about being alone in the darkness of the prairie with only a fire for light and the moon for a chaperon. She made it a habit to turn in early, pleading that spending eight hours in the saddle made her tired, but it was a lie, and they both knew it.

She was afraid to be alone with him, afraid of her feelings, afraid of surrendering to the ever-present hunger in his eyes. She had vowed to go to her marriage bed a virgin, and she meant to keep that vow. It would have been so much easier, she thought, if Caleb wasn't so damnably handsome, if his smile was less beguiling, if his voice didn't make her heart sing and her pulse beat fast.

They were about a week from home the morning Callie snuck away from camp and headed for the river located at the foot of a short, steep hill. It was the first time they'd camped anywhere near water in the last several days and the prospect of a bath, even in cold water, was a temptation she couldn't resist.

At the water's edge, she paused a moment to watch the sun climb over the horizon, staring in awe as the sky changed from indigo to gray and then exploded in a riot of color that no artist could ever paint.

She loved this country, she thought, loved the vast, gently rolling prairie and the endless sky, the wildflowers that swayed in the breeze, the animals that she glimpsed from time to time. No wonder the Indians had fought so hard for this land. No wonder the whites had coveted it.

She undressed quickly and plunged into the river, gasping as the cold water closed around her. Shivering, she washed her hair and soaped her body, then held her breath as she ducked beneath the surface to rinse.

On shore, she dried herself with the shirt she'd worn the day before, then hurriedly donned clean undergarments, a plaid shirt, and a pair of dungarees. She was beginning to enjoy the freedom that dressing like a man allowed her. It was so nice not to be hampered by corsets and billowing petticoats.

Sitting on a flat-topped tree stump, she pulled on her socks and boots.

She was braiding her hair when she heard a low growl behind her. She froze instantly, every muscle tense, as she heard a rustling in the underbrush to her right.

Fearing what she might see, yet compelled to look, Callie glanced over her shoulder.

She saw it in rapid blinks. A tawny coat. A long tail whipping back and forth. Yellow teeth. A pale pink tongue coated with saliva.

She opened her mouth to call for Caleb, then thought better of it, afraid that the slightest move, the slightest sound, might provoke the big cat.

Her heart, already racing, pounded even harder as the mountain lion jumped up on a nearby rock, then crouched as if to spring.

# Chapter Twenty

Caleb stared at Callie's bedroll, wondering where she'd gone off to so early in the morning. Usually, he had to shake her awake. Then, thinking she might be answering a call of nature, he went to gather some wood for a fire.

And still she didn't return. Tossing the wood into the pit he'd dug the night before, Caleb grabbed his rifle and followed Callie's footprints, cursing softly when he realized that she was headed for the river.

He was halfway down the slope when he saw the mountain lion crouched on a flat-topped rock near the water's edge, its tail whipping back and forth, its ears laid back. He took a step to the left and felt his breath catch in his throat as he saw the cat's prey.

Callie. She was perched on a stump in a low spot near the river. Her face was as pale as death, her eyes wide and frightened as they stared, unblinking, at the big cat.

Caleb took several steps forward, placing each foot carefully so as not to alert the mountain lion to his presence before he lifted the rifle to his shoulder.

He was sighting down the barrel when the mountain lion whirled around on its haunches and sprang forward.

Caleb swore as the huge tawny cat leaped toward him. He fired while the animal was in midair, and then the cougar was on him, its weight driving him backward.

Callie screamed as Caleb and the mountain lion crashed heavily to the ground. Jumping from the stump, she grabbed the rifle that had been knocked from Caleb's hand.

She had never fired a rifle before, never held one in her hands, but she had watched Caleb and now, with an urgent prayer in her heart, she lifted the heavy weapon to her shoulder, jacked a round into the breech, sighted down the long barrel, and squeezed the trigger.

For a moment she thought she had missed, and then the big cat went limp and rolled over onto its side.

Dropping the rifle, Callie ran toward Caleb and fell onto her knees beside him.

Blood. All she saw was blood. On his face. On his shirtfront.

"Caleb," she murmured. "Caleb!"

His eyelids fluttered open, and he grinned at her. "Nice shot."

She'd never known such profound relief. "I thought you were dead."

Carefully, Caleb sat up. "Not yet."

"But . . . all that blood . . . ?"

"Most of it's from the cat. I hit him before he knocked me down. Your shot finished him off."

"Thank God," she murmured. And then she saw the long, bloody furrow in his left arm. It ran from the top of his shoulder almost to his wrist.

Caleb followed her horrified gaze. "Damn," he muttered. He hadn't even realized that the cougar had got him. He stared at the laceration in his arm, at the blood that was welling from the wound, and swore again.

Rising to his feet, he walked down to the river and dipped his arm in the water. The water was clear and cold, cleaning the wound and slowing the bleeding. From his wrist to his elbow, the scratch wasn't bad, but there was a place in his upper arm, roughly three inches long, that was going to be a problem.

Callie stood nearby, watching him. He was so calm, so unshaken, it was as if the wound belonged to someone else. Or so she thought until he turned away from the river and she saw the pain in the depths of his eyes.

"I've got an extra shirt in my saddlebags," Caleb said. He sat down on the stump she had used earlier. "Think you could get it and tear it into strips?"

Callie nodded.

"There's a small bottle of whiskey in there, too."

Callie looked at him, a question in her eyes.

"Just bring it."

The pain in his voice spurred her to action. As fast as she could, she scrambled up the steep slope. She found the whiskey in his saddlebags, then began to rummage through her own, withdrawing two lengths of heavy white cotton cloth and a packet that contained a needle and a spool of thread. She ripped one length of cloth into long strips, wrapped the strips and the whiskey in the second length of cloth, then hurried back down the hill.

Caleb frowned as she knelt beside him and bit off a length of thread.

"You must know that needs stitching," Callie remarked, her voice shaking almost as badly as her hands.

"And you're going to do it?" Caleb asked dubiously.

Callie nodded.

"Ever done anything like this before?"

"No. Have you?"

"Yeah. Here," he said, taking the needle and thread from her hands, "let me do that." He managed to thread the needle in one try. "Where'd you get the cloth?" he asked as he handed her the needle.

A bright flush stained Callie's cheeks. "I brought it along for . . . for . . . I just brought it in case of an emergency."

Caleb nodded, readily understanding what the cloth had been for and her embarrassment at his mentioning it. "Hand me that bottle, will you?"

Callie handed him the whiskey, watching as he took several very long swallows, then shrugged out of his shirt. She stared in stunned silence as he doused the raw wound with whiskey. His face went white, and he swore a vile oath as the liquor touched his mutilated flesh.

"Here." He handed her the whiskey bottle. "Soak the needle and thread in that rotgut before you start."

"All right." Her hands were still shaking as she dribbled whiskey over the needle and thread, trying not to think of that narrow bit of shiny steel penetrating living flesh.

Caleb let out a deep breath. "I can do it if you can't."

"You? How?"

"One stitch at a time."

Callie stared up at him in disbelief, knowing that at some time in his past he had been hurt and there'd been no one he could turn to for help. "I'll do it."

She took a deep breath, willing her hands to stop shaking.

"Take a drink, Callie. Not too much."

She did as she was told and felt the fiery liquor burn a path to her stomach, suprised that it soothed her, that her hands stopped trembling.

Sitting beside him on the stump, she placed Caleb's arm across her knees. She concentrated on the task at hand, trying to pretend it wasn't human flesh she was sewing. Caleb used his right hand to hold the edges of the wound together as she carefully stitched the deep gash in the upper part of his arm, her stomach churning as the white thread turned crimson with his blood.

Caleb's face was drawn and pale, his body sheened with sweat, by the time she tied off the thread. Wordlessly, she handed him the bottle.

He drained the contents in one long swallow. "Thanks."

"You should lie down," Callie remarked. She wrapped the second length of cotton around his arm to keep the wound clean and dry.

"Yeah." Easing himself off the stump, he stretched out on the grassy bank beside the river and closed his eyes.

For a moment, Callie sat where she was, willing her queasy stomach to relax; then she made her way to the river and washed the blood from her hands.

When she returned to Caleb's side, he was asleep. She gazed down at him for a long time, admiring his broad shoulders and chest, his long muscular arms and legs. He was beautiful to look at—long and lean, solid as the mountains.

It was midafternoon when Caleb awoke to find Callie sitting on the stump mending the rip in his shirt sleeve. He watched her for a long moment, his stomach muscles tightening as he watched the needle dart in and out of the cloth. She was a good seamstress, he mused. The stitches she took in his shirt were as tight and neat as those she had used in sewing up his arm.

Sensing his gaze, Callie looked down at Caleb. "How do you feel?"

"Hungry. Think you could fix us something to eat?"

"Sure." She eased the needle into the collar of the shirt and slid off the stump.

Caleb stood up, glancing over at the mountain lion's carcass. "It's a shame to leave that hide," he remarked. "It's prime." He looked at Callie. "I don't suppose I could persuade you to skin it?"

"No."

He didn't argue.

He was breathing hard by the time they reached the top of the hill. His whole upper body ached from where the mountain lion had landed on him, and he wondered if he'd cracked a rib or two. There was an ugly bruise on his right shoulder where he'd hit a rock when the cat slammed into him, and another on his left thigh, but he wasn't complaining. He was lucky to be alive.

Caleb sat with his back against a tree, pretending the pain in his arm belonged to someone else as he watched Callie prepare something to eat. As soon as the meal was over, he stood up, saying it was time to move on, but Callie insisted that he needed to rest, and he relented without giving her much of an argument. He was sore. He was tired. Tomorrow would be soon enough.

Callie moved their bedrolls into the shade, and he took another nap. When he woke, Callie was sitting beside him, his shirt, washed and mended, folded in her lap.

Caleb grinned at her. "You're the first woman who's ever done that."

"Done what?"

"Mended one of my shirts."

"Really? Didn't your mother darn your socks and patch the holes in your clothes?"

"Not after we moved to Cheyenne. She just tossed them out and bought new ones. Before that, I didn't wear shirts or socks."

Callie nodded. She'd forgotten that Caleb had grown up in a mansion, surrounded by wealth. He'd probably never had to wear second-hand clothes or shoes with holes in them, but Callie remembered times when she'd had to wear dresses that were too small or too short, or clothes that her mother had received from some charity organization. It had been humiliating, but not as humiliating as wearing nice clothes and knowing how her mother had earned them.

Caleb had a low fever the next day. She knew his arm pained him more than he let on, but he didn't complain, and he didn't argue when she suggested they stay put another day.

Callie checked his arm the following morning, always afraid she'd see the telltale red streaks that meant infection, afraid her stitches wouldn't hold and that she'd have to do the whole grisly thing over again. But the wound seemed to be healing fine.

Of course, he'd have a scar. When she mentioned it, he just shrugged, as if it were of no consequence, but Callie couldn't help feeling a sense of regret. He had an arm that could have been sculpted by Michelangelo and it seemed a shame to mar such perfection, but Caleb seemed unconcerned.

"It could have been worse," he remarked, flexing his hand.

"Worse?" Callie asked skeptically. "How?

"If you hadn't been there, I'd have had to stitch it up myself."

Callie looked away. If she hadn't been there, it probably wouldn't have happened.

The next few days passed uneventfully. Callie continued to keep a close eye on Caleb, pleased when his fever went down, when his wound continued to heal without any complications.

It was midafternoon and they were only a few miles from the ranch when dark clouds began to gather overhead. Moments later, a cold wind blew out of the north.

"It's gonna rain," Caleb called over his shoulder. "I know a place where we can hole up."

"Where?"

"There's a line shack about a mile from here. If our luck holds, we'll get there before the storm breaks."

Their luck didn't hold. Ten minutes later, they were soaking wet. Lightning slashed the dark clouds. Thunder shook the earth, making Callie jump with each booming crash.

Fifteen minutes later, Callie saw the gray outline of a squat, square building through the curtain of rain.

She didn't argue when Caleb helped her from the saddle. Handing him her horse's reins, she ran to the line shack, opened the door, and stepped inside, grateful to be out of the rain.

The shack wasn't much to look at, just four wooden walls and a sturdy roof. The floor was made of raw planks; there was a single window opposite the door. A fireplace took up most of one wall, and there was a small, square table made of pine, with two rough-hewn chairs. A narrow bed topped with a straw tick and a dingy brown blanket was built into the west wall. A large wooden box held a mixed variety of tinned meat and fruit.

Caleb entered the shack a few minutes later, his arms laden with their saddlebags. "Get out of those wet things," he said, dropping the saddlebags beside the stove. He thrust a blanket into her hands. "I'll light a fire."

Callie stared at him. "You can't stay here while I change."

He looked at her as if she'd gone slightly loco. "You don't expect me to go outside?"

"Yes, I do."

"Well, I'm not. In case you've forgotten, it's raining like the devil."

They glared at each other for several moments; then, with a sigh of exasperation, Callie turned her back on Caleb and pulled off her boots. She was wet to the skin. The damp denim pants clung to her legs, making it difficult to get them off. Her socks seemed glued to her feet.

Mouth set in a determined line, she sat down and peeled her socks from her feet, then wrapped herself up in the blanket, muttering under her breath all the while about the raging elements and arrogant, insufferable men.

Caleb turned his back to Callie and shucked off his own wet clothes. He was reaching for his saddlebags when he felt Callie's curious gaze. For a moment, he stilled completely, his breathing suddenly erratic. He could feel her watching him, feel her gaze moving over his back and shoulders, down his buttocks and thighs.

"So many scars," Callie mused, hardly aware that she said the words aloud. "Where did they come from?"

"My father," Caleb replied harshly. He whirled around, feeling as if his soul were bared to her gaze. "Have you seen enough?"

Callie blinked up at him, her cheeks flaming with embarrassment. She hadn't meant to stare at him, had only meant to steal a glance, but once she'd caught a glimpse of him, she couldn't turn away. He was a beautiful man, well-proportioned and muscular, with only the scars on his back to mar what was surely a study in masculine perfection.

"I . . . I didn't mean to . . ." Callie shook her head. "I . . ." Her expression grew soft and sympathetic. "Did it hurt very much?"

"Like the flames of hell."

"I'm sorry, Caleb."

Clutching the blanket, she crossed the distance between them.

For a moment, their eyes met, then she stepped behind him and let her fingertips trace the web of scars on his broad back.

Caleb sucked in a sharp breath. No woman had ever touched him with such compassion, and as Callie's fingertips outlined each mark left by the lash, he felt as if she were drawing out all the old hurts that had festered within him for so long.

He let his breath out in a long, slow sigh and then, slowly, he turned to face her.

"Callie."

She gazed up into his eyes, and in the depths of his gray gaze she saw the answer to the doubts that had plagued her.

"Caleb, I . . ."

"Don't pull away, Callie. I won't hurt you."

"Won't you?"

He bent his head and kissed her, softly, entreatingly. "Trust me, Callie, just this once."

She shook her head, afraid to trust him, afraid of the wild rush of emotions that were warring within her. If she said yes, she'd learn what it was like to be with a man. She'd learn the mysterious secrets that all women longed to know; she'd discover why her mother had refused to leave Duncan Stryker.

If she said yes, she'd find out what it meant to need a man, just like her mother . . .

"No." She backed away from him. "I can't."

"Callie . . ."

She clutched the blanket tighter, her eyes wide and scared. "Don't. Please don't."

Slowly, deliberately, Caleb backed her into a corner, then drew her into his arms. He could feel her trembling, knew she was afraid of him, afraid of herself. Afraid of becoming what her mother had been. But he didn't care. Not now, when she was warm and soft in his arms. Not now, when he wanted her so bad he ached with it.

"Callie."

He kissed the side of her neck, his arms tightening around her. Her nearness, the scent of her rain-damp hair, the taste of her skin, turned his blood to flame. She was a woman, made to be loved, and he wanted her.

Callie stiffened in his embrace, frightened by the urgency of his kisses, by the untamed desire that flared in his eyes. He was Man, primal, earthy, and she was Woman, made for man.

She gazed up at him, knowing that she was lost, knowing that he meant to have her.

"No, Caleb," she whispered. "Please don't. We'll be married soon . . ."

He didn't answer. Instead, he kissed her again, kissed her until she was limp in his arms, until she was kissing him back, holding on to him as the only solid thing in a world gone wild.

A distant roar of thunder echoed the feral beat of her heart. And still he kissed her, bending her to his will, until she could think of nothing else. His lips were warm and firm, his tongue like the lightning that flamed in the sky.

She let the blanket drop to the floor as her hands reached up to grasp his shoulders. His skin was hot beneath her fingertips, and she let her hands slide down his arms, across his chest. She could feel him trembling, as she was trembling, and then he was lifting her, carrying her to the narrow bed, stretching out beside her. And all the while his mouth was on hers, teasing, caressing, promising.

She closed her eyes, refusing to look at him, refusing to admit that she wanted him to touch her, to hold her. It was wrong, so wrong.

"Callie, don't shut me out." He kissed her eyelids. "Look at me."

She had no intention of looking at him, but, slowly, her eyelids opened and she found herself staring into his eyes, eyes as gray and stormy as the sky. Eyes filled with desire, with longing. With love?

She whispered his name once, and then she began to explore the hard-muscled flesh she had admired only a short time ago. Touching him brought a smile to her face. His body was magnificent, hard and lean. She felt him shudder, heard him sigh, and reveled in the knowledge that her untutored hands could bring him pleasure.

And Caleb was touching her in return, learning the texture of her skin, the soft curves, the hidden hollows, memorizing the places that made her gasp with surprised delight, and those that made her sigh with wonder.

He held his own desire on a tight rein, wanting this time, her first time, to be a journey she would not regret. Only when she was trembling beneath him, her nails raking his back as she moaned his name, did he possess her.

One quick thrust tore her maidenhead. He swallowed her low cry of pain in a kiss, and after a moment he began to move within her again, slowly, gently, until the brief hurt was forgotten and she was clinging to him again, climbing with him toward a peak wrapped in sunshine and rainbows.

Caleb held back, his whole body aching, until she shuddered beneath him, and then, as his own release came, he clung to her, whispering her name, vowing that she would never be sorry.

Caleb held Callie in his arms, reluctant to let her go. There was much that needed to be said, much that he wanted to say, but somehow he could not form the words. Perhaps, if he was lucky, she wouldn't need the words.

They were as close as two people could be for several minutes, and then Caleb felt her withdraw from him, both physically and emotionally.

He didn't try to hold her. "What's wrong?"

"Nothing." Her voice was subdued, remote. "Everything."

"Callie . . ."

She stared at him, the pleasure of only a moment before forgotten in the guilt that flooded her soul. Guilt because she hadn't resisted more. Guilt because she had liked every kiss, every caress. He didn't need to marry her now, she thought bitterly. No man would want to marry her now.

Hurt and confused, she lashed out at him. "You had to do it, didn't you?" she said in the same detached tone. "You had to prove I'm just like my mother."

"Don't even think such a thing, Callie," he said gently, his voice filled with understanding. "You're nothing like your mother."

"Aren't I? Do you think Duncan made love to her here, in this dirty little bed?"

"I don't know. What difference does it make?"

"Should I buy a red dress?"

"Callie, one indiscretion doesn't make you a whore."

"Oh? How many does it take?"

"I didn't mean to shame you, you must know that. We'll be married as soon as we get back to the ranch, if you want."

"That won't change what I've done," Callie murmured. "Nothing will change that." She stared at him, her expression bitter.

"Callie, don't. You've done nothing to be ashamed of."

"I've made all the mistakes I intend to make today. I'm going home."

Home, she thought. She didn't have a home. Maybe she never would.

"Don't be a fool," Caleb admonished, irritated because he couldn't understand the depths of her anguish. "It's still raining."

"I don't care."

She slid out of bed and dressed under his gaze. It was all she could do not to cry, not to strike him with her fists and demand to know why he had treated her so shamefully.

She heard him call her name as she opened the door, but she didn't turn around. Jamming her hat onto her head, she ran outside to get her horse.

# *Chapter Twenty-one*

Caleb swore under his breath as Callie bolted out the door. Stubborn woman! Storming out into the rain like that.

Getting out of bed, he drew on a pair of dry pants and a shirt, clapped his hat on his head, pulled on a pair of socks, and stamped his feet into his boots.

Cussing mightily, he put out the fire, grabbed their saddlebags, and left the shack. He hoped to find her huddled in the rain, but she was gone. He knew a quick moment of satisfaction that she'd been able to catch and saddle her horse without his help, and then he cussed again. Stubborn woman, he thought irritably. And then he smiled. That was one of the things he liked about her.

In a matter of minutes, he was riding after her, cursing a blue streak all the while and grinning like a kid who'd just discovered the difference between men and women.

He caught up with her four miles later.

Callie glared at Caleb as he rode up. She'd known he would follow her, but she'd hoped to reach the ranch before he did. Instead, her horse had lost its footing on the slippery ground. The animal had gone down, throwing Callie over its head. She was unhurt except for a bruised derrière and several scrapes on her arms and legs. The horse hadn't fared so well. It was lame.

"You all right?" Caleb asked.

"Yes."

He swung out of the saddle and examined the black mare's right foreleg. It wasn't broken, but there was no way Callie could ride the mare back to the ranch.

Caleb turned to face Callie. "We'll have to ride double."

"Is she hurt bad?"

"No." He looped the mare's reins over the saddle horn, knowing she'd follow the buckskin home. "You ready to go?"

Callie nodded. She didn't argue when Caleb gave her a leg up. She was tired and cold and sick at heart, and all she wanted now was to go home, crawl into bed, and pull the covers over her head.

Her breath caught in her throat as Caleb swung up behind her. His arm brushed the curve of her breast as he reached forward to take up the buckskin's reins. He was close, so close. His chest caressed her back; his hard-muscled thighs cradled her own. He clucked to the buckskin, and the horse moved forward.

It was impossible not to touch him, impossible

to pretend she was unaffected by his nearness. When the buckskin stumbled, Caleb's arm closed around her waist, holding her against him. His chest was solid, and all too comforting. Why didn't he love her? Why did she love him?

They rode for hours without saying a word. Every time Caleb touched her, she remembered what it had been like in his arms. She had never dreamed that such ecstacy existed, never imagined anything so wonderful. In Caleb's arms, with his body joined intimately to hers, she had felt like she belonged to someone, really belonged, for the first time in her life. Had Duncan made her mother feel like that? If so, it explained why Leila had refused to leave him.

Thinking of her mother brought a flush to Callie's cheeks. What if Leila had felt that oneness with every man she slept with? The very idea made Callie sick to her stomach. What if any man could make *her* feel like that? But even as the thought crossed her mind, she knew it wasn't true. Richard Ashton had kissed her, touched her, and she had felt nothing but revulsion.

Callie took a deep breath. What had Caleb felt while lying in her arms? Had he felt that special oneness she had experienced, or had she been just another woman to warm his bed?

She was off the horse and running for the front door as soon as they rode into the yard. She had to get away from him, to be alone with her thoughts.

Caleb let her go. Dismounting, he led the horses to the barn, rubbed them down until they were dry, and forked them some hay. Standing in the doorway, he removed his hat and ran his hand through his hair. He stared up at the house, his gaze going to Callie's room.

Callie. Sweet child-woman, stubborn as the day was long. How was he going to convince her that they hadn't done anything wrong?

Resolutely, he headed for the house. Waiting wouldn't make it easier.

He didn't bother to knock, just opened her bedroom door, stepped into the room, and shut the door behind him.

Callie was in bed, the covers drawn up to her chin, staring at him through eyes as blue and wide as the Wyoming sky.

"Go away," she said.

"Not until you hear me out."

Not wanting to hear what he had to say, but knowing he was going to say it anyway, she crossed her arms over her chest and glared at him.

"I'm sorry," he said, his voice gruff. "I was wrong, and I'm sorry."

She continued to stare at him, her mouth set in a thin line, her whole attitude one of distrust and self-loathing.

"Callie . . ."

Crossing the room, he sat on the edge of the bed and took her hand in his. It was small and cold.

"I never meant to hurt you."

He swore under his breath. He'd never been any good at expressing his feelings, and the way Callie was looking at him, as if she wished the floor would open and swallow him whole, didn't make it any easier.

He took a deep breath, then let it out in a ragged sigh. "I love you, Callie. I never meant to shame you. You've got to believe me."

His words, as unexpected as flowers in winter, as

welcome as rain after a long draught, melted the ice around her heart.

"You love me?" she asked breathlessly.

Caleb nodded.

"You mean it? You aren't just saying it because you're feeling guilty about what we did?"

"I don't feel guilty about what we did. It was right, Callie. You know it as well as I do."

She felt the heat climb in her cheeks. It *had* felt right, inevitable.

"We'll go into town tomorrow and make arrangements for the wedding, okay?"

Callie nodded, her heart beating a happy tattoo. And then she frowned. "My dress hasn't arrived yet."

"Do you want to wait for it?"

"No."

"I imagine Fanny will want to be at the wedding," Caleb mused.

"Tell me again."

"What?"

"That you love me."

"I love you, Callie."

"Will you tell me often?"

"Every day, if you like." A wry grin tugged at the corners of Caleb's mouth. "I'd better go."

"I guess so," Callie agreed, though in truth she wished they were already married, that she could draw him down beside her and feel his mouth on hers.

He gave her hand a squeeze. "Goodnight," Caleb said, his voice thick.

"Do you think you could kiss me goodnight?"

"I won't be responsible for the consequences."

The desire in his eyes, the gentle teasing in his voice, flooded her with warmth.

"Soon," she said, her voice as thick with longing as his.

"Soon," Caleb agreed. And knew the next few nights would be the longest of his life.

Callie woke with a smile on her lips, feeling as if the morning sunshine had stolen into her heart. Caleb loved her! And she loved him. Perhaps she'd loved him from the very first day.

She dressed quickly, then hurried into the kitchen to prepare breakfast, eager to go into town, to make arrangements for the wedding. Mrs. Caleb Stryker. The words sang in her mind and echoed in her heart.

The sound of his footsteps sent a thrill of expectation spiraling through her. And then he was standing behind her, his arms circling her waist, his lips nuzzling the side of her neck.

"Good morning," he whispered huskily.

"Good morning."

"Up early, aren't you?"

"I couldn't sleep," she confessed.

"Me, either." His lips moved up the side of her neck, nibbling at the sensitive skin behind her ear. "You taste good enough to eat."

"And waste this perfectly good breakfast?" she teased, and marveled that she could say such things, that she felt so at ease in his arms. *He loved her.*

They ate quickly, and then, while Callie washed up the dishes, Caleb hitched the horse to the buggy.

Callie's smile was as bright as the sun when she stepped outside. Desire lanced through Caleb as he took her arm and helped her into the buggy. Lord, she was beautiful. And he loved her. . . .

He realized with startling clarity that it was true, that the words he'd spoken last night had come from his heart.

They stopped at the church and made arrangements with the priest to be married the following Saturday morning, then Caleb went off to see about getting the horse shod while Callie went to invite Fanny to the wedding.

Callie sat at one of the back tables in the restaurant. It seemed strange to be there as a customer, and she had to stifle the urge to jump up and clear the table whenever a patron left.

She smiled as Fanny came to sit with her.

"We've got time to talk now," Fanny said, wiping her hands on her apron. "The dinner crowd won't be coming in for about an hour. So, tell me, lamb, how are you doing?"

"Fine, Fanny."

"Is he treating you all right?"

A faint blush stained Callie's cheeks. "Yes."

Fanny nodded. "He's a good man."

"He asked me to marry him."

"Did he now?" Fanny exclaimed, looking pleased. "And what did you say?"

"I said yes. We're being married Saturday morning by Father Cardella. You'll come, won't you?"

"Wouldn't miss it, but that doesn't give you much time to get ready. There's invitations to be sent, and food to prepare . . ."

"We're not having a big to-do," Callie said. "It'll just be me and Caleb, and you."

A frown creased Fanny's brow. "I see. Are you sure you don't want a big wedding, with bridesmaids and flowers and a cake six feet tall? After all, he can afford it."

"I know, but . . ." Callie shrugged. "I don't have any friends in town besides you, and Caleb said he doesn't have any at all, so . . ."

"Well, at least you can have a cake. I'll bake it myself."

"Thank you, Fanny."

"And you'll be needing something to eat after the ceremony," Fanny added. "I'll take care of that, too."

"You don't have to."

"Hush, now." Fanny made a gesture of dismissal. "I want to."

"Fanny, you're so good to me."

Callie looked up at the clock on the wall. "I'd better be going. I'm supposed to meet Caleb out front at four."

"Do you love him, child?"

"Yes."

"And he loves you more than life itself?"

"Yes, I think he does."

"Then I'm happy for you both, lamb." Fanny reached out and took Callie's hand in hers. "He's had a hard life, Callie. He may not be an easy man to live with."

"I know, but . . ."

"But he's more handsome than any man has a right to be, and as charming as the devil."

"Yes."

"I wish you all the happiness in the world. And I'll be there Saturday morning with bells on."

"Thank you, Fanny. I knew I could count on you."

Callie gave the older woman a hug, then left the restaurant.

Outside, she glanced up and down the street, wondering where Caleb was.

She waited a few minutes, then walked down the boardwalk to peer into the window of Ohnhaus & Donovan's shoe store. She was admiring a pair of black leather boots with red silk tassels when a familiar voice made her stomach clench.

Turning, she saw Richard Ashton standing beside her, a smirk on his face.

"Well, well, Miss McGuire," he drawled. "And how are you this fine day?"

"Quite well, thank you, Mr. Ashton."

"So formal," he said with a sneer. "I hear you're getting married to that half-breed."

"What if I am? It's none of your business."

"I'm making it my business. You have no right to marry him."

"Who are you to tell me who I can and can't marry?" Callie exclaimed indignantly.

"Does he know who you are? Does he know that your mother was his father's whore?"

"How dare you!"

"You little tramp! Do you think marrying Stryker will make people forget who you are, what you are?"

Richard grabbed her by the arm and yanked her up against him. "I want you, and I mean to have you. Now."

"No!" Callie tried to break his grasp on her arm, but he was too strong for her. "Let me go!"

"Not until I'm through with you."

"You're through now."

Richard whirled around at the sound of Caleb's voice.

"Let her go," Caleb said.

"She's too good for the likes of you," Ashton stated.

"I can't argue with that."

Caleb stepped from the saddle and tossed the buckskin's reins over the hitch rack.

"You've got a short memory, Ashton. It seems I warned you once before to keep your hands off Callie."

The look in Caleb's eyes had made other men quail with fear, but Richard stood his ground.

"I'm not afraid of you, bounty hunter."

"You should be," Caleb retorted, his gaze moving contemptuously over the younger man.

Richard Ashton was young and rich and soft. His hands had probably never held anything heavier than a wineglass.

Richard glanced around, hoping that someone would step in and take his side, but the boardwalk was empty save for the three of them. He swallowed hard, remembering that Stryker had threatened to whip him within an inch of his life if he ever laid a hand on Callie again.

He was about to back down when Roy Gaines and Davis Carlson stepped out of Ohnhaus & Donovan's, only to come to a sudden halt when they saw Caleb walking purposefully toward Richard.

Caleb saw the two men out of the corner of his eye and knew, instinctively, that neither posed any threat.

Turning his full attention back to Richard, he said, "Let her go."

Sudden, unreasoning panic flooded Richard Ashton's mind as he stared into Stryker's cold gray eyes. Unbidden came all the stories he'd heard about the man, stories of scalping and mutilation, of cold-blooded killings.

With a cry, he pushed Callie aside just as Stryker reached for him. Wild-eyed, he looked to Roy and Travis for help, but neither man seemed inclined to interfere.

Caleb grabbed Ashton by the shirtfront and slammed him against the wall of the shoe store.

"This is my last warning. Don't ever lay a hand on Callie again."

"Go to hell," Richard retorted, and with a speed that surprised everyone, including himself, he drew a derringer from his coat pocket.

A sharp report echoed and re-echoed in the sudden stillness.

"Richard!" Callie screamed. "How could you?"

"I didn't." He shook his head emphatically, his gaze darting from Caleb's suddenly pale face to Callie's. "I didn't pull the trigger. I swear."

For a moment, Caleb stood there, his hand still clutching Ashton's shirtfront.

As from far away, he heard Callie scream.

Roy Gaines swore under his breath.

Davis Carlson ran down the boardwalk, hollering for Doc Maynard.

Caleb stared at the gun in Ashton's hand. No smoke spiraled from the barrel. Through a red haze of pain, he realized that the gunshot had come from someone else.

Fighting off the darkness that was swirling around him, he murmured Callie's name, and then everything went black.

Callie sat beside the bed, her hands clasped in her lap as she listened to Caleb's labored breathing. He lay face-down on the bed, the bandage swathed around his upper back very white against the dark bronze of his skin. Doctor Maynard had stopped the bleeding, then Roy and Davis and a man Callie didn't know had lifted Caleb into a flatbed wagon and taken him to the mansion.

That had been over two hours ago, and Caleb was still unconscious. Doctor Maynard had given her the medical terminology of the damage that had been done while he treated the injuries, but none of it made any sense. She knew only that someone had shot Caleb in the back and that the bullet had passed through his shoulder without hitting any vital organs. On leaving, the doctor had warned her about the danger of infection and admonished her to wash her hands in hot, soapy water before she changed the bandages.

The doctor had also mentioned that the effects of the anesthesia probably wouldn't wear off until late that night. Still, she couldn't help but be frightened. Caleb looked so pale, and he lay so still.

Callie stood up and pressed a hand to her back. Suddenly feeling restless, she picked up the pile of Caleb's clothing and carried it downstairs. His shirt was ruined, and his pants were soaked with blood. She doubted all the soaking in the world would erase that awful red stain. So much blood. Just looking at it made her nauseated.

She filled a bucket with cold water and was about to drop Caleb's pants into it when she felt a bulge in the pocket. Reaching inside, she drew out a folded envelope. She was about to put it on the kitchen table when she noticed that it was addressed to Miss Leila McGuire.

Callie stared at her mother's name for a long moment, wondering what was inside. An old love letter, she thought, since the handwriting was obviously Duncan Stryker's, and then she frowned. Why would Caleb be carrying around an old love letter?

Her hand was trembling as she opened the envelope and withdrew the contents. The first sheet of paper was indeed a letter to her mother.

The second was a codicil to Duncan Stryker's will.

Callie read the document three times, unable to believe her eyes. The Rocking S belonged to her!

She sat down on one of the kitchen chairs, the paper crushed to her breast. The Rocking S was hers! Why hadn't Caleb told her? Perhaps he'd been saving it for a surprise, a wedding present, she mused. And then she went cold all over, as if someone had drained all the blood from her body.

He'd had no intention of telling her.

She put the thought from her. That was silly. Why wouldn't he tell her? They were going to be married.

"No." She shook her head, refusing to believe what she knew to be true.

Rising, she dropped Caleb's blood-stained pants into the pail of cold water and tossed his other clothes into the laundry basket to be washed later. She filled the coffeepot with water and cut herself a piece of cake, which she toyed with but didn't eat. When the water was hot, she added tea and let it steep, then poured some into a cup and carried it into the parlor.

Taking a place on the sofa, she stared at the portrait of Caleb's parents, at the beautiful black-haired woman and the handsome fair-haired man, and wondered what had gone wrong with their marriage.

And then she smiled, a small, cold smile. The Rocking S belonged to her. She'd never have to worry about her future again. She had all the security she'd ever wanted, all she'd ever need, and no one could take it away from her.

Caleb tossed restlessly, his fevered mind filling with vague images of his past, images of hide lodges pitched along the banks of a winding river, of his mother sitting beside a small fire putting the finishing touches on a pair of moccasins she'd made for him. He saw himself astride a raw-boned paint stallion, riding across the plains in search of game, and he smiled because he was wild and free, because he would always be wild and free.

Abruptly, the scene changed, and he was dressed in the trappings of a white man, his freedom curbed by shiny floors and tall ceilings and walls that shut out the sun and the moon. His father was there, tall and austere and handsome, demanding that he forget his old life, that he forget the language and ways of his mother and embrace the way of the white man.

His hands balled into tight fists, and he writhed on the bed as he relived the day his father had cut his hair.

"You'll not speak that heathen tongue in my hearing again," Duncan had shouted. "You'll not wear those smelly buckskins another day. And you'll never wear a feather in your hair again."

"I'll wear whatever I damn well please!"

It had taken four cowhands to hold him down

while Duncan hacked off his hair. It had been the worst humiliation of his life.

The images scattered and changed. He was running away from home. Working for the freight company. Killing his first man. Chasing outlaws on both sides of the border. Drinking. Gambling. Whoring . . .

"Callie . . ." He whispered her name and the images dissolved like smoke in the wind.

He started to sit up, but a searing pain lanced through his chest and he fell back against the pillows, his breath coming in short, hard gasps.

"Lie still."

"Callie?"

"I'm here." There was a brief flare of light as she struck a match; a soft glow filled the room as she lit the lamp and turned up the wick. "How do you feel?"

"I've been better. And worse."

"Here." She held a glass of water to his lips. "Drink this."

He drained the glass, more thirsty than he'd realized.

"Go back to sleep."

He stared at her, puzzled by the coldness in her voice, the distant look in her eyes, but before he could ask her what was wrong, darkness closed in around him once more, dragging him down, down, into blessed oblivion.

The sun shining through the window coaxed him awake. He glanced around the room, but there was no sign of Callie.

With a sigh, he lifted a tentative hand to the thick bandage swathed around his chest. He was lucky to be alive, he thought, and wondered who had tried to kill him, and why.

The bedroom door swung open, and Callie entered the room. "How are you feeling this morning?"

"Better."

"Are you hungry?" She nodded at the tray balanced in one hand. "I made you some broth and a cup of tea."

"Thanks."

She sat on the edge of the bed to feed him, but he took the spoon from her hand. "I can do it."

"Very well. I'll be back later to change the bandage."

He ate slowly, grimacing as he emptied the bowl. Broth! And tea! He wasn't an invalid. Why hadn't she brought him something he could sink his teeth into?

She returned thirty minutes later carrying clean bandages, scissors, and a jar of salve.

He closed his eyes, his body tensing as she removed the old bandage, checked the wound, and applied a thin coat of salve.

"What is it, Callie?" he asked curtly. "What's wrong?"

"Nothing."

"Don't lie to me, dammit! What's wrong?"

She looked at him for the first time since entering the room.

"Do you want to talk about lies, Mr. Stryker?"

The look in her eyes twisted the knife a little deeper. Caleb glanced around the room, wondering where his clothes were, and then everything made sense.

She'd found the envelope.

"I can explain."

"Can you?"

Her eyes, once as blue and warm as a summer sky, were now as cold as winter ice.

"Probably not. I guess this means the marriage is off?"

Callie choked back her tears, wishing she'd never found that blasted envelope, wishing she could think of something mean enough to call him, something that would hurt him as she had been hurt. She'd been a fool to believe he was marrying her because he loved her. *Men only wanted one thing from a woman,* she thought bitterly. Two things, in her case. Her virginity and the ranch. And he'd wanted the Rocking S badly enough to marry a woman he didn't love to get it. The thought cut her heart to the quick.

"Dammit, Callie, the ranch should have been mine!"

"Your father didn't think so."

Black rage filled Caleb's eyes, and behind that rage was a hurt so deep, so soul-shattering, that Callie's heart twisted with pain. She'd hurt him, she thought, but it didn't make her feel better, it only made her ache inside.

"It's the only place where I ever felt at home," Caleb said, his voice thick with anger. "And my old man knew it."

His hands curled into tight fists. "Take the mansion, instead."

"No."

"You don't know the first thing about running a cattle ranch."

"I'll learn," Callie said, the tone of her voice clearly

indicating that the subject was closed. "I'll be back later with your dinner."

With that, she hurried from the room, unable to endure the force of his anger, or the hurt that his anger couldn't hide.

# Chapter Twenty-two

He had a fever when she went to check on him later that afternoon. He'd tossed the covers aside, and her first thought was that she was glad he was asleep because, stark naked, Caleb Stryker was a sight to behold.

Her second thought was that she was glad he was lying on his stomach!

Hurrying to the side of the bed, Callie was about to draw the covers over him when she paused, letting her gaze wander over the broad expanse of his back. His skin was the color of warm copper, very dark against the white bandage. She stared at the closely knit web of scars that criss-crossed the taut flesh across his shoulders and back.

Her throat constricted as she tried to imagine the pain, the humiliation he had endured. The sense of betrayal he must have felt at being whipped by his own father.

*I will not feel sorry for him.*

Quickly, she covered him with the blanket before she could see any more. She didn't want to feel sorry for him. She didn't want to feel anything.

He began to thrash about on the bed. Rolling over onto his back, he sat up, his gaze darting around the room.

"Underwood! Don't do it!"

He was having a nightmare.

Callie placed her hand on his shoulder and shook it gently. "Caleb, you're home. It's all right."

Lifting his head, Caleb glanced around the room. The dream had been so vivid, so real, he could almost smell the gunsmoke, feel the pain as the bullet from Red Jack Underwood's revolver tore into his arm, hear Underwood's harsh cry as Caleb opened fire.

He swore softly when he saw Callie staring at him. Damn. Why'd she have to come in and find him thrashing about like a baby crying in the dark?

"Are you all right?" she asked.

He could see the questions in her eyes. To her credit, she kept her mouth shut and poured him a drink of water from the pitcher on the side table. She held it for him while he drank, as if he were a doddering old man.

Callie frowned as her hand brushed his. His skin was hot, so hot.

"Lie down," she said, putting the empty glass on the table. "I'll be right back."

Hurrying downstairs, she went into the kitchen and filled a basin with cold water, found a cloth, and hurried back to Caleb's room.

He watched her suspiciously as she dipped the cloth in the bowl. "You gonna give me a bath?"

"No. You've got a fever. I'm going to sponge you off with cold water."

Before he could argue, before she lost her nerve, she drew the blanket down to his waist and began to sponge him off, hoping the cool water would bring down his temperature.

She tried not to care that he was in pain, but she couldn't ignore the ache in her heart as she bent to her task. It occurred to her that he still might die from his wounds. Even in this day and age, in a town as civilized as Cheyenne, people still died of fever and infection.

He was watching her, his eyes fever-bright, as she drew the damp cloth across his left shoulder and down his arm, but she refused to meet his gaze.

He groaned softly as she touched an area near the wound in his other shoulder and she felt a sudden queasiness in her stomach as she remembered standing beside Doctor Maynard as he examined the two ugly wounds. She had seen gunshot wounds before, though always from a distance. Living above a saloon made such a thing a common occurrence, but none of the others had ever affected her. She had always thought herself impervious to the sight of blood, until the blood was Caleb's.

"Do you have any idea who shot you?" she asked.

"No."

The sheriff had been around, asking questions, but last she'd heard, he hadn't been able to learn anything.

She laid the cloth aside and reached for the bottle of laudanum the doctor had left.

"What's that?" Caleb asked suspiciously. "Poison?"

"Laudanum."

"I don't want it."

"Why not? It'll ease the pain and help you sleep."

Caleb shook his head. "No."

Callie frowned in exasperation. "It'll make you feel better."

"I didn't think you cared how I felt."

"I don't," she retorted sharply, "but the sooner you're on your feet, the sooner I can go out to *my* ranch."

Caleb muttered something extremely vile under his breath, and Callie turned on her heel and left the room, slamming the door behind her.

Downstairs, she went into the kitchen and fixed herself a cup of tea. It was then that the questions she had put out of her mind came back to haunt her. Why hadn't Caleb told her the ranch was hers? Had he decided to marry her simply to keep control of the ranch?

She fought the urge to cry. She would not weep for him! She would not shed one single tear. And when he was back on his feet, she would go out to the ranch, *her* ranch, and never see him again.

Caleb struggled to sit up, ignoring the pain that accompanied each movement, cursing the weakness that kept him bed-ridden, cursing whoever it was who had shot him. He'd been ambushed twice, even stabbed a couple of times in the past eight years, but nothing quite as bad as this.

He stared out the window, memories of the ranch crowding his mind. He'd roped his first cow there, castrated a bull, branded yearlings. He'd ridden over every acre of range, mending fences, checking waterholes, rounding up strays. Once, he'd thought to spend his life on the Rocking S. But his father had changed all that.

Unconsciously, he lifted a hand to his hair. "Damn you, Duncan," he muttered under his breath. "Wasn't it enough that you humiliated me in front of men I respected? Did you have to give away my birthright too?"

He felt his anger grow as he thought of Callie, stubbornly refusing to let him have the ranch in exchange for the mansion. Didn't she realize she could sell the mansion for more money than she could spend in a lifetime?

Stubborn woman! She didn't know a blessed thing about running a cattle ranch, but she was determined to hang on to it, simply because she'd always wanted to live on a ranch.

And yet, he couldn't blame her for wanting the Rocking S. He wanted it himself. And he intended to have it, one way or another.

The sheriff came to call the next day.

"You know of anybody who's got a reason to be out gunning for you?" the lawman asked.

"I've been a bountry hunter for the last eight years," Caleb retorted, his voice thick with sarcasm. "What do you think?"

"Well, I'll keep checking around."

Four days in bed was all Caleb could stand. The doctor had stopped by a couple of times, examining Caleb's injuries, declaring that the wounds were inflamed but clean, putting Caleb's right arm in a sling to make sure he didn't exert any pressure on the injured area, assuring him that the fever would pass, admonishing him to drink plenty of water.

Caleb had grunted in reply and drunk beer instead.

The air was blue with the sound of his cursing by the time he managed to pull on his pants and boots using only one hand. A shirt was too much trouble, and he flung it aside, and the sling with it.

He ran a comb through his hair, grimaced at his reflection in the mirror, and left the room.

He could hear Callie singing as he stepped into the hallway, and he figured she was in the kitchen, cooking breakfast.

He descended the stairs slowly. His whole right side was sore; four days in bed had left him feeling weak and light-headed.

Callie's song came to an abrupt end when she saw him standing in the doorway. "You're supposed to be in bed," she said, her tone curt.

"I'm supposed to be a lot of things," he replied as he sat down at the kitchen table. "That coffee hot?"

With a sigh of resignation, she reached for a cup and slammed it on the table. She was more careful as she poured the coffee.

Caleb grinned wryly. "Thanks."

Callie glared at him, wondering how he could drink his coffee like that, as black as sin and as hot as Hades.

Her gaze moved over him, noting the width of his shoulders, the absence of the sling. She started to remark on it, then changed her mind. If he didn't want to wear it, he wouldn't.

She watched him take a sip of coffee, thinking that the cup, made of blue flowered china, looked incredibly fragile in his large hand. Unbidden came the memory of his hand in her hair. . . .

She jerked her thoughts from that direction and studied his face, contemplating the faint lines of pain and fatigue around his mouth and eyes. He really shouldn't be out of bed, she thought, then wondered why she cared.

Turning away from the table, she mixed the ingredients for flapjacks.

Caleb watched Callie as she worked, wondering what he could say to mend the rift between them, wondering how he could convince her to let him have the ranch.

He felt his desire for her stir to life as she set the table, the warm, womanly scent of her mingling with the aroma of frying bacon and coffee. He'd held her, kissed her, tasted her, and it had only whet his appetite for more. Her kisses were sweeter than honey, more satisfying than a cup of hot coffee on a cold night, more intoxicating than brandy.

Callie sat down across from Caleb, refusing to meet his gaze. It was Saturday. If Caleb hadn't been shot, if she hadn't found Duncan Stryker's letter, it would have been her wedding day.

The day after the shooting, she'd gone into town and told Father Cardella that the wedding was off. She'd gone to see Fanny as well. Fanny had clucked softly, enfolding her in a motherly embrace, and Callie had burst into tears, the whole story pouring out of her like floodwaters overflowing the banks of a river.

Fanny had listened quietly, offering no advice, taking no sides, letting Callie think it through for herself, and when her tears subsided, Callie knew she wanted to keep the ranch. Right or wrong, her mother had earned it, and Callie intended to keep it. Other women ran successful ranches; she could, too!

She looked up at the sound of Caleb pushing away from the table.

"Think you could help me put on a shirt?"

"Where are you going?"

"For a walk."

"Do you think you should go out?"

"I need to get out of the house, Callie," he said. "I don't like being cooped up. Are you gonna help me or not?"

With a nod, she stood up and followed him to his room. He tossed her a dark gray shirt and she slipped it over his arms and shoulders, then fastened the buttons. If this had been their wedding day, she might be undressing him, she thought, and felt her cheeks grow hot.

"Callie . . ."

She looked up, her gaze meeting his, and knew that he was thinking the same thing. For a timeless moment, she couldn't move, couldn't think. She looked into Caleb Stryker's eyes, past the hurt and the pain, past the anger, and saw only his hunger.

It made her heart beat a wild tattoo, made her insides ache with a warm, sweet pain she didn't understand. She felt suddenly weak, out of breath. His eyes were gray, like storm clouds, yet they burned like silver fire, threatening to engulf her in flame.

"This should have been our wedding day, Callie," he said, his voice low and husky.

"I know."

He bent toward her, his good arm circling her waist to draw her close.

"One kiss," he murmured.

Helpless to resist the sound of his voice or the heat in his eyes, she swayed toward him. Her eyelids fluttered down as his mouth closed over hers. He tasted of coffee and syrup, bitter and sweet, and she melted against him, her arms twining around his neck.

Caleb groaned low in his throat, his need for her clawing at him, urging him to take her. He wondered briefly why he hadn't destroyed that blasted codicil before she had a chance to find it. It would have made everything so simple. They could have been married, and she'd never have been the wiser. But, fool that he was, he'd taken it with him into town, curious, in spite of himself, to find out if it was still valid. Hoag had assured him that it was. It occurred to him that, had he destroyed that one damning piece of paper, marrying Callie would have been unnecessary. But that would have been too low-down a trick, even for him. Besides, he wanted to marry her, though he didn't think he'd ever be able to convince her of that now.

His tongue slid into her mouth, savoring the taste of her, as he backed her toward the bed. He wanted her, wanted her warm and willing beneath him. He wanted her for his wife.

With his hand at her back to support her, he lowered her to the mattress, then stretched out beside her, ignoring the faint twinge of pain that lanced through his injured side.

She made a low mewing sound in her throat as he kissed her again, and yet again. He drew her close, their bodies lying side by side, touching from shoulder to ankle. She was like liquid silk against him, soft and pliable, and he yearned to bury all the old hurts, the old angers, the old fears, in her sweetness, to endure what the Spanish called "the little death" and be reborn in her arms.

Callie yielded to his kisses, too caught up in the wonder of his touch to worry about right or wrong. He was kissing her again, his lips working their familiar magic, his tongue igniting little fires wherever it touched. His body was hard and firm against hers, his voice like deep black velvet as he whispered her name.

She strained toward him, knowing that only he could ease the honeyed ache that left her weak and yearning for something that hovered just out of reach.

She was drowning in pleasure, smothering in sensations that made it hard to breathe. And then his hand was reaching inside her bodice, stroking the curve of her breast. She gasped with pleasure, her stomach fluttering with excitement and trepidation, all her senses, her whole being, waiting, waiting. . . .

She opened her eyes and met his gaze, hungry and hot, and suddenly her mother's voice rang out in the back of her mind, warning her that men only wanted one thing from a woman unless that woman was his wife.

This was to have been her wedding day.

He had planned to cheat her out of the ranch.

With a strangled sob, Callie twisted out of his embrace and practically flew out of the bed.

"No!" she cried, straightening her bodice and smoothing her skirt. "You won't seduce me with your lying kisses again!"

"Callie, wait."

"No. I'm going out to the ranch, *my* ranch, and if you follow me, I'll have you shot on sight for trespassing."

"Dammit, Callie, if you'd just listen . . ."

But she was already gone. Moments later, he heard the front door slam, and then there was only the empty echo of her silence.

# *Chapter Twenty-three*

Caleb wandered through the mansion for the next two weeks, too angry to care what he ate, his nerves raw with unfulfilled desire. He drank too much, slept too little, and thought constantly of Callie, cursing the day he'd met her, wishing she were there beside him.

He endured the doctor's final examination, nodding impatiently when the sawbones admonished him to take it easy for another week.

So, he mused, resuming his pacing when the doc left the house, Callie thought he was despicable for not telling her about the ranch. Well, she wouldn't have any doubts at all after he paid a little visit to the bank.

George Webster was a short, rotund man with shrewd blue eyes and a shock of wavy brown hair. He invited Caleb to sit down, inquired politely about his health, then sat back and waited for Caleb to tell him the purpose of his visit.

Caleb came quickly to the point. "The bank holds a mortgage on the Rocking S. I want to know how much it will cost me to buy it back."

"I believe the loan was for five thousand dollars," Webster replied. "But I understand that you are no longer the owner."

"That's true, but the new owner can't afford to pay it off, and I don't want the bank to foreclose."

"I see."

"There's just one problem. I don't have five thousand in cash, so I'd like to borrow five thousand, using the Stryker mansion as collateral."

Webster frowned. "Do you think that's wise, taking out a loan on property you own to pay off a mortgage on property that belongs to someone else?"

"I don't believe it's any of your business," Caleb retorted.

A flush crept up Webster's neck. "The note on the ranch is due a week from today. I'll have to ascertain that Miss McGuire is unable to meet the deadline before I discuss terms with you."

"You do that. You can tell her someone is willing to buy the note and extend it for another year, but don't tell her it's me."

"Very well."

"I'll see you next week."

Webster nodded. Rising, he offered Stryker his hand, shook Caleb's firmly, and hoped he never found himself looking into the half-breed's cold gray eyes over a gun barrel or across a poker table.

* * *

Callie sat on the edge of the chair, her gaze intent upon George Webster's face. "Five thousand dollars! Are you sure?"

"Quite sure."

"But where am I supposed to get that much money in such a short time?"

"Things are not quite as bad as they appear. There is a party interested in buying your note and extending it for one year."

"There is? Who?"

"I'm not at liberty to divulge his name at this time."

"And I have nothing to say about it?"

"I'm afraid not. The bank has held the note long enough. We are, of course, eager to recoup our investment."

"But . . . what if I can't pay off the note next year?"

"That will be between you and the investor I spoke of. He may extend the note indefinitely, or he may demand payment."

"And if I can't meet it, I'll lose the ranch?"

"I'm afraid so."

"Thank you, Mr. Webster," Callie mumbled.

Leaving the bank, she stood on the boardwalk, her mind whirling. What was she going to do now? It occurred to her that Caleb knew all about that note! She felt her anger rise, then quickly disappear. He'd told her about it weeks ago.

*It seems my mother mortgaged the ranch to raise money to lobby for Indian rights in Congress.*

The words rang loud and clear in the back of her mind.

She glanced across the street at the Three Queens, wondering if Caleb was inside, wondering if she could summon the nerve to ask him for a loan.

She frowned thoughtfully as it occurred to her that Caleb Stryker might very well be the investor Mr. Webster had spoken of. It would be just like Caleb to buy up the note, then toss her out on her ear when she couldn't come up with the money. And he wouldn't have to wait a year. He could demand payment at any time.

She was considering the advisability of marching into the Three Queens to see if Caleb was there when she saw Richard Ashton riding toward her.

She quickly turned away, hoping he hadn't seen her, but it was too late. Reining his horse to a halt, he dismounted and hurried toward her.

"Callie, how pretty you look!"

"Mr. Ashton, please leave me alone."

"Callie, why do you keep fighting me? You must know that I'll have you sooner or later. No other man in this town will make an honest woman of you."

"And you will, I suppose?"

"I might."

Callie stared at Richard. He was looking immensely prosperous in a dapper brown suit that was the exact color of his eyes. His cravat was silk, perfectly knotted at his throat. He wore a brown bowler hat, shiny brown boots, and kidskin gloves. The diamond stickpin in his cravat was probably worth hundreds of dollars.

"Can I buy you a glass of lemonade?" Richard asked.

"All right."

He took her arm, and they walked down the boardwalk to a small but elegant restaurant.

"So tell me, Richard," Callie said after Richard

ordered two glasses of lemonade and two slices of spice cake, "how are you?"

"I'm fine. I hear the bounty hunter recovered."

"Yes."

"I hear the wedding's off. Are you still working for him?"

"Hardly."

Richard took a long drink from his glass, his gaze resting on Callie's face. She was such a pretty thing. Usually, he liked tall, buxom women, but Callie's figure was small and perfect. Her skin was the color of rich cream, her hair the red-gold of autumn leaves, her eyes a clear, vibrant blue. He wondered how many men she'd had, and why she continued to turn him down. The thought that she'd been whoring for that half-breed ate at his pride and redoubled his determination to have her, one way or another.

"We're having a party at our place Saturday night," he remarked. "I'd like to see you there."

"Me?" Callie stared at him in open astonishment.

"You."

"No."

"Why not?" He smiled at her, his expression warm.

"I can't."

"Sure you can. You'll be my guest. If you're worried about what to wear, I'll have something sent over."

"Your father would have apoplexy if I so much as darkened the door."

"My father will take one look at you and understand perfectly."

"That's what I'm afraid of."

"Well, I just thought you might like to better your position in town. After all, once you've mingled with the townspeople, they'll hardly be able to cut you on the street. And maybe, if they see you in a nice dress in good company, they'll realize that you're not like your mother after all."

"And what's in it for you?"

"I'll get to dance with the prettiest girl in town." And after he'd plied her with champagne and pretty words, he'd get what he'd been wanting since Callie was fifteen.

Callie shook her head. She'd never thought of herself as a coward, but she didn't have the nerve to attend a party at the home of Charles Ashton.

"Isn't there some way I can convince you to be my guest? Can't I bribe you with a new dress, or a bauble of some kind?"

He smiled, displaying even white teeth. "Anything you want, Callie, just name it and it's yours. All you have to do is dance with me Saturday night."

Her mouth went dry as she found herself considering his offer. "Anything?"

Richard nodded, certain she was about to give in.

"I want five thousand dollars."

He almost choked on his lemonade. "Five thousand dollars!"

Callie covered her mouth with her napkin so he couldn't see her smile. "Is there a problem?"

"No. Do you want cash, or will a bank draft do?"

"You aren't serious?"

"Why not? People will talk about it for years, how Richard Ashton once paid a girl an exorbitant amount of money for one dance."

Callie pushed her plate away and reached for her reticule. "You must think I'm a fool. We both know you only want one thing from me, and it isn't a dance."

"Maybe I've changed, Callie."

"I'll believe that when men fly to the moon."

"It's true." He took her hand in his and gave it a squeeze. "Won't you trust me, Callie? I know I've acted badly in the past, but that's all over now."

Callie drew her hand from his. Richard Ashton could be quite charming when he put his mind to it, she mused, but she simply didn't believe a word he said.

"Thank you for the lemonade and the cake," Callie said, pushing away from the table. "I think I'd better go now."

"I'll walk you back."

"No, that won't be necessary. Good afternoon, Mr. Ashton."

"Good afternoon, Miss McGuire."

Outside, Callie shook her head. Five thousand dollars for a dance, indeed! What kind of fool did he take her for?

He'd changed, all right, but only his tactics.

Callie was sitting in the ranch kitchen late Saturday afternoon, sipping a cup of tea, when she heard a knock at the front door.

A woman was standing on the porch, a large box in her arms.

"May I help you?" Callie asked.

"I'm Ruth Manning. Mr. Ashton sent me."

"I don't understand."

"I'm Mrs. Ashton's maid. I've come to help you get ready for the party." She reached into the box and withdrew a long, narrow envelope. "Mr. Ashton said to give you this."

Callie's heart began to beat rapidly as she opened the envelope. Inside she found five thousand dollars in large bills and a note that said, "See you at eight. R."

Ruth Manning shifted the box in her arms. "Shall we get started?"

"I . . . I think there's been a mistake."

"We don't have much time, Miss McGuire," the woman said, sweeping past Callie. "I think we should get started."

Throwing caution to the winds, Callie decided she would accept Richard's offer and beat him at his own game.

For the next three hours, Callie was at Ruth Manning's mercy. Not that it wasn't a delightful experience. The woman insisted that Callie soak in a hot bubble bath. She washed Callie's hair, helped her into a robe, then manicured Callie's nails while her hair dried. Next, she gave Callie a massage "to relax you." When Callie's hair was dry, Ruth experimented with several styles, finally sweeping the long, red-gold mass away from Callie's face, fastening it in place with two large jeweled combs, so that it fell down Callie's back in a mass of soft waves.

Reaching into the large box, Ruth withdrew a pair of lacy pantalets, a chemise, and a satin petticoat. She helped Callie into her new underthings, then, reaching into the box once more, she drew out a gown of the finest silk. It was sapphire blue in color, with a high neck, long sleeves, a slightly belled skirt, and a modest bustle adorned with white satin flowers.

But the biggest surprise was the diamond necklace Ruth fastened around Callie's throat. The gems sparkled in the lamplight, glittering like stars fresh from heaven. There were matching earbobs and a bracelet.

Callie stared at herself in the mirror, unable to believe her eyes. The gown was the exact color of her eyes, the perfect foil for her ivory skin and red-gold hair. The dress was modest in the extreme, exposing not an inch of flesh, yet it was undeniably provocative, clearly outlining every curve.

Ruth Manning took a step back, her hands on her hips. "You look exquisite," she said, obviously pleased with her handiwork. "The dress is yours to keep, but the diamonds will have to be returned."

"Yes, of course," Callie murmured. She stared at her reflection. No one, seeing her now, would ever recognize her as Leila McGuire's daughter.

"That gown looks like it was made for you, and that necklace—well, you look like royalty, Miss. I think Mr. Ashton will be pleased."

"Thank you, Mrs. Manning," Callie murmured, but it wasn't Richard she was thinking of, it was Caleb Stryker. What would he think if he could see her now, dressed like a duchess?

"Miss?"

Callie glanced over her shoulder. "I'm sorry. Did you say something?"

"It's time to go."

Callie took a deep breath. She was certain she was making a mistake, but something compelled her to follow Ruth outside. If Richard Ashton wanted to pay her five thousand dollars for a dance, so be it. And if he thought he was going to get more than a dance, he was sadly mistaken.

A fancy buggy was waiting outside. A footman wearing dark green livery assisted her into the back seat of the conveyance, helped Ruth into the opposite seat, and they were off.

Callie smiled as she sank back into the seat, feeling like Cinderella on the way to the ball—except she wasn't going to meet a handsome prince, she was going to dance with a dragon.

# *Chapter Twenty-four*

Caleb was sitting on the front porch, smoking a cigar, when he saw Ashton's buggy coming down the street. At first he paid it no mind, but then he caught a flash of red-gold hair that could only belong to Callie.

Rising, he walked down the stairs and peered into the gathering darkness. It was Callie, all right, looking more beautiful than he'd ever seen her. She passed by the house without a glance in his direction and he frowned, wondering what she was doing in Ashton's buggy. Then he swore under his breath. She had to be going to the birthday party Charles Ashton was throwing for his wife, Dolores.

He stared down the street. He could see numerous carriages gathered in front of the Ashton mansion. All the important people in Cheyenne had been invited.

He chuckled softly as he imagined Callie walking into a room full of Cheyenne's elite. She'd be as out of place as a hen in a foxhole, he thought, and then he grunted softly. Maybe not. She looked like a fairy princess in that blue dress. Likely no one would recognize her as Leila McGuire's daughter until it was too late, and having once received her in the Ashton home, the townspeople would hesitate to snub her in the future.

But what was she doing accepting an invite to Ashton's in the first place? She'd always claimed to detest Richard Ashton, and he was certain that was who the invitation had come from. Why had she changed her mind?

Slowly, he returned to the porch, only to stand with one hand on the rail, staring into the darkness, his thoughts filled with an angel dressed in a sapphire-blue gown.

Callie stepped from the carriage, her eyes growing wide as she took in the colorful Chinese lanterns that lit the walkway leading to the Ashton mansion.

At the door, a servant asked to see her invitation.

"I . . ." She lifted a hand to the diamond necklace. "That is . . ."

"It's all right, Hawkins, she's with me."

Relief washed through Callie as Richard hurried toward her, impeccably attired in a black suit and white cravat.

"Callie, you look lovely," he said, taking her hand in his. "Come along, I want you to meet my folks."

Charles Ashton had been wealthy all his life, and it showed. Confident and self-assured, he smiled at

Callie as he took her hand. "Richard, who is this lovely young woman, and where have you been hiding her?"

"This is Claire Thompson, father. Claire, this is my father, Charles Ashton, and my mother, Dolores."

"I'm pleased to meet you Mr. Ashton. Mrs. Ashton."

"You look familiar, my dear," Charles Ashton remarked, still holding her hand. "Have we met before?"

"I don't think so, sir. I'm sure I would have remembered."

"Do enjoy yourself, my dear," Dolores Ashton said, patting Callie's arm. "Richard, you make her feel at home, you hear?"

"Yes, Mother. My pleasure. Come along, Claire."

Callie frowned up at him when they were away from Richard's parents. "Why didn't you tell them who I really am?"

"I thought you might feel more at ease if no one knew who you were."

"Someone is sure to recognize me. What then?"

"I don't think so. You look like a princess in a fairy tale. And those diamonds make your eyes sparkle."

"They're lovely. Thank you."

"Ruth did tell you they were just on loan?"

"Yes. Don't worry. I won't run off with them."

"I'm not worried."

Richard took her arm and they made their way into the ballroom. The Ashton home was even grander than Caleb's, if that was possible, filled with crystal and fine china, ornate mirrors, delicate vases. She was certain the dark, lustrous furniture must have come from castles in Spain.

There was a coat of arms above a marble fireplace, and next to the hearth stood a life-sized statue of a knight. There were imported carpets and tapestries and dozens of knick-knacks made of china, crystal, and exotic woods.

Richard introduced her to several couples. Some names, like Whipple and Nagle, she recognized; others meant nothing to her. She didn't see anyone she knew, but that was hardly surprising. People who traveled in the Ashtons' social circle weren't likely to mingle with the likes of Leila McGuire.

Callie felt uncomfortable for the first few minutes, but then she caught a glimpse of herself in a mirror and it restored her self-confidence. She looked pretty. So far, no one had recognized her. For this night, she would be Claire Thompson, a lady to the manor born. She would dance and laugh, and if she didn't say too much, she might just get by with her pretense.

And Monday morning, she'd go straight to the bank and pay off the note.

An hour later, they were called to dinner.

Callie could hardly keep from gawking as Richard escorted her into the dining room. Silver candelabras were placed at intervals on the long, damask-covered table. The china was the finest Callie had ever seen. Long-stemmed crystal glasses sparkled in the candlelight. The silverware was highly polished, heavy in her hand.

And the food! It just kept coming, course after course, each more pleasing to the palate than the last. She wondered if Duncan Stryker had thrown such lavish parties, if these same people had gathered under his roof. She had a crazy urge to stand up and announce that she was Leila McGuire's daughter, just to see what kind of a reaction it would elicit.

She glanced at Richard and saw him smiling at her.

"Having a good time, Claire?"

"Yes, thank you."

"Andre's a wonderful chef, don't you think?"

Callie nodded. "Quite adequate," she remarked, mimicking the haughty voice of the lady seated to her left.

Richard smothered his laugh with his napkin, then squeezed Callie's knee.

"No one would ever guess that you didn't belong here."

"But I do belong," Callie replied. "You paid me five thousand dollars to be here, remember?"

"I meant it as a compliment," Richard said. "Anyone would think you've been attending these soirees your whole life. The way you act, the way you talk—why, any one would think you were born to royalty."

"But I was," Callie whispered, forcing a smile. "My mother was the queen of the Miner's Rest, didn't you know?"

Richard frowned. "Don't talk like that. Someone might hear you."

Suddenly she didn't care if the whole world heard her. What was she doing here, anyway, pretending to be someone she wasn't?

She should have stayed home, she thought, and then remembered that it was because of the Rocking S that she was here.

When the meal was over, Richard took her arm and they went into the ballroom. It was the biggest room Callie had ever seen.

When the orchestra began to play, Richard led her out on the dance floor and they waltzed around the room. He was a wonderful dancer, though not as graceful as Caleb. She remembered how Caleb had danced with her in her room, his arms holding her close, but not too close, his turbulent gray eyes filled with desire.

She felt a sudden longing to be held in his arms again, to hear his voice, know the touch of his hands, taste his kisses. With cold-blooded determination, she reminded herself that he had lied to her about the ranch, that he had proposed to her simply to gain control of property that was rightfully hers.

"Hey?"

The sound of Richard's voice drew her back to the present. "I'm sorry, did you say something?"

"Would you like a glass of champagne?"

"Yes, thank you."

She stood near an open door while he went to fetch their drinks, smiling at those who passed by. She felt as if she were living someone else's life, as if Callie McGuire had ceased to exist the minute she entered the Ashton mansion. It was a strange feeling, like being inside someone else's skin.

She felt a twinge of apprehension when she saw Mrs. Ashton walking toward her.

"Hello, Claire," Dolores said. "Are you having a good time?"

"Yes, thank you."

"We haven't see you before. Have you known Richard long?"

"A few years."

Dolores Ashton frowned. "Is your family from around here?"

"No, I'm from Denver." The lie slid easily past her lips, reminding her of other lies. Caleb's lies.

"I see." Dolores Ashton smiled as she saw her son coming toward them. "Ah, here's Richard now. I'll leave you two alone. Do enjoy yourself, Claire."

"Thank you, ma'am."

"Is my mother playing matchmaker?" Richard asked as he handed Callie a glass of champagne.

"No. What makes you think that?"

"Oh, she's been trying to marry me off for years. She thinks it's time I settled down and gave her grandchildren."

"And you don't think so?"

"I'm too young to get married."

"Me, too."

Callie sipped her champagne, loving the way the bubbles tickled her nose.

"This is wonderful," she murmured, draining her glass.

"Here," Richard said, handing her his drink. "You can have mine, too."

"Don't you want it?"

"I'll get some more later."

For the next hour, Callie danced and drank champagne. She smiled at Richard, thinking that perhaps he wasn't as bad as she'd painted him. He laughed at her jokes, kept her glass filled with "the bubbly," as he called it, and paid her outrageous compliments which he assured her were nothing but the truth.

Callie was breathing rather hard, having just completed a lively polka, when he suggested that they go outside.

"Oh, that's a good idea," Callie agreed. "I could use some fresh air."

Taking her arm, Richard led her out onto the veranda, then down two flights of stairs to the gardens.

He slipped his arm around her waist as they walked down a twisting path lined with rosebushes.

"I think you might have had a little too much to drink," he remarked when she swayed against him.

"Do you think so?" Callie asked. She blinked up at him. "But it was so good."

"You're not used to spirits, are you?"

"No. My mother wouldn't let me drink. She wouldn't let me gamble, either." Callie giggled. "Once, she shot a man in the foot because he tried to kiss me."

"Have you been with a lot of men?"

Callie shook her head. "None. Mother wouldn't allow it."

"You don't have to lie to me."

"I'm not lying."

"What about Stryker?"

"What about him?"

"Didn't he . . . I mean, you lived in his house."

Callie stared at him coolly, offering no reply. Her relationship with Caleb was none of Richard's business.

Richard frowned, wondering if he'd been wrong about Callie McGuire. Maybe they'd all been wrong. Maybe she wasn't like her mother at all.

Then again, maybe she was just playing hard to get.

Coming to a halt, he drew her into his arms.

Callie gasped in surprise as Richard pulled her close, but before she could protest, his mouth closed on hers. She put her hands on his shoulders and tried to push him away, but he held her fast, his lips grinding against her own.

He was breathing hard when he let her go. "You've been kissed before."

"So?"

"So I almost believed that innocent act of yours, that's all."

"What do you mean?"

"All that talk about being a virgin. What do you take me for, a fool?"

"Just because I've been kissed doesn't mean I've . . ."

She shrieked as his hand closed over her arm. Then he was dragging her into the shadows, pushing her against the garden wall, his body pressing relentlessly against hers.

"I paid five thousand dollars for this night," he growled, "and I intend to get my money's worth."

"Let me go!"

"Not a chance."

She tried to push him away, but the weight of his body held her immobile. She could feel the heat of his breath on her face as he bent toward her, and then he was kissing her again, his lips tasting of champagne and cigars, his hands hard and cruel on her shoulders as he ground his pelvis against hers.

Repulsed, she twisted her head to the side and then, taking a deep breath, she brought her knee up hard and fast, catching him square in the crotch.

Air whooshed out of Richard's lungs in a painful gasp. Stumbling backward, he dropped to his knees, a string of curses falling from his lips.

Lifting her skirts, Callie ran down the path toward the side gate. Lifting the latch, she hurried out onto the street, turned left, and ran as fast as her legs would carry her. The sound of Richard's voice spurred her on, and she headed for the only haven she knew, praying that he was home, that he would give her shelter one more time.

Caleb blinked at Callie in surprise. He'd been thinking about her all night, picturing her at the Ashtons' party, dancing with Richard, having the time of her life.

He'd never expected her to show up on his doorstep in the middle of the night.

"Lose your way, princess?" he asked.

"No. May I come in, please?"

"Sure."

He stepped back and motioned her inside, then followed her into the parlor. In the lamplight, he could see that her cheeks were flushed, her lips bruised. "Can I get you a drink?"

"No, thank you."

"So, what can I do for you?"

"Nothing, I . . . I was just . . ."

"Just out for a stroll and you decided to stop by and pay your respects? At one o'clock in the morning?"

"Yes . . . well, no, I . . ." She stared up at him, wondering what to say. For the first time, she noticed that he needed a shave. His shirt was badly wrinkled, as if he'd slept in it.

"I take it your little get-together with Richard didn't go as planned."

She glared up at him, hating the insinuation in his voice. She squared her shoulders and lifted her chin, ready to do battle. "I had a very nice time."

"Uh-huh. And that's why you came running down here in the middle of the night, to tell me what a good time you had."

Callie heaved an exasperated sigh. What was the use of trying to pretend?

"He tried to . . . to, you know, and I kicked him. There."

A faint grin tugged at Caleb's lips. "You're awfully good at kicking people 'there' as I recall. Sharp little knees. Very effective. What I don't understand is why you accepted his invitation in the first place."

"That's none of your business."

Caleb shrugged. For the moment, he put Richard Ashton from his mind and drank in the sight of Callie instead. The blue of her gown made her eyes sparkle like sapphires. She'd lost some of her hairpins in her wild flight, and her hair fell over her shoulders in a red-gold mass of curls.

"You look beautiful, Callie," he murmured, closing the short distance between them. "Your eyes are as blue as a high mountain lake in midsummer. And your hair . . ." He let his fingers slide through a silken ringlet. "It's as soft as doeskin, as bright as a flame."

Callie blinked up at him, stunned by his words. They were soft and sincere, almost poetic.

"And your lips . . ." He traced the line of her mouth with the tip of his finger. "So soft. So pink . . ."

It never occurred to her to push him away. He reached out to take her in his arms, and she swayed against him, lifting her face for his kiss, her eyelids fluttering down as his mouth covered hers.

Fire, hot sweet fire, roared through her veins, bringing to life every sense, every nerve, until she was tingling all over. He tasted of whiskey and tobacco. Richard Ashton had tasted much the same, yet his kisses had repulsed her while Caleb's made her heart beat fast and her pulse race with longing.

He drew away from her, just a little. Breathless, she gazed up into his dark eyes, feeling herself trapped in the web of his stare.

"Caleb, I . . ."

Her words were cut off by a sudden pounding at the front door.

"I wonder who that could be," Caleb mused.

"He wouldn't come here!"

"Wouldn't he? Let's go see."

Callie followed Caleb to the entry hall and stood back as he opened the front door.

"Where is she?" Richard demanded.

"She?"

"Don't play games with me, Stryker. Where's Callie McGuire?"

"Have you lost her?"

"Listen, you—"

"She's here." Caleb's voice cut across Richard's, silencing him. "And she's going to stay here."

"Not tonight. Tonight she's mine."

"Callie, do you want to go home with him?"

"No."

"You heard what she said. Now get off my porch before I shoot you for trespassing."

"Wait!" Callie unfastened the diamond necklace and bracelet and removed her earbobs. "Here," she said, thrusting the jewelry into Richard's hands. "Take these with you."

Ashton shoved the diamonds in his coat pocket, then glared at Caleb. "You won't get away with this, Stryker."

"Careful now, son. You're scaring me."

"You'll be sorry for this, you dirty half-breed. You don't belong in this town, with decent people."

"Go home, Ashton. The party's over."

"You haven't heard the last of this!"

Muttering an oath, Caleb slammed the door in Ashton's face.

"You shouldn't have done that," Callie said. "He's a very vindictive man."

"You afraid he'll come gunning for me?"

She shook her head. The mere idea was ludicrous.

"It's late," she said, suddenly overcome with weariness. "Would you mind if I stayed the night? I don't have any way to get back home."

She felt a flash of anger as she thought of the Rocking S, and how he'd lied to her. If she hadn't found the codicil to Duncan's will, she'd be Mrs. Caleb Stryker now, never knowing that the only reason he'd married her was for the ranch. The thought still hurt. She'd been so sure he cared for her, at least a little. But it wasn't affection he felt for her at all. He'd coveted the ranch and he'd been willing to marry poor little Callie McGuire to get it. She wondered briefly why he hadn't destroyed the letter and the will, then pushed the thought from her mind. It was over and done, and she'd never trust him again.

"Callie . . ."

He took a step toward her, and she backed away, afraid of the yearning that rose up inside her. She was tired and discouraged and the thought of being in his arms was all too tempting.

"Good night, Caleb."

She could feel him watching her as she made her way toward the stairs. It felt right to be in this house again, to run her hand over the banister, to walk down the hall to her room, the room next to Caleb's.

Sitting on the edge of the bed, she removed her dancing slippers, unfastened the blue silk dress and pulled it over her head, then removed her petticoats. Clad in her chemise and pantalets, she crawled under the covers and closed her eyes, wishing she'd never found the codicil to Duncan Stryker's will, wishing she'd never left this house.

# Chapter Twenty-five

She was gone the next morning.

Caleb let out a long sigh as he closed her bedroom door. He hadn't really expected Callie to stay, but some small part of him had hoped she wouldn't run off without at least saying good-bye.

He shook his head, disgusted with himself. He was getting maudlin in his old age, he mused as he went back into his own room. What he needed was a woman and a bottle, and when he'd satisfied those two basic appetites, it was time to go back to bounty hunting. That was something he knew, something he was good at. He ought to get the hell out of town before it was too late, before he found himself sniffing at Callie's skirts, begging her to forgive him. He didn't need her. He'd never needed any woman, and he never would.

He stared at his reflection in the mirror over the dresser.

"You poor stupid fool," he muttered. "You look like the devil."

For a moment, he wondered again who had taken a shot at him, and why.

Abruptly, he turned away from the mirror and headed downstairs. Bounty hunting was the answer, he told himself firmly. He'd pay off the loan on the Rocking S, find a buyer for the mansion, and get the hell out of town.

Caleb stared at George Webster. "What are you saying?"

"I'm saying, Mr. Stryker, that several things have happened in a short period of time. Miss McGuire came to see me first thing yesterday morning. She had five thousand dollars in cash, and she used it to pay off the note on the ranch. She now owns the Rocking S free and clear."

"Where the devil did she get five thousand dollars?"

"I didn't ask."

"I guess I won't be needing that loan after all."

"Yes, and it's just as well. I'm afraid your request for a loan was turned down."

"Turned down? Why?"

"I'm not at liberty to say."

"It wouldn't have anything to do with the fact that Richard Ashton is one of the bank's major stockholders, would it?"

Webster shuffled through the papers on his desk. "I'm not at liberty to say."

"I think you've said plenty. Give my regards to

Ashton next time you see him," Caleb said with a sneer. "Good day, Mr. Webster."

He left the bank, slamming the door behind him, then paused on the boardwalk, frowning thoughtfully.

Five thousand dollars. Where would Callie get five thousand dollars? Ashton, he thought. Ashton was the only one in town who'd lend her a dime.

*Tonight she's mine.* Ashton had spoken those words as though she'd been bought and paid for. And maybe she had. Maybe she'd taken the money and then changed her mind. That would explain why Ashton had been so angry.

Caleb shook his head. He couldn't believe it. He knew Callie too well to believe she'd bed Ashton or anyone else for five thousand dollars.

Or maybe he didn't know her at all.

"Hell," he muttered crossly, "why didn't she come to me?"

*And you'd have given it to her, I suppose,* his conscience chided. *Just like the last time. She only needed a thousand then, and look what happened.*

He cursed under his breath. Of course she wouldn't come to him. He'd lied to her about the ranch, lied to her about why he wanted to marry her. Hell, he'd been lying to her from the start. And to himself, as well.

Caleb stared at the empty bottle in his hand. Too many cigarettes and too much whiskey had left him with a hangover the size of the Grand Canyon and a mouth that tasted like the inside of a spittoon. Muttering an oath, he threw the bottle across the floor. Nothing helped, he thought.

Sleeping didn't help. Every time he closed his eyes, Callie's image rose in his mind, her eyes soft and blue, her skin smooth and creamy, her hair a wealth of color that tempted his hand.

Drink didn't help. He'd dived headfirst into a bottle of scotch and he could still see her face, still see the hurt in her eyes when she'd accused him of lying to her.

With a sigh, he closed his eyes.

"*Ina,*" he murmured. "What should I do?"

*What you have always done, cinski.*

"*Ina?*"

*I am here.*

He opened his eyes, expecting to see his mother's face, but there was only darkness in the room.

"I must be a lot drunker than I thought," Caleb mumbled, then went suddenly still as he felt a hand in his hair. Her hand.

*It will be all right.* He heard the sound of her voice, low and soft near his ear. *Don't let your pride get in the way again.*

He felt her spirit whisper past him, a tangible presence in the darkened room; he caught the faint scent that had been hers alone, and then she was gone.

Caleb blinked into the darkness. A dream? Too much booze? Slowly, he shook his head. She'd been there, beside him.

"Thanks, Ma," he murmured, and fell into a deep, dreamless sleep.

He woke feeling better than he had any right to feel. Going upstairs, he took a bath, washed his hair, and shaved for the first time in days.

He knew what he wanted now, and he meant to have it, even if he had to get down on his hands and knees, even if he had to crawl on his belly like a snake.

Dressing quickly, Caleb buckled his gunbelt in place, grabbed his hat, and left the house. The buckskin wasn't happy to see him so early in the morning. He stamped his feet and tossed his head, then swelled up like a bullfrog when Caleb swung the saddle in place. Caleb punched the mare in the flank, then quickly tightened the cinch.

"I know, I know," Caleb said as he swung into the saddle. "It's early and you haven't had breakfast. But neither have I."

He was riding down 16th Street when he saw Angela Bristol standing outside Doctor A.J. Gray's office.

He reined the buckskin in that direction. "Hey, Angie, what's wrong?"

"Cal . . . Oh, Cal, it's Dad. He . . ." The rest of her words were swallowed up by tears.

Dismounting, Caleb hurried toward her. "Angie, what happened?"

"His heart . . . it just . . . quit. He's gone, Cal. Dad's gone!"

Caleb gathered Angie into his arms and held her while she cried. He couldn't believe it. He'd always thought Joe Brigman would live forever.

"When did it happen?"

"Late last night. Mother said he was going over the ranch accounts when he just slumped forward. She thought at first that he'd fallen asleep. Oh, Cal, I can't believe he's gone."

"I know. Come on, I'll take you home."

"We won't have a home, now that's Dad's gone."

"Don't be silly. You and your mother can stay at the ranch as long as you want."

"That's very generous of you, Cal, but I don't think your fiancée will want us to stay."

"Let me worry about that. How'd you get to town?"

"In the buggy. It's out back."

"Come on, I'll take you home."

Caleb tied the buckskin to the back of the buggy, lifted Angie onto the seat, and vaulted up beside her. Taking up the reins, he clucked to the team.

"What do you think your mother will do now?" Caleb asked after a while.

"I don't know. She said something about going back East to stay with her sister."

"You'll go with her, I guess."

Angie looked up, her gaze meeting his. "I don't want to."

"Angie . . ."

"You know what I want."

"I hardly think this is the time to talk about it."

"I think it's the perfect time. What's wrong between you and your fiancée, Cal?"

"I'm afraid that's none of your business, Angie."

"Why don't you call off your engagement and marry me?" She placed her hand on his thigh and squeezed it softly, suggestively. "I'll make you happy."

Caleb grunted softly. He'd made a mess of things, but he hoped to change that.

"Angie . . ."

"Just think about it."

"No." He took her hand from his thigh, held it a moment, then let it go. "I love Callie. Nothing you can say or do will ever change that."

"You're making a mistake."

"I don't think so. Angie, why don't you give Tom

another chance? Your dad thought he was the right man for you. Maybe he was right."

"Maybe. Tom's a wonderful man. Honest and hard-working. But he doesn't make me feel the way you do."

Caleb shook his head in frustration. "It won't work, Angie. I'm sorry."

"Me, too."

They rode the rest of the way back to the ranch in silence.

When they reached the Brigman home, Caleb lifted Angie from the carriage, then walked her into the house.

Joe's wife, Emily, met them at the door. She was a pretty woman, with graying brown hair and light blue eyes.

"Good morning, Caleb."

"Emily. I'm sorry about Joe. If there's anything I can do, you be sure and let me know."

"Thank you, Caleb. Would you like something to drink? Coffee, or perhaps a glass of lemonade?"

Caleb shook his head. The last thing he wanted was to be trapped in the house with Angie.

"The funeral will be day after tomorrow at the Methodist church."

"I'll be there."

He gave Emily a hug, told Angie good-bye, and left the house.

Moments later, he was heading for the ranch house. And Callie.

Callie's heart skipped a beat when she opened the front door and found Caleb standing there, hat in hand. She blinked up at him, unable to think of a thing to say. What was he doing here?

"Can I come in?" Caleb asked.

She knew she should tell him no. Instead, she opened the door.

Stepping into the entry hall, Caleb tossed his hat on the rack in the corner, then followed Callie into the kitchen.

"Sit down," Callie said, hating the way her heart warmed at the mere sight of him. "I was just peeling some apples for a pie."

Caleb pulled a chair from the table and straddled it, resting his arms on the back.

"What brings you out here?" Callie asked.

"I saw Angie in town. She told me about her father, and I brought her home."

Callie nodded. "It was so sudden. There was nothing we could do." She lifted her hand in a gesture of helplessness. "He was gone before the doctor got here."

"You'll be needing a new foreman."

"Yes, I guess so."

"I'd like to volunteer for the job."

"You!"

"Why not? Nobody cares about this place more than I do."

"But . . . that means you'd have to live here."

"Is that a problem?"

"You know it is."

"Callie . . ."

"No. I don't want to hear anything you have to say. I trusted you once."

"Dammit, Callie, if you'll just listen—"

"No, I'm through listening to you. You lied to me."

"I never lied to you."

"You never told me the truth, either. Why didn't you tell me the ranch was mine?"

"I was afraid you wouldn't marry me."

"I don't believe you."

"It's true. All right, I admit it, at first all I could think of was the ranch. It should have been mine. The old man knew how much I wanted it, and I decided if I had to marry you to get it, then I'd marry you."

"That's very flattering."

"Let me finish. After you called off the wedding, I realized I wanted you more than the ranch."

She wanted to believe him, but she didn't dare. He'd lied to her before. He was probably lying now.

"The day we were to be married, I kissed you, remember?"

Callie nodded. How could she ever forget that day, that kiss?

"Was that a lie?" he asked.

"I don't know."

"I want you for my wife, Callie."

She shook her head. "It won't work, Caleb. You lied to me about the ranch, and I'll never trust you again. I think you'd better go now."

"I'm staying, Callie, as your new foreman, whether you like it or not."

"You can't come in here and tell me what you're going to do. This is my ranch, remember? I'll choose my own foreman, if you don't mind."

"I do mind. I'm going crazy in the mansion. I need something to do. I won't bother you, Callie, I promise."

She was softening, he could see it in her eyes, so he played his hole card.

"Besides, I'll feel safer out here than in town after what happened the other day." It wasn't quite a lie, just a long stretch of the truth.

An image of Caleb, covered with blood, rose up in her mind. "Did the sheriff ever find out who shot at you?"

"No."

She stared at the bowl of apples in her lap, wondering what she should do. It was sheer madness to let Caleb stay. Even though she hated him, she couldn't deny the attraction that hummed between them. Even now, she longed to reach out and touch him, to take him in her arms and hold him close, to feel his lips on hers. She couldn't see him every day, talk to him, hear his voice, and hold on to her anger.

"I'll bunk with the cowboys," Caleb said. "Tomorrow I'll take a look around, see what needs to be done. I imagine you'll be going to the funeral?"

"Wait a minute! I haven't said you could stay."

"Shall I beg?"

He clasped his hands to his chest and looked at her through soulful eyes.

"Please, Callie, please let me stay."

"Stop it!"

He threw her a victorious smile. "I'll see you tomorrow, bright and early."

A wave of helplessness washed over Callie as she watched him walk out the back door.

He was here, on the ranch.

She'd see him every day.

But even as she railed at her own weakness, the thought of seeing Caleb, of being near him, made her heart beat deliciously fast.

Picking an apple out of the bowl, she began peeling it. Caleb liked apple pie.

# *Chapter Twenty-six*

Callie removed her hat and took the pins from her hair. Going to the window, she gazed down into the yard. Funerals were so depressing. She hoped she wouldn't have to go to another one for a long time. She thought of Duncan Stryker's funeral, attended by Cheyenne's most influential citizens, and then she thought about her mother's funeral. There had been only a few people at the grave-side service, and none of them would have been welcomed in the homes of Cheyenne's elite.

Most of the merchants in town had turned out for Joe Brigman's funeral. He'd been a resident of Cheyenne for years, well-liked and respected by all. Joe's wife, Emily, looked as if she'd aged ten years in the last three days. Angela, however, had managed to look quite lovely in her black mourning dress and veil.

Emily had invited Callie to the house after the funeral, but Callie had pleaded a headache and declined. Caleb had gone, of course, with Angela Bristol clinging to his arm.

Callie grimaced. Angela had hovered around Caleb, leaning heavily on his arm while the minister read over the grave, weeping against his shirt front when the service was over. It was obvious that Angela Bristol wanted Caleb in the most elemental way. It infuriated Callie that seeing the two of them together made her positively green with jealousy.

Sitting at the dressing table, she began to brush her hair, her mind filling with images of Caleb: Caleb offering condolences to Emily Brigman; Caleb standing beside the grave, his deep gray eyes filled with sadness as he said a last good-bye to the Rocking S foreman; Caleb helping Angela into the buggy for the ride back to the ranch.

She shook away the tendrils of jealousy that threatened to tie her heart in knots, but she couldn't shake Caleb's image from her mind. She saw him dancing with the Indians, looking as wild and untamed as any of them, remembered how he'd looked bending over her, whispering delightfully shocking things in her ear as he seduced her.

She blinked back tears. She had wanted to be his wife, had wanted to share the ranch with him. She had imagined them raising a family, had looked forward to riding out to the reservation each year to take cattle and supplies to the Indians.

She stared at her closet door. Inside, wrapped in layers of white tissue, was the wedding dress she'd never wear. She'd cried for hours the day she picked it up. Steeped in sorrow, she'd tried it on, her fingers lightly stroking the delicate material.

She should have sent it back, she thought, and then shrugged. She'd keep it as a reminder of . . .

She looked up, startled, at the sound of her bedroom door swinging open. Looking in the mirror, she saw Caleb standing in the doorway.

"You should have knocked," she admonished waspishly.

"I did."

"Oh, I guess I didn't hear you. What do you want?"

He swore softly, amazed that one little bit of a girl had so completely beguiled him. No other woman had ever taken root so deeply in his heart, or been so hard to win. He'd never had trouble with women before. Even when they learned he was a half-breed, it didn't matter. From the time he was twelve, he'd seen the way girls looked at him.

At first, he hadn't understood, but then, one day when he was about fifteen, he overheard a couple of grown women discussing him. He'd gone home and looked in his mother's full-length mirror, conscious of his appearance for the first time. It amused him that white women found him attractive, that they were intrigued by the color of his skin, that they admired the width of his shoulders, the way he smiled. It was knowledge he had put to good use from time to time.

Caleb frowned. Callie didn't trust him anymore. She might never trust him again. But he meant to have her, by fair means or foul. She might not have faith in him, he mused, but she wanted him, maybe more than she knew. He was keenly aware of her long furtive glances, the way she trembled whenever he was near. He saw the tiny flame of desire that burned in her eyes, felt the attraction that hummed like a telegraph wire between them whenever they touched.

A slow smile curved the corners of Caleb's mouth. He would have Callie McGuire, one way or another. He would have her because he loved her—loved her stubbornness, her innocence. She had a face that hid nothing, eyes that were young, so young. And he wanted her as he wanted good whiskey to drink and fresh air to breathe.

"I asked you what you wanted," Callie reminded him, wishing he would stop looking at her as if she was a rabbit and he a hungry wolf.

"The south range, Miss McGuire," Caleb said. "I asked you what you wanted to do about the south range?"

"You're supposed to be the foreman," she snapped. "Do whatever you think is best."

She glared at Caleb, hating him for making her love him, hating herself for caring. She couldn't keep from remembering the night they had spent in the cabin, couldn't keep her body from remembering how wonderful it had been to lie in his arms while he taught her what it meant to be a woman.

A long moment passed, and the expression in Caleb's eyes changed. He hadn't forgotten that night in the cabin, she realized, not for a minute. If she but said the word, he would take her in his arms, here and now, and do it all again. To her chagrin, she wished he would do just that.

Caleb gazed at Callie, easily reading her thoughts. He considered telling her that he loved her, but he had a feeling he could swear that he loved her from now until the end of time and she'd never believe him.

The trouble was, she had no reason to believe him.

"Is that all, Mr. Stryker?"

"Yeah."

With a sigh, he left the room and closed the door behind him.

Callie avoided Caleb as much as possible during the next three weeks, speaking to him only when necessary, and then only about matters that pertained to the ranch.

She had listened as he told her about branding and castrating and the round-up next spring, about driving the cattle to the railhead and the current price of beef, about the feasibility of buying a new bull.

On one visit, he had mentioned that there was a hole in the roof of the barn, then went on to say that one of the cow ponies had stepped in a prairie dog hole and broken its leg and had to be destroyed.

And now Caleb was here again, one shoulder braced negligently against the door jamb between the kitchen and the parlor, his hat pushed back on his head, looking lean and masculine and very, very desirable. Callie blinked at him, aware that he'd asked her a question, something to do with hay and feed.

Callie frowned. She had no idea what he had asked her, but it didn't matter. She was certain he was just trying to make her feel stupid because there was more to running a cattle ranch than she'd ever dreamed of, and she was ignorant of most of it. No doubt he hoped she'd admit she had no business keeping the Rocking S and would sell it to him. But that would never happen.

While she was trying to decide how to handle such a disturbing revelation, Angela Bristol came to call.

Callie couldn't hide the look of dismay on her face when she opened the front door and saw Angela. The woman couldn't have picked a worse time for a visit. Callie had been in the midst of cleaning the hearth when Caleb came to call, and her apron was covered with soot. Her hair, quickly twisted into a knot on top of her head, was hanging precariously to one side.

"Good afternoon," Angela said brightly. She held up a covered basket. "My mother made bread today and thought you might like a loaf."

"Thank you. That was very kind of her."

Callie let out a deep breath, and then, none too graciously, invited Angela inside. "Would you like a cup of coffee?"

"Yes, thank you," Angela said, handing Callie the basket. A smile, as warm as a Texas summer, lit her face when she saw Caleb in the parlor. "Hello, Cal," she purred.

"Angie."

Callie stared at the two of them and grimaced. Fresh bread, indeed! Angela Bristol had come here for the sole purpose of seeing Caleb. She was dressed immaculately in a day dress of apple-green muslin that made her eyes sparkle and her skin glow. A wide sash of emerald-green satin spanned her narrow waist; a ribbon of the same color was tied in a perky bow at the side of her head.

Standing next to Angela, Callie felt like one of Cinderella's ugly stepsisters.

"I'll make the coffee," Callie said, and taking the basket, she went into the kitchen.

She quickly ground some coffee beans, filled the pot with water, added the coffee, and put the pot on the stove.

While she waited for the coffee to heat, she took off her grimy apron, washed her hands, and removed the pins from her hair. Not for Caleb, she told herself as she combed her fingers through her hair, and not because Angela was there.

When the coffee was hot, she took down a tray, loaded it with cups and saucers, the sugar bowl, a small pitcher of cream, and the coffeepot, and carried it into the parlor.

Angela was sitting beside Caleb on the sofa, gazing raptly into his face, her smile so sweet it was almost sickening.

" . . . and I just don't know what I'll do," Angela said, placing her hand on Caleb's forearm. "I'll be so alone."

"You can stay at the old house until you find another place," Caleb said, gently disengaging Angela's hand from his arm.

"Oh, Cal," Angela gushed. "You're so kind."

"Yes, isn't he?" Callie remarked.

She set the tray on the table beside the sofa, then looked at Caleb, her expression grim.

A faint smile tugged at the corners of Caleb's mouth. She hadn't said a word, but he knew Callie was thinking he had a lot of gall, telling Angela she could stay on at the ranch when it no longer belonged to him.

Angela looked up at Callie. "You don't mind, do you?"

"Of course not." Callie forced the words through her teeth, wishing she had a gun so she could shoot Caleb Stryker.

"How soon is your mother leaving?" Caleb asked.

"Day after tomorrow," Angela replied, her attention again focused entirely on Caleb. "Do you think you could help us load her trunks on the wagon?"

"Sure. I'll stop by tomorrow night."

"Coffee, Mrs. Bristol?" Callie asked, thrusting a cup under Angela's nose.

"Why, yes, thank you."

"Cream? Sugar?"

"Yes, please."

A knife seemed to be twisting in Callie's heart as she watched the way Caleb and Angela Bristol looked at each other, as if they were alone in the room. She wasn't jealous! She couldn't be jealous. She just didn't like being ignored in her own home. But if Angela Bristol batted her eyelashes at Caleb one more time, Callie thought she might hit her over the head with the fireplace poker.

Angela took her leave thirty minutes later. Callie slammed the door after her, then began gathering up the cups and saucers, slamming the dishes down on the tray, refusing to admit she was jealous of the other woman.

"Hey, Callie, take it easy."

"I'm fine."

Caleb couldn't smother the grin that twitched at his lips. "Want to tell me what's wrong?"

"Nothing's wrong. What could possibly be wrong?" She planted her hands on her hips and glared at him. "That woman! How dare she come into my house and act as though she belongs here and I don't."

"You wouldn't be jealous, would you?"

"Jealous? Don't be absurd!"

Callie took a step backward as Caleb closed the distance between them, intimidated by his nearness and by the look in his eye.

"I don't want Angie," he said, his voice as soft and warm as melting butter. "I never did. I want you. Just you."

Callie stared up at him. She wanted to run away, but her feet seemed frozen in place and she could only stand there, helpless, as he slanted his mouth over hers and kissed her.

He didn't close his eyes, and neither did she.

His eyes were as gray as the storm clouds that were hovering low in the sky. His mouth was warm and firm, and when she tried to pull away he cradled her head in his hand, holding her immobile as he continued to kiss her. It wasn't a kiss of passion or desire, merely a touching of his lips to hers, but Callie felt the heat of it clear to her toes.

Slowly, he lifted his mouth from hers.

"I want you," he said again. "Not the ranch. Just you."

His lips took possession of hers again, his arms circling her waist.

The strength went out of Callie's legs and she swayed against him, her hands pressed against his chest. Why was she fighting him?

His hands were stroking her back, sending little frissons of pleasure skittering along her spine, weakening her resolve. His mouth was warm and hot, branding her lips, searing her soul.

Her hands slid around his neck and she leaned against him, wanting to be closer.

He'd said he wanted her. Dared she believe him? How could she doubt him? His kiss deepened as his arms tightened around her, making her senses reel. She was drowning in pleasure, reveling in his nearness. She loved the touch of his hands, the taste of his lips. His tongue caressed hers, lightly enticing, and she was sorely tempted to give him what he wanted, everything he wanted. . . .

Callie twisted out of his embrace, her breath uneven as she glared up at him.

"No! It won't work. Not this time."

"Callie . . ."

"I don't believe you. You lied to me before. For all I know, you're lying now." She shook her head as he reached for her. "I think you'd better go."

A soft curse escaped Caleb's lips as he grabbed his hat and stomped out of the room.

Callie shivered as a cold blast of air swept through the room and settled in her heart.

She didn't see him for the next four days, but she knew of his whereabouts.

When she went out to gather eggs Tuesday morning, Slim McCoy mentioned that Caleb had driven Angela's mother into town to catch the train east, then driven Angela back home. Callie nodded curtly, trying not to think of Angela and Caleb alone in the house.

When she went to milk the cow Wednesday evening, Big George Geary told her that if she needed Caleb, he was over at the Brigman place, helping Miss Angela move furniture.

On Thursday, Slim informed her that Caleb had taken Mrs. Bristol into town to look at curtain material.

They returned Friday afternoon, according to Harvey Smith.

She didn't care. She refused to care. But she couldn't help wondering what they'd done in town for two days. Had they spent the night at the mansion? Had Angela slept in Caleb's bed, made him breakfast in the morning?

She stamped her foot, angry at the thought of Caleb with another woman, and angry because it made her angry.

He could do whatever he wanted. He was nothing to her. He had lied to her about the ranch. He wanted her. Oh, he admitted that all right, but if he loved her, what was he doing spending so much time with Angela Bristol? And why did it hurt so much?

She managed to remain cool and aloof when he came to the house the following night. All was well on the ranch, he said. The cattle were looking good. There would be plenty of hay for supplemental feed if they needed it during the coming winter, he remarked, then added that Old Fred Turley had predicted a mild winter.

"Thank you, Mr. Stryker," Callie said when he finished his report. "Good night."

"Callie . . ."

"Good night."

"All right, dammit, have it your way," he muttered, and settling his hat on his head, he left the house.

Callie stared after him until the night swallowed him up. Would he go to Angela Bristol now? Did he spend his nights with that woman? He was supposed to sleep in the bunkhouse. Did he? The cowhands seemed so eager to tell her everything else, it seemed odd that they never mentioned where Caleb spent his nights.

She threw herself into housekeeping as the autumn leaves began to fall. She mopped and waxed the parlor floor, dusted and polished the furniture, washed the kitchen cupboards inside and out, and all the dishes as well. On a clear day in mid-September, she shook out all the rugs and washed and ironed the curtains. She rearranged the furniture in the parlor and in her bedroom.

It rained on and off for the next two weeks, and she passed the time cleaning the bedrooms. The yellow one was nice, sunny and bright, and she guessed it had been a guest room. There didn't seem to be any personal belongings in the room, just a bed, a small chest, and a chair. The pink bedroom reminded her of a nursery that had been made over into a spare bedroom. There was nothing in the room to indicate it had once been a child's room, but she couldn't shake off the feeling that the room had known not only great joy, but a deep sadness as well.

The brown-and-white bedroom had been Caleb's. She knew it as surely as she knew the color of her hair. The bed was long and narrow, covered with a sturdy brown-and-white quilt. The curtains at the window were light brown, without lace or frills. There was a dark oak dresser, a commode, and a comfortable-looking brown leather chair.

She reminded herself that this was her house now, as she opened the dresser drawers. The first three were empty and she couldn't stifle a hint of disappointment. She had hoped to find some remnant of Caleb's past tucked inside one of the drawers.

Her breath caught in her throat when she opened the last drawer. Inside she found a buckskin shirt, leggings, and a pair of moccasins. She removed the clothing almost reverently. The shirt was soft to her touch. Long fringe dangled from the sleeves. The leggings were made of heavier buckskin, also fringed. The moccasins were unadorned but well-made.

Impulsively, she took off her shirtwaist and slipped into the buckskin shirt. It was a trifle large, but too small to fit him now, and she tried to remember how old Caleb had been when he left the Lakota.

Next, she held the leggings against her, but they were much too long; the moccasins were too big.

Still wearing the shirt, she moved about the room, running her hand over the quilt, looking out the window, trying to imagine how Caleb had felt when he lived here. She'd never known her own father, and she thought how sad it was that Caleb had hated his father. Such a waste, she mused, such a loss. She'd have given anything just to know who her father was.

She was staring out the window, watching the rain, when she realized that she was no longer alone in the room. She took a deep breath, willed her heart to stop pounding, as she turned around to face him.

"You thinking of joining up with the Sioux?" Caleb asked, gesturing at the buckskin shirt.

"No, I . . . I was just . . ."

"Snooping?"

"Certainly not," she replied indignantly. "This is *my* house, remember?"

"As if you'd ever let me forget," he retorted, and Callie winced at the barely contained bitterness in his voice.

"Did you want something, Mr. Stryker?"

"You know what I want."

"Angela Bristol?" Callie remarked with a sugary smile.

"You."

Callie swallowed hard, wishing he'd leave her alone, wishing that his nearness didn't make her think of dark nights and warm, masculine arms.

"Is that what you came here to tell me?"

"No. I came to tell you that you've got a visitor."

"A visitor?"

"Richard Ashton is waiting for you in the parlor."

"Richard! What does he want?"

"Why don't you ask him and find out?" Caleb looked at her and grinned. "You might want to change your clothes first."

"I will, thank you."

With a nod, Caleb left the room, closing the door behind him.

Callie entered the parlor a few minutes later. "Good afternoon, Mr. Ashton," she said coolly. "What brings you out here on such a dreary day?"

"I came to see you, of course," Richard replied. "May I sit down?"

"I'd rather you didn't."

"Listen, Callie, I'm sorry about what happened at the party. I'd had a little too much champagne."

He shrugged. "You can't blame a man for trying to kiss a beautiful woman."

"Yes, you can. Good day, Mr. Ashton."

"Callie, I know we haven't gotten along too well in the past, but I'd like to change all that. I came out here to ask you to marry me."

"Marry you!" Callie stared at him as if he'd suddenly grown two heads and a tail.

"It's no secret that I've wanted you for years."

"I know, but . . . marriage!" Callie shook her head. "I don't think I'll ever marry anyone."

"Will you at least think about it?"

"No. It would never work. Your parents would never approve. You couldn't even tell them who I was at the party that night."

"They know now."

"They do?"

"Yeah. My mother was furious that I'd deceived her. I'll admit, she's not crazy about the idea, but she'll come around."

"And your father?"

"He's all for it. He was quite taken with you, you know. Think about it, Callie. You'd be a wealthy woman. We could travel all over the world. Italy, Spain, England, France."

It was tempting, Callie thought, except for one thing. She didn't love Richard. She would never love him.

"I know it's sudden," Richard remarked, "but think about it, won't you?"

"I'd rather not drag it out. I'm afraid the answer is no."

"It's because of him, isn't it?" Richard said, his voice edged with anger.

"I don't know what you mean."

"You know darn well what I mean. It's Stryker. You're still trying to get your hooks into him, aren't you?"

"Definitely not." Callie crossed the room and opened the front door. "I think you'd better leave."

"I'll go," Richard said. "But I'm not giving up."

It was all Callie could do not to slam the door after him. The nerve of the man, proposing to her after the way he'd behaved the night of the party. Why would he want to marry her?

"Is he gone?"

Callie whirled around to see Caleb standing in the kitchen doorway.

"Have you been eavesdropping, Mr. Stryker?"

Caleb shrugged. "I was having a cup of coffee. I couldn't help overhearing. Are you thinking about accepting his offer?"

"Of course not."

"He's gonna be a wealthy man someday."

"I don't care. If and when I marry, it won't be for money."

"No?"

"No. I want to marry a man I love, a man I respect, one who loves and respects me."

"Got anyone in mind?"

His voice, low and husky, made her stomach quiver and her heart skip a beat. His eyes, dark and smoldering, were watching her intently; his hands, shoved into his pockets, were balled into tight fists.

"No," she answered. "No one."

"Are you sure, Callie?"

His words reached out to her, wrapping around her like skeins of fine silk. She heard the longing in his voice, the faint note of hope.

Stubbornly, she jerked up her chin, refusing to be seduced out of the ranch by the sound of his voice. "Quite sure."

His expression changed then, the warmth in his gaze turning cold and hard, as if he had shut an invisible door between them.

"Good-bye, Callie." His tone was cool now, distant.

Callie stared at him, frightened by the gulf that had opened between them. Had he looked at outlaws like that, his face impassive, his eyes as gray and cold as dead ashes?

"Good-bye," she murmured. There was a faint note of sadness in her voice, and as she watched Caleb leave the house, she wondered if he'd heard it, too.

# *Chapter Twenty-seven*

Angela smiled at Caleb as she handed him a cup of coffee. He was spending more and more time at her house.

At first, she had flirted with him shamelessly, hinting that all he had to do was ask the right question and all the barriers would be lowered, but he hadn't responded to her brazen invitation, and so she had changed her tactics. He wasn't looking for physical satisfaction, she realized, just a place to go, someone to talk to. And she intended to be that someone.

Another woman might have been insulted, even hurt, but not Angela. She was a patient woman. She'd wanted Caleb Stryker since she was twelve years old and she meant to have him. Soon, he would realize he'd made a mistake in pursuing that whore's daughter, and then he'd come to her.

In the meantime, he was here, in the parlor, filling the room with his presence. He had been handsome as a boy, but he was a man now, rugged, hard, filled with a degree of quiet assurance and self-confidence that she found highly attractive. She knew it was improper for her to be alone in the house with him, but Caleb had never been one to worry about propriety, and she was too pleased to have him there to care what anyone else might think.

She thought of his past, replete with tales of shoot-outs and dangerous encounters with outlaws, and knew such exploits should have repelled her, but they only added to his mystique. And the fact that he was a half-breed—dark, mysterious, forbidden—made him more exciting than any other man she had ever known.

Her first romantic fantasies had been about Caleb. He'd been the first boy to kiss her, the first one to notice her, and she'd never forgotten him. During the course of her marriage, she had often closed her eyes and pretended it was Caleb making love to her. She had wanted him then, and she wanted him now.

"More coffee?" she asked.

"No, thanks. It's getting late. I should be going."

She wanted to beg him to stay; instead, she stood up and handed him his hat. "Will I see you tomorrow night?"

"Sure." He smiled down at her. "Thanks, Angie."

"For what?"

"For listening. For not judging." He gave her a quick kiss on the cheek. "For the coffee. Good night."

"Good night." She stood at the door, her fingers

lightly rubbing the place where he had kissed her as she watched him ride out of the yard.

Tomorrow she'd go into town and buy some material for a new dress. A blue dress, she thought. It had always been his favorite color. Perhaps, if she was lucky, she would wear it for him Thanksgiving day. Perhaps, by then, she'd have something to be truly thankful for.

Richard Ashton was crossing the street when he saw Joe Brigman's daughter leaving the mercantile. Changing direction, he hurried after her, frowning as he tried to remember her name. Annie? Amelia? Angela!

"Mrs. Bristol. Angela, wait up."

Angie glanced over her shoulder, surprised to see Richard Ashton hurrying to catch up with her. She hardly knew the man.

"May I help you?" she asked politely.

"I . . . uh, wondered if you'd take a message to Miss McGuire for me."

"What sort of message?"

Richard smiled. "A personal one."

"Oh?"

"You look like a woman who can keep a secret," Richard remarked. Taking her arm, he led her down the street, away from prying eyes and ears.

"What sort of secret?" Angie asked.

"Are you and Callie good friends?"

"Not really."

"Oh. I'd assumed that was the reason you were staying out at the ranch."

Angie studied Ashton's face. He was a handsome man, not as rugged-looking or virile as Caleb, but then few men were.

"Can *you* keep a secret, Mr. Ashton?"

"If necessary."

"I'm staying because of Caleb."

A slow smile tugged at the corners of Richard's mouth.

"I see. Maybe we can help each other. Come on, let's go someplace where we can talk in private."

Callie stared at Caleb, unable to hide her disappointment. He was going to spend Sunday with Angela.

"She's all alone now that her ma's gone," he said, looking at Callie intently, "so I thought I'd keep her company. You don't mind, do you?"

"Of course not," Callie answered stiffly. "You're free to do whatever you want."

"That's right," he said brusquely.

Callie blinked back tears as he left the house. He didn't want Angela Bristol to be alone, Callie thought bleakly. Apparently he didn't care that she'd be alone.

Well, she wouldn't stay at the ranch, she thought She'd have Big George hitch up the buggy and take her into town to spend the day with Fanny.

And that was exactly what she did.

It was a pleasant day, cool and clear, but as Callie made small talk with Fanny, she couldn't help thinking of Caleb spending the day with Angela, the two of them alone in the old house.

Fanny insisted that she spend the night, and Callie didn't argue, knowing she'd never make it back to the ranch before dark. But the truth was, she simply couldn't face going home to an empty house.

The next afternoon, after lunching with Fanny,

she went into town, intending to stop at Killian's Mercantile and pick up a few things as long as she was there.

She was about to enter the store when she saw Angela Bristol walking toward her.

"Good morning, Miss McGuire."

"Good morning," Callie replied politely, conscious of other people on the street.

"Where's Caleb?" Angie asked, a smug smile on her face.

"Don't you know?"

"As a matter of fact, I do."

With great effort, Callie restrained the urge to slap Angela across the face. "Good day," she said curtly.

"A friend of mine asked me to ask you to reconsider his offer."

*Richard,* Callie thought angrily. "When you see Mr. Ashton again, tell him the answer is still no."

"You'll never have Caleb," Angie said. "Why don't you give him up?"

"I don't want him," Callie replied, almost choking on the lie.

"I'm glad. I've been waiting for Caleb my whole life."

"He's yours," Callie snapped. "But the house you're living in is mine. I want you out of it by tonight!"

"But—" Angie bit back her protest. "I'll leave," she said, her voice filled with venom, "and I'll take Caleb with me."

Fighting back tears of rage, Callie went to the livery and hired a buggy and driver to take her home. She dashed the tears from her eyes with the back of her hand. Curse that woman! She could have Caleb, and welcome to him!

Callie's shoulders slumped dispiritedly. What would she do if Caleb left? She didn't know anything at all about running a ranch except what Caleb had taught her, and she still had a lot to learn.

Determination stiffened her spine. She didn't need Caleb Stryker. She'd hire someone else to be the foreman—Big George, perhaps. Or maybe she'd do it herself. She almost laughed out loud. Who was she trying to kid? The men weren't going to take orders from her, even if she knew what orders to give.

Caleb was waiting for her when she got home. They had hardly spoken since the night Richard came to call. Caleb had withdrawn from her in a way that was frightening, and final. He made his nightly reports at the front door, refusing to enter the house. He never spoke her name, never touched her or looked at her in that provocative way that had once made her insides melt and her knees weak. It was as if they were strangers, as if the intimacy they had shared on a rainy night had never happened.

"Is something wrong?" Callie asked after thanking the driver.

"Richard Ashton came by to see you this morning."

"Oh. What did he want?"

"I don't know. I thought maybe you did."

"I don't." She started toward the house. "Is that all?"

"Yeah."

A muscle worked in Caleb's jaw as he fought down the urge to grab Callie and give her a good shake. He was angry with her, and even more angry with himself, because he didn't know how to reach past the ever-widening gulf between them.

"I saw Angela in town," Callie said, her voice curt. "I told her to leave the ranch today."

"Why?"

"Because I don't like her."

"Jealous?"

"Of course not."

"Then why make her leave? She's got no place to go."

"I'm sure she could find work at one of the saloons. Of course, then you'd have to pay for her time."

Caleb uttered a savage oath, and Callie took a step back, frightened by the rage that flared in the depths of his eyes. And then her own anger sparked to life.

"What's the matter?" she asked sweetly. "Isn't she worth the ride to town?"

Caleb glared at her, his fists clenched, too angry to speak.

"I want her gone by tonight," Callie said, and swept past him before he could say another word.

Moments later, Angela rode into the yard, her eyes red-rimmed.

"Oh, Caleb," she sobbed, and practically fell off the horse into his arms. "I have to leave."

"I know."

He held her for a moment, wondering if he wouldn't be smart to give up on Callie and take what Angela was offering.

"Where will I go?" Angie sobbed quietly. "What will I do?"

"I'll think of something. Go on home and pack. I'll see you tonight."

She smiled at him through her tears. "Oh, Caleb, I don't know what I'd do without you."

He lifted her into the saddle and gave her arm a squeeze. "Go along now. I'll see you later."

"Promise?"

"Yeah."

"You're so good to me," she said, and leaning forward, she kissed him. "See you tonight."

Glancing past Angie, Caleb swore softly as he saw Callie standing at the window, her face pale, her blue eyes shimmering with tears. She held his gaze for a long moment before she dropped the curtain in place and turned away.

It was just after dusk when Caleb arrived at the old house. He found Angela inside, sitting on the edge of the worn brown sofa, a forlorn expression on her face.

"Ready to go?" he asked.

She managed a brave smile. "I would be, if I had somewhere to go."

"You can stay at the mansion."

"Oh, Caleb, I couldn't."

"You got any better ideas?"

Slowly, she shook her head.

"Let's go then."

She didn't have anything to take other than a large valise and a couple of boxes that contained her clothes and a few personal effects. The furniture belonged to the Rocking S; the other things, knick-knacks and the like that had once brightened the house, had belonged to her mother.

She scooted close to Caleb as he took up the reins and clucked to the horse.

"It's cold," she remarked.

"Here." He took off his jacket and draped it

around her shoulders. "That better?"

"Yes, thank you."

"What will you do now, Angie?"

"I don't know. I guess I'll have to go stay with mother."

"You might like the East."

Angela wrinkled her nose. "I don't think so." She slid a glance at Caleb, thinking that she had no intention of going East or anywhere else. "I guess I'll have to find some sort of employment. Do you need a housekeeper?"

Caleb grunted. That's what he'd hired Callie for, he mused with a wry grin, and look how that had turned out!

"I'll have to do something to earn my keep," Angie remarked. "If you won't hire me, I'll have to find someone who will."

"You're hired."

"Will you be coming to town often?"

"I don't know."

"Caleb, why don't you stay there with me? Callie doesn't want you. Why do you stay? Oh, Cal, we'd be so good together. I'd do anything for you. Anything."

"Angie . . ."

"Think about it?"

He nodded, knowing if he didn't give in, she'd nag him all the way into town. And maybe she was right. Maybe he should leave the ranch. Callie didn't want him. Maybe she never would.

It was late when they reached Cheyenne. Caleb helped Angie from the buckboard, unloaded her belongings, and carried them into the house.

Angie could only stare as Caleb showed her around. She'd never been in a house that was so large, so grand. She'd dreamed of such a place, envied those who lived in such elegance, and now she was here. Perhaps for good.

"Make yourself at home," Caleb remarked. "If you need anything, just go over to Brewsters and have him put it on my account."

"That's very generous of you, Cal."

"Well, I can't have you starving to death, can I?"

"You could. You don't owe me anything."

"You're my friend, Angie. About the only one I've got."

They were standing in the hallway outside the bedroom she'd chosen to sleep in. Now she gazed up at him, her green eyes aglow.

"I'd like to be more than your friend, Cal," she whispered, and standing on tiptoe, she pressed her lips to his.

For a moment, he didn't respond, and then his arms went around her and he drew her close. She was warm and oh, so willing. Her lips were soft, yielding, inviting. Her body was soft against his, silently entreating as she leaned her hips into his. It felt good, holding a woman in his arms, a woman who didn't deny she wanted him, a woman who didn't say no when she meant yes.

Sensing that he was on the verge of surrender, Angie pressed herself against him, a soft moan of longing rising in her throat as her fingers kneaded the strong muscles in his back. At last, she thought, the moment she had been dreaming of, waiting for.

And then, abruptly, he took his mouth from hers and stepped away.

"I can't, Angie."

"Why? I want you. I know you want me."

Caleb stared at her. Was it Angie he wanted, or just a warm body to soothe his pride? Into his mind came a picture of Callie as she'd been that night in the line shack, her eyes cloudy with passion, her lips swollen from his kisses, her hair shimmering in the firelight.

"Cal?"

"It won't work, Angie. I'm sorry."

She wanted to yell at him, to vent her anger and frustration in screams of rage.

Instead, she took a deep breath and said, "I understand. Good night, Caleb."

When he rewarded her with a look of admiration, she knew she'd done the right thing.

"Good night, Angie. I don't know when I'll be back."

"I'll be here." She gazed up at him, her eyes shining with unshed tears. She moistened her lips with the tip of her tongue; the movement was sensual, provocative. "I'll always be here."

Caleb nodded, feeling a sudden weight settle on his shoulders. He had a woman he wanted, and a woman who wanted him, and he thought it would take the wisdom of Solomon and the patience of Job to untangle the mess he'd made.

# Chapter Twenty-eight

Callie sat at the front window, staring out at the rain. What had started as a mild shower had quickly turned into a full-fledged storm. Thunder cracked across the heavens, lightning split the skies, while the wind blew angrily across the face of the land.

She pulled the blanket tighter around her shoulders, too comfortable to get up and add more wood to the dwindling fire. As usual, when she wasn't busily engaged in some household task, her thoughts turned to Caleb and Angela. She'd heard that Angela was staying at the mansion. Was Caleb in town even now, with her? Was he sitting at the front window with Angela, watching the storm, or were they snuggled on the sofa, sharing a glass of brandy before a cozy fire?

Callie tried to shake the images from her mind; instead, Caleb's ruggedly handsome face rose up before her, his gray eyes dark, his arms reaching for her, his lips warm and inviting. All too clearly, she remembered that night in the cabin. Until then, she had never yearned for a man's touch, never spent her nights dreaming of being in a man's arms or wasted whole days imagining what it would be like to be Caleb Stryker's wife.

*Next time,* she thought, *next time he takes me in his arms, I'll say yes.*

A little gasp of shock and dismay erupted from Callie's lips. What was she thinking? It was sinful, lying with a man who wasn't your husband. It was bad enough she'd made one mistake, but at least that had been done in the heat of the moment. But to set out to deliberately do something she knew was wrong was certainly a transgression of the worst kind.

But she was so lonely. Especially now, with the rain pounding on the roof and the wind howling around the eaves. She wanted someone to talk to, someone to cuddle with. She wanted Caleb.

No, she was just lonely, that was all. She hadn't seen anyone except Big George for three days. Closing her eyes, she willed herself to sleep.

Caleb stood in the bunkhouse doorway, a cigarette dangling from the corner of his mouth as he watched the rain. He'd been in town having dinner with Angela when the rain started. He'd taken one look out the window at the lowering skies and left the mansion, wanting to be at the ranch in case a blizzard hit.

Caleb took a deep drag on the cigarette. It was a hell of a storm, and he'd always loved a storm, even though it usually wreaked havoc on the ranch, bringing down trees, flooding the rivers, scattering the herd. But tonight he wasn't thinking about the ranch or the cattle. Tonight he was thinking of Callie, wondering how she was getting along up at the house.

He felt an all-too-familiar ache as he pictured her sitting in front of a cozy fire or curled up in bed. He yearned to hold her in his arms and kiss her sweet lips. He cursed himself for being a fool, for not satisfying his need with Angela, who was all too willing to jump into bed with him. Not that he wanted Angela, but at least she was honest enough to admit she wanted him.

For a moment, he thought of saddling the buckskin and going back to town. He was tired of yearning for a woman who didn't want him, tired of playing the monk when there was a beautiful woman waiting at his house, eager to please him.

Muttering an oath, Caleb dropped his cigarette into the mud, disgusted with himself because he knew he'd never be satisfied with Angela or any other woman. He wanted Callie, beautiful stubborn Callie, with the face and the heart of an angel and the body of a temptress.

A knock at the door jerked Callie from the brink of sleep. Rising, she gathered the blanket around her and went to the door, expecting to see Big George.

She blinked up at Caleb several times, wondering if her imagination was playing tricks on her. "Is something wrong?"

"No, I just came up to make sure you're all right."

"I'm fine."

Callie couldn't take her eyes from him. He loomed tall and dark in the doorway, as primal as the storm that raged behind him. His skin glistened with raindrops; his eyes were as gray as the clouds. All her senses came awake at his nearness and it was all she could do not to reach out to touch him.

"Mind if I come in?"

Alarm bells went off inside Callie's head. Inviting him into the house would be to invite trouble—and temptation, of the worst kind. She stepped back so he could cross the threshold, then closed the door behind him. Shutting out the world. And her conscience.

"I thought you were in town," she remarked, resuming her seat by the window and gathering the blanket tightly around her.

"I left when it started to rain." He smiled at her. "I am the foreman, you know. I thought I should be here in case you needed me."

Callie nodded. She needed him all right, needed him in the most elemental sense of the word. "Do you think the storm will last long?"

"No telling."

He took off his hat and tossed it on the rack by the door, then sat down on the overstuffed chair on the other side of the window.

"It could blow over tonight, or last another week. If it starts to snow, I'll have the men load a couple of wagons with hay and take it out to the cattle."

Callie nodded, hardly aware of what he was saying. His shirt was damp, clinging to his torso, outlining the hard planes and muscles of his chest and arms. His hair was blue-black in the firelight, his skin a deep bronze. And his eyes, those fathomless gray eyes that stripped away the layers of pretense and saw the truth. . . .

Less than an hour ago, she'd told herself she wanted him, that if he came to her again, she'd give him what he wanted. What she wanted. But now he was here and she was again beset by doubts. If only he hadn't betrayed her trust. If only he'd tell her again that he loved her.

Caleb drew a long breath, held it, and slowly released it. It had been only a few days since he'd seen her last. How was it possible that she'd grown more beautiful, more desirable? He looked into her eyes and saw the loneliness lurking there, the passion she refused to acknowledge. Her hair fell in waves down her back and over her shoulders, shimmering like flames of fire.

Abruptly, he stood up and walked to the hearth, knowing he had to put some distance between them. He stood there for a moment, one hand braced on the mantel as he gazed into the flames; then he added some wood to the fire, which wasn't nearly as hot as the blood racing in his veins.

He shouldn't have come here. Looking at her, wanting her, and not touching her was torture of the worst kind.

He turned, intending to tell her good night, but the words wouldn't come. Instead, he crossed the room. Kneeling at her feet, he took her hands in his and kissed first one and then the other.

"Callie?"

The blanket fell away from her shoulders as she shook her head. "No. Please, don't. I can't . . ."

He didn't say anything else, just knelt there in front of her, still holding her hands in his, the yearning in his eyes more eloquent than words.

And she knew she couldn't fight him any more. She wanted him desperately, completely, and they both knew it.

She was about to tell him so when there came an urgent knock at the front door.

"Mr. Stryker! Mr. Stryker!"

Caleb rose to his feet and went to the door, quietly cursing Big George's timing. "What is it?"

"Barn's on fire. Don't know how it started. Lightning, maybe."

Caleb didn't listen to the rest. He ran down the porch stairs, heading for the barn, noting absently that now, when they could use the rain to douse the fire, it had stopped.

Men were pouring out of the bunkhouse when he arrived, grabbing buckets, filling them at the water trough outside the barn. Flames darted out the broken window. He could hear the frightened whinnying of the horses trapped in their stalls.

Caleb grabbed a bucket and ran into the barn. The roof and walls were too wet to burn, but inside the barn the flames were spreading. He threw the water on a bale of smoldering straw, then opened the door of the stall nearest him. Removing his neckerchief, he wrapped it over the buckskin's eyes and led the mare out of the barn. Big George passed him, followed by several other men, most of them carrying buckets of water.

Caleb turned the buckskin loose and hurried back into the barn, intent on saving the horses. The smoke was thick now, stinging his eyes, making it difficult to see. He opened a stall door and grabbed the horse's halter, dodging the frightened animal's flying hooves. It took several minutes to blindfold the horse and get it outside.

When all the animals were out of danger, the men turned their attention to battling the fire.

It took the better part of an hour to completely douse the flames. By then, the loft and most of the barn's contents had been destroyed. Only the outer walls and the roof remained intact.

"Uh, boss."

Caleb glanced over his shoulder to find a bandy-legged cowhand standing behind him.

"What is it, Smitty?"

"Might not mean anything," Smitty remarked, keeping his voice low, "but I found an empty kerosene can behind the barn. It's not the brand we usually buy."

"Thanks, Smitty. Keep it to yourself, will you?"

"Sure, boss."

Caleb turned his attention to the other cowhands. All were soaked with sweat, their faces and clothes black with soot and ash. Slim McCoy had a nasty burn on one arm, and Harvey Smith had a couple of cuts on his right hand. Big George was nursing a bite on his shoulder and cussing the big Clydesdale they used for pulling the hay wagon. No one else seemed to have sustained any injuries.

"Should have let that big hunk of crow-bait burn," George muttered, wincing as Cookie smeared salve over the wound. "We could have eaten off him for a month."

Caleb grinned, knowing that Big George would rather eat dirt than harm a hair of the Clydesdale's hide. His gaze swept the cowhands. They were men to ride the river with, he thought, men who rode for the brand and did what had to be done no matter what the risk.

"Good work, men," was all he said, but they knew what he meant.

"I think they've earned a day off."

Caleb glanced over his shoulder to find Callie standing behind him. He felt a surge of pride as he took in her appearance. Her hair fell in tangled waves across her shoulders, her face and hands were streaked with sweat and soot, and her skirt was damp from where water had splashed onto it, the hem heavy with mud. Knowing how Callie felt about the ranch, he shouldn't have been surprised that she had pitched in to help.

"You heard the boss lady," Caleb said. "No work tomorrow."

The men nodded in appreciation as they bid Callie good night and trudged back to the bunkhouse.

"It could have been worse," Caleb remarked, seeing the look of dismay on Callie's face. "If it hadn't been for the rain, we'd probably have lost the whole thing."

"Yes." She lifted her chin and squared her shoulders. "I'll order some lumber and some new glass for the window tomorrow, and we can get started rebuilding the interior."

"Yes, ma'am."

"And I'd like you to take a bottle of the best bourbon we've got to the men and tell them thank-you for me."

"Yes, ma'am," he said again.

She hated it when he treated her like that, coolly formal and polite, as if he were just one of the hands, as if nothing had ever happened between them, and then she realized that she was just as guilty.

"I'll get the bottle," she said tersely.

Caleb followed her across the yard, waiting on the porch while she went inside to get the liquor.

"Is this good enough?" she asked, thrusting a bottle of bonded Kentucky bourbon into his hand.

Caleb glanced at the label. It was Duncan Stryker's favorite brand, ordered special from St. Louis.

"Probably better than most of them are used to," Caleb assured her.

"Will one bottle be enough?"

Caleb nodded. "More than enough."

She gazed into his eyes, seeing the memory of what had passed between them earlier that night, the knowledge of what would have happened if they hadn't been interrupted. Had it been fate, or simply bad luck, that had kept her out of his arms?

"Callie . . ."

"Good night, Mr. Stryker."

So they were back to formalities, Caleb mused grimly. Maybe it was time to admit defeat. Time to high-tail it out of Cheyenne before this stubborn child-woman drove him completely insane. But even as the thought crossed his mind, he knew he couldn't leave her. She was in his blood, as much a part of him as the color of his skin.

"Good night, Miss McGuire. Sleep well."

Callie nodded, knowing she wouldn't be able to sleep at all.

# *Chapter Twenty-nine*

Richard Ashton turned up his coat collar against the cold as he waited on the porch of the Stryker mansion. Callie McGuire had become a challenge he couldn't turn his back on, a quest to test his manhood, a crusade to prove he could have anything he set his heart on. In all his twenty-two years, he'd never been denied anything he put his mind to. Whether it was a horse that caught his fancy, a woman he desired, or a rare painting he coveted, he'd always achieved his goal, thanks to his money, his looks, or both. Only Callie McGuire continued to elude him.

He'd been to the mansion several times in the last few days to confer with Angela as they tried to decide how they could achieve their goals. Angela wanted Caleb; Richard wanted Callie. Neither was particularly squeamish, or honorable, when it came to getting what they wanted.

Richard's breath caught in his throat when Angela opened the door. He'd always thought of her as beautiful, though he'd had no interest in her other than as an ally, but tonight she looked radiant in a flowing gown of dark-green silk that made her eyes sparkle like emeralds. Her hair fell over her shoulders in waves of honeyed gold. There was a faint hint of color on her cheeks and lips, and the fragrance of French perfume lingered in her hair.

She'd been expecting Stryker, he thought irritably.

"Good evening, Richard," Angela said, smiling up at him. "I didn't expect you tonight."

"I can see that," he muttered as he stepped into the foyer and removed his hat and coat. "Maybe I'd better leave."

"I'm not expecting anyone else either," Angela said quickly, then shrugged. "I ordered this gown several weeks ago. It arrived late this afternoon and I was just trying it on."

She pirouetted, her arms held out, a smile on her face as the voluminous skirt belled out around her ankles. "Do you like it?"

"What you really want to know is if Stryker will like it."

"No, Richard," she said softly, "I want to know what *you* think."

Ashton frowned at her. "I like it."

"I'm glad. Come on in," she said, smiling up at him again. "Would you like a drink?"

"Sure."

He followed her into the parlor and sat down while she fixed him a drink.

"I guess you've come to talk about Callie," Angela remarked, taking a place at the opposite end of the settee. "Have you thought of a way to get her alone?"

"Not yet."

"You will. A man like you always gets what he wants."

Angela smiled at him yet again. Once, she'd thought she'd never find anyone to take Caleb's place, but in the last few days, she'd begun to wonder if maybe she was chasing a dream that would never come true. Richard Ashton had everything she'd ever wanted: wealth, respectability, a good family, the biggest mansion in Cheyenne. If he wasn't as tall and handsome as Caleb, he made up for it in other ways. Still, she wasn't blind. She knew he could be cruel, that he wouldn't hesitate to retaliate against anyone who wronged him, but she also knew that he'd take care of what was his, that he'd be generous to the woman he married.

All that day, she'd thought about Richard and Caleb, comparing the two men in her mind, weighing their faults against their virtues. In the end, she knew she'd rather have Caleb, but she also knew he'd never be hers. Caleb Stryker was the kind of man who loved hard and loved only once, and as difficult as it was to admit, she knew he'd never love her.

"Perhaps I could convince Caleb to spend the night here. I could pretend to be sick or something, and you could go out to the ranch and spend the night with Callie."

Richard nodded. "Maybe."

He stared at her mouth as she spoke, wondering what it would be like to run his tongue over her provocative pink lips. She took a deep breath, and he watched the swell of her bosom, barely concealed by a thin layer of green silk.

Angela sat up a little straighter, fully aware of Richard's thoughts. "Would you care for another drink?"

He nodded, his nostrils filling with the scent of her perfume when she passed in front of him. It occurred to him that she was a highly desirable woman, one he wanted to know better.

When she handed him his glass, he ignored it and took her free hand in his, pulling her toward him.

He had expected her to object, to remind him that he had no right to take such liberties.

He would not have accepted such a response from Callie McGuire. Despite her beauty and the fact that he wanted her, Callie was still the daughter of a cheap tart and probably no better than she ought to be despite her tiresome protests to the contrary. But he considered Angela Bristol a respectable widow. Besides, in Angela, he recognized himself, a person who saw what she wanted and went after it.

And at the moment, she wanted him. He could see it in her eyes, in the quick flush that rose in her cheeks.

Richard caressed the curve of her cheek with the back of his hand. "Where's your room?"

"Upstairs. First door on the left."

No games, no coy protests, no pretense.

Richard rose to his feet. Taking the glass she had offered him earlier, he drained it in a single swallow; then, tossing the empty glass on the floor, he swept Angela into his arms and carried her up the carpeted stairway, his lips already seeking hers.

She would be a pleasant diversion until he got hold of the woman he really wanted.

# *Chapter Thirty*

Callie stared at her reflection in the mirror. It couldn't be true. She couldn't be pregnant. Not after just one indiscretion. And yet, even as she tried to deny it, she knew it was true. She'd suspected it for days, but she'd refused to admit it, even to herself. But there was no denying it any longer.

She was going to have a baby, and Caleb Stryker was the father.

She'd been so preoccupied with Caleb and his affair with Angela Bristol she hadn't paid any attention to the fact that her monthly curse was very, very late. At first, she'd attributed it to nerves, the stress of discovering Caleb had lied to her, the strain of trying to run the ranch. She'd never been very regular anyway. But she couldn't fool herself any longer.

She was pregnant. Her breasts were tender and swollen. She was tired all the time. She was nauseated in the morning, and sometimes in the evening. Oh, she knew the signs all too well. You couldn't grow up as she had and not know the symptoms.

Callie placed her hands over her belly, which was, thankfully, still flat. But that wouldn't last much longer. Soon she'd begin to show, and everyone, including Caleb, would know she was going to have a baby.

A cold sense of dread settled over her. She'd have to tell him sooner or later, she thought apprehensively, but how could she face him?

Going into her bedroom, she sat down on the bed and buried her face in her hands. Why had she ever let him touch her? It had been wrong, and now she was paying the price.

She could just hear Martha Brewster and Maude Colton raking her over the coals. *Just like her mother,* they'd say smugly. How could she face the townspeople? How could she face Caleb?

She hadn't seen him for over a week. As soon as the last storm passed, he'd gone out to check on the cattle—or so he'd said, but she couldn't help wondering if he was staying at the mansion with Angela Bristol.

Callie frowned. Everyone knew Angie was living in the Stryker mansion, that Caleb was supporting her.

But Angela Bristol was the least of her problems now, Callie thought as she placed her hands over her stomach. She counted backward, trying to remember exactly when Caleb had made love to her. The middle of August. It had been the middle of August and now it was nearing the end of October. Ten weeks.

It was hard to believe he had made love to her, that they had once been intimate. Now they rarely spoke. Caleb was unfailingly polite when he came to the house, staying just long enough to bring her up to date on ranch affairs. She knew he went into town with the other hands on Saturday night, and even though she'd driven him to it, she died a little inside every time she thought of Caleb spending the night in Angela Bristol's arms.

She missed him. She missed the few weeks of happiness they had known before she found out he'd lied to her. She missed cooking for him, missed his company at dinner, his teasing remarks.

She glanced at her stomach, trying to imagine it rounded with new life. A baby. She was going to have Caleb Stryker's baby in the spring.

How could she tell him now, when they hardly spoke, when he looked at her as if he hated her?

Caleb let out a long weary sigh as he walked out of the barn. Ten days of riding the range, checking the waterholes and the cattle had left him feeling surly and out of sorts.

In the past, he'd loved riding over the ranch, loved the vastness of it, the quiet, the camaraderie he'd shared with the other men. But that had been before Callie McGuire entered his life.

Now, he wanted only to be with her. She'd vowed she didn't care for him, that she didn't trust him, would never trust him. And maybe that was all true, but she couldn't deny she wanted him. He knew she'd never say it aloud, but the need was there, in the depths of her eyes. He saw it each time he reported on the affairs of the ranch, and it made it almost impossible to keep his hands off her, but he had his pride and he'd vowed never to touch her again unless it was her idea.

He had hoped that, once he admitted he'd lied to her, once he'd apologized, she'd forgive him. But she was too hard-headed, too stubborn, to take a chance on him again. And maybe he couldn't blame her. So he'd turned to Angela for comfort, letting her fuss over him even though it made him feel like a cad because he knew there'd never be any other woman for him except Callie, and she wouldn't give him another chance.

Stubborn woman.

The words sounded in the back of his mind as he walked toward the main house. A light in the window beckoned him, and for a moment he imagined that he and Callie had gotten married as planned, that he was coming home from a long day on the range, that she would be waiting for him, a smile of welcome on her face. She'd pour him a drink and listen while he told her about the day's activities. Later, they'd have dinner, then sit in the parlor until it was time for bed. She'd be mending one of his shirts, he'd be going over the ranch accounts, but they'd both be looking forward to bedtime.

He shook the image from his mind as he knocked on the front door of the ranch house.

Moments later, Callie opened the door.

"You're back," she murmured, and felt her heart skip a beat at his nearness. Right or wrong, she felt better just knowing he was at the ranch again.

Caleb nodded. "May I come in?"

"Of course."

Following him into the parlor, she thought how tired he looked. There were lines of fatigue around his mouth and eyes. His clothes were travel-stained, and bits of dried mud clung to his boots.

Caleb nodded at the liquor cabinet that stood in the corner. "Mind if I have a drink?"

"Help yourself."

Callie sat down on the sofa, watching as he took a crystal decanter from the glass-fronted oak cabinet and poured himself a shot of whiskey. For the first time, she wondered what it must be like for Caleb to be working for her. This had been his home. It must be awkward, humiliating, to have to ask for permission to take what should rightfully be his. The ranch, the cattle, the whiskey he was drinking—it had all belonged to Caleb's father.

She shook the guilt from her mind. It wasn't her fault Duncan Stryker hadn't left the ranch to his son.

Caleb drained the glass in a single swallow, then poured another before he turned to face Callie. He thought how lovely she looked, sitting there with the firelight behind her. He'd thought of her every day since the day he met her. He wanted to share his life with her, confide in her, tell her his hopes and dreams, his fears. He wanted to love her and protect her and yes, share the ranch with her. And he might have had a chance if only he'd been honest with her about the will from the start.

*Water under the bridge,* he thought glumly.

"Is everything all right?" Callie asked, wondering at his morose expression.

"Fine. A mountain lion pulled down one of your cows. I'll send a couple of the men out to bring it down.

She grimaced as she heard his emphasis on the words "your cows."

"Do you have to kill it?

"Birth and death," Caleb said with a shrug. "On a ranch, it's a fact of life."

Callie folded her hands in her lap, wishing she could think of some clever way to tell him he was about to be a father, but the words stuck in her throat.

Caleb frowned at Callie as he sipped his drink. She looked different somehow, though he couldn't quite put his finger on it. She looked kind of sad, yet there was a glow about her that hadn't been there before, as if she knew a secret.

Had she accepted Ashton's proposal while he was gone?

The thought slammed into his gut like a fist. He'd kill Ashton before he let him marry Callie.

"Anything new here?" he asked, his voice casual.

A faint blush tinged Callie's cheeks. "Why do you ask?"

"I've been gone more than a week," he reminded her. "It seems like a logical question."

She knew exactly how long he'd been gone, but she didn't say so.

"There's nothing new. Fanny came by for a visit last Friday. She said to tell you hello and asked when you were coming into town for dinner."

"Is that all?"

Callie nodded. Her visit with Fanny had ended in tears as she told the older woman everything, unburdening herself of all the doubts and hurts that had plagued her since she learned about the codicil. Fanny had held her and comforted her, urging her to tell Caleb about the baby, assuring her that Caleb would do the right thing. At the time, Callie had been certain she didn't want Caleb to marry her because it was the "right" thing to do. But now . . .

If only she could lay her head on his shoulder and pour out her doubts and fears about being a mother. She didn't know anything at all about raising a baby. And the thought of childbirth filled her with dread. She'd heard such horror stories at the Miner's Rest, ghoulish tales of women who died after hours of labor, of girls who had tried to abort unwanted babies and bled to death.

She stared at Caleb, thinking that she'd rather die in childbirth than ask him to marry her, but she couldn't let her baby be born out of wedlock. She knew what that was like.

An old ache rose in her heart as she wondered who her father was, and if her mother had loved him. No matter how many times Callie had asked, Leila had refused to tell her who her father had been, and Callie had finally decided Leila didn't know. Somehow, that hurt more than anything.

Caleb watched the changing emotions on Callie's face. What was she thinking? Usually, her thoughts were as transparent as water, but not tonight.

Callie glanced up and caught Caleb watching her intently. How could she tell him about the baby? What if he didn't care? What if he laughed and refused to marry her?

"What is it, Callie?"

It was the first time he'd called her by her given name in weeks, and it made her heart ache for what might have been.

"Spit it out, Callie. What aren't you telling me?"

"Nothing." She forced herself to smile. "I'm just tired, I guess. If there's nothing else, I think I'll go to bed."

She stood up, waiting for him to make some suggestive comment about sharing her bed, even though she knew he wouldn't. Those days were far behind them, but she couldn't help hoping just the same.

He was still watching her intently, his eyes probing deep into her own. She met his unblinking stare, wondering if he could read her mind, if he could probe the depths of her heart and soul and see the loneliness inside, the fear, the wanting.

She swallowed hard, forcing herself not to look away, to keep her expression impassive. She couldn't tell him about the baby. She didn't want him to marry her because he had to, but because he wanted to, and now it was too late for that. She'd ruined everything.

"Good night, Mr. Stryker."

"Good night, Miss McGuire."

So they were back to "Miss McGuire," Callie thought unhappily. She watched him turn and head for the door, saw his hand close on the knob.

"I'm pregnant."

The words, as soft as a sigh, stopped Caleb in his tracks. "What?"

He didn't turn around, and Callie was grateful that she didn't have to see the look on his face.

"I'm pregnant," she repeated. "Almost three months."

She saw his hand tighten on the door knob, saw his knuckles go white.

"So what do you want from me?"

It wasn't the response she had hoped for, but at least he hadn't asked who the father was.

"I want . . . that is, I'd like you to . . . I mean, I think we should . . ."

She felt her cheeks grow hot. Asking him to marry her was even harder than she'd imagined.

Slowly, Caleb turned around, his gaze sweeping over her as he examined her from head to foot. Her breasts did look fuller, her waist a little thicker.

He drew a deep breath and exhaled it slowly. She was pregnant, and he was the father; he had no doubt about that.

"What do you want from me, Callie?" he asked again.

His voice was very soft, almost gentle, strangely at odds with the cool expression on his face.

"I don't want my baby to be fatherless."

"It won't be. I'm his father, and I'll take care of him."

The flame in her cheeks burned brighter. "That's not what I meant."

He wanted to go to her, take her in his arms, assure her that he loved her, that everything would be all right. But he couldn't get the words past his pride.

"Are you asking me to marry you, Miss McGuire?"

"Caleb, please don't make this any more difficult than it is."

"As I recall, I asked you to marry me not long ago. Several times, in fact. And you said you wanted someone you loved, someone you respected. I assumed that didn't mean a half-breed bounty hunter."

She wanted to curl up and die. Instead, she lifted her chin and squared her shoulders. Not even for the sake of her unborn child would she beg this arrogant, insufferable man to marry her.

"You assumed right," she said, her voice as frigid as a high mountain stream in midwinter. "Good night."

She started to leave the room, tears of humiliation welling in her eyes, only to be jerked to a halt as Caleb's hand closed, none too gently, over her arm.

"We're getting married, Callie. Just as soon as possible."

"No. I don't want to marry you."

He pulled her around to face him. "It no longer matters what you want. That's my child. I won't have it born on the wrong side of the blanket."

He fixed her with a hard stare, his eyes filled with self-reproach. "It'll have enough to contend with just having me as a father."

His hand tightened on her arm as she tried to pull away. "You won't have to share my bed, and you can divorce me as soon as the baby's born, but we're getting married day after tomorrow."

"You can't make me," Callie retorted, forgetting that only minutes ago marrying Caleb was the very thing she had wanted most in the world.

He stared down at her, his gray eyes cold, his expression ominous. "Can't I?"

A blind man could have seen the warning in his eyes.

"I'll ride into Cheyenne tomorrow and bring the priest out to the ranch," Caleb said in a tone that left no room for argument. "We'll be married first thing Tuesday morning."

# *Chapter Thirty-one*

Caleb stood beside Callie. Her hand, enfolded in his, was cool and trembled slightly. Her face was almost as pale as her wedding gown. She hadn't wanted to wear the dress, but Caleb had insisted.

"I paid for it," he'd reminded her in a voice as hard and cold as stone. "And you'll damn well wear it."

He glanced briefly at Fanny and then at Orville Hoag, who had been invited to witness the ceremony. Fanny smiled at him, her expression warm and reassuring. Hoag looked solemn and thoughtful.

As the priest began to speak, Caleb had eyes only for Callie. Her "I do" was hesitant and barely audible; she refused to meet Caleb's eyes when he placed a wide gold wedding band on her finger.

And then the priest said the words that made Callie McGuire his woman, his wife.

"You may kiss the bride," Father Cardella said, beaming at the couple standing before him.

Caleb cradled Callie's face in his hands and kissed her. He had meant to keep it light, meaningless, but as soon as his lips touched hers, the desire he'd held in check for the last two months burst into flame and he wondered how he'd keep his hands off her now that she was his lawfully wedded wife.

Callie felt Caleb's kiss sweep through her, hotter than lightning, threatening to melt the ice that had formed around her heart like a protective barrier. She didn't trust him, even now, and she would not, could not, love him, not any more.

She felt disoriented when he finally let her go, and then Fanny was hugging her, telling her she was a beautiful bride, wishing her happiness. Orville Hoag shook her hand, wished her well, and bade everyone good-day, apologizing because he had to get back to town.

Father Cardella kissed Callie on the cheek, shook hands with Caleb and Fanny, and took his leave, saying he hoped to see the newlyweds in church on Sunday.

"Well, I suppose I should go, too," Fanny remarked, troubled by the undercurrents that flowed between the bride and groom.

"No, please stay," Callie said urgently. "I'll fix lunch."

Fanny glanced at Caleb, then back at Callie. "All right, lamb. But I'll fix lunch."

"Thank you, Fanny." Callie's relief was obvious to everyone. "I'll just go change."

"Caleb, why don't you help me in the kitchen?" Fanny suggested.

He grinned at her good-naturedly, knowing she

didn't need any help at all. Following her into the kitchen, he sank down on one of the chairs. "I'm not going to hurt her, you know."

"You've hurt her already," Fanny replied.

"She told you, huh?"

Fanny nodded. "I'm not taking sides, Caleb, I'm not saying who's right and who's wrong. . . ."

"I was wrong, Fanny. I admit it. I admitted it to Callie. But she won't forgive me."

"She's a good girl, Caleb. You be nice to her."

"I'll try."

"Don't try. Do it. She deserves a good life after the way she grew up, never knowing who her father was, listening to all the nasty gossip about her mother and your father. She's not thick-skinned like you are. She's a fine, decent girl and she deserves more out of life than she's gotten so far."

"Yes, ma'am."

"I'm serious, Caleb."

"I know. I never meant to hurt her, Fanny. I'd make it up to her if she'd let me."

"I know. You were always such a good boy."

Caleb laughed at that, the first good laugh he'd had in weeks.

"You didn't think I was such a good boy when I threw a rock through your parlor window, or when I knocked your wash off the line."

"Hopefully, you've grown up since then and my windows and wash are safe."

Caleb grinned, then grew serious. "She doesn't trust me, Fanny. Maybe she never will."

"Be patient with her, Caleb. She's been hurt, but she loves you."

"She tell you that?"

"Not in so many words." She smiled as she saw

Callie standing in the doorway. "Come on in, lamb. Everything's ready."

They ate cold roast beef and potato salad and washed it down with champagne. Fanny kept up a constant stream of chatter, taking the burden from Callie and Caleb. When the meal was over, she shooed Caleb out of the kitchen.

"You stay put," Fanny said when Callie started to clear the table. "I'll have these washed up in no time."

"I can help."

"Don't argue with me, young woman. You get all the rest you can while you can. I've had six babes and I know what I'm talking about. Once that little one gets here, you won't have time to sit down and take it easy."

"You're so good to me, Fanny. But then, you always were."

"It's easy to be nice to nice people."

Fanny filled a pan with water and put it on the stove, then scraped the dishes and wiped the table. She was a wise woman and knew when to speak and when to keep silent.

When the dishes were done, Fanny kissed Callie on the cheek, gave Caleb a hug, and took her leave, hoping they'd be able to work things out between them. It was obvious to her that they'd both been hurt. And just as obvious that they were very much in love with each other. She just hoped they figured it out before it was too late.

Callie stared at the front door for a moment, fidgeting with a fold of her dress, wishing Fanny hadn't had to leave. She was suddenly uncomfortable, being alone in the house with Caleb. She belonged to him now. The ranch might be hers, but she belonged to Caleb.

Crossing the room, she sat down on the curved settee and picked up a mail order catalogue, slowly turning the pages. She didn't have to look at Caleb to know he was watching her. If only things were different between them. If only he had married her for love instead of out of duty, how different things would be.

Caleb let out a long sigh. Shoving his hands into his pockets, he turned away from Callie and gazed out the window. Callie was his, and in a way the ranch was his, even though, legally, the Rocking S still belonged to her.

He grinned wryly. If they lived anywhere but Wyoming, Callie's assets would have passed to him when they married, but in Wyoming, a woman was allowed to own property in her own name. Still, he had what he wanted most. Callie was his wife, lawfully and legally. And he had the satisfaction of knowing that the Rocking S would remain in the family, that his child would one day inherit the ranch that he loved so much. The thought should have made him happy, but victory tasted like ashes in his mouth.

He looked at Callie, her head bowed over the pages of the catalogue. She was carrying his child, but she hadn't wanted to marry him. She'd held him at arm's length, vowing that she hated him, didn't trust him, didn't want him, and suddenly it didn't matter. He wanted her, and he'd waited long enough.

Callie gasped as she felt Caleb's fingers dig into her shoulders, and then he was sweeping her into his arms, carrying her down the hall into the big bedroom.

He paused in the middle of the room, his eyes blazing.

"I know I promised you wouldn't have to share my bed," he said, his voice rough, "so we'll share yours. I told you before, I'm not a boy to play foolish games. I don't intend to spend my wedding night alone.

"Hate me for it if you want," he murmured, his lips drifting over hers. "You hate me anyway. . . ."

She started to protest, but he silenced her with a kiss, plundering the recesses of her mouth. He carried her swiftly to the bed and undressed her, his gaze moving over her body, his expression daring her to try to stop him.

Callie watched as he shed his clothes to stand naked before her, a man in the prime of life, tall, rugged, and fully aroused.

She felt a moment of sudden, unreasoning fear, and then he was beside her, drawing her into his arms. He seemed not to care what she wanted, intent only on pleasing himself, as if she were his prisoner with no rights at all. And yet she had never felt so loved. His kisses were sometimes gentle, sometimes rough, but always satisfying.

He was Man, protector, provider, predator.

She was Woman, helpmate, giver of love and support, the bearer of life.

Together, they were perfect.

He took the lead, and she followed, followed him to the depths of desire, to the soaring heights of ecstasy, and knew she had finally come home. Heart overflowing, she wept softly.

Racked with guilt, Caleb held her while she cried,

the sound of her tears twisting the knife in his gut a little deeper. No wonder she was crying, he thought. He'd taken her roughly, against her will, using her as though she were no better than a . . . he swore under his breath, unable to say the word.

Not wanting to face her, he slid out of bed and pulled on his pants.

"Caleb . . ."

"What?"

"Where are you going?"

"Out." He yanked on his shirt and headed for the door. "Don't worry, it won't happen again," he said, and was gone before she could ask him to stay.

For Caleb, the days that followed were difficult. He worked long and hard, trying to bury his yearning for Callie in hard work, hoping exhaustion would keep his desire at bay. He rode the range, dreading winter, looking forward to spring, when the days would be filled with rounding up the cattle, branding calves, riding fence, checking the rivers and waterholes.

He spent so much time in the barn currying the horses and repairing tack that the men began to complain that he was going to put them out of work. But he just laughed their remarks aside. He was the boss, after all. If he wanted to spend his time in the barn, that was his business.

Still, no matter what task occupied his hands, all he could think of was Callie. She was pregnant with his child, and he had taken her against her will as if she were just some saloon girl he'd hired for the night. He longed to apologize, but he was too ashamed to face her. Maybe he was no better than his old man, after all.

He'd never thought of himself as a father and couldn't picture himself in the role. He didn't know anything about kids, had never even held a baby. Or wanted one. But he wanted Callie's child, and he hoped for a son, someone who would love the ranch the way he had always loved it. The way Callie loved it.

The long autumn nights were a torment. Sometimes Callie went to bed early, leaving him alone in the parlor. But more often she sat on the sofa before the fireplace, sewing things for the baby, or doing the mending, or reading one of Shakespeare's plays. He often caught her looking at him, as though she longed to tell him something, but he never asked her what was on her mind, and whatever she wanted to say was left unsaid.

Often, while he pretended to be going over the ranch accounts, he watched her, noticing the little changes that were taking place in her body. Her ankles were a little swollen; her breasts were getting larger, heavier, and he pictured her sitting in the big old easy chair by the window, nursing their baby.

He ached to touch Callie, to hold her close, to nuzzle the breasts that would suckle their child. He watched her waistline thicken, and he tried to imagine his child living and growing within Callie's body, sheltered beneath her heart, nourished by her body.

Callie. He had to find a way to breach her defenses, to reach past her distrust and make her realize that he hadn't married her because of the ranch or even because of the child, but because he loved her. He owed her an apology, too, he thought, and putting if off wouldn't make the words come any easier.

Tomorrow, he thought. Tomorrow he'd take his courage in hand and tell Callie what was in his heart. He just hoped she'd believe him, because he couldn't endure the tension between them another day.

Callie sat up, startled to find Caleb standing beside her bed.

"Get up," he said. "We're going for a ride."

"A ride? Where?"

"Meet me downstairs. Dress warm." Without waiting for her to reply, he left the room.

Callie frowned. What was he up to now? For a moment, she considered burrowing under the covers, but her curiosity was stronger than the urge to go back to sleep.

Rising, she dressed as quickly as possible considering her expanding girth and increasing lethargy. Thirty minutes later, she met Caleb in the kitchen.

"Ready?" he asked, and at her nod, he opened the door and followed her outside.

The buggy was waiting. Lifting Callie onto the seat, Caleb draped a blanket over her shoulders, covered her legs with another blanket, then swung up onto the seat beside her.

"Where are we going?" Callie asked again, but Caleb just shook his head and told her to wait and see.

With an exasperated sigh, Callie folded her arms and sat back. It was a lovely day, bright and clear. The sky was blue, the air cool and crisp.

She smiled faintly as they drove across the

Rocking S. As always, she felt a sense of peace and fulfillment as she reminded herself that it all belonged to her. The ranch represented roots, a foundation to build on, all the security she had been denied as a child.

After an hour, Caleb parked the buggy beneath a cottonwood tree. Vaulting to the ground, he pulled the blanket from Callie's lap and spread it on the ground, then lifted Callie from the buggy. When she was seated, he reached under the seat and withdrew a basket.

"Breakfast," he explained, and opening the basket, he withdrew a half-dozen assorted biscuits and tarts, bread and butter, jam and honey. There were hard-boiled eggs, a couple of apples, and a jug of sweet cider. "I hope you're hungry."

"I'm always hungry," Callie muttered, reaching for a strawberry tart. "Where'd you get all this?"

"I asked Cookie to throw something together."

Callie, always ravenous, ate in silence, enjoying the food and the beauty of the day. She avoided Caleb's gaze, wondering why he had brought her out there, wondering at the almost tender expression in his eyes. It was the first time they'd been alone together outside of the house since that night when he'd carried her to bed, the first time he'd sought her company during the day. Usually, he was out on the range with the men or in the barn. Sundays, he spent his time playing poker in the bunkhouse with the hands. And, of course, he made numerous trips to town. To see Angela Bristol, she suspected.

Callie frowned irritably. The last time she'd seen Angela had been in town several weeks ago. Angela had gone out of her way to get Callie's attention, had made sure she noticed the lovely fur-lined cloak she was wearing. A gift from Caleb, Angela had said. For her birthday. Callie had wanted nothing more than to slap the smug expression from the other woman's face. *You may be married to him,* Angela's look had seemed to say, *but it's me he wants.* And how could Callie doubt it?

"More cider?"

Callie looked up, startled from her reverie by the sound of his voice. "No, thank you."

"What were you thinking about?" Caleb asked curiously. "You looked angry enough to chew nails."

"Nothing."

"Don't you think it's time we stopped lying to each other?"

"I don't know what you mean."

"Don't you? If I reach for you, will you push me away or will you admit it's what you want?"

A slow heat engulfed her, spreading under his watchful gaze. She shook her head, determined to deny the truth of his statement, but the words wouldn't come.

"We got off to a bad start, Callie. I'd like to make it right between us if I can, but I need your help."

He closed the distance between them and cupped her face in his hands.

"I want you, Callie. I think I talked you into that phony engagement because I wanted to feel that you were mine without having to admit that I needed you, but it's true. I know that now."

He covered her mouth with his hand, knowing she was about to argue with him.

"It's you I love, Callie, you I want, not the ranch.

If you don't believe me, sell the place and we'll live in town, or anywhere else you want."

Callie blinked up at him. He'd said he loved her. Did he mean it?

"I know I owe you an apology for what happened the other night, but I can't apologize for it, Callie. I'm not sorry, and I'd do it again."

Callie took his hand from her mouth, started to let it go, then held it in her lap, gazing at the color of his skin, so dark against her own.

"Caleb, I . . ."

"Believe me, Callie. Just this once."

"I want to, but . . ."

He placed a finger beneath her chin and tipped her head up so that he could see her face. "Go on."

"What about Angela and you? All that time you spent together?"

"It didn't mean anything, Callie. I was just lonely, that's all. Nothing happened between us."

"What about . . . ?" Callie bit down on her lip, then met Caleb's gaze. "What about the cloak you gave her?"

Caleb frowned. "What cloak?"

"The one you gave her for her birthday."

Caleb shook his head. "I didn't give Angela anything for her birthday. I don't even know when it is."

He swore under his breath when he saw the doubt in her eyes.

"Dammit, Callie, you've got to believe me. Angela's just an old friend, that's all. There was never anything between us, I swear it."

He took her hands in his and gazed steadily into her eyes. "You've got to believe me," he said fervently. "You're the only woman I want. The only woman I've ever wanted."

Callie searched his face, looking for deceit, but all she saw was hope and an aching tenderness that melted the last misgivings from her heart.

"Please, Callie, won't you trust me one more time?"

She nodded, too close to tears to speak.

Hardly daring to believe that she was willing to put the past behind them, Caleb framed her face in his hands and kissed her gently, tasting the salt of the tears she could no longer hold back.

"I've been a fool," he whispered.

"I have. I kept pushing you away because you'd hurt me."

"I know."

"But that hurt, too. And then, that night after we made love, our wedding night, you left. I tried to tell you that it was all right, that it had been wonderful, but you wouldn't let me, and that hurt worse than anything."

"I was ashamed to face you after what I'd done, Callie, but if you'll give me another chance, I'll never hurt you again."

He took her in his arms then, his kiss as warm as the sunshine that danced in her hair, as tender as a sigh.

Drawing back a little, he gazed deep into her eyes. "I'll never hurt you again," he repeated fervently.

And this time she believed him.

The days that followed were the happiest Callie had ever known. She spent every waking moment with Caleb, certain she would never get enough of him.

She would never forget the wonder, the joy, of waking up beside him that first morning, of seeing him smile at her, his eyes filled with the knowledge of what they had shared the night before, of what they would share in the years to come.

In the days that followed, he made love to her in ways she had never imagined. Sometimes, in the early hours of the morning when the sky was aflame and the earth was quiet and still, he made love to her gently and tenderly, whispering to her of his love and devotion, declaring that she was as beautiful as a Madonna.

Sometimes he made love to her in the black of night, arousing her passion to such heights that she thought she might die of needing him.

He was like a dark phantom, then, a shadowy being she could not see clearly, one that challenged all her senses as he spoke to her of desire, unleashing primal urges she had never dreamed existed.

And sometimes he made love to her in the light of day, slow, sweet love that stretched for hours while he caressed her, or brushed her hair, or took sweet oil and massaged her body, his big brown hands lingering over the soft swell of her belly as he talked of their unborn child. For Callie, these were the best times of all.

And now, it was early morning and their delayed honeymoon was at an end. Callie lay beside her husband, wishing he didn't have to go back to work. Watching him sleep, she lightly traced the planes and angles of his face.

"Beautiful," she whispered. "Do you know how

beautiful you are, Caleb Stryker? Do you know how much I love you?"

She let the tip of one finger glide over his lower lip, then let her fingertips slide down his neck, over his broad chest.

She paused a moment, drinking in the sight of his strongly muscled arms, the width of his shoulders.

"So strong," she murmured, then let her fingertips continue their journey, traveling downward, over the flat belly ridged with muscle, slowly following the path of curly black hair until it disappeared from sight under the sheet.

"Don't stop."

A faint blush rose in Callie's cheeks as she realized he'd been awake the whole time.

"Why didn't you tell me you were awake?" she scolded.

"And miss hearing that I'm beautiful?" He was smiling at her, his dark eyes alight with silent laughter.

Callie scowled at him in mock annoyance. "I was lying."

"Were you?"

"Yes. You're the ugliest man I've ever seen. Why, I've seen frogs that were more handsome."

He was laughing out loud now. "Frogs, huh?"

"Yes, and big hairy rats. And . . . and lizards."

Before she knew what was happening, he was lying atop her, most of his weight supported on his elbows so he didn't crush her, both her hands trapped in one of his. "I draw the line at lizards," he growled, raking his stubbled chin over her cheek. "Take it back."

"No. Even old Mort Holley is better looking than you."

"Pity our poor child, then," Caleb remarked, and burst out laughing.

Callie's laughter blended with his, and then she grew pensive.

"What's wrong? Am I hurting you?"

Eyes dark with concern, he released her hands and sat up.

"No. I was just thinking of all the time we wasted being angry when we could have been . . ."

Caleb raised one eyebrow. "Could have been what, Mrs. Stryker?" he asked, his voice suddenly husky. "Could have been doing this?"

He kissed her mouth. "Or this?"

His lips nuzzled the soft skin beneath her ear lobe. "Or this?" His mouth moved to her breast.

Callie gave a little gasp of pleasure as his tongue stroked her skin. She had never felt such bliss, never known such love existed. She belonged to Caleb, heart and soul, mind and body. She knew now why her mother had refused to leave Duncan Stryker, knew why she had endured the scorn of a whole town. Right or wrong, Leila had found love in the arms of a married man, and Callie no longer blamed her for refusing to leave town, for refusing to leave Caleb's father. She understood so much more now.

And as Caleb rose over her, his dark eyes warm with love and desire, Callie forgave her mother for everything.

# Chapter Thirty-two

Angela Bristol sat on the damask-covered settee, her hands folded tightly in her lap, while she watched Richard Ashton's face. He had been curious, even pleased, when she appeared on his doorstep wearing the fur-lined cloak he had given her for her birthday. He was no longer pleased.

"I suppose you expect me to marry you," he said, his voice harsh.

"Well, it is your child I'm carrying."

"Hah! For all I know, Caleb Stryker could be the brat's father."

"I wish he were," Angela retorted, though she wished no such thing. She had grown to care deeply for this man, had thought he cared for her. "But it's yours, and you know it."

"I don't know it."

Angela smiled at him, but her eyes were cold. "When have I had time to see Caleb or any other man? *You've* been at the mansion every night for the past two months. And most days, too."

Ashton swore under his breath. Damn the little minx, she was right. Since that night he'd carried her up the stairs, he hadn't been able to resist her. Not only was she a lovely woman, but she had no inhibitions in bed. She didn't play coy little games, pretending she didn't like his touch. She didn't make him beg for her favors, or pretend to be shocked or disgusted when he couldn't wait until bedtime, but drew her down on the parlor floor and made love to her all night long. She was a lusty wench, he mused, there was no doubt of that. And though he was loathe to admit it, he knew the child had to be his. The problem now was what to do about it.

Angela rose to her feet and drew her cloak around her shoulders.

"Where are you going?" Richard demanded.

"I'm going home. I've said what I came to say."

"That's it?"

"Did you expect me to beg you to marry me, Richard? You should know me better than that. Will I see you tonight?"

Ashton frowned, disappointed in spite of himself. He *had* expected her to cry and carry on.

"Well?" Angela said, her hand on the polished brass door knob. "Will you be coming over this evening or not?"

Richard stared at Angela, at the haughty lift of her chin. Maybe he had been wrong about her. Maybe she did like to play games, but he was damned if he could figure out what kind of game she was playing now. "I don't know."

"Good day, then," she said, and swept gracefully out the door.

Ashton stared after her. He took a deep breath, and the lingering fragrance of her perfume tickled his nostrils. What did she really want? Maybe she wasn't pregnant at all. Maybe she was just trying to trap him into marriage. Other women had tried the same ruse and failed.

His brows drawn together in a thoughtful frown, he closed the door.

Angela walked briskly down the street, wondering what to do next. She would not beg Richard Ashton to marry her. She would not ask him for charity. She would not stay in this town and be the subject of brutal gossip. So, what was she going to do?

The answer came to her clearly. She would go to Caleb and ask him to give her enough money to get out of town. She'd leave Cheyenne, go to another town, and start a new life. She'd tell people that she was a widow, that her husband, a brave and handsome man, had been killed in the line of duty while trying to stop a bank robbery.

Yes, she thought. Caleb was the answer.

Callie stared at Angela Bristol. "What is it?" she asked, struggling to keep her envy from showing on her face. Angela was wearing a dark green day dress that perfectly outlined her slender figure and made her eyes sparkle like emeralds.

Callie's gaze dropped to her own burgeoning belly. She was almost six months pregnant now. Standing beside Angela made her feel like a cow.

"I'd like to see Caleb," Angela replied.

"He isn't here."

"Not here?"

Callie frowned at the quiet desperation in Angela's voice. "He went into Laramie to see about some cattle. Is something wrong?"

"When will he be back?"

"I expect him late this afternoon. Maybe you could come back tomorrow?"

"I'll wait," Angela said, and swept past Callie into the parlor.

Callie stared after Angela, stunned by the woman's rude manner. Then, with a sigh, she closed the door and followed Angela into the drawing room. "Can I get you something?"

"Tea would be nice."

Callie smiled politely. "With or without arsenic?" she muttered under her breath as she went into the kitchen.

Angela glanced around the room while she waited for Callie to return. She'd always loved this room with its huge stone fireplace, massive furniture, and dark-hued carpet. As a child, she had dreamed of living here, of raising her children in this house.

She felt her insides churn with envy as Caleb's wife entered the room. It wasn't fair that a whore's daughter should have everything she had once dreamed of: the best ranch in the country, the man Angie had loved all her life, a baby who wouldn't be a bastard.

Callie placed the silver tray on the table, then sat down, poured two cups of tea, and handed one to Angela. "Sugar?"

"No."

So much for politeness, Callie thought. "Why do you want to see Caleb?"

"I just thought he'd like to know he's going to be a father."

The lie slid past Angela's lips. Unbidden and unexpected, it was satisfying nevertheless.

Callie placed her arm across her abdomen. "Of course he knows he's . . ." The words died in her throat as a horrible suspicion formed in her mind. "What do you mean?"

"I'm pregnant."

Callie's gaze darted to Angela's trim waist and flat stomach. "No."

"Yes, and Caleb's the father."

Angela watched Callie's face turn pale, taking perverse pleasure in the other woman's pain. Misery did, indeed, love company, she mused.

"You're lying." Callie felt the blood drain from her face. It couldn't be true. And yet, he had spent all those nights with Angela in the mansion. . . .

Feeling suddenly guilty for telling such an outrageous falsehood, Angela stood up.

"Tell Caleb I'll wait for him at the old house, won't you?"

Callie nodded, unable to speak past the nausea rising in her throat. She sat there for several minutes after Angela left, too numb to move, then she ran into the kitchen and bent over the sink, her stomach heaving.

Angela was pregnant, and Caleb was the father.

Richard Ashton swore under his breath as he sat up in bed. He'd been dreaming, dreaming about Angela.

Lighting the lamp beside his bed, he reached for a cigar, wondering when life had gotten so complicated. Pregnant. She said she was pregnant. It was a distinct possibility, considering all the time they'd spent together in the last few months. Still, she was a woman, and women had been trying to ambush him into marriage all his adult life, attracted by the Ashton name and his family's wealth. All except Callie. He hadn't been able to woo her or bribe her or buy her, though she had outfoxed him where that five grand was concerned. Maybe that was why he had refused to give up on her, he thought. Maybe, if she'd said yes like all the rest, he'd have tired of her.

He pictured her in his mind: red-gold hair, blue eyes, a soft figure that went in and out in all the right places, skin the color of fresh cream . . . Yes, she was pretty enough, but if he was going to be entirely honest, he had to admit that he found Angela Bristol more attractive and that he much preferred her company. True, she wasn't as young as Callie, or as innocent, but he rather liked the fact that Angela knew what a man wanted and how to give it to him.

Richard frowned. Maybe he'd been a fool to send Angela away. Maybe she *was* pregnant with his child. His heir.

He swore under his breath. A son, he thought. She was a strong, healthy woman. What if she produced a son? Did he want his child to carry the awful stigma of bastardy? Good Lord, what would his father say?

Richard blew out a column of blue smoke, then regarded the glowing end of his cigar. In the morning, he'd go to Angela and propose. He'd set the date for sometime in January, two months from now. If she was indeed pregnant, she'd be starting to show by then, and they'd be married.

But heaven help her if the child had tawny skin and hair as black as Satan's heart!

Caleb let out a sigh of relief as he rode into the ranch yard an hour after dusk. Damn, it was good to be home. Swinging out of the saddle, he handed the buckskin's reins to one of the men, spent a few minutes catching up on what had happened in his absence, then headed for the house, anxious to see Callie, to hold her in his arms. Lord, how he had missed her!

He ran up the steps, smiling as he opened the front door. Then he frowned. The house was dark and quiet. Too quiet. Tossing his hat on the rack, he ran a hand through his hair, wondering where Callie was.

"Callie?"

"In here."

He followed the sound of her voice into the kitchen. "Why's the house so dark?"

"I've been in the dark for months," she replied cryptically.

Puzzled by her reply, Caleb crossed the floor toward her. "Hey, pretty woman," he said, his voice low and soft, "did you miss me?"

Callie's heart lurched at the sound of his voice. Carefully, she lifted a pan of hot water from the stove and placed it on the table. She heard his footsteps coming up behind her, and then his arms were sliding around her nonexistent waist, his hands reaching up to cup her breasts.

"I missed you," Caleb murmured, his breath tickling her cheek.

"Did you?" Callie asked. Her voice was brittle, as stiff as her back.

For a moment, Caleb didn't move. Then he placed his hands on Callie's shoulders and turned her around to face him.

"What's wrong?"

"You tell me."

His gaze swept over her, lingering a moment on her swollen abdomen before resting on her face. There were dark shadows under her eyes, and her face was pale and haggard.

A nameless fear rose within him. "Callie, are you all right?"

"I feel fine."

"The baby . . ."

"Is fine."

She stared up at him, her hands balled into tight fists, her eyes empty of all emotion.

"Then what is it?"

"Angela Bristol is waiting for you at the old house."

"Waiting for me?" Caleb frowned. "Why? What does she want?"

"What does she want?" Callie repeated, and her voice was as clear and cold as ice.

Caleb shrugged. "How should I know?"

"Don't play games with me, Caleb Stryker. I should have known better than to trust you. You're no better than any other man, no better than your father."

"What the hell are you talking about?"

"I'm talking about Angela. And you."

Caleb felt his anger rise, and then, remembering that Callie was pregnant, he took a deep breath. Fanny had warned him that expectant mothers sometimes got bizarre notions and should be humored.

"There's nothing between us," he said reassuringly. "There never was. I told you that before."

"I see. Then perhaps you'll explain something to me?"

"If I can."

"How is it that Angela Bristol is carrying your child?"

"What?"

"You heard me. She came here to let you know that you're going to be a father. Again."

Caleb shook his head. This had to be a joke. Only Callie didn't look like she was going to laugh. Ever.

"Well?"

"It's not true. Callie, you've got to believe me."

"Why should I? When have you ever told me the truth?"

"I never really lied to you about anything. There were just some things I didn't mention."

"Like the fact that your mistress is pregnant!"

"She is not my mistress." Caleb ground the words out between tightly clenched teeth.

"She's waiting for you," Callie said, her voice as cold as winter frost. "Go tell her your pretty lies."

A muscle worked in Caleb's jaw; then, without another word, he slammed out the back door.

He made it to the old house, on foot, in record time, his anger eating up the distance. Angela, pregnant. She had the devil's own nerve to come here claiming the child was his. He'd never laid a hand on her.

He didn't bother to knock. "Angela!"

"In here, Caleb."

She was sitting in the kitchen, staring out the back window. A squat white candle burned on the table, casting her profile in shadow.

"You want to tell me what the hell is going on?" Caleb demanded.

"I'm pregnant," Angela replied tonelessly. "Didn't she tell you?"

"She told me. Why'd you tell Callie I'm the father?"

"I don't know. I didn't mean to. It just slipped out."

Caleb swore. "Just slipped out!" he exclaimed. "Like hell! Do you realize what you've done?"

He paced the floor in long strides, his face dark with rage. "Dammit, Angie, I should cut out your lying little tongue!"

Angela knew a moment of real fear as he turned to glare at her. Caleb Stryker was a fearsome sight when he was angry. And he was angry now. He'd killed men, she thought. Maybe he'd kill her, too, and put her out of her misery. She wouldn't blame him. She'd done a terrible thing, and she had no excuse for what she'd done, no excuse other than soul-shattering envy.

"I'm sorry, Cal," she said penitently. "I'll go tell Callie the truth."

"Why, Angie? Why would you tell her such an outrageous lie?"

"I don't know! I didn't mean to, but when I saw her standing there . . ." Angela shook her head. "She has everything, Cal, everything I ever wanted. Everything that should have been mine."

Caleb rested one shoulder against the door frame, all the anger draining out of him. He knew only too well what it was like to want something you couldn't have. All his life, he'd wanted his father's love and acceptance, his forgiveness. He should have gotten over it long ago, but it still ate at him, gnawing at his insides like a tiny worm that couldn't be destroyed.

Angela slumped in her chair, her heart heavy with discouragement. If only her husband hadn't died, life would have been so different. She'd been happy with Stan; she would have been happy with Cal. Given a chance, she might have been happy with Richard, but she'd never know that now.

A fresh wave of pain tore at her heart. It had hurt when he refused to believe the child was his. What kind of woman did he think she was? Except for her husband, Richard Ashton was the only man she'd ever slept with. But that was all in the past now.

"I need some money, Cal. I want to leave town."

"Sure. I guess you'll be going back East to stay with your mother."

"No."

"Why not?"

"I can't face her. She'd be so ashamed. Anyway, there's no room at my aunt's house."

"Where will you go?"

"Chicago."

Caleb frowned. "Chicago? Are you crazy?"

"No one knows me there. I can get a job, start a new life."

"Sure, there are lots of jobs waiting for women in your condition," he muttered sarcastically. "Well, forget it, I'm not letting you go."

"I don't see how you can stop me."

He crossed the room in two long strides and knelt before her. "A woman in your condition shouldn't be making long trips, especially alone." He took a deep breath, held it a moment and then, his decision made, he released it in a long sigh. "You can stay here."

Angela looked at him in surprise. "Here? You can't be serious?"

"Here or at the mansion, whichever you want. At least until the baby's born." He held up a hand to silence her objections. "We've always been friends, Angie. That hasn't changed, and I won't have you running around with no one to look after you. After the baby's born, I'll give you a stake and you can go to Chicago if you're still of a mind to go."

Tears of gratitude welled in Angela's eyes as she took his hand in hers. "Oh, Cal, you've always been so good to me. I'll . . ."

"Well, well, isn't this a pretty scene."

Caleb lurched to his feet at the sound of Callie's voice. A soft oath escaped his lips as he realized how guilty he must look, kneeling at Angie's feet. The red flush creeping up Angie's neck didn't help any.

"Sorry I interrupted," Callie said. "But I had to see it for myself."

"Callie, I can explain."

"Don't bother."

Caleb glanced down at Angela. "Tell her the truth, Angie."

"I lied to you before," Angela said. "The baby's not Caleb's."

"Did he tell you to say that?"

Angela managed to look offended. "Of course not."

"So, you were lying before?"

"Yes."

"How do I know you're not lying now because Caleb asked you to?"

Caleb took a step toward Callie, but she put her arm out as if to ward him off.

"Don't come near me. I've had enough of your lies. And hers, too."

"Callie, the baby's not Caleb's, I swear it."

"Oh? Then who's the father?"

Angela's gaze slid away from Callie's face. "I'd rather not say."

Callie nodded, her face expressionless. "It doesn't matter. Don't come home, Caleb. You're no longer welcome in my house."

Her voice was low, toneless. There was no emphasis on the *my*, but he heard it anyway.

Callie glanced briefly at Angela, then focused her attention on Caleb again. He'd hurt her, and she wanted to hurt him in return. And she knew just how to do it.

Lifting her chin and squaring her shoulders, she said the one thing she knew would hurt him more than anything else.

"I'm selling the ranch," she declared, and hurried from the room before he could stop her.

Caleb swore under his breath. Sell the ranch! She was bluffing, he thought. She loved the place. But so did he, and she knew it. What better way to get back at him for his supposed infidelity than to sell the one thing in the world that mattered to him?

"Oh, Cal, you don't think she'd really sell the ranch, do you?" Angela asked, coming to stand beside him.

Caleb shook his head ruefully. "I don't know, Angie. She might. She sure as hell looks mad enough."

"You'd better go after her, Cal."

"She doesn't want me. Maybe she never did."

"You don't believe that."

"No, I guess not."

"I'm sorry. I didn't mean to cause you trouble. I never thought she'd believe me."

"It's not your fault. It's mine. All mine. So, where do you want to stay?"

"Here," Angela replied without hesitation. She couldn't go back to town, couldn't take a chance on running into Richard. She never wanted to see him again. "You really love her, don't you?"

"Yeah."

Angie felt a twinge of regret. She'd never meant to cause Caleb trouble. He'd always been good to her, and she loved him, would always love him. It was just so hard to know that Callie had everything while she, Angela, had no one.

She smiled wistfully as she placed a hand over her abdomen. Soon, she thought, soon she'd have someone all her own to love.

"I guess you'd better go home now and see if you can't straighten things out with your wife."

Caleb nodded, thinking that it would take a miracle to make things right with Callie this time.

# *Chapter Thirty-three*

The windows were dark by the time he returned to the main house. The front door was locked; the back door too. His clothes and other personal belongings had been thrown into the yard, along with his rifle, his moccasins, and the boots he wore on those rare occasions when he took Callie to church.

He stared up at their bedroom window for several long moments and then turned away. If that was the way she wanted it, so be it!

Retracing his steps to the barn, he threw a bridle on the buckskin, swung up on the mare's bare back, and rode away from the ranch. He needed time alone, time away from moody females and solid walls and responsibility. Time away from clocks and cattle. Maybe he never should have married Callie, after all. Maybe it had never been in him to be a husband or a father. Maybe he should have stuck to bounty hunting. It might have been dangerous. It might have been lonely. But it had been a hell of a lot less complicated!

He felt all the anger and frustration drain out of him as the miles slipped by. The night was quiet, peaceful, soothing. The breeze was fragrant with the scent of damp earth and sage. He heard the muffled sound of an owl's wings, the distant cry of a coyote, the faint bawling of a calf.

Reining the buckskin to a halt, he took a deep breath; then, dismounting, he lifted his arms above his head and offered a silent prayer to *Wakan Tanka,* asking the God of the Lakota to bless him with wisdom, with patience and understanding.

His only answer was dark silence.

Removing his shirt, Caleb drew the knife from the sheath at his belt and raked the edge of the blade across his chest. A warm trickle of blood followed in the wake of the blade.

A whisper of cold air stirred the leaves in the trees.

"Hear my prayer, *Wakan Tanka.* Forgive me for the years I have neglected the Life Way of the People. Forgive me for the blood I have shed . . ."

He winced as he drew the knife across his chest again. " . . . for the lives I have taken, for the people I have hurt."

Again, Caleb raked the knife across his flesh, offering his blood and his pain as a sacrifice to the Great Mystery.

"Bless my woman and my unborn child. Help me to be patient with my woman's fears, understanding of her heartache, tolerant of her doubts. Bless her with strength, and my child with life."

A fourth time, Caleb drew the blade across his chest. "Life is a circle. The buffalo and the wolf are my brothers, the birds are my cousins. *Mitakuye oyasin.* All are my relatives. Help me to remember that I am but a small part of thy creation. Grant me wisdom. Grant me understanding. Grant me patience."

Head thrown back, Caleb stood in the moonlight. His arms ached, the cool night air stung his wounds, and still he stood there, waiting.

There was a sudden gust of wind, and the moon disappeared behind a cloud. For a moment, he stood in a darkness so complete it was like being blind. Then the cloud disintegrated, a shooting star plummeted from the sky, and the moon smiled down on him once more.

Filled with a sense of peace, Caleb lowered his arms. "*Ate, Pilamaya,*" Caleb murmured softly. "Thank you, Father."

Callie sat at the bedroom window, staring out at the darkened yard. Hours had passed since she saw Caleb ride away, and now an awful fear enveloped her, a cold terror that grew ever stronger.

What if he had gone for good? What if he believed she meant to sell the ranch and he'd decided to leave Wyoming? But no, surely if he believed her, he'd want to buy the Rocking S for himself.

She tried to convince herself that he wouldn't ride out of her life forever. He might leave the ranch; she had ordered him off it. But surely he wouldn't leave Cheyenne. Surely he wouldn't leave his child.

No, he would never do that. No matter how he

felt about her, he would stay and provide for his child. And for Angela's child.

She couldn't bear the thought of never seeing him again. No matter that he'd lied to her, betrayed her, broken their wedding vows, she still loved him. Would always love him.

Oh, it wasn't fair! Why did he have the power to hurt her so badly? She rested her head on her forearm and closed her eyes. She'd been so happy these past weeks, so sure he loved her, would always love her. And now this . . .

With a start, Callie sat up. She was being unfair, she realized. Even if Angela was pregnant, it had all happened before the picnic, before Caleb declared his love for her, before their marriage had been truly consummated.

"Oh, Caleb," she murmured. "Forgive me. Please come home."

She gazed out the window, staring in wonder as a cloud drifted across the moon. A falling star trailed its brilliance across the sky and then the moon was shining again, bathing the earth in a halo of pale silver light.

A short time later, Caleb rode into the yard.

The dappled moonlight illuminated him, showering his dark hair with silver highlights, reminding her of a medieval knight returning from battle. She frowned when she saw that he was shirtless. When he dismounted, she saw several dark streaks across his chest.

He wasn't a knight, she thought, but a warrior, and he deserved to be welcomed home.

Rising from her chair, she hurried from her room and ran out of the house, calling his name.

Caleb turned at the sound of her voice, dropping

the buckskin's reins as Callie hurled herself into his arms.

"Are you all right?" she cried, hugging him tight.

"I'm fine."

She drew back, her gaze moving over his chest. "You've been hurt."

Slowly, Caleb shook his head. "I've been praying."

"I don't understand."

Caleb drew a soft breath, wondering how to explain it to her, how to make her understand. Draping one arm around her shoulders, he drew her close to his side.

"The Indians have a ritual called the Sun Dance," he began. "It's a religious ceremony, one the white man viewed with revulsion. During the most sacred part of the ceremony, the warriors are connected to the Sun Dance pole and they dance until they free themselves."

"Connected how?" Callie asked.

"The medicine man cuts a slit above each breast and inserts a small piece of wood or bone to which he attaches a long strip of rawhide. The other end of the rawhide is fastened to the pole, and while the warriors dance, they pull against the rawhide until it tears from their flesh."

"That's awful."

"Maybe, but they believe that *Wakan Tanka* hears their prayers. Their pain, their blood, is a token of their sincerity, a plea for the blessings of the Great Spirit."

"That doesn't explain why you're bleeding," Callie said, horrified by the picture he had painted.

"Yes, it does. I haven't prayed for a lot of years, Callie, and I offered *Wakan Tanka* my blood and my pain so He'd know my prayer was sincere."

Callie gazed up at her husband. "What did you pray for?"

"Don't you know?" His voice was as soft as a kiss, as quiet as a caress.

"For me?" She could hardly speak the words.

Caleb nodded. "Among other things. Callie, I never touched Angie, I swear it."

"I know. Can you forgive me for being a fool?" Callie asked in a choked whisper. "I'm sorry I didn't believe you. I should have known you wouldn't do anything that would shame me, or dishonor Angela."

"Callie, you don't need to apologize. You had every reason to doubt me."

"No. You told me once that you weren't like the men my mother knew, but I didn't believe you. I guess I was afraid to believe you, afraid you'd hurt me. I'm sorry, Caleb. I'll never doubt you again."

His arm tightened around her shoulders and he hugged her close, savoring her nearness as much as her words. "Do you still want to sell the ranch?"

"No. I only said that because I was angry and hurt."

"Are you sure, Callie? We don't have to stay here if you'd rather leave."

Callie drew away a little so she could see his face. "Are you trying to make me crazy, Caleb Stryker?" she demanded. "You know you don't want to leave this place, so let's not hear another word about it."

"Yes, boss," he replied, grinning down at her. "Can we go to bed now?"

"Not until I've cleaned those cuts." She stared at his chest, awed by the thought that he had put a knife to his own flesh, that he had done it while praying for her. "Does it hurt terribly?"

"A little," he admitted.

"Come on, let's go inside."

"In a minute." He glanced at his belongings, still strewn all over the yard, then grinned as he imagined Callie tossing everything out the door. "Looks like I've got some cleaning up to do."

"I'll help," Callie offered contritely.

They quickly gathered up Caleb's belongings and carried them into the house, depositing them on the floor inside the front door.

"I'll put everything away tomorrow," Callie said as Caleb placed his rifle in the rack above the fireplace.

A short time later, Caleb sat in one of the kitchen chairs while Callie washed his chest with warm water and dried it with a clean towel.

His breath hissed from between clenched teeth as she swabbed the cuts with carbolic.

"Damn, woman," he growled. "That stuff burns like the devil."

Callie made a face at him. "How can you carve yourself up with a knife and then complain about a little sting?"

"That was different. I was holding the knife." He grabbed the rag out of her hand. "That's good enough."

"Are you sure?"

"I'm sure." He tossed the rag onto the table, then drew Callie into the vee between his thighs, his hands resting, palms down, on her belly. He looked up at her as he felt their child move beneath his fingertips. "Does it hurt?"

"No. It feels wonderful." Callie grinned at him.

"I'm sure it's a boy, he kicks so hard."

Caleb waited, hoping the baby would move again. It was hard to believe there was a living being growing within Callie's body, a child that they had created together. He had witnessed the miracle of birth only a few times in his life. Always, it had left him with a feeling of awe bordering on reverence. Oddly enough, taking a life had often left him feeling the same way, reminding him of the tenuous bond between life and death.

Rising to his feet, he lifted Callie into his arms and carried her down the hall to their bedroom. Wordlessly, he undressed her, his gaze moving over her, worshipping her as the giver of life, a co-creator with the Great Spirit.

He tried to tell her how much he loved her, but words failed him, and so he told her with tender caresses instead, hoping she would hear the words he couldn't say.

His fingers stroked her breasts, imagining them filled with milk to nourish their child. He let his hands wander over her rounded belly, where their baby slept, safe and secure. His hands massaged the arms that would cradle their son. He kissed her lips, lips that would smile as their child learned to walk and talk, lips that would kiss away a little boy's hurts.

Lips that could soothe a grown man's doubts and fears. He groaned her name as desire overcame awe, and the passion of now overcame the promise of tomorrow. She was woman, his woman, and he ached for her with every fiber of his being.

Afraid to hurt her, he started to pull away, but Callie drew him close, her arms wrapping around him.

"It's all right," she whispered, her voice filled with desire.

"Are you sure?" Not for the world would he hurt her or the child.

"I'm sure. Love me, Caleb."

"Always," he murmured, and buried himself in her sweetness, pledging his love anew with each kiss, renewing his promise of devotion with each caress.

Callie clung to him, breathless, mindless, as the rest of the world faded away until only Caleb remained, the muscles in his arms rock-hard beneath her restless fingertips, his breath warm upon her neck, his hands playing over her body, making her sigh with ecstasy.

And when she was trembling on the brink, certain she would die from the wonder of his touch, he carried her over the edge and together they merged into that brief moment when two souls become one, when two halves are made whole.

# Chapter Thirty-four

Standing at the clothesline, Callie drew a deep breath, her face turned up to the sun.

How good life was! The winter she had dreaded had been like a dream. While the wind howled and rain pummeled the roof, she had found refuge in Caleb's arms. Christmas had come in a flurry of snow, covering the earth in a blanket of white. They had shared it, just the two of them, exchanging gifts—a pair of fur-lined gloves for Caleb because she'd noticed he didn't have any, a delicate silver heart-shaped locket for Callie. Later, they had eaten supper by candlelight, made love by firelight. It had been the best Christmas she'd ever known.

And then, suddenly, it was spring.

It was like a miracle, Callie thought. Only a few weeks ago she'd been certain the sun would be forever shrouded in clouds, and now the world was busily renewing itself. Sweet grass covered the prairie like a verdant blanket, a bright profusion of flowers covered the hills, and the trees, newly garbed in shades of green, were filled with the chirping of baby birds.

The sow had ten plump little piglets, and there were downy yellow chicks everywhere. One of the mares had twin foals; miraculously, both fillies survived. Lambs frolicked behind the house.

In the evening, they sometimes saw a fawn following its mother down to the river. Soon, it would be round-up time, and the calves would be branded.

Secure at last in the strength of Caleb's love, Callie's jealousy vanished, and she often invited Angela to spend the day at the house. Now that she no longer thought of the other woman as a threat, she found herself feeling sorry for Angela. Several times, she'd tried to find out who had fathered Angie's baby, but Angela refused to tell anyone, including Caleb.

Sitting in the parlor, mending clothes or sewing tiny sacques for Callie's baby, they complained of the aches and pains that went hand in hand with pregnancy, lamenting the loss of their figures, the nausea, the tenderness of their breasts, their peculiar cravings at odd hours of the night.

Callie confessed to being afraid of childbirth.

Angela confided that she was more afraid of town gossip, of having to raise her child alone in an unforgiving world.

Both complained of having cabin fever.

Callie dropped the last of the wash into the basket at her feet, feet she could no longer see over her big belly. The baby was due in mid-May and she was as big as a house, so big she couldn't even put on her own shoes. So big she was beginning to wonder if she'd ever be thin again. She knew it was highly improper for her to be seen in public, but she was past caring. She wanted to buy a frilly new hat and some material for a baby quilt. She wanted to eat a meal she hadn't prepared. She wanted to see Fanny.

And so it was on a bright morning in early spring that Caleb found himself escorting his very pregnant wife and Angela into Cheyenne. Callie wore a dress with a high waist and a flowing cloak that covered her body from her neck to her ankles and pretended that no one would notice she was in the family way.

Angela cleverly managed to conceal her condition beneath a loose fitting gown and a shawl.

Two hours later, Caleb was ready to call it a day. They'd had pie and coffee at Dyer's Restaurant, and they'd stopped to visit Fanny. Callie had bought a perky bonnet adorned with silk flowers, ribbons, and an ostrich plume from Hills & Goodsell, as well as several yards of cotton and batting from I. Herman & Co. Angela had bought a box of scented powder and several yards of muslin to make a new dress that would accommodate her expanding girth.

And now they were walking down 16th Street and Callie was peering in the window at Dobson's Confectionery, debating whether she wanted bonbons or licorice.

Caleb let out a sigh of exasperation, silently vowing that he'd never again accompany two pregnant females into town.

Callie had just decided on bonbons when Angela let out a gasp. Grabbing Caleb by the arm, she tried to hide behind him.

"What's wrong?" he asked.

"Don't let him see me," Angela exclaimed.

"Who?"

"Richard."

"Richard?" Caleb frowned. "Ashton, you mean?"

"Yes."

Caleb glanced down the street, scowling blackly when he saw Ashton striding purposefully toward them. He slid a look at Angela's pale face, and suddenly everything made sense.

"He's the father, isn't he?"

She started to deny it, then nodded.

"When? Where?"

Angie's cheeks blossomed with embarrassment. "At the mansion."

"At the mansion!" Caleb exclaimed. "You used my house to meet that weasel?"

"I . . . we . . . that is, he wanted Callie, and I wanted you, and we got together to see if we couldn't figure out some way to come between you. It just happened." Angela shrugged apologetically, deciding it wouldn't be wise to tell Caleb just how many times it had happened.

Angie turned to Callie for support. "It just happened," she repeated.

"Do you love him?" Callie asked.

"No, I hate him, the cad! Please, Cal, make him go away. I never want to see him again."

Without waiting for a reply, she pushed open the door of Dobson's Confectionery and ducked inside.

Callie slid her arm through Caleb's as Richard approached.

"Get out of my way, Stryker," Richard ordered curtly.

"She doesn't want to see you."

"This doesn't concern you," Richard said.

"I'm afraid it does. Angie's a friend of mine, and I'm responsible for her."

Ashton tilted his head back and stared at Caleb disdainfully.

"What's the matter, 'breed? Isn't one white woman enough for you?"

Caleb took a step forward, his eyes narrowed with rage. "I ought to kill you for that."

"You can try later. For now, get out of my way. I have a personal matter to discuss with Mrs. Bristol."

"She doesn't want to see you," Caleb repeated, biting off each word.

"I'd like to hear that from Angela, if you don't mind."

Caleb's hands clenched at his sides as he felt the anger building within him. "Callie, go inside."

Callie shook her head. "Caleb, don't."

"Do as I say. Ashton and I have a little unfinished business to settle."

A wry smile twisted Ashton's lips. "Glad to oblige you any time, anywhere."

"Here," Caleb said tersely. "Now."

Callie shrieked as Richard swung at Caleb and missed. Caleb's fist shot forward, swift as a striking snake. There was a nasty crack, and blood gushed from Ashton's nose. Richard stumbled backward, and Callie hoped the fight was over.

It wasn't. Caleb lunged at Richard, his fist driving into Ashton's face a second time. Then the two of them were tumbling down the stairs, trading blows as they rolled back and forth in the street. In minutes, a crowd had gathered.

Callie watched helplessly, her hands covering her ears to block out the sound of knotted fists striking flesh. There was blood dripping from Caleb's nose and mouth now and a jagged gash on his cheek, caused by the big onyx ring Richard wore on his right hand.

Callie grimaced as Caleb drove his fist into Richard's back, winced as Richard hit Caleb in the face. She glanced at the crowd, hoping someone would put a stop to the fight, but the men were watching with unbridled excitement, the women with barely suppressed fascination. The sheriff was nowhere in sight.

For all the horror of it, Callie couldn't help but admire her husband. He seemed to be enjoying the fight. His eyes were shining with the heat of battle, and he seemed impervious to Ashton's blows. There was blood on his face, on his shirt, on his knuckles, but he seemed oblivious to it all, his whole being focused on his opponent.

Caleb was breathing hard as he grabbed a handful of Richard's shirtfront and hauled him to his feet, and Callie wondered how much longer the fight could go on. Both men seemed exhausted and ready to drop in their tracks.

Caleb was drawing back his fist, an exultant grin on his battered face, when Angela ran down the stairs and started hitting him on the back.

"No!" she shrieked. "Leave him alone! Can't you see he's through?"

Caleb swore under his breath. "Angie, get out of here!"

"No. Leave him alone—please, Caleb!"

"No, dammit! He insulted Callie."

Caleb drew in a lung full of air as he wiped his face on his shirt sleeve. "He pulled a gun on me. Hell, he probably started the fire at the ranch, too."

Caleb shook Angie's restraining hand from his shoulder. "Leave me be!"

Richard Ashton shook his head as if to clear it. "What are you talking about, you stupid Indian?" he sputtered, gasping for breath. "I didn't have anything to do with that fire."

"Don't lie to me, you mangy cur."

Richard swiped at the blood dripping from his nose. "I'm not lying," he insisted with as much dignity as he could muster under the circumstances. "You're talking nonsense. Why would I want to set fire to the ranch?"

"Revenge," Caleb bit off the word.

Richard shook his head, then groaned. "It wasn't me."

The two men glared at each other for a tense moment. Caleb drew a deep breath, released it in a long sigh, and then, abruptly, he released his hold on Ashton's shirt and stepped back. "I believe you."

Richard Ashton sank to his knees, and Angela dropped down beside him, pressing a dainty pocket handkerchief to his mouth while tears rolled down her cheeks.

Caleb stared at the crowd that was still gathered around. "Angie, let's go," he said curtly.

"I can't leave him."

"What?"

"He needs me."

Angela put her arm around Richard's waist and helped him to his feet, clucking to him like a mother hen.

And Richard Ashton had the gall to grin at him, split lip, broken nose, and all.

"You're going with him?" Caleb asked in disbelief.

Angie nodded, smiling as Richard put one arm around her shoulders.

"We're getting married," Ashton said, wincing as he pressed a hand to his rib cage.

"Oh, Richard!" Angie exclaimed. "Do you mean it?"

"Yeah." He took the bloody hanky from her hand and pressed it to his nose. "C'mon, Ange, let's go home."

Caleb swore under his breath as he watched the two of them walk away. "She said he was a cad. She said she never wanted to see him again."

"She's in love," Callie said, smiling. "Women say funny things when they're in love. You should know that."

Reaching into her reticule, Callie withdrew a lovely handkerchief made of Irish linen. It had been a gift from Fanny. With regret, she dampened one corner with her tongue, then wiped the blood from her husband's battered face as best she could, thinking that he looked as if he'd been kicked by a mule. His nose, his left cheek, and his lower lip were swollen and bloody; his right eye was already turning black and blue.

Men, she thought ruefully. "Come on, let's us go home, too, so I can clean you up properly."

Shaking his head, Caleb followed Callie down the street. "Women," he muttered. "I'll never understand them."

# *Chapter Thirty-five*

Caleb sat on a chair in the kitchen of the mansion, wincing slightly as Callie disinfected the cuts on his face, then soaked his bruised knuckles in a pan of cool water.

"You didn't tell me you thought someone set the fire," Callie remarked.

"I didn't want to worry you."

"Who would do such a thing?"

"I don't know."

"But you think it was the same person who took a shot at you, don't you?"

"Yeah." He swore softly as Callie poured carbolic over his knuckles. "That's enough," he admonished, jerking his hand away. "The cure hurts more than the cause."

"Caleb, you don't suppose . . ."

"What?"

"Well, it's possible you made some enemies in the last eight years."

Caleb grunted. "Possible? I'd say darn likely."

"Maybe someone's trying to get even."

"I thought of that."

"Do you have any idea who it might be?"

"No. I've killed more than my share of men. I suppose they all had families somewhere."

"Has anyone ever tried to get revenge before?"

"A few times," he admitted, and Callie's stomach clenched as she thought of the numerous scars on his back and chest, souvenirs of bullet wounds and knife wounds.

Seeing the worry in her eyes, Caleb took her hands in his and gave them a reassuring squeeze. "Don't worry about it, Callie, it's probably nothing."

"Nothing!" She pulled her hands free. "Somebody took a potshot at you. Then the barn is set on fire. Oh, and the cut cinch. And the rattlesnake in your bedroll . . ."

Concern flared in her eyes with the realization that so many accidents couldn't possibly be accidents. "Oh, Caleb . . ."

She stared at him as the true horror of it all sank in for the first time.

"Callie, I can take care of myself."

He drew her into the vee of his thighs and buried his face in the cleft of her breasts.

"And you, too." But even as he spoke the words, he wondered how he'd protect her from an enemy that had no face and no form.

They spent the next couple of days at the mansion. For Callie, it was a rare treat to relax, to have nothing to do but sleep late and spend all her time with Caleb. He took her shopping; he took her out to luncheon and to dinner. One day they browsed through George Holt's bookstore; Callie bought a copy of *Portrait of a Lady* by Henry James; Caleb bought *Ben Hur.* At Ohnhaus & Donovan, Caleb ordered a pair of custom-made boots. Callie purchased a new bonnet from Hills & Goodsell, then they went to Kapp's Restaurant for a late supper.

The following afternoon they spent almost two hours browsing through F.E. Warren & Co., admiring the imported carpets, the furniture and china. Callie picked out a brightly colored print wallpaper for the room that would belong to the baby, a silver candy dish, and a delicate music box that played a Strauss waltz.

When Callie admired a necklace in the window of Zehner, Jackson & Buechner, Caleb bought it for her, and when he admired a new Winchester rifle in Bergersen's window, she returned the favor.

It was such fun, she thought, to have money, to be able to actually buy what she admired instead of just looking at it and wishing. Caleb was tall and handsome. Despite his reputation, despite the fact that he was a half-breed, women turned to stare at him wherever they went, and each time Callie felt a little thrill because he belonged to her, only her.

Callie was sitting in Colton's Restaurant, indulging in a slice of chocolate cake and a glass of lemonade, when she saw the young cowboy, Whitley, peering into the window. He waved when he saw her, his expression pensive, and then stepped into the restaurant.

"Afternoon, Mrs. Stryker," he said, removing his hat.

"How are you, Whitley?"

"Fine, thank you, ma'am." He gestured at the cake. "Is that as good as it looks?"

"Better. Why don't you join me?"

Whitley shook his head. "No, thank you, ma'am, it wouldn't be proper."

"Fiddlesticks. Fanny, bring this young man a slice of cake, please. And a glass of lemonade. Or would you rather have coffee?"

"Lemonade's fine."

"So, tell me," Callie said, "how have you been?"

Whitley hung his hat on the corner of a chair and sat down across from Callie.

"I'm doing all right, ma'am. I got me a job at the Bar J."

Callie nodded. The Bar J was their nearest neighbor to the south. "I thought you were going back to Texas."

"Soon," Whitley said. "I have a little unfinished business to settle here in Wyoming first."

"Oh." Callie smiled at Fanny as the older woman brought Whitley's order to their table. "Told you it was good," she said, seeing him smile as he took a bite.

"Yes' ma'am. It's prime."

"Well, I guess I'd better be going. I'm supposed to meet Mr. Stryker in front of the Inter-Ocean at one-thirty."

"I'll walk you over," Whitley offered.

"It isn't necessary," Callie said. "Stay and finish your cake."

"No, I insist."

"Very well."

Outside, Callie turned east, toward 16th Street.

"No," Whitley said, taking her firmly by the arm. "We're going this way."

"I told you I have to meet Caleb."

"I'm sorry, Mrs. Stryker, but you're coming with me."

Callie looked into Whitley's pale blue eyes and shuddered at what she saw there.

"Don't scream," Whitley warned.

His gaze moved swiftly over her. He frowned when he noticed, for the first time, that she was in the family way. But it was too late to turn back now.

"Just come along quietly," he said. "I don't want to hurt you."

"Where . . . where are we going?"

"Not far."

His fingers held her arm in a viselike grip as he urged her down the street and into an alley where two horses were waiting.

"Whitley, please . . ."

"I'm gonna tie your hands now."

Fear snaked its way down Callie's spine. All trace of the amiable young man she'd known on the trail was gone, and in his place stood a stranger with a voice as unyielding as steel and eyes as cold as ice.

Deftly, he lashed her hands together, then lifted her onto the back of a small-boned chestnut mare. Taking the mare's reins in his hand, he mounted his own horse and led the way out of town.

Caleb paced back and forth in front of the Inter-Ocean, wondering what the devil was keeping Callie. For the second time in ten minutes, he opened the door and looked inside, his gaze darting around the lobby, but there was no sign of Callie.

He heard the courthouse clock chime two, and he muttered an impatient oath under his breath. Where was she?

Thinking she might have stopped in to see Fanny, he went to Colton's Restaurant.

"Why, yes, she was here," Fanny said. "But she left over an hour ago."

"Did she say where she was headed?"

"Why, no." Fanny frowned. "Is something wrong?"

"She was supposed to meet me at two, but she never showed up."

"I see."

Fanny toyed with the folds of her apron, wondering if she should tell Caleb that his wife had shared a table with a young man. She didn't want to cause any trouble for Callie. On the other hand, she didn't want Caleb to worry needlessly, either.

Caleb glanced at the clock on the wall. "Are you sure she didn't say anything?"

"I hope I'm not telling tales out of school," Fanny remarked, "but she left with a young man."

Caleb's head jerked up, his dark eyes glinting dangerously. "What young man?"

"I've never seen him before."

"What was his name?"

Fanny pursed her lips, trying to recall if she'd heard the man's name, then shook her head. "I don't know."

"What did he look like?"

"Well, let me see, he was about nineteen or twenty, with light-colored hair and real pale eyes. Wore a big Texas hat. And stovepipe chaps."

"Did you see which way they went?"

"No, Caleb, I'm sorry, I didn't."

Caleb nodded. He gave Fanny's shoulder a squeeze, then left the restaurant. Callie and a young man. He felt as if his insides were being torn apart as he thought of her with another man. Then he swore under his breath. When would she have had time to meet another man? It couldn't be Ashton; he was off with Angela. And what man would want her now, when she was carrying his child in her belly?

He questioned every person he met and finally someone remembered seeing Callie. She'd been walking west. Yes, she'd been with a young man.

Caleb headed west toward the end of town, his brow furrowed. A young man with light hair and pale eyes. A Texas hat. Stovepipe chaps.

"Sounds like Whitley," Caleb muttered.

"Hey, Stryker!"

Turning, Caleb saw Orville Hoag striding toward him.

"Orville."

"You wouldn't be looking for your missus, would you?"

"Have you seen her?"

"Yeah. About an hour and a half ago. She was riding out of town."

"Alone?"

"No, there was a man with her. Never seen him before."

"Which way?"

"Due west."

Hoag motioned for Caleb to follow him. They turned down an alley and went about twenty feet when Orville stopped and pointed at the ground.

"He's riding a big blood bay. That's his print, there."

"Thanks, Orville."

"Anything I can do to help?"

"Send word to the ranch, will you? Tell Big George I might be gone for a couple days longer than I planned."

"Sure thing."

"I left my buggy in front of the Inter-Ocean. Take it over to the Bon Ton, will you, and ask Tony to look after the horse?"

Orville nodded, chilled by the predatory look in Stryker's eyes. Whoever the stranger was, he felt sorry for him.

*Hurry. Hurry.* The words pounded in Caleb's mind as he raced for home. At the mansion, he changed out of his city clothes and slipped into his trail gear. He buckled on his gunbelt, checked the loads in his Colt, and went out to saddle the buckskin.

Fifteen minutes later, he was riding down the alley. Whitley had at least a two-hour head start on him, but it wouldn't do him any good.

Callie grabbed the saddle horn as Whitley urged his horse into a lope, praying that the chestnut wouldn't step into a hole, praying that riding astride this late in her pregnancy wouldn't hurt the baby.

They'd been riding for almost two hours when Whitley reined his horse to a halt and offered Callie a drink from his canteen.

The water was warm, but she drank it greedily, crying out when Whitley tore the canteen from her grasp.

"Take it easy, Mrs. Stryker."

"Why are you doing this? Surely you know Caleb will come after you?"

"I'm counting on it."

"But why?"

"He killed my pa."

"What?"

"Three years ago. And now I aim to kill him." Whitley shook his head. "I would have called him out, but I've seen him draw and I knew I didn't have a chance against him."

"The snake," Callie murmured. "The cut cinch—it was you."

"Yeah. I wanted him to worry a little, like my pa worried. Like my ma worried."

"Whitley . . ."

"He tracked my pa for a week, then he shot him. But Pa didn't die right away. I know, 'cause I was there."

Whitley stared past Callie, his eyes hard and cold. "The breed caught up with my pa near the Rio Grande. I was hiding behind a clump of sagebrush. Pa didn't know I was there. Stryker called my pa out, and when my pa refused to surrender, there was a fight. Pa's bullet creased the breed's arm. Stryker caught my pa in the belly. He was a long time dyin'."

"I'm sorry," Callie murmured, "but you must know your father was a wanted man."

"He was innocent! They said he robbed a bank and killed a guard, but it was a lie."

"Are you sure?"

"Of course I'm sure! My father was a good man. He wouldn't do a thing like that." He glared at

Callie, his eyes wild with suppressed rage. "Let's go," he said curtly. "We've wasted enough time."

He kicked his horse into a trot, and Callie bit down on her lower lip to keep from crying out. The jarring of the horse made her breasts hurt. Her back and shoulders ached from riding for so long. Cold sweat, born of fear, trickled down her spine.

At dusk, Whitley drew rein in the shelter of a rocky overhang in a shallow canyon. There was no way to approach from above; twin piles of jumbled rocks formed a path of sorts, so that there was only one approach to the place he'd chosen.

He helped Callie from the saddle, spread a blanket for her to sit on, and tossed her a hunk of beef jerky, a thick slice of bread, and his canteen.

The sight of food made Callie's stomach churn. She took a drink of water, hoping it would wipe the taste of bile from her mouth, and then she asked the question that had been tormenting her for the last several hours.

"Whitley, what are you going to do when Caleb arrives?"

"I'm gonna make the breed suffer," he replied tersely. "The way my pa suffered. I'm no gunman. I can't shoot it out with him face to face and hope to survive."

"So you shot him in the back."

A faint flush crept into Whitley's cheeks. "It was a cowardly thing to do, I admit it, but like I said, I don't have a chance in hell of besting him in a fair fight. And I mean to kill him, Miz Stryker, make no mistake about that."

A brief flash of regret showed in his pale eyes.

"I'm sorry you had to be involved, but it was the only way I could think to get him to follow me that wouldn't get me killed."

"Whitley, please . . ."

"Don't waste your breath. I swore an oath on my pa's grave that I'd avenge him, and I mean to do it."

There was no use arguing with him. She sat on the blanket, her hands numb, her wrists chafing from where the rope rubbed against her skin.

At dusk, Whitley tied her hands behind her back and secured his kerchief over her mouth so she couldn't cry out a warning.

"I don't expect him tonight," he explained. "I don't reckon even a snake like Caleb Stryker can track in the dark." He draped a blanket over Callie's shoulders. "You might as well get some sleep," he advised, and drifted into the shadows, leaving Callie on the blanket, alone and afraid.

Callie woke at first light, stiff and sore from lying on the ground, but her discomfort was soon swallowed up in the memory of where she was and what was sure to happen when Caleb came for her.

She sat up as Whitley knelt beside her. Removing the kerchief from her mouth, he offered her a drink of water.

"We'll have breakfast later," he said, capping the canteen. "He should be along soon."

"Whitley, please . . ." she began, but he quickly drew the kerchief over her mouth again, stifling her pleas.

She watched as he took cover behind a boulder,

his rifle in his hand, and there was nothing she could do but sit there like a Judas goat, her throat filling with unshed tears as she waited for Caleb to come for her.

# Chapter Thirty-six

Caleb sat his horse, watching the sun climb in the sky. He wiped the sweat from his brow—it was unseasonably hot. At dawn, he'd circled the area where Whitley had gone to ground, ascertaining that there was only one way in and one way out.

The kid had chosen a perfect place, Caleb mused, and he'd picked the perfect bait to set the trap. And though Caleb was pretty certain Whitley wouldn't hurt Callie if his intended prey didn't show up, he knew he couldn't live with the consequences if he was wrong. And so he rode between the wall of boulders, knowing he probably wouldn't ride out again.

And then he saw Callie, bound and gagged, sitting on a blanket at the base of a rocky overhang. He reined the buckskin to a halt, his gaze moving over her for a long moment, noting the way the early morning sun danced in her hair, the way her eyes lit up when she saw him, then narrowed with worry. She shook her head, warning him away, but he only smiled as he clucked to the buckskin.

The skin between his shoulder blades began to tighten as he rode into the mouth of the canyon. He could feel Whitley behind him, lurking somewhere in the boulders to his left.

Bringing the buckskin to a halt, Caleb dropped the reins and held his hands well away from his guns.

"I'm here," he said, his voice echoing off the canyon walls.

"Toss your rifle and your six-gun to the right, then get off your horse, real slow."

Caleb did as he was told, his gaze on Callie all the while. "Now what?"

"Get your hands up where I can see 'em. That's better. You don't even know who I am, do you?" Whitley asked, his contempt thick in his voice.

"Why don't you tell me?"

"You killed my father down on the Rio Grande. Three years ago. Do you remember him, bounty hunter? His name was Murdock. Joe Murdock."

"I remember him."

"Do you remember how he died?"

A sudden chill crept down Caleb's spine as he remembered the day Murdock died. It had been summer, and hot as Hades. The Rio Grande had been running low; the sky had been warm and clear, as blue as Callie's eyes. But it was the blood he recollected most, bright red and plentiful, bubbling from the gunshot wound low in Murdock's belly. "I remember."

"That's how you're gonna die, bounty hunter."

Caleb tensed as the voice drew nearer. Too late, he saw the warning in Callie's eyes. Her face dissolved in a sea of bright light, and then there was only darkness and the distant echo of a muffled scream.

When he woke, he was staked out on a patch of hard, dry ground, Indian-style. The sun was high in the sky, and he squinted against the blinding rays, conscious of a deep thirst and a dull throbbing in the back of his head.

"Caleb."

He turned his head at the sound of her voice, wincing as a bright shaft of pain lanced through his skull. She was sitting on the blanket as before. The gag had been removed from her mouth, and Whitley had retied her hands in front so she could reach the canteen he had placed beside her. The overhang shaded her from the sun.

"Are you all right?" he asked.

"Yes."

He started to ask if she thought the baby was all right when he heard the sound of Whitley's footsteps.

"She's not hurt," Whitley said, "though I should probably kill her, too. My ma was pregnant when she heard how you'd killed my pa. She lost the baby and almost died herself."

"The shoot-out was your pa's doing," Caleb said, knowing he was wasting his breath. "He could have come along peacefully."

"So they could hang him? He was a good man, my pa. He never robbed no bank."

"The law said he was guilty," Caleb replied. "It wasn't for me to decide otherwise."

"You're gonna pay, damn you! You're gonna suffer just like he did, and then I'm gonna leave you out here to rot."

"Then do it and be done with it," Caleb retorted. "But let Callie go."

"I'll do it, all right," Whitley said. "But not now. I want you to think about it, the way my pa thought about it, knowing you were after him, knowing he'd never get away."

Whitley gazed up at the sun, then nodded to himself. He'd avenge his pa, but first he'd let the bounty hunter roast awhile. A little taste of Hell, he mused, removing his hat to wipe the sweat from his brow. After all, he could only kill the breed once, and he didn't want to do it too soon. Best to savor the moment as long as he could before he went back to Texas and told his ma that his pa's death had been avenged.

Callie sat in the shade of the overhang, her gaze focused on Caleb. His shirt was drenched with perspiration; sweat sheened his face and trickled down his neck. His breathing was shallow, labored, and his eyes closed against the glare of the sun. He ran his tongue over his lips, which were dry and cracked, but other than that, he didn't move.

People died of too much sun, she thought. Even people who had skin as dark as an Indian's, people who had lived most of their lives outdoors.

She glanced at Whitley, sitting a few feet away, his rifle across his knees. A faint smile played over his lips as he stared at Caleb. In the last few hours, she had tried several times to convince Whitley to release Caleb, to let them go home, to forget his vow of revenge, but it had all been in vain. Once she had stood up, intending to give Caleb a drink, but Whitley had stopped her.

Callie shifted uncomfortably on the blanket. Perspiration trickled down her back and pooled between her breasts, but she knew that her discomfort was as nothing compared to what Caleb was suffering. She, at least, had shade and water, while he was at the mercy of a blazing sun.

Caleb drew a shallow breath and expelled it slowly. He could feel Callie watching him, feel her anguish. With a low groan, he opened his eyes and looked at her, offering her a tight smile of reassurance.

"Don't cry," he said, his voice sounding brittle in his ears.

"Whitley, you've got to stop this now," Callie said. "Please."

"No, ma'am."

"He's dying."

"Not yet." Whitley patted the gun holstered on his right thigh. "Soon, though. Real soon."

"Then do it now," Callie begged. "He's suffered enough."

But Whitley just sat there, his hand caressing the butt of his Colt, his eyes fixed on Caleb's face.

"You won't be gut-shooting any other innocent men, bounty hunter," Whitley murmured. "Not after today, you won't."

It was no use, Callie thought. Whitley was going to make Caleb suffer through the heat of the day and then he was going to shoot him in the belly and watch him die a slow, agonizing death.

She pulled against the rope that bound her hands, ignoring the pain that darted up her arms. She twisted her hands back and forth, struggling to be free, and the rough hemp bit into her wrists, drawing blood. She ignored that, too, desperate to free herself so she could help Caleb before it was too late.

But the ropes had been tied by an expert, and she was powerless to loosen them.

She gazed at Caleb, her eyes filling with tears. "I love you," she whispered, and he nodded slightly, his lips, now cracked and bleeding, silently repeating the words.

He was going to die, she thought, and there was nothing she could do about it.

Whitley whirled around as a high-pitched feminine shriek reverberated off the canyon walls. "What the hell . . . ?"

"The baby," Callie said, panting heavily, and then screamed again. "I think I'm losing the baby."

She drew her knees toward her chest and began rocking back and forth, moaning all the while.

Whitley stared at her, a soft curse whispering past his lips as he hurried over to Callie and knelt beside her. He watched her rock back and forth for a minute and then, with a shake of his head, he cut her hands free and eased her down on the blanket.

"What should I do?" he asked anxiously.

"I don't know."

She whimpered piteously, then wrapped her arms around her stomach and closed her eyes.

"I need a doctor. Please, Whitley, get me to a doctor before it's too late."

"Yes, ma'am," he said.

He watched her writhe on the blanket for several moments; then, drawing his gun, he turned toward Caleb. "Just as soon as I put a bullet in his belly."

Caleb drew a deep breath, his gaze focused,

unblinking, on Whitley Murdock's face.

Whitley wiped the sudden sheen of cold sweat from his brow as he leveled the Colt at the half-breed and thumbed back the hammer. He'd never killed a man, and the thought of taking a life, even the life of the man who had killed his father, made him sick to his stomach.

"I'll take care of her," Whitley promised.

He swallowed the bile rising in his throat as his finger curled around the trigger, squeezing slowly, only to let out a startled shout as Callie threw herself across Caleb's body.

The gunshot echoed loudly off the canyon walls. Then there was a deafening silence.

Whitley stared at Callie in horror. A bright red stain blossomed near her shoulder, spreading outward in an ever-widening circle.

Whitley glanced at Caleb, whose face had gone deadly white.

"I'm sorry," the boy babbled, "I didn't mean to shoot her . . . I didn't mean it. . . ."

"If she dies, I'll come out of the grave after you," Caleb said, his voice lethal.

"She won't die," Whitley said, his gun falling, unnoticed, to the ground at his feet. "She can't die. I never meant her no harm."

He hurried forward, lifting Callie in his arms. "Mrs. Stryker?" He lowered her to the ground, then lightly patted her cheek. "Oh, Lord, Mrs. Stryker."

Caleb drew a labored breath. "Untie me."

"Yessir," Whitley said.

Drawing his knife, he cut Caleb's hands and feet free, then gently lifted Callie and carried her to the blanket.

Feeling weak as a newborn colt, Caleb stood up, swaying slightly as the world spun out of focus. He blinked several times, then he went to kneel beside Callie, his hand brushing a wisp of hair from her brow.

"Whitley, bring me your canteen."

The boy ran to do as he was told, and Caleb unbuttoned Callie's dress, drawing back the bloodstained cloth to disclose the raw, ugly wound located high in her left shoulder.

"Callie . . ." He whispered her name, his insides knotting with fear. The wound didn't look all that dangerous, but there was a possibility that the loss of blood would send her into shock, that she might have the baby out here, in the wilderness.

He murmured her name again, his voice filled with anguish.

Callie's eyes fluttered open, and she smiled at him. "I'm all right, Caleb," she said, reaching for his hand. "It's just a scratch."

"The baby . . . ?"

"The baby's fine," she assured him with a smile. "I had to think of something to distract Whitley."

"You little fool, you could have been killed."

"But I wasn't." She pulled Whitley's gun from beneath the folds of her skirt, holding it between her thumb and forefinger as though it were a particularly repulsive rodent.

"Where'd you get that?"

"I picked it up when he was untying you. Maybe you'd better take it."

Caleb glanced from Callie's face to the gun she'd thrust in his hand, not knowing whether to kiss her for saving his life or strangle her for scaring the devil out of him.

"Here's the canteen," Whitley said, and then, seeing the gun nestled comfortably in Caleb's hand, his face turned fish-belly white. "You gonna kill me?"

"I don't know," Caleb replied. "I haven't decided. Suppose you just sit down where I can keep an eye on you while I bandage up my wife's arm, and then we'll talk about it."

Whitley did as he was told. Once, his gaze strayed to the rifle booted on his saddle, but a warning look from Caleb kept him where he was.

Callie groaned a little as Caleb washed the blood from the crease in her shoulder, bandaged it with a strip of her petticoat, then fashioned a sling from Whitley's kerchief.

"I guess you'll be all right," Caleb said, relieved that the wound wasn't as serious as he'd first imagined. "Are you sure that business about the baby was just an act?"

Callie patted her stomach with one hand. "I'm sure," she said. "We're fine." She glanced over at Whitley. "You're not going to hurt him, are you?"

"I ought to kill him."

"But you won't."

"I guess not."

"Here." Callie thrust the canteen into his hands. "Drink this. Slowly," she admonished, her gaze moving worriedly over his face. "Are you sure you're all right? You don't look so good."

"I don't feel so good," he admitted.

Now that Callie was out of danger, he was feeling the ill effects of a day spent in the sun.

"Maybe you should lie down?"

"I think you're right," Caleb murmured, and slipped into unconsciousness before his head hit the ground.

He woke cradled in Callie's arms, his head resting on her breast. For a time, he gazed into the depths of her eyes, content just to lie there. He could feel the beat of her heart beneath his cheek. Her arms were warm and comforting. Soon, she would hold their infant to her breast, but for now, he felt like a child himself, in need of solace. His head ached, his lips were swollen and cracked, and the skin of his face was blistered.

"I love you," he murmured.

"I know."

"Are you all right?"

"Fine. My arm's a little sore, that's all. How are you feeling?"

"I'll live. Where's the kid?"

"I sent him home."

"You what?"

"I sent him home."

Caleb swore under his breath as he struggled to sit up.

"He's gone, Caleb. Just lie still. You weren't going to hurt him, anyway."

"The devil I wasn't."

"Caleb, he's just a boy. You can't blame him for wanting to avenge his father's death. And there was no harm done, not really."

"No harm done! How can you say that? You could have been killed."

"But I wasn't. And you'll be fine in a few days." Her hand stroked his forehead. "I couldn't let you kill him, and I couldn't let him kill you."

A wry grin twitched at the corner of Caleb's mouth. "You'll do to ride the river with, Mrs. Stryker. You've got more brass than Bill Hickock, and more nerve than Curly Bill."

"Is that supposed to be a compliment?" Callie asked, smiling at him.

"The best." He sat up, groaning softly. "Callie . . ." He laid his hand on her cheek, bent forward, and kissed her gently. "I . . ." He grinned at her self-consciously. "I've never been one for pretty words or flowery speeches, but I want you to know, when I was staring into the barrel of Whitley's Colt, it wasn't dying that made me sad, but the thought that I'd never see you again. Never hold you again. I love you, Callie. I think maybe I loved you from the start."

"Oh, Caleb, I love you, too." She leaned toward him, and then drew back.

"What's wrong?"

"Your mouth. I don't want to hurt you."

"Not kissing you will hurt more," he murmured, and he drew her into his arms.

He had intended to kiss her gently, just once, but the touch of her lips, the taste of her, enflamed his senses. He had seen the face of death in the yawning maw of young Murdock's Colt and now he reached for life, his arms tightening around Callie. The swell of new life beneath her heart filled him with tenderness and he caressed the growing mound of her belly, pressed his head to her breast.

Slowly, reverently, he undressed her, there on the blanket, his gaze warm with love and awe as his hands adored her, worshipping her beauty, her power to create life. Bending, he kissed the bloodstained bandage on her shoulder, remembering how she'd thrown herself across his body. The thought that she would have died in his place humbled him as nothing else ever had.

He murmured her name as her hands moved over him, soothing him, her touch like a balm, healing his hurts as no physician ever could, banishing his aches, making him forget everything but his need for this one woman above all others.

He groaned with pleasure as her hands worked their sweet magic, until he was quivering with desire, and then he returned the favor, arousing her with his hands and his lips, with soft words of love.

When she started to tug at his belt, he placed his hand over hers. "Are you sure, Callie? Your shoulder . . . ?"

"I'm sure."

He was trembling with restraint when he possessed her, afraid of hurting her, afraid to unleash the full force of his desire, until she began to move beneath him, touching him in the secret places only she knew, driving him past the ability to be cautious.

Her tongue tickled his ear, slid down his neck, laved the point of his shoulder. With a strangled cry, he drove into her, possessing her in the most primal way, proving to her, to himself, that she was his, would always be his, and that nothing but death itself would ever part them.

# *Chapter Thirty-seven*

They returned to the ranch late that night. The following morning, Caleb sent for Doctor Maynard, insisting that Callie's wound be examined, and even when the sawbones proclaimed her to be in perfect health, Caleb made Callie stay in bed. He waited on her hand and foot, massaging her back, rubbing her feet, brushing her hair, refusing to let her do anything more strenuous than read a book.

Only when he was certain she had suffered no ill effects from their ordeal did he allow her out of bed.

Two days later, they received an invitation to Angela's wedding. Callie wasn't sure she wanted to attend, but Caleb insisted, and so it was on a bright clear day in April that they went into Cheyenne.

It was by far the biggest wedding the town had ever seen. The church was fragrant with flowers and overflowing with people.

Angela looked lovely in a gown of soft pink silk that was cleverly designed to hide her pregnancy.

After the ceremony, Angela's first kiss went to Richard. She bestowed the second on Caleb, full on the mouth, to the cheers and catcalls of several onlookers. Then she smiled at Callie.

"Take good care of him," she said.

Callie nodded, her hands clenched at her sides as she resisted the urge to scratch Angela Bristol Ashton's eyes out.

The gesture was not missed by Caleb, who put his arm around his wife's shoulder and gave her a rough squeeze.

"Behave yourself, Mrs. Stryker," he whispered. "Angie and I are just friends, remember? Nothing more."

"Well, that kiss was a little too friendly for my taste."

"Jealous, are you?" Caleb mused with a satisfied smirk. "Good."

"I am not jealous," Callie replied haughtily. "I just don't want anyone gossiping about my husband."

Caleb laughed softly. "Have it your way, sweetheart."

The reception was held at the Ashton mansion and everyone who was anyone was there. Callie had never seen anything like it. The tables, covered with fine lace and linen and laid with gleaming silver and crystal and china, held more food than she had ever seen: platters of sliced meat and cheese, huge bowls of fruit and chilled vegetables, breads and rolls, caviar and champagne.

The wedding cake, six layers high and decorated

with pink roses, both real and made of icing, occupied a table of its own. There were several other, smaller cakes, also decorated with pink roses.

A ten-piece orchestra played in the ballroom, and several wandering minstrels entertained in the gardens and in the company parlor.

Caleb held Callie close as they waltzed around the crowded ballroom. "I'm sorry, Callie," he murmured.

"Sorry?" She looked up at him. "For what?"

"I cheated you out of the kind of wedding you should have had."

"You didn't cheat me out of anything."

"Are you sure?"

"I'm sure. I have everything I've ever wanted."

Caleb nodded, but he didn't look convinced.

"Honest, Caleb. All this is nice, but it's just window dressing. The most important thing is how you feel about me in here." She pressed her hand over his heart.

"We could go home," Caleb said, his eyes glinting wickedly, "and I could show you how I feel." He placed his hand over hers. "In here, and elsewhere."

As usual, her whole being responded to Caleb's smile. Her heartbeat quickened, butterflies danced in her stomach, and every nerve ending came suddenly alive, yearning for his touch. "I'd like that," Callie said breathlessly, and in no time at all, Caleb was leading her outside, handing her into the carriage, carrying her over the thresh-old of the mansion.

And it was like the first time all over again.

Caleb insisted that they stay in town until after the baby was born. Callie asserted that she was fine, that first babies never came in a hurry. Certainly this one was overdue. She told him that she wanted to have the baby at the ranch, but Caleb turned a deaf ear to all her arguments. He wasn't taking any chances on losing her or the baby.

Callie had to admit that it wasn't so bad, living in town. Since Caleb didn't have to go out and ride the range, she had him all to herself, day and night.

They stayed up late and slept late. Caleb taught her to play poker and blackjack and monte. He entertained her with tales of gunfighters and gunfights, telling her of Billy the Kid, who was reported to have killed twenty-one men, not counting Indians and Mexicans, before his twenty-first birthday. Caleb said he'd met The Kid once, down in Lincoln County when Billy was working for John Tunstall. John Chisum had called The Kid "the pink of politeness, a courteous gentleman," but Caleb said he'd seen Billy close up, and the boy looked hard enough to chew steel and spit nails.

Caleb said he'd met Bob Ford a couple of times in St. Joe, the same Bob Ford who had shot Jesse James in the back on April 3, 1882.

Callie listened intently as Caleb told of meeting Virgil Earp in Tombstone the year before the shootout at the O.K. Corral. He'd been there on business, Caleb had told her, dropping off a prisoner.

It was amazing to Callie that her husband had met such men, but then, perhaps it had been inevitable, considering his line of work at the time.

The most gruesome tale Caleb told her was about an outlaw known as Big Nose George, who had been arrested for robbing a stagecoach near Miles City. He was taken to Rawlins, a wild and woolly Wyoming town, to stand trial, only a mob decided not to wait for a trial. They stormed the jail and lynched him. One of the spectators was a doctor, who cut down the body after the mob dispersed. The good doctor made a death mask of the victim and then skinned him and tanned the hide. It was rumored that Osborne made a new medical instrument bag out of part of the outlaw's hide.

Callie refused to believe such an outrageous tale, even though Caleb assured her it had really happened.

Though Callie enjoyed hearing Caleb's wild tales, she preferred the quiet evenings they spent before the fire, dreaming dreams of the future, speculating on whether their child would be a boy or a girl, arguing over names. Sometimes Callie read aloud from Shakespeare or Dickens, though Caleb didn't care much for either author and much preferred reading the *Cheyenne Leader.*

Surprisingly, they spent a good deal of time with Angela and Richard, either going out to the theater or staying home to play cards. Callie couldn't help thinking that they made a strange foursome, considering all that had happened between them, but she was glad of Angela's company. Caleb was sympathetic to the aches and pains of her advanced pregnancy, but only Angela really understood.

As the days passed, Callie's anxiety over the coming birth grew. She tried to tell herself that childbirth was perfectly natural. Women had babies every day. Her own mother had given birth and survived, but she was still afraid, afraid of the pain that the good ladies in town were so eager to tell her about, afraid she would die, afraid the baby would die.

Now, sitting at the window with her hand pressed over her belly, she stared out into the darkness, hoping and praying that all her fears would be for naught. She glanced at the big bed where Caleb lay sleeping peacefully and felt her heart quicken at the mere sight of him. She would miss him dreadfully, she thought, even in heaven. He had become her whole life, his smile as dear as the sun. She had never dreamed a man could be so tender, so thoughtful. This late in her pregnancy, they could no longer be intimate, but he often held her and cuddled her, telling her that he loved her, that she was beautiful even though she knew it was a lie. She had a mirror, after all.

He rubbed her back when it ached, dropping feather-light kisses along her neck, whispering love words in her ear. When she craved chocolate in the middle of the night, he rode into town, got poor Mr. Peabody out of bed, and brought her back a box of imported chocolates. He held her close when she cried for no reason at all and rocked her like a child when she couldn't sleep. Once, he even sang to her, his voice deep and rich, if slightly off key.

The first pain was hardly noticeable, just a twinge in her back. Her low gasp of surprise brought Caleb instantly awake.

"Callie?"

"I'm over here."

He was beside her in a moment, his big hands cupping her shoulders. "What are you doing out of bed?"

"I couldn't sleep."

"Is it the baby?"

"I don't know."

Effortlessly, he picked her up, then sat down in the rocking chair, cradling her in his arms. "Pretty night," he mused.

"Yes." The sky was dark and clear, studded with stars that twinkled like tiny candles. She'd heard a story once, long ago, something about starlight and fairies, but she couldn't remember how it went, only that it had a happy ending.

They sat there in the dark for a long while, her head on his shoulders while he stroked her back. He felt her tense as the second pain came. Gradually, the night deepened and the pains grew closer together and more intense.

She clung to him then, needing the reassurance of his strength. When her water broke, he helped her out of her gown, toweled her legs dry, pulled a clean gown over her head, and helped her into bed.

She reached for him immediately, clutching one of his hands in both of hers, squeezing hard as another pain knifed through her.

"That was the worst one so far," she said, panting slightly. "Oh, Caleb, I'm so afraid."

"Don't be." He sat beside her on the bed, his face impassive so she wouldn't know that he was afraid, too. "I think I'd better go get Mrs. Strickland."

"Don't leave me."

"I'll be right back, Callie. Ten minutes, that's all."

"Promise?"

"I promise."

For Callie, the minutes passed like hours. Caleb was her courage, her strength. Without him, fears crowded into her mind. What if she was in labor for days? What if the baby was born dead? What if she died?

"Caleb, come back. Caleb. Caleb. Caleb!" She screamed his name as a sharp pain threatened to tear her in half, and suddenly he was there beside her, holding her hands in his, telling her that everything would be all right.

"You'd better go downstairs now, Mr. Stryker," the midwife advised. "This is no place for a gentleman."

Caleb couldn't have agreed more. Placing a kiss on Callie's forehead, he left the room.

Downstairs, he paced the floor as fathers had been doing for centuries. He could hear Callie's muffled cries, and each one was like a knife in his heart.

Bowing his head, he offered a silent prayer to *Wakan Tanka,* praying that Callie's suffering would soon be over, that she would be delivered of a healthy child. Never again, he thought as he heard her scream again. Never again.

And then, as another cry rent the stillness, he raced up the stairs.

Mrs. Strickland's eyes widened in horror as Caleb burst into the room. "Mr. Stryker, you mustn't—"

"Mustn't be damned." Caleb knelt beside the bed and took Callie's hands in his. "Callie?"

"It hurts."

"I know. Hang on to me, Callie."

"You won't leave me?"

"No. Don't fight the pain, honey. Here now, bear down with the next one. That's my girl."

Mrs. Strickland cleared her throat. "Excuse me, Mr. Stryker, but I think I'm better qualified to handle this than you are."

"Maybe so, but I'm not leaving."

With a soft snort of disapproval, the midwife crossed her arms over her ample breast and sat down in the chair next to the window.

"Caleb, why is it taking so long?"

"It hasn't been very long, honey. Only a couple of hours."

"It seems longer."

"I know. But they tell me you'll forget the pain as soon as you hold the baby in your arms."

"I don't believe it," she said, trying to smile, but the smile quickly disappeared as several contractions ripped through her.

"Push, honey," Caleb urged. "Push."

Mrs. Strickland moved to the foot of the bed, tossed the blankets aside, and lifted Callie's gown. "I see the head," she exclaimed. "Push, Mrs. Stryker."

Caleb bit back a groan as Callie's hands tightened on his, her fingernails digging into the palms, drawing blood. Her back arched off the bed as she gave one last mighty push, and their child slid into Mrs. Strickland's waiting hands.

"It's a boy," the midwife announced. After cutting the cord, she wrapped the infant in a blanket and placed it in Callie's outstretched arms.

"A boy," Callie murmured. "We have a son."

Caleb nodded, his gaze on Callie's face. The lines of pain were gone now, and her eyes glowed with love as she examined their son, counting tiny fingers and toes, stroking his cheek, laughing softly as the baby yawned.

"He's beautiful, Caleb."

"Yes. And so are you." He bent to kiss her then, his heart swelling with such happiness that it was almost painful.

"Do you want to hold him?"

"Yeah." The baby was incredibly tiny. Tears of joy welled in Caleb's eyes as he gazed into the baby's deep blue eyes. *A son,* he thought. *I have a son.* He looked at Callie, wanting to tell her how much he loved her, but she was already asleep.

"I'll take the wee one," Mrs. Strickland said. "I'll bring him down to you after he's bathed."

Caleb nodded, though he was reluctant to part with his son, even for a moment.

Downstairs, he stood at the window and watched the birth of a new day, quietly thanking *Wakan Tanka* for a healthy child, for a loving wife.

Thirty minutes later, Mrs. Strickland handed the baby to its father, then went back upstairs to look after Callie.

Caleb sat down, the baby cradled in his arms, and wondered how his own father had felt when he was born. Was it possible that Duncan had felt this same sense of love, of wonder—and if so, where had those feelings gone?

Watching the sunrise with his son clinging tightly to one finger, Caleb felt all the old anger and hatred slowly seep away. What was done was done, and it couldn't be changed. But somehow, with a new life in his arms, the past no longer mattered.

# *Epilogue*

Caleb stared at his wife, a smile tugging at the corners of his lips. "When did you do this?"

"A few days before Ethan was born."

"Callie, I don't know what to say."

"Don't say anything. You've given me so much, I—"

"I haven't given you anything," Caleb protested. "You're the one. You've given me everything any man could ever want."

"Caleb Stryker, do you meant to sit there and tell me our son is nothing? That your love is nothing?"

"No, but . . ." He stared at the deed to the ranch, at the finely written line stating that the property known as the Rocking S was jointly owned by Callie McGuire Stryker and Caleb Stryker.

"After all, it really is yours as much as mine." She smiled up at him. "Think of it as my dowry."

Speechless, Caleb drew Callie into his arms and held her tight.

If not for his father, he never would have met Callie, never would have known how empty his life had been.

In a way, Duncan Stryker had given his son everything he had ever wanted, and more.

# *Dear Reader:*

I hope you enjoyed *Cheyenne Surrender.* I have recently completed my second fantasy romance, which is tentatively titled *Beneath a Midnight Moon.* It was wonderfully fun to write. I finished it in five months, and I hated to see it end, hated to say good-bye to my hero, Hardane of Argone. How I love that man!

I hope you'll love him too. His story begins like this:

He came to her in dreams, always different yet always the same, his fathomless gray eyes filled with quiet desperation and a silent plea for help.

Was he real, this dark-skinned man with long inky black hair, or only an image sketched from the paint box of her imagination, a phantom warrior woven into the shadowed tapestry of her nighttime fantasies. . . .

What do you think?

I love to hear from you. You can write me at

P.O. Box 1703
Whittier, CA 90609-1703.

SASE appreciated.

Madeline

**"Powerful, passionate, and action-packed, Madeline Baker's historical romances will keep readers on the edge of their seats!"**

***—Romantic Times***

# WARRIOR'S LADY

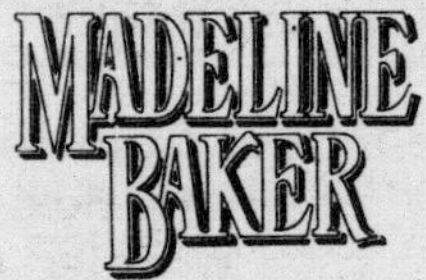


A creature of moonlight and quicksilver, Leyla rescues the mysterious man from unspeakable torture, then heals him body and soul. The radiant enchantress is all he wants in a woman—gentle, innocent, exquisitely lovely—but his enemies will do everything in their power to keep her from him. Only a passion born of desperate need can prevail against such hatred and unite two lovers against such odds.

_3490-5 $4.99 US/$5.99 CAN

**LEISURE BOOKS**
**ATTN: Order Department**
**276 5th Avenue, New York, NY 10001**

Please add $1.50 for shipping and handling for the first book and $.35 for each book thereafter. PA., N.Y.S. and N.Y.C. residents, please add appropriate sales tax. No cash, stamps, or C.O.D.s. All orders shipped within 6 weeks via postal service book rate. Canadian orders require $2.00 extra postage and must be paid in U.S. dollars through a U.S. banking facility.

Name________________________________________

Address______________________________________

City ____________________ State______ Zip______

I have enclosed $______in payment for the checked book(s).

Payment must accompany all orders.☐ Please send a free catalog.